A Queen Too Many

by Ken Hayton

Published by Alison Findlay
Publishing partner: Paragon Publishing, Rothersthorpe
First published 2010
© Alison Findlay 2010

ISBN 978-1-907611-08-7

Book design, layout and production management by Into Print
www.intoprint.net
01604 832149

Printed and bound in UK and USA by Lightning Source

Cover picture by Gill Hayton
The cover was inspired by a picture of blackwork embroidery from 1590 and by my late husband's love of butterflies. We had such fun researching this last book, before he became ill, and I hope it gives pleasure to all who read it.

Prologue

It was a scant twenty miles by sea from Dundrennan in Scotland to the Cumbrian coast at Workington but it had been a miserable journey. The short sharp seas, which had been generated by the sudden westerly breeze, had produced an uncomfortable effect, especially where the water was funnelled into the mouth of the Solway Firth, and the passengers were showing signs of their unaccustomed subjection to such conditions. Not all of them, as the captain of the fishing boat allowed. The two fine gentlemen were clearly upset by the weather; one had commenced vomiting almost as soon as they left the shore, whilst the other, a dark saturnine character with a humourless face, was clinging to the rigging and gazing fixedly at the horizon. Not that there was anything to see, it was too dark for that, but that gaze kept his head and vision directed straight ahead, which was the best attempt that could be made to avert the predicament of his companion. The lesser mortals amongst his passengers had been pressed into service on the boat, as far as they were able, and for at least some of them this had prevented the onset of sea-sickness by virtue of their preoccupation.

But the woman, he had to admit, was not affected in the least. In fact she gave every appearance of revelling in the wild weather and gazed about her keenly, marking the handling of the boat and more than once exchanging a smile with himself, as he handled the wheel and directed the crew. The captain had been surprised at his own reaction to this interchange of glances. A hard-bitten man of the world, he was not one to be suborned by the flirtatious behaviour of a young woman but he had capitulated within minutes of their first encounter. She was beautiful, to be sure, but it was the spirit that shone through her current adversity which had won him over. Her vivacity had overcome the reduced circumstances in which she now stood and the travel-stained untidy apparel and her unkempt personal appearance did nothing to lessen her attraction. A shrewd man, he was sure that he was not the first male to be so affected by her and, he thought, he would certainly not be the last. He was right on both counts.

As for the lady herself, she was completely aware of the effect she had produced on the skipper of their boat. It was something she was entirely accustomed to and therefore no surprise. She regretted her appearance, dishevelled, ill-dressed and bereft of any jewellery or adornment and she was aware of the fact that her recent history would be well known even to this seaman from the fringes of Scottish society. Her very bearing demonstrated that she was above the disadvantages of all that. She bore herself regally, as indeed she should, for she was a queen. No matter that she had recently fled, somewhat precipitately and uncharacteristically so, from the field of battle. No matter that she had signed, under duress, the articles of abdication whilst in prison. In her own eyes and in the eyes of many others she was still Mary, Queen of Scots.

Chapter 1: Walburn

Things were certainly different at Worton. Back home in Walburn he had felt himself to be one of the elite. After all, his father was the miller and they owned a horse. Not a young and swift horse, nor indeed a smart or elegant horse but an un-enterprising, un-exciting horse who worked well, was patient and easily manageable. He was called Wallee, which was a corruption of wall-eye, a physical attribute of this unlovely but docile old animal. William had cause to know the horse well for he was often sent by his father to deliver flour to neighbouring farms and villages, with Wallee pulling the battered old cart whilst he trudged alongside. They visited Stainton, Downholme and Bellerby villages besides isolated farms and, in addition, the local fortified mansion of Walburn Hall. William especially liked delivering to the Hall. It was, after all, only a few hundred yards from their home and there was often a piece of pie or sweetmeat for the young lad from the mill, as the dairy maids and cook were all besotted with this bright young boy with his fair hair, blue eyes and delicate, almost feminine, features. Even the Lord of the Manor, Sir Francis Lascelles, had conceived a soft spot for this well-spoken and well behaved young boy. Not that William was a paragon of the virtues, but he was intelligent enough to know when good behaviour was likely to reap the best rewards.

His father had come to rely upon William, with his ability to reckon quickly and keep accurate tallies. By the age of ten he was clearly able to manage these trips on his own and, despite his slender build, the necessary manhandling of heavy sacks caused him to produce a musculature beyond his years. He enjoyed these excursions, not only because of the occasional bits of hospitality but because he met other boys and girls of a similar age to himself. Had he really stopped to think about these things, William would have realised that his own village was dying, if not already moribund. There were no children in Walburn. Many of the little cottages were empty and piles of stones showed where previous dwellings had been abandoned, especially opposite the Hall, where a whole street of tofts had fallen into decay. At one time it had obviously been a bigger and busier settlement, a well-organised and relatively prosperous farming community. Now it was a failing remnant of a village in which the inhabitants were mainly older people who scratched a bare subsistence from the surrounding land. Over the years, the majority of younger and fitter folk had migrated to the more successful villages of Stainton and Downholme. But he liked his home, enjoyed helping his father to work the mill, which still handled corn from those larger villages and their surrounding farms. When at liberty, he loved the solitude of the surrounding hills and forests. He was passionately fond of wildlife and spent hours patiently waiting for animals to appear whilst he sat in the fork of a tree overlooking some little pond. He was familiar with all the birds of the fells, the wheeling lapwing, the soaring curlew with its mournful, bubbling cry and the drumming snipe. Similarly he knew well the birds of fields, copses and waterside, glorying especially in the rich summer song of the stratospheric skylark and the cheery chirping of the swallows that darted in and out of the old, deserted buildings. If ever there was any small upset between father and child it was because of William's propensity for disappearing into the wilds when his help was needed at the mill. But he was generally a biddable and conscientious boy and they got on well together. A pleasant enough life for a young lad then; but it had all come to an end just after his twelfth birthday, some five years ago when his father had brought him to Worton.

It had started with the arrival of a pedlar in the village, who had called at the mill seeking to assuage a burning thirst. He had sat at the entrance to the corn-drying kiln drinking large quantities of water and looking quite unwell. William's mother, Martha, had brought him into their dwelling, against the inclinations of her husband, and fed him some broth after which he lay down and slept fitfully. The following morning he started to vomit more or less continuously and it was noted that his body was covered in swellings and pustules, the latter in the form of concentric roseate circles. John Robinson had not hesitated. Calling William to him from the brook side, where he was lying on his stomach watching caddis fly larvae hauling their mosaic-like homes across the pebbles, he had thrown a blanket over the horse, hauled up his son behind him and ridden off to Worton. William had not been allowed to enter their dwelling. There had been no opportunity to gather any belongings, no chance to say a farewell to his mother. His father had said little to him on the journey, other than a vague explanation that he was going to see his uncle Joseph, who might be able to look after him for a short spell. When pushed further he said that he expected a bad sickness to come to the village and it would be better if William did not return until after it was over. This was quite exciting as William had little recollection of his uncle Joseph, who he had not seen since he was a very small child, and he had never visited Worton nor ever journeyed so far away from home.

They passed through the villages of Bellerby and Leyburn, both of which William knew well, and then Wensley which he had also visited, it being the market town of Wensleydale. It seemed strangely quiet today and his father, looking slightly worried, had pushed on quickly through to the dale beyond. This was all new country to William and there was much to interest his curiosity. As they approached the village of Aysgarth, the noise from the river valley clearly indicated that there was a waterfall hidden beneath the trees. By the volume of the sound it was large and doubtless an impressive spectacle, but his father was not to be persuaded to make a detour to sightsee; he was obviously anxious to press on. They arrived at Worton in the early afternoon and William was impressed by the Hall where his uncle Joseph lived. It seemed huge and there were several farm buildings around, one of which clearly housed horses. Strangely, his father left him sitting on Wallee, enjoining him to remain there and not dismount. Then he stood at the gate into the yard and called out. After a while an elderly woman appeared and asked him his business at which John Robinson announced who he was and asked to speak with his brother, declining the invitation to enter the house. The woman went in and reappeared in the company of a man, instantly recognisable as the brother of William's father. Taller perhaps and a little older but with features so similar and with a broad, welcoming smile such as his father could produce, so that William warmed to him immediately.

There followed a scene which mystified young William for, as his uncle approached his father with outstretched hand, the latter held up his hand and commanded his brother to stop. He did so, in some surprise, and there then followed a subdued conversation, which William could not hear, but which was grave and manifestly of importance. At one point he saw his uncle nodding his head vigorously and then his father showed signs of great relief. He seemed to make as if he would embrace Joseph but then stepped back and turned towards his son.

"Jump down lad, jump down," he said. "Your uncle Joseph bids you welcome and will be happy to look after you until I can return for you. Now, mind your manners, try to be of use to your uncle and take care not to vex him with foolish behaviour." To William's surprise, he was kissed on the cheek by his usually undemonstrative father, who then mounted Wallee and urged the horse away. He turned to wave to the little group and then rode off but not before William had noticed the glint of tears in his eyes.

All that had been five years ago in the summer of 1563 and his father had never returned from Walburn. Only ten days after he had arrived at Worton Hall, his uncle had called him into the parlour and there, with sympathetic candour, he had informed William that both his parents were dead. Not only his parents but the entire remaining population of the little hamlet had perished from the dreadful plague so that it was now a truly deserted village. It was not just Walburn that had suffered. The little market town of Wensley had also been hit hard and the population had either succumbed or fled so that it was now a ghost town. Fortunately the disease seemed to have burnt itself out in that limited area and had not penetrated further up the dale. William had grieved as would any little boy who had lost his mother and father, the more so perhaps because he was intelligent enough to realise that, but for his father's action, he too would have died in that dreadful epidemic.

Furthermore, his father had returned voluntarily to be with his mother, when he might perhaps have stayed on in the comparative safety of Worton. But no, he had clearly been at pains not to come into contact with his brother and risk passing on the infection. All was now clear to the young boy and, saddened as he was, he was also proud of the selfless way in which his father had behaved and, as he had been spared, he was resolved to help others in some such way when he grew up. Now, however, he was a member of a new household and determined to obey his father's last instructions to fit in and make himself useful.

It was indeed very different at Worton Hall and William now understood what it was to be truly a member of the elite. His uncle had married well, to Anne, a member of the Metcalfe family who lived at Worton Hall. Whilst farming at nearby Thornton Rust, Joseph had met and courted this young lady, who was very beautiful, if rather frail. As a yeoman farmer, he had been prosperous enough to meet the exacting standards of the local Metcalfe clan and was deemed to be an acceptable husband for the young Anne and they had lived together at his farm in Thornton Rust for some years. Upon the sudden death of both her parents, Anne had inherited their quite considerable wealth and the Hall at Worton, into which they had moved. There, a child had been conceived but neither the little girl nor the mother had survived the confinement and now Joseph was left alone in this large, rambling house. He had taken a servant from the village called Hannah to live in as house-keeper but there was no doubting the air of emptiness and loneliness that pervaded the big house. The arrival of William had changed all that. Well behaved as he was, there was nonetheless an occasional boisterousness, typical of any twelve-year old, which enlivened the old Hall. Joseph found this especially pleasing. People who were not pleased by these developments were the rest of the Metcalfe clan, who looked upon Worton Hall as one of their possessions that had somehow been stolen away from them by this Robinson upstart. No matter that Joseph's inheritance of his wife's estate had been legitimate and beyond any legal reproach, they nonetheless felt that the property should revert to the Metcalfe family who had held it for generations. And now a new young Robinson had appeared on the scene and gave every appearance of being likely to remain there. There were plenty of dark mutterings at Nappa Hall when Sir Christopher entertained other members of the extensive Metcalfe clan but that was as far as things went.

After the death of his brother, Joseph had given his nephew a little time to grieve in his own way and this had taken the form of long disappearances into the countryside where the boy had sought solace in the observation of nature, as he had done at home. Sometimes he was on foot but often he rode Gaynor, a lovely horse which his uncle had kindly made available to him. Together the boy and horse travelled all around the dale and William came to know both animal and district very well indeed. He often smiled sadly as he compared his new mount to the faithful but uninspiring Wallee. His uncle Joseph was rich enough to employ two labourers on the farm at Worton and there was no necessity for the boy to work although he did lend a hand especially when sheep were being moved. Eventually, however, Joseph had decided to find a more useful occupation for his young ward and they had had a long conversation on the subject of his future. His uncle had quickly appreciated the boy's facility with numbers. Doubtless as a result of his frequent contacts and dealings with adults he had acquired something of an adult conversational ability but he could neither read nor write. There was no doubt in Joseph's mind that he was intelligent enough to master these accomplishments and so he proposed to William that he should go to school. This was a shock to the lad, who had never ever considered such a course of action to be open to him and he was not sure that he liked the idea. But his uncle explained the many advantages of an education and the possible avenues it would open up to him so that in the end he was persuaded. It was consistent with his character that one of his first questions was how it could be afforded as his father had left him no means at all. Joseph explained that he, himself, did have the means and, with no son of his own, it would be his pleasure to put them at the disposal of William to further his education. It would be, he said, his own testament to the memory of his deceased younger brother.

The more they discussed the possible outcomes of an education, the more enthusiastic William became and he vowed not to let down his uncle who was being so generous. There was only one problem. There was no suitable school in Wensleydale and Joseph was determined to send the boy to the best establishment he could find in the region. There being none sufficiently near to allow of William attending as a day pupil, Joseph felt enfranchised to cast his net ever wider and eventually he decided upon an establishment which had been set up nearly twenty years ago by Archbishop Holgate of York. The Archbishop's grammar school had an excellent reputation and was situated just outside the city walls. To be sure, it was a long journey to the City of York but coaches plied regularly from Ripon whence it could be reached in a day. This was a wonderfully exciting prospect for a boy who had never ventured out of his native dale before. The lure of seeing the big city quite overcame any misapprehensions he may have had about mixing with a different class of boy, most of them no doubt more worldly wise and sophisticated.

Well, he had gone. He had met and mixed with the other boys finding them neither frightening nor superior to himself in any sense, either academically or physically. He had quickly adapted to life in the city and, truth to tell, it palled quite quickly so that he was always glad to return to his beloved Wensleydale for the holidays. Now here he was, five years later and on the verge of his seventeenth birthday, standing at the field gate and gazing with pleasure up towards the head of the dale where the high fells crowded close together, their summits often lost, as they were today, in low cloud. It was an enchanting view of a countryside which he had explored thoroughly in the company of his special friends Kit and Bess Fawcett. They, brother and sister, lived with their parents at Cuebeck Farm, just up the hill from Worton and the three of them had got on famously from the first time they met. Kit was of a similar age to William and they shared a passion for the countryside and its creatures, although whilst William was content to observe, Kit was more inclined to pursue and catch. Not so fortunate as William, their father required them to work on the farm. When they could be spared from their tasks, and sometimes when they could not, they roamed together all over the dale which Kit knew like the back of his hand and, at only eight years old, Bess could not be persuaded to stray from the side of her beloved brother. They became an inseparable trio and Joseph was to discover that the tranquillity of Worton Hall could be totally shattered by the antics and raised voices of the youngsters. But William and his young guests were always respectful and obeyed quickly enough when he requested a little peace. These were happy days: days of exploration of leafy glades, populated by little rabbits which, strangely, were black unlike those which William remembered from Walburn; rocky crags with watchful birds of prey circling above them and little deserted plateaus with circles of stone to show where t'owd man had once lived. Water was always a great attraction and they fished in the streams, stripped and dived into the bigger pools on the river, emerging to dry unselfconsciously naked in the warm sunshine.

Despite the interesting times he was experiencing in York and the friendships he had made there, William was always glad to return to the dale when his holidays came around. Perhaps it was something of the actor within him that allowed him to adapt so easily to the different environments in which he found himself. York was a truly different world in which conversations were more sophisticated in terms of the language employed if not the content, whilst pronunciation too was equally different. Whilst he never quite lost his dales accent, his ear was sufficiently good to pick up and copy the city style of speech and treatment of vowels. It has to be said that his street education included the knowledge of a few robust and unsavoury expressions but he knew well not to introduce them into exchanges with tutors and staff. William was very conscious of his own ability to adapt quickly to the company in which he stood and he practised it easily and unselfconsciously. It was not done to ingratiate but only to equate himself better as a member of the society in which he found himself at any given time.

And now here he was back at Worton looking forward to renewing his adventures with the Fawcett children. Equally Kit and Bess counted the days to his return and they all fell into their old ways without hesitation, each year bringing new discoveries and delights which they shared. Until just recently that is. William frowned as he recalled the event that had caused a small rift, a fleeting problem he hoped, for it was he who had been responsible for the difficulty which had arisen.

It had been the day immediately following his return to Worton in early July. They had taken a few pieces of bread and cheese on an expedition down the dale, tramping along the river bank until they had reached the falls at Aysgarth. Here they had turned over stones to try to discover the little crustaceans, which were lately appearing in the streams of Wensleydale, but having no luck, William and Bess decided to go for a swim, whilst Kit stayed to chase small trout which had remained trapped in a pool at the top of the falls. William was about to make a remark to Bess about the warmth of the water and, glancing up, he froze, his mouth hanging open in shock. This was not the Bess of last summer. In place of the androgynous tomboy, all gangling legs and arms, was an undeniably female creature, all curves and rounded softness. The little buds of last year had developed into fully formed breasts, admittedly small but of exquisite shape. To confirm the totality of the metamorphosis, there was the dark fuzz at the base of the abdomen, which drew his gaze like a magnet. Perhaps alerted by some element of tension in the sudden silence, Bess looked up and perceived the direction of William's gaze. The weathering effects of the summer sun were totally inadequate to conceal the comprehensive blush that suffused her features and, gathering her clothes to her, she rushed off without a word. William was too embarrassed to call her back and minutes later Kit appeared to tell him that Bess had declared her intention of going straight home.

"She seemed upset and rather cross. Had you been teasing her Will? " he asked with a laugh. William shook his head.

"Not a word did I say Kit," he protested and so Kit was inclined to dismiss the incident as yet another of his sister's ever increasing and inexplicable mood swings.

That had been over a week ago and since then Bess had declined to join the boys in any of their expeditions or activities. William did not know if he should apologise and, if so, for what. He thought it better to leave the matter as it was and not refer to it in any way. Bess would come round he was sure. But she was taking a long time to do so. This morning both his friends were helping their father on the farm and William, at a loose end, was reduced to embarking upon a solo expedition into the country. No matter, he had always done so as a young boy and solitude was not a problem for him.

Chapter 2: Bolton

Her Majesty, Queen Elizabeth of England, was a very troubled and irate woman. The cause of her irritation and also the source of most of her problems at this time was her cousin, Mary Stuart. This wretched woman had, by her impulsive and outrageous behaviour, created a dilemma for the English Queen that would not be easily resolved. It was bad enough that her reputation for moral laxity and sexual excesses had been exacerbated by the growing rumours that she had connived at, if not actually participated in, the assassination of her husband, Lord Darnley, but now the troublesome woman had arrived in England, throwing herself, she said, on the mercy of her sister Queen.

Elizabeth had always had a certain sympathy for her cousin. Although they had never met, they were related after all and, furthermore, they had endured a common difficulty as being lonely, regnant Queens, without the benefit of family support. The apparent ease with which Mary had been stripped of her power and compelled to sign articles of abdication had outraged the English Queen, who believed implicitly in the sacred right of a monarch to remain on the throne. There was no way in which she could countenance the idea of wilfully abandoning Mary to the less than tender mercies of her enemies. What was worse, however, was the reminder of how easy it might be to unseat herself from the English throne should a powerful enough rebellion be raised against her. She was insufficiently confident of her own ability to remain in control of this emergent protestant country of hers in the event of a religious uprising. Mary Stuart was a committed member of the Roman Catholic faith and Elizabeth did not need Cecil, her most trusted and valuable advisor, to point out that Mary's Catholicism was a constant focus for the encouragement of dissidents and potentially a threat in the form of a dangerous alliance with one of the powerful Catholic powers of France or Spain.

And now this charismatic Scottish Queen had arrived in the north of England, where she had been fêted by northern Catholic nobility, who competed for the honour of sheltering her. Joined by more of her own Scottish supporters, she had been escorted with a great show of respect and courtesy to Carlisle Castle. Before leaving Workington, she had written an emotional appeal to Elizabeth saying: 'I entreat you to send to fetch me as soon as you possibly can, for I am in a pitiable condition, not only for a Queen, but for a gentlewoman.' This had prompted an immediate reaction in the form of the despatch to Carlisle of Sir Francis Knollys, vice-chamberlain of Elizabeth's household, and Lord Scrope who was the governor of Carlisle. They carried sympathetic letters from Elizabeth and also clothes befitting the station of her unexpected and, to be frank, unwanted guest. But subsequent correspondence had been less satisfactory. Mary had been insistent that she should be allowed to meet with the English Queen who had demurred with the explanation that, as long as Mary remained under the cloud of the accusation of murder, she could not for her reputation's sake publicly meet with her cousin. This matter had to be cleared up as quickly as possible in order to regularise their relationship. Thus deprived of an opportunity to exert her personal magnetism on Elizabeth, Mary resorted to subtle hints that she may have to enlist the aid of other powers. It was dangerous, not to say foolhardy, to try to influence Elizabeth by such threats. The reports from Sir Francis did nothing to reassure the English Queen. Clearly Knollys had fallen under the spell of the royal refugee and he greatly admired her spirit but this did not prevent him from providing an accurate assessment of the lady's character and pointing out the problems of harbouring such a woman, desperate for vengeance and re-instatement, and willing to stop at nothing to achieve this.

Elizabeth pondered over all this, toying with the idea of returning her cousin post-haste to Scotland with the title of Queen but without the power to govern. She realised, however, that not only would this be unacceptable to Mary but it would also alienate the Regent, Moray, and the protestant nobles, who were essential in preventing that dreaded alliance between Scotland and France. Detention in England was therefore necessary in the short term and, as she had taken on board the fears of Knollys that Mary's speed and skill on horseback was a great security risk, a move deeper into England was considered the best policy. It had to be somewhere away from the potentially rebellious borders, away from the coastal escape route to the continent and in a place from which it would be difficult to take a direct route back to Scotland. The choice was the seat of Lord Scrope: Bolton Castle in Wensleydale.

....

It would have been impossible to see the young stag against the perfectly matching background of mixed vegetation had it not been for the slight heaving of his flanks. Young he may have been, but he was old in the ways of the hunt and had not survived to attain his first points without crossing the paths of men – and their dogs. Those dogs could be heard now about a quarter of a mile away, occasionally barking but not in the full-blooded tones of the chase. They had lost the scent at the point where he had entered the river and he had waded along its course against the current for a few hundred yards before emerging again on the same side. He was headed for the thick, almost impenetrable forest at the head of the dale and there was still a long way to go. But now he was blown and needed a few minutes at least to recover so, feeling himself to be temporarily safe, he stood motionless against the bank of alder which arose from the scrub land. He was by no means safe. At that moment two pairs of eyes, each oblivious of the other, were fixed upon him. William had been walking softly through the woods when he had heard the deer emerge from the water and climb the bank. He had stood motionless as the animal came to rest at the far side of the glade and watched sympathetically as it stood there recovering its strength. He too could hear the dogs and knew that he would not be granted this vision for long. Higher up the hill, from where Thomas had lurked, bow in hand, waiting for a passing hare or rabbit to appear, he had also been lucky enough to see the deer. Now he had notched his arrow and was rising slowly, ever so slowly, from his crouched position to get a clear shot. William was edging forward to get a better view. Thomas had reached a point of good equilibrium and sighted along his arrow. William's incautious foot stepped upon a dry twig; Thomas discharged the bow; it was too late and the shaft clattered harmlessly against the alder stems as the deer fled into the trees.

The sound of the breaking twig had not only alerted the stag to its danger but had pinpointed the position of the person responsible to the furious Thomas, who charged down the bank and seized him by the collar of his jerkin.

"Who the devil are you boy and what d' ye mean by spoiling my sport? You are a trespasser and by God I'll thrash 'ee before I kick you off our land." He swung a wild and vicious blow at William's head, which the lad easily dodged returning a blow of his own which landed painfully on his assailant's ear. It was a close contest. Thomas, at sixteen years, was big and burly whilst William, just turned seventeen, was thin and wiry. Each took a lot of punishment in the exchange of blows but still they fought on until Thomas sought to bring the fight to a quicker conclusion. Seizing the cudgel which hung at his belt, the better to dispatch a wounded rabbit, he swung the weapon down upon William's head, missing his aim slightly but causing the lad to stagger blindly and fall to the ground. Another blow was aimed but by raising his left arm William warded it off. It was at great cost. The sound of the breaking bone was heard by both. The next blow being aimed at his head might well have killed him but for a stentorian shout of "Hold there!" The combatants froze and saw that they were under the gaze of a company of mounted huntsmen who had penetrated the clearing unnoticed. The man in charge, who was clearly delineated as such by both attire and demeanour, rode forward and demanded

"What the devil are you lads about that you seek to end each others' life in this violent fashion?"

"Thomas Metcalfe, my Lord, of the Metcalfes of Nappa Hall." It was said proudly, and with a touch of defiance born of a tremendous self-confidence. "And this here is a poacher, from where I know not, but I discovered him in the act of stalking one of your deer. I had thought to give him a beating to teach him a lesson but perhaps your Lordship would wish to hang him on the spot?"

His Lordship was sufficiently percipient to realise that the spectacle of a young man dangling from a rope at his behest would do nothing to enhance his image in the eyes of the accompanying party.

"No, no, young Metcalfe, a beating will suffice," he said and Thomas moved forward again with the clear intent of inflicting more punishment on William.

"My Lord Scrope!" The woman's voice cut clearly across the glade and every head turned towards her. It was a voice imbued with the expectation of being heard and receiving deference, a deference which his Lordship reluctantly conceded. "Yes Ma'am?" he enquired.

"Methinks the case is not sufficiently proven," she continued. "Master Metcalfe it is who holds the bow, whilst the other lad has no weapon unless he sought to ensnare a 'dear' by fluttering his long eyelashes at her." The jest was appreciated and served to lessen the tension considerably. Lord Scrope spurred his horse forward and in much softer tone enquired

"Your name lad, and your dwelling?"

"William Robinson, my Lord, of Worton Village."

"By God, it is indeed John Robinson's son!" came confirmation in a voice which William knew well. "The wrong side of the river for ye my lad; what do ye here then?"

William looked up at Sir Francis Lascelles, Lord of the Manor of Walburn.

"My father brought me here, Sir Francis, when the sickness came to our village and I have lived with my uncle since then."

"Ah, so Joseph has housed you has 'ee? Well now my Lord, I am sure there was no harm in the lad's mind. A bit of a dreamer and the despair of his late father but living now it seems with Joseph Robinson who is a true and honest gentleman, with a fine farm at Worton." He swivelled in his saddle to address another of the party. "Dammit man, I believe you might be related by marriage. We can't have cousins brawling so, eh!"

The huntsman so addressed was Sir Christopher Metcalfe, father of William's late assailant, and he scowled at the comment but said nothing.

Lord Scrope broke the short but awkward silence and addressed William.

"Well then, be off with you boy and we'll say no more on't. An' I catch you here again I may think different." Lord Scrope wheeled his horse around and William made to stand but gave a loud gasp of pain as his arm jolted against the bole of a tree. The lady slipped neatly off her saddle and came to him in some concern.

"What is it my lad? you look as wan as a goose feather."

She looked kindly upon him but spoke with an accent which he could not place. He had never heard its like before.

"This arm, my Lady, I think t'is broke."

One look at the unnatural angle of the forearm confirmed his statement.

"Aye, it is indeed boy," and she glowered at the unrepentant Thomas and then turned.

"My Lord Scrope, you have a man skilled in dealing with such a mishap?"

"Yes Ma'am, I do."

"Then I pray you give me leave to bring him to the castle."

Without waiting for an answer she called to another member of the party: "My Lord Herries, do you bind up the arm with some support and ride him before you. I shall go on ahead and instruct the physician."

With that, she nimbly remounted and spurred away leaving William to gaze after this kindly apparition, this woman clad in plain hunting costume but enlivened by a shawl of brilliant green and who sat her horse so well and rode as assuredly as any man. The remainder of the party followed along leaving the thin-faced, sharp-eyed Lord Herries to minister to the broken limb, which he did by lashing it to a stout branch of elm. William endured the ordeal in silence and did no more than wince as he was hauled up onto the horse behind Lord Herries who nudged the animal into a steady walk. There was a parting shot from the sole remaining occupant of the glade.

"Stay away from Nappa Hall, young Robinson, or I shall deal wi' thee properly next time, cousin or no!"

"Nae friend of yours laddie!" smiled the rider grimly as he set a gentle and steady pace along the easiest route he could find. William had no difficulty in his identification of the Scottish accent which had been employed.

"I fear that's true my Lord, " William managed a smile, "though we had ne'er met afore this and I swear I had no wish to harm the stag. Rather was it he who loosed an arrow – I heard it fly and fall."

"I think we all believe it to be so, laddie, and that is why we tak ye to be well mended as befits a true, if vanquished, warrior."

William was not sure that he enjoyed being teased in this manner but he smiled dutifully. His escort meanwhile seemed to be greatly interested in him and his family, asking where he lived in Worton and whether his uncle was in good standing with Sir George. William assured him that his uncle was well respected by Sir George and indeed all the villagers and that his farm, on the banks of the Ure, was a prosperous one, which gave them a good living. He was clearly as proud of his family's standing in the community as his erstwhile adversary was of his.

"A goodly sized farm d'ye say laddie? And are there stables there?"

"Oh yes my Lord, we have stabling for three horses and all are fine animals."

"Better and better, " muttered his noble companion under his breath and then aloud, "I should think your uncle will be well pleased to see his boy returned to him having been properly cared for."

"He will be most grateful, my Lord, as so, indeed, am I. My Lady and yourself have been most kind to me." Lord Herries laughed shortly and said "Not 'my Lady' boy 'tis 'Your Majesty,'" and when William looked up at him in astonishment he explained.

"It is Mary, the true Queen of Scotland who has taken you into her care!"

It took a long time to reach Bolton Castle, seat of Lord Scrope, and it was dark when they did so. William, stiff and very sore from his injury, had to be helped down from the horse and led from the courtyard through a doorway which gave onto a winding staircase. In a chamber on the next floor there burnt a log fire and rush torches. A grave looking old man stripped off his shirt and examined the arm gently.

"Lucky, boy, lucky," he pronounced solemnly. "It is a clean break and has not penetrated the skin. At your age t'will mend quickly but you must needs take care not to shock it again. I am going to bind it now tightly with a compound which hardens. That will help the bone to set straight and will prevent it from moving. After six weeks we shall remove this splint for you but until then it stays in place."

The binding was a little painful but when completed the arm felt more secure and the application of the strange mixture, which the physician had pounded up and mixed in a large bowl, was tedious but not at all distressing.

Towards the end of the process they were joined by a small audience. It was Queen Mary accompanied by Lord Herries and another nobleman, Lord Fleming. William struggled to free himself from the grasp of the physician and fell onto his knees before the Queen.

"My Lady – I'm sorry – Your Majesty, I beg you to accept my humble thanks for all this care you give me and what is more for saving my life at the hands of that Metcalfe." His chameleon-like ability to adopt the cultural behaviour and language of his present social surroundings came to the fore. He spoke as he had occasionally heard the gentry address one another and he was a good mimic with an excellent ear so he carried it off well. For sport he had amused his parents as a little boy with this sort of talk as he play-acted some fanciful drama of an evening and they had laughed and enjoyed the joke, although his father had warned him against putting on too many airs. The Queen meanwhile was delighted and laughingly told him that for a miller's son he was well spoken and knew how to please a lady. The physician seized hold of him again, clucking loudly about the risk to his splint, and respectfully ushering his visitors out of the room.

"We give way, Sir Leech," said Willam's royal patron and, turning to him with a smile, she said "I bid you a restful night Master Robinson and hope to see you better on the morn."

She did indeed see him better on the next morn but not as William had understood the words.

He did not sleep well. The arm was painful, his head ached and he felt bruised and battered. The old physician attended him early and noted that he looked flushed and his brow felt hot. A cold bath was prescribed and William wondered how this could be achieved in his current condition. He was soon to find out. A servant was summoned who helped him negotiate the winding stair and led him out into the courtyard. Here he was ordered to strip himself of all his clothes and then step into the stream of water which issued from the pump operated by the servant. It was desperately cold and, gasping, he rotated painfully in the stream seeking to wash away the grime and stains he had accumulated in the fight in the forest. Emerging from the cold downpour, he was thrown a rough cloth with which to dry himself and, as he towelled vigorously away to restore circulation to his frozen body, he was startled to hear a female voice call out

"Good morrow Master Robinson, you look in better case, and doubtless better odour, after your cleansing."

William hastily adjusted his towel but he feared he was too late and this was confirmed by the subdued giggling of the two maids in the small party that stood in a doorway opening onto the courtyard. Queen Mary, for it was of course she, smiled and said "Dress yourself sirrah then attend me in my chamber." As she turned to leave William made to bow but, to his acute embarrassment, his clumsiness caused his towel to fail in its defensive role and he remained uncomfortably crouched as he fumbled to retrieve it. The Queen laughed, "Methinks you are at least covered with confusion, if naught else." and she swept back into the castle, leaving a thoroughly discomfited William to complete his drying and dress himself.

When he was eventually conducted into the Queen's chamber he found her attended by the same Lord Herries who had carried him back on his horse and an amiable but elderly gentleman, who he found later to have been Sir Francis Knollys. The Queen was dressed in striking mixture of green, gold and brown. The fairly plain kirtle was divided at the bottom to reveal a forepart decorated in contrasting greens formed into a formalised pattern suggesting the leafy boughs of the woodland. Tiny green slippers peeped from beneath the border.

William had been practising and his bow this time was more successful. He answered respectfully as the Queen enquired after his injury and was relieved to hear from her that Lord Scrope had sent a messenger to his uncle at Worton, telling him of the circumstances of his retention at Bolton Castle and promising that he would be restored to his home as soon as possible.

"And are ye well enough to return?" asked the Queen.

"Aye, thanking you, your majesty," William replied. "I am thinking my uncle will be anxious to see me."

"Well then, we must let thee depart but 'twill be necessary for our good doctor to see thee again in a few weeks to look at that limb."

William repeated his thanks for her kind attention, declared that he would be for ever at her service and prayed that the opportunity to serve her in some way would present itself. The Queen smiled, somewhat mischievously and said she might well think of something.

Bowing his way out of her presence, William left the chamber in the company of Lord Herries, who checked his further progress with a question: "Ye have declared that ye 'd wish to serve her majesty if so required. Is that true young master?" William assured his Lordship that he would be more than happy to discharge his obligation to the Queen and indeed Lord Herries himself for their help and kindness in his trouble. For the second time that day William felt himself to be subjected to close scrutiny but this time the gaze was directed at his character rather than his physique. He seemed to have passed some sort of test for the face of Lord Herries relaxed into an unaccustomed smile and he said "Aye Laddie, I do believe you would and mayhap I will call upon ye one day to make good your promise." William made shift to leave the castle with the discomfort of his broken arm more than counterbalanced by the glow in his heart. He thought he was in love.

The entire hamlet, or so it seemed, turned out to watch his return to Worton, escorted by one of Lord Scrope's men at arms. His uncle was angry at his trespass onto the Metcalfe land and his discovery there.

"There is bad blood between that family and myself William and now you have drawn attention to yourself as a member of the hated Robinsons, you will be included in their catalogue of enemies. Our very life here at Worton Hall may have been endangered by your rash enterprise into their woods. It was good of Sir George to speak out for you and uncommon condescension on the part of the Scottish Queen to take such an interest in your welfare. But don't let it go to your head my boy!" He was not to know that it already had gone to William's head. He had met a Queen, a real living and breathing queen who had taken notice of him, commanded assistance for him and indeed intervened to save his life. Kit and Bess meanwhile were suitably impressed by his adventure and sought to know all the details. Kit was envious of his opportunity to see the inside of Bolton Castle, a structure that brooded over the dale with a distinct aura of threat and authority. He wanted to hear full details of the stag and William's opinion as to where it was heading. The answers he received to that enquiry were deliberately vague as the prospect of his friend being caught and accused of poaching deer seriously frightened William. Bess on the other hand wanted a complete description of every garment worn by the Queen on each occasion he saw her but she too was disappointed in his answers. Apart from a few colours, and specifically the vivid green shawl, he was unable to describe the fashions with anything like the detail demanded by his young inquisitor. The one really good result of this episode was the happy resumption of the threesome with all awkwardness between William and Bess forgotten.

The conference which took place in Mary's chamber at Bolton Castle was riven by disagreement from its outset. Only three persons were present and each took a different view of events and how to deal with them. The principal matter for discussion was the offer which Lord Herries had brought back from London that day, 30th July. It was a curious offer constructed by Queen Elizabeth and her chief advisor, William Cecil. The prime objective was to persuade Mary to submit her cause to a quasi-judicial hearing and to entrust her case to be not judged, but overseen by her sister Queen, who promised to summon her adversaries to attend and answer as to why they had deposed their legitimate ruler. If they could not do so, as she believed was the case, then Elizabeth would reinstate Mary on the Scottish throne.

All this sounded very enticing but there were conditions: Mary had to renounce any claim to the English throne during the lifetime of Elizabeth. She should abandon the league with France and receive common prayer in Scotland rather than the Mass. Mary was inclined to accept the offer. Her claim to the English throne was an embarrassment under the present circumstances and could be dropped instantly. Others, of course, might pursue it on her behalf but she would be personally distanced from this. The league with France was more in the spirit than the actuality and might be revived in the future if needed. It seems she placed little value on the continuation of Mass in Scotland despite her strong Catholic upbringing. Clearly she was prepared to be pragmatic in terms of her faith, with the prospect of restoration to the throne as the bait.

Lord Fleming, however, was outraged at the demands. He said he would not be able to bargain away his faith for the temporal gain. The only good thing was the clear statement of support for Mary's claim to the throne and he admitted that the reputation of the English Queen for honest dealing and the keeping of her pledges was well known. He also knew of her strong belief in the divine right of monarchs to rule and to this extent he believed in her integrity. But the right to remain Catholic was paramount. He advocated refusal of the offer.

Lord Herries took a more cynical attitude to the situation. He pointed out that a man's faith was between himself and his God, that clandestine religious practice could become more overt as the passage of time cemented the reality of the Queen's rule over her country and that the support of Elizabeth was essential to any realistic hope of restoring Mary to the throne. The 'conference' as it was euphemistically called was likely to be convened in York, handy for her representatives to attend and relay information relatively quickly. He then presented his fears about the situation. Should the hearing find against Mary then her cause was lost in England. Being unwilling to return Mary to persecution in Scotland and being unwilling to allow her to escape to France, her dreaded enemy, Elizabeth would be compelled to keep her under permanent restraint in England; perpetual imprisonment in effect, however it might be dressed up as hospitality.

Faced with this dreadful possibility, the Scottish firebrand erupted into threats of raising rebellion in England believing public sentiment would be with her. She had many Catholic friends in this country she said, who would rally to her cause. Herries shook his head emphatically. That was her greatest danger, he said. The supporters of whom she spoke did indeed exist but they did not have the power to match Elizabeth, nor the network of intelligence agents such as that under the direction of the cunning and powerful Cecil.

"Should any such plot be discovered your majesty, t'would not be imprisonment but execution which would be your fate."

He then made the statement which momentarily paralysed the other two and plunged them into gloom. "I truly believe that the findings of the conference will go against your majesty. The man Cecil will see to it. He and not Lord Moray is your most dangerous enemy. He would have it that your case fail, that you are removed deeper still into England, safely immured in a secure castle and, in the fullness of time, quietly murdered."

Mary's hitherto unbowed self-confidence failed her at this moment.

"Am I then lost, My Lord?" she asked simply.

"Not so ma'am. We must await the findings with at least some hope but we must prepare for failure. We must plan, your majesty, for your escape."

....

It was several weeks later when William attended Bolton Castle to be seen by the physician. He had been apprehensive about the removal of the splint but in fact it had been much easier than he had expected. A couple of sharp blows had split the hard covering without in any way damaging his newly mended arm and he felt a wonderful sense of freedom at the removal of this encumbrance. He was disappointed that none of the principals were present at the castle, most of all of course the charismatic and glamorous Queen Mary. The only figure of note he encountered was Sir Francis Knollys who hailed him as he crossed the courtyard, enquiring pleasantly as to his condition and congratulating him upon his speedy recovery. He explained that the others had ridden over to Walburn Hall for a day's hunting as the guests of Sir George and would be back only in time for a late dinner. He paused and looked William straight in the eye.

"Ye'll doubtless feel greatly indebted to the Queen," he said. When William stammered something barely intelligible about being forever in her service, Knollys smiled somewhat grimly and said that this was a reaction of many other men before him and some had come to grief as a result. William took his leave politely and made off back to Worton wondering a little at the old man's words and the reason behind this short interview. He had a strange impression of having been studied and included in a sort of mental notebook. However, he reasoned that in time he would be dismissed and forgotten as being of no account. In that he was mistaken.

In the meantime consideration had to be given to his future and he was astounded to hear his uncle Joseph's suggestion that he undertake legal training. This incredibly generous man had to reassure William that the expense of his training could be easily borne and it would not only be a tribute to the memory of his brother but a pleasure to watch his nephew's progress in the world.

"Your master at York sings your praises my boy," said Joseph with a smile. "He tells me you have studied hard and applied yourself to your work with no more than the occasional misdemeanour."

William started a little at this for he had been sure that all his little escapades at York had been unremarked but this, it seemed, had not been so. The all-seeing eye of the headmaster must have picked up something and he was thankful that most of his transgressions had been mischievous rather than venal. In fact the only incident of any moment had been the scaling of one of the east towers of the Minster in an attempt to recover his cap, which had been hurled into the air by a rumbustious class fellow and snagged on a gargoyle. He had been making good progress when a shout from below alerted him to the fact that the proctor had spotted him and was ordering him to descend. To be fair, this individual was more concerned about the danger to the boy than the risk of damage to the building but nonetheless William climbed down swiftly and craftily, managing to swing sideways over the wall to the Bishop's garden at the last minute before dropping to the ground and making his escape through the shrubbery.

He had certainly avoided capture at that time but he could guess that, when eventually recovered, the name inside his cap had revealed his identity. If so, he wondered why he had not been taken to task over the incident? He was not to know that the proctor and his headmaster had chortled together over a glass of malmsey, marvelling at his audacity and resourcefulness. The headmaster had planned a small token punishment and ceremonial return of the cap when William came back next term. But William was not going back. Instead he was to be articled to Mr Allcot, a noted attorney in Durham, a city much given to legal practice of one sort or another.

It seemed that his uncle had been fairly sure of William's acquiescence in this plan for him to undertake legal training in Durham for he had already been in contact with Mr Allcot and made several provisional arrangements. Although he knew nothing of the normal system of apprenticeship, it seemed to William that he was extraordinarily fortunate in the terms that were being offered. To be sure, the payment he was to receive was very small but then he was to benefit from the instruction he would receive at the hands of his principal. In addition, he would be provided with full board and would have a room to himself in the house.

What was even more incredible was that he would be able to stable his horse, Gaynor, on the premises although the cost of feeding would be his responsibility as would the care and exercising of the animal. Uncle Joseph promised to supplement his meagre income to help cater for this expense.

William was hard put to it to express his gratitude to his uncle, who waved away his thanks with an embarrassed air and making some comment about hoping his faith in William would be justified. The boy promised him earnestly that it would indeed be so.

So now, with the summer waning, he was set to embark upon a new phase of his education and, although he would be sorry to leave the dale, the prospect was exciting. He was glad to be leaving with things put right between Bess and himself. Nothing more had been said or even hinted at about the affair at Aysgarth Falls and the incident, although not forgotten, had been put to the backs of their respective minds. Some of the former easy relationship had returned but there was a difference which was impossible to deny. Looking at her now, William saw a lovely young woman rather than the little playmate of last year and furthermore a young woman who was conscious of her new status and expected to be treated in a more adult fashion. He was looking forward to the festival of Christmas which would allow him to return home for a few days and spend time with his Fawcett friends.

It was on his last day at home that the visitors arrived. Joseph had been surprised and a little disconcerted by the appearance of Lords Herries and Fleming at his house. It was unusual to say the least for nobility to condescend to recognise a plain yeoman socially, regardless of his degree of affluence but perhaps, he thought, it was different with the Scottish. In any event they had introduced themselves courteously enough and, when they had explained the purpose of their visit, a baffled Joseph had replied

"Aye, My Lords, he will be about in the fields and I shall send for him directly. I have a pleasant enough sherry sack which your Lordships might enjoy, otherwise nought but a quantity of perry which we country folk drink but which might not be to your taste." He was gratified by their acceptance of his hospitality and, as they sipped their sherry brought by a flustered Hannah, they questioned him affably about his farm holding, complimented him upon his house and stock and showed particular interest in how many horses he owned. At no time however did they explain their reason for wanting to interview his nephew and when William did make his appearance they requested politely that they be allowed to speak to him privately. At this Joseph looked really worried but he was reassured by Lord Fleming who smiled and said gently

"Nay, good Master Robinson, the lad is not in trouble; we need to question him on a certain matter of local knowledge to which he is privy." So, at this point Joseph excused himself, saying he would be in the dairy if required and the two Lords turned their attention to a bemused William.

It was Lord Herries who opened the interview going straight to the nub of things:

"Are ye of the Catholic faith?"

"No, My Lord. Our own Queen has decreed that we worship in the English Church."

"Are ye aware that my Lord Fleming and I are of the Roman Church?"

"I did not know, my Lord, but I had thought that might be so."

"And this does not offend ye?"

William smiled.

"Why no, my Lord! I think we all speak to God, mayhap in a different language but t'is the same God and there are still many hereabouts who do adhere to your own Catholic faith."

"And your uncle?"

"T'was my uncle who taught me to think that way my Lord."

Herries exchanged glances with Fleming.

"Good, good," he continued. "I think we are all here aware of such a Roman Catholic gentleman who resides in this area."

William froze. Was this a ruse to incriminate a recusant? The persecution of such people was well known and there were often disaffected Protestants who were prepared to denounce them. He knew well to whom Lord Herries was referring, having seen as a boy the coming and goings of hooded and cloaked figures at Walburn Hall and once stumbling across a wicker basket containing a chalice and bejewelled crosses.

"My Lord, I cannot fully perceive the drift of your mind," he said quietly.

Lord Herries laughed appreciatively.

"Aye but ye do, laddie, ye do, and I take it well that ye have the caution not to reveal the name of Sir Francis of Walburn. Fear not. He is in our confidence touching the matters of which I may now speak, having established your loyalty and discretion."

"I am loyal to my Queen and country," said William firmly.

"I doubt it not my lad," was the reply. "But ye do have a loyalty to friends and those to whom you may be beholden?"

This was really a question, not a statement and William was obliged to reply in the affirmative.

"It may be young Master Robinson, that my Queen, our Queen of Scotland, stands in need of help, which ye might be able to render, but which might go a trifle against your conscience to perform."

Totally mystified, William had to enquire what sort of assistance could possibly merit such a description.

Lord Herries replied bluntly:

"We would have you help her Majesty to escape her imprisonment."

William was stunned.

"My Lord Scrope holds the Queen prisoner?" he exclaimed.

"Aye t' is so boy but done at the behest of your Queen Elizabeth," answered Lord Fleming. "A sad thing when a monarch is prevented from returning to her kin and country, is it not so?"

But William had learnt a few things of current interest from his uncle and he was able to counter this loaded question with one of his own.

"My Lord Fleming, is it not true that the Lady Mary is no longer Queen of the Scots, having given up her claim to the throne?"

The brief, uncomfortable pause was broken by Herries who said

"Aye, ye are well informed William, but would ye say t'was a just and moral thing to hold the lady here in England, when she should be returned to the side of her son, the King?"

"And this would be a return to Scotland my Lord?" enquired William.

"Of course boy, where else?" asked Fleming caustically.

"I did wonder about France, my Lord," was the soft reply.

Herries was suddenly frightened of this perspicacious young man and the dangerous knowledge he possessed. In the short silence which followed he was already pondering as to how this lad could be quietly and safely disposed of but the problem quickly disappeared.

"I will help my Lords," said William quietly but firmly. "I believe the Lady Mary saved my life and showed me great kindness, as indeed did you, My Lord Herries, although I might wonder now at your own motivation." This latter was spoken with a smile which was almost a grin and which served to choke off the angry retort which Herries was formulating. "Whatever, my Lord, you have the right of it. I am indebted to the Lady Mary and yourself such that I cannot refuse to give whatever assistance I can. I have but one caveat." He was proud of that word which he had learnt from his teachers at York.

The silence was an enquiry.

"I will not take a life, my Lords, in the execution of this enterprise, nor would I willingly do physical harm to any of my fellow dales folk or damage their property. Now how may I serve you?"

There was a genuinely appreciative smile on the face of the ruthless Scottish peer when he replied.

"I had not realised, my young master, the depth of the intellect with which I was engaging when I planned to seek your help. Your sincerity I cannot doubt and your scruples do you credit; they will not be abused. Your honesty deserves my own. I do fear for the very life of my Lady Queen. An enquiry is to be opened at York, which might turn against her."

"Do you fear the commission will not deal fairly with the case of Lady Mary?" enquired William in disbelief.

"It is not the commissioners I fear William. There will also be present the Lord Cecil, however, and him I greatly fear. He has the ear of Queen Elizabeth and I believe he will poison her mind with tales of a possible revolt against her reign. Should she be so persuaded then I do fear the consequences. T'would be to the good if we could return to our country to dispel such false rumour."

"Yes my Lord," William agreed readily because he was beginning to believe that the rapid departure of this Scottish intriguer and his party would be best for his own country and most especially his own part of that country.

"Very well," said Herries. "We need a plan and I have one."

In essence the plan was a simple one but it relied upon a good deal of luck. Sir Francis would invite them to a hunting party. A notoriously savage and huge wild boar which roamed Downholme Park would be the bait to ensnare Lord Scrope, an enthusiastic huntsman. The day would be completed by a feast in the evening and liberal refreshment would be offered to the accompanying men at arms in the Bolton party. The Scottish Queen would be housed in a private chamber from which she could escape without being seen, although Sir Francis had given no details as to how this would be achieved. The Lords Herries and Fleming would not be in the party, having declared their intention of attending the hearing in York. In fact they would have stayed close by and remained hidden throughout the day. They would meet up outside the walls of Walburn Hall at some predetermined hour of the night with spare horses for the Queen and William himself. William's part was to guide them through the dark up the length of Wensleydale and thence through Maller-stang to Appleby and Penrith. From there they would strike west to Workington where a boat would be waiting to ferry them back to Scotland.

The Scottish Lords looked at William for his reaction to their proposed method of escape and he paused for a while, as he digested the plan. Finally he shook his head.

"It seems a goodly plan, my Lords, but I see two difficulties. I fear you may be overhauled by the men of Bolton once your flight is discovered. They could ride in relays at speed to raise the alarm ahead and you would be found."

"True," said Herries. "We can only hope that there will be delay before the absence of the Queen is discovered. The story could be put about that she is unwell after the evening's feasting and wished to stay abed for the morning. And your other misgiving?"

"T'is myself, my Lord. I fear I am not best fitted to guide you on this path. True, I know the dale well but, once at the head I am no better placed than yourself. I have never travelled the route over the fells to Mallerstang and, as to Penrith beyond, I know it not."

Fleming intervened.

"Then t' is no use, my Lord. We must place our faith in the goodwill of Queen Elizabeth, as I have ever counselled, rather than hazard all on a scheme beset with such difficulty."

"Methinks there is scant goodwill from that quarter," snapped Herries in reply and turning to William he asked "You think the plan unworkable then?"

"No, my Lord, it can be done with but two differences."

"Aye, so then?" he was prompted.

"We need a better guide than I and there is one such upon whom I can rely."

Herries looked doubtful.

"Another conspirator increases the risk of discovery William – I like it not."

"My Lord, Kit is a friend of these five years and we are like brothers. He would not fail me and he knows of my debts to you and will be happy to help me discharge them."

"Mayhap he would serve then. But your other thought on the matter?"

"We must not just delay the pursuit my Lord. We must utterly misdirect it."

Herries enquired how this could be achieved and William explained that there was a route to the north, much more frequently taken by travellers. It involved going through Richmond and then either continuing north up through Northumberland or swinging west onto the pass through Stainmore to reach Penrith and thence Carlisle. The escaping Queen and her escort should indeed make a silent departure going west up the dale but, after a suitable passage of time, noise would be made to alert the watch, who would then be treated to the sound of a party of horses galloping off to the north. The decoy party would continue through Richmond, making enough disturbance to alert the watch but without being seen. It would be sufficient to lead the pursuers onto the road to Gilling to cement in their minds the belief that the party was definitely heading for Scotland.

It was the turn of Herries to shake his head. "T's a good notion but we cannot raise such a number of horses without attracting attention and conjecture as to their use," he said sadly.

"But I can, my Lord!" said William. "My uncle has three from which I have been given the permanent use of one and I doubt not that Kit could borrow his father's horse for the night."

Over the past few minutes Lord Herries had witnessed his bold plan being demolished and then completely rebuilt. Instinctively he knew it could work and he turned to William with a question.

"Can ye take me to meet this Kit laddie?"

"Why yes my Lord – but now Sir?"

"Indeed now. There may be no room for wasted time."

"As to time, my Lord, I must enquire when you propose to carry out this plan. I leave for Durham in two days and will not be able to return until the Christmas festival, and then but for a few days."

Once again Lord Herries was shaken by yet another unforeseen difficulty.

"What keeps you in Durham so long?" he enquired.

"I am indentured to an attorney, my Lord, and will hope to continue my studies there to become one myself."

Lord Herries laughed despite his disappointment.

"An attorney indeed! And ye will make a fine one, William, I doubt not."

He thought for a moment and then continued. "There is naught certain about this undertaking yet William. Mayhap my Lord Fleming here is correct and we can expect better hope of support for our Lady from your Queen. But I have fears that this commission might bring about a sudden change for the worse and we may have need to carry off the plan without your help. I would hope however that there will be no need for action until the Christmas celebration occurs and indeed there will be better excuse for a party at Walburn

Hall. What time will you have here in December?"

"But four or five days, my Lord," was the reply.

"It must suffice. Now, take me to your Kit!"

Chapter 3: Durham

In many ways this city was like the only other one of his acquaintance, York. There were grand houses, busy streets, a river and a cathedral. But whilst York was flat, Durham was built upon a hill, nay a cliff, and the cathedrals were totally different in nature. William was hard put to it to decide which he preferred; the elegant, gothic spires and the glittering white limestone of the Minster in York or the awe inspiring mass of the brooding Norman edifice with its grey stone and its position on the cliff at Durham. Each was impressive and eventually William decided that each looked right in the general context of its setting. All this he had seen as he entered the city riding over the Framwellgate Bridge, approaching as he had from the south west. Now he must set about discovering the chambers of Mr Allcot and his home for the next five years.

According to his instructions he was to ascend Smith Street, passing all the busy forges and metal working establishments before entering the continuation of this road, which was named Silver Street and thereafter turning to the right he would enter Saddler Street. This he was to follow until a right hand turn into Owengate led him to the office of his new master. He found it easily enough and to the left was an archway, which led into the stable yard, through which he rode and which was backed by the massive walls of the castle. Finding nobody there he tied Gaynor to the post and went in search of the occupants of the house. There seemed to be several doors opening from the yard and, not knowing which to take, he decided to walk around to the street and present himself at the front door. There was a very large and shining brass handle that he pulled, generating the disproportionately small sound of a tinkling bell within. At length the door opened to reveal a little man of indeterminate age, and a pair of rheumy eyes either side of a sharply pointed nose peered at him.

"This is the residence of Mr. Allcot, attorney at law. Do you have an appointment?" The question was put politely enough but in the manner of one who was able to be selective about whom he admitted.

"Indeed I have," replied William, determined to hold his own in this situation. "Pray inform Mr. Allcot that Mr. Robinson is here, Mr William Robinson of Worton."

"Very good, Sir." There was a decided increase in deference which pleased William although he knew it was a cheap trick that would not survive their further acquaintance. The retainer shuffled off and, knocking at a door, entered without waiting to be called. There was an exchange of words, which although inaudible rose on both sides in obvious consternation. Eventually an older man with an air of distraction came out of the room and made for the door.

"Enter Sir, enter," he called. "I must needs offer my apologies for your name is not in my book of engagements for today. The foolish Peters here has doubtless failed to inscribe it therein to my shame and your discomfiture. I tell him that he must strive harder to emulate his illustrious and holy namesake who guards the gates on high and never makes such a mistake. Now how can I assist you Mr err…Mr Worton is it?"

All this was delivered with a smile and a very much more welcoming attitude than that of his employee. William suffered a sharp feeling of remorse for his foolishly highhanded speech at the door and he hastened to make amends and explain his true position.

"No Sir, no, t'is I who am in the wrong and I do apologise to you and Mr Peters here for misleading you so badly. I do indeed have cause to be here but it as your apprentice that I come, not as a client. William Robinson, of Worton, Sir, at your service."

There was a pause during which the expression of Peters became even sourer than before but the countenance of Mr Allcot broke into an amused smile.

"Of course, Mr Robinson. I was not sure just when to expect you and I do fancy that you are a day or so early. No matter, it bespeaks an enthusiasm which I hope will not be too short lived. You are as welcome as any client my boy, indeed more so, for I am so o'er whelmed with work as to be quite unable to undertake more cases. We must settle you in and I shall put you straight to work!"

Peters was instructed to superintend the stabling of Gaynor and show William to his room. William was at pains to address the man respectfully and to apologise again for the misunderstanding. That worthy, finding himself addressed by the unaccustomed honorific of 'Mr', became somewhat mollified and his expression softened to a mere gloominess, which William guessed was the best he could expect. In his room, which was comfortable enough, he placed his bags upon the bed and, after performing a quick ablution, he descended again as quickly as possible, having discerned in his master an anxiety to put him to work as soon as possible. He was proven correct in this for, being admitted to the study where Mr Allcot worked, he was seated at a small side table which bore a pile of papers.

"I need to have three copies of each of these documents, William. T'is boring work but necessary and they need to be in a fair hand. You can write clear and well?"

"I believe so, Sir, although t'is not my best accomplishment, I do confess."

"Well, well, we shall see. Finish that pile and we shall examine your handiwork over dinner. Now I crave your silence as I work on this brief."

There followed a few days of sedentary labour for William, not unpleasant but involving his more or less permanent immurement within Mr Allcot's house. Unaccustomed to this withdrawal from fresh air and outdoor existence, William was beginning to chafe a little and looked forward to the break which Sunday would bring. To be sure, a good deal of his work was repetitive and boring but there were many points of interest to an enquiring mind. Working as they did in the same room, William was conscious from the very first day of the necessity of his maintaining silence and forbearing from asking too many questions. Instead he made copious notes as he proceeded with a view to enquiring later as to the meaning of the many legalistic terms which cropped up. He was pleased to discover that his knowledge of Latin, painfully acquired during his time at school in York, now proved to be of great value in some instances.

There was a mid-day break for food and drink, of a somewhat frugal nature, and during which his principal continued to be pre-occupied with his work. Conversation was limited and William sensed that his own contribution should be limited to absolute essentials. It was clear that this short period at the table was an unwelcome, if necessary, distraction from the business of the day and indeed the business of the day did continue again, as before, until the hour of five in the afternoon. At this time, work ceased and William was informed that dinner would be served promptly at seven o'clock. He retired gratefully to his room where he simply rested upon his bed, the grey autumnal evening light having hampered his ability to observe the outside world through his little window. A half hour or so before the appointed time William arose, washed and changed into his smartest clothes before descending to sit in the anteroom and await the arrival of Mr Allcot. He had prepared himself for a virtually silent meal punctuated by only the most essential items of speech. He was utterly astonished by the actuality of the occasion.

Mr Allcot appeared in splendid if mutedly colourful attire and with his change of appearance there also came a dramatic change in his demeanour. He was solicitous, he was witty, he was expansive. Within this welcoming atmosphere William was encouraged to raise the questions which had occurred to him during the day's work and they were answered with enthusiasm. Each explanation was enlivened with an example from Mr Allcot's vast experience so that, rather than a catalogue of answers, the conversation flowed, albeit under the direction of the master. The meal over, sweetmeats were served with an accompanying cordial drink of deceptive mildness and conversation turned to more personal topics. It became clear that Mr Allcot and his uncle Joseph had enjoyed a long time professional relationship and a great measure of respect between the two had developed. Over the years Joseph had invested in property, modestly at first but more adventurously in subsequent years, and Mr Allcot had acted for him on most occasions. A correspondence had sprung up between them and Joseph had written to presume upon their friendship in the matter of placing his nephew as an apprentice. Mr Allcot gave no indication of the glowing praise that Joseph had bestowed upon William in his letters, and which he had largely attributed to an exaggerated avuncular affection. He was forced to admit to himself that, on the brief evidence available to him, the boy was extremely well behaved, respectful and sensitive. He was by no means dull and exhibited a fine talent for conversation. Beneath this, it was clear, was a deep intelligence which had been nurtured by a good education. He was inclined to congratulate himself upon the acquisition of, not only a useful adjunct to his practice, but a pleasing and interesting companion.

William was drawn out on his history to date and was listened to sympathetically as the story of his tragic early days unfolded. One thing which became clear to Allcot was the gratitude which William felt towards his father and his uncle in retrieving him from a catastrophic situation and placing him upon a path to advancement and achievement. There was no mistaking the genuineness of his feelings in this respect and Allcot warmed to the lad in response. He learnt of the passion which William felt for the outdoors and his love of wildlife generally and encouraged him to believe that this predilection and the legal profession were not necessarily mutually exclusive. In fact he extolled the delights of the northern dales of Tyne, Wear and Tees, which he had enjoyed many years ago as a boy and was enthusiastic about the prospects open to the lad, possessed as he was of a fine horse which would facilitate his exploration of the area. But, having plumbed the depths of the young man's psyche and heard of his many pleasures, exploits and acquaintances, Mr Allcot had the sensibility to divine that there was a gap in the narrative. Something was being held back; it was probably quite recent and too sensitive a subject to be aired to a comparative stranger. He hoped he would eventually be admitted to a closer relationship in which knowledge of the matter and any problems arising therefrom could be revealed.

For his part, William had been pleasantly surprised by the relaxed atmosphere in which he found himself during the evening meal and afterwards as they sat and conversed. The contrast between this and the almost monastical silence of the working day was amusing but he could appreciate the difference in circumstance which required this to be so. If life was to continue in this fashion during his sojourn in Durham then he was content. But he was still looking forward to his day of freedom on Sunday. He had been told that he would be expected to attend morning service, not in church but in the Cathedral.

"For two reasons my boy. Appearances, which are important to the well being of the practice, and because it is close by and much easier to walk to!" After that he would be free to enjoy the remainder of the day as he willed.

Sunday, when it dawned, was one of those delightful September days with sunshine, clear skies and yet a sharp nip in the air. A goodly number of people attended the service attired in their best finery and this proved to be an antidote to the almost overwhelming impression created by the stark surroundings within the cathedral. William was immediately struck by the contrast between this and the only other great house of worship he had encountered, York Minster. In York the feeling of reverence was engendered by the beauty and fluidity of the architecture. The building was awash with light which poured through the many lovely stained glass windows illuminating the brilliant white of the limestone structure. But the reverence was tempered by a strange feeling of friendliness, approachability perhaps being a better description. The congregation, the casual visitor, felt almost at home here and there was room for light-heartedness of spirit. The occasion of the mission to retrieve the lost cap came to mind and William could not imagine even the bravest student attempting such an escapade at Durham. Here everything was severe and forbidding. The architecture was massive, solid and rarely delicate. There was nothing in the way of decoration. William was to learn that the Prince Bishop Pilkington, the very first protestant to hold that office, had taken his responsibilities as he saw them very seriously and removed any objects which smacked of idolatry or popery. Apart from one splendid coloured window, the only object of interest which caught William's eye was an elaborate clock. He found he could not examine it well from his current position and resolved to return and study it at leisure. As for the rest, it was an austere edifice of worship, its solemnity perhaps appropriate for the resting place of the great Saint Cuthbert; magnificent but grim. It seemed that the congregation were here on sufferance rather than as welcome visitors.

As it was, the brightly coloured clothes worn by both sexes contrasted beautifully with the sombre grey stones of the massive building and there was an undoubted air of enjoyment about the occasion almost as though the festive season of Christmas was being anticipated. No overt gaiety and laughter perhaps, but smiling faces were all around. After the service William found himself being introduced to selected groups of people as the new assistant at Mr Allcot's practice. The word 'apprentice' was never used and, possibly as a result of this, he found he was being accorded a respect which he had never expected and which he hardly felt he deserved. But it was exceedingly pleasant to mix socially with persons who were clearly not without import in this busy city and to exchange civilities with them as though he had been doing so all his life. Ever the born actor and readily adaptable to new circumstances, William acquitted himself well and thought he had made a good impression. He quite missed the knowing smile on the lips of his mentor.

What he did not miss, however, was the apparent abundance of pretty young girls, all dressed to impress the likes of himself. Never had he seen such a multitude of female attraction gathered together in one place. And he was conscious of the fact that he, too, was being appraised by the ladies. Surreptitious glances from under lowered lids were sometimes accompanied by a blush as eyes met, whilst some of the older women were frankly assessing him as a potential son-in-law. This latter thought was slightly uncomfortable and he made efforts to distance himself from these women. Once again he missed the growing amusement on the face of Mr Allcot.

After a while he was able to take his leave of the social circles and, promising to return to the house before dark, he set off to explore the city. The shops were all closed of course and workplaces deserted but there were plenty of folk out enjoying the sunshine. There seemed to be a general movement down the street called Elvet towards the river and in lieu of a definite plan of action William followed the crowd. There on the banks he found a lively enough scene. The river opened up into a wide pool at this point. There were crude stalls erected from which ales and pies were being sold and gangs of youths were occupied in a variety of games. The activity which was causing the most amusement was a jousting contest of sorts in which small boats were being rowed about the river bearing a standing 'knight' who sought to knock his opponents into the water by belabouring them with a sack full of straw. Some of the sacks were splitting under the impacts and straw was littering the surface of the river and sticking in the hair of the protagonists but now and again a well-delivered blow produced the intended result and a body fell heavily into the chilly water. There were howls of mirth as the sorry victims hauled themselves onto the shore and tried desperately to mop themselves dry and restore circulation.

Eventually the field had reduced to just two survivors who did battle earnestly. William noted how the oarsmen tried to manoeuvre their craft so that their 'knight' could attack from behind; not sporting perhaps but certainly effective. At length one such tactic produced a final swimmer who, after gyrating desperately in trying to maintain his balance, abandoned the attempt and dived gracefully into the water. The winner was cheered loudly and after acknowledging the plaudits he was rowed to the bank. His final opponent meanwhile had reached the shore just where William was standing and he stepped forward to lend a hand in heaving him onto dry land.

"A brave try my friend!" was William's greeting. "You had bad fortune."
"No, I was outmatched yet again by that scoundrel Jed. He always contrives to beat me," was the rueful reply.

"But you provided great sport for we who watched from the safety of the river bank. Let me buy you a measure of ale in token of that entertainment." William had instinctively liked the youth who stood dripping before him and wished to cement the acquaintance.

"I thank 'ee kindly," said the lad, "But I must needs dry myself. I shall be with 'ee betimes to claim my drink!" and with that he shot off to a nearby clump of bushes behind which was hidden a rough bundle of clothes and a drying cloth. In a few minutes he was back again, grinning broadly and reddened of countenance from the vigorous towelling down he had inflicted upon himself. He led the way to a tent from which small bowls of ale were being dispensed and, after an enquiring glance at his companion, he ordered two such measures for which William paid cheerfully.

As is usually the case between lads of this age, the exchange of formalities was brief and to the point. Names were swapped and William learnt that he was conversing with one James Milburn who was known however by all and sundry as 'Sculley'. On enquiring the reason for this strange nickname he was told that it was on account of his having worked casually for some time as a scourer of pans and general cleaner at one of the city hostelries, which he had been compelled to do whilst he awaited the opportunity to acquire an apprenticeship with a local silversmith. This had been procured for him some three years ago by the Parish, as was now encouraged by the recent Statute of Labourers and Artificers, and had been a decided improvement in his lot. As an orphan living on the Parish, life had been hard and dreary, whilst he was now gainfully employed and with prospects of a career ahead of him when he concluded his apprenticeship in another four years. He had no doubt that he would satisfy the guild's examiners at that time.

Throughout Sculley's cheerful account of his circumstances, William had become increasingly aware of the contrast between them in terms of dress and outward signs of affluence or lack of same. Whilst he was wearing smart and moderately elegant apparel, his attention was drawn to the simple attire of his new friend. The doublet was of country russet in a dark blue, with a low hung skirt. The sleeves were of a dull grey with polished pewter buttons. Breeches and hose were of simple homespun wool and the plain leather shoes had polished pewter buckles to match the sleeves. All was clean and well tended but certain signs of wear could not be concealed. Sculley however was totally unconcerned by the obvious disparity in their outward appearances, although William did detect a glance at his own silver buttons and buckles, but it was an inspection based upon professional interest rather than of envy.

It became William's turn to explain himself and he did so from the starting point of their common condition of being orphans. He admitted to his own good fortune in finding himself in a situation of financial security and being able to attend a good school thanks to his kindly and generous uncle. He had expected to feel slightly uncomfortable in reciting his own background of financial and social advantage but any such feeling was dispelled quickly by Sculley's enthusiastic congratulations and the whistle of pure admiration, when he learnt that William was articled to Mr Allcot.

"Not that I knows him of course, but I had him pointed out to me and a grand looking fellow he is to be sure."

"Yes indeed," replied William. "I have only been in his employ for a few days but already I have found him to be a kind and friendly man, although very hard working and serious during the day."

As William described his uncle's home in Wensleydale and the country pursuits which he and his friends pursued, he thought how alien this would seem to a city bred youth with his sharp street wisdom and familiarity with urban life. He was astonished to find that this was not the case. Sculley listened with great interest to his accounts of the animal life and in particular the wealth of birds in the surrounding countryside. In fact he drew William on with questions which exhibited the fact that he was no stranger to wildlife and finally admitted that he made as many excursions into the country as was allowed him with his limited free time and that his own particular interest lay in the butterflies of the region.

William, whilst being aware of these brightly coloured insects, had not developed a major interest in them so he in turn listened to Sculley's impassioned description of the beauty of his favourite specimens. In the absence of any known nomenclature, Sculley had invented his own names for these little airborne jewels and William found himself trying to picture the butterfly from Sculley's imaginative names. The 'Orange Corners' were instantly identifiable as were the 'big', 'little' and 'streaky' whites but he had difficulties with some of the others and was delighted when his newfound friend proposed an expedition the following Sunday. "T'is late in the year, mind, so we may not be fortunate," confessed the lepidopterist. William made light of this possibility and said that there would still be plenty of birds to observe.

It was at this juncture that William became conscious of an uncomfortable sensation of emptiness in the region of his stomach. It was a long time since his early and limited breakfast. He needed food and sought to find a way to include his new friend in an expedition to seek something out. He resolved to employ the strategy of seeking advice which he felt would somehow put him in debt to the other lad.

He rose to his feet.

"Sculley, tell me if a man can find wholesome food in one of these tents?" he implored. "I have desperate need of, well shall we say, a mutton pie or some such refreshment." William had actually observed such a facility when he had first ventured down to the riverside. He jangled some coin in his purse and said "I think I have means to buy two such items; would you honour me by sharing such a feast?" and he removed his cap and made a bow with all the flourish of a royal courtier. Grinning broadly, Sculley too rose to his feet and adopted a reserved and condescending pose.

"I am minded to grant you such an honour, Sirrah, if you will consent to my choosing the hall in which we may seek our indulgence." They both laughed and in comradely fashion exited from the beer tent and marched directly into one next door which served the aforementioned culinary delicacies.

They ate heartily and William was pleased that there seemed to be no awkwardness in Sculley's acceptance of his munificence. The conversation flowed and after the meal William was taken on a tour of the area and was introduced to a bewildering number of young people, all of whom seemed to be bosom friends of his escort. There might have been some reservations amongst these persons less fortunate than himself but they were dispelled quickly by Sculley's wit and good humour and his refusal to take too seriously his companion's supposedly elevated situation in life. His very presence acted as a talisman which allowed William to converse freely and naturally with all he met and more than once he was driven to admire the natural gift of his friend to create a pleasant atmosphere. With his curly black hair, ruddy countenance and seemingly permanent expression of good humour, he radiated bonhomie. Sculley even introduced him with enthusiasm to Jed, his erstwhile and successful opponent on the river. William became aware of a penetrating and challenging stare which preceded the remark,

"Well, Sculley, perhaps your friend might fancy his chances against me on the river next Sunday, if he feels strong enough that is?"

William met the stare full on and said with a smile,

"Oh yes, I am more than strong enough, but today Jed I watched you closely and I noted your great skill. In that I cannot match you. Yet." There were smiles now on both sides but William was aware that a challenge had been thrown down and he had accepted it, albeit with an incorporated time factor.

The afternoon passed quickly in a whirl of friendly sociability but at the close it started to rain and everyone made a dash for shelter. There was just time for a reaffirmation of their tryst for the following Sunday and then William made his own hurried way home. Mr Allcot was asleep in his study but Peters was available to inform him that the Sunday evening meal would be taken at 6 o'clock as the master had an evening appointment with friends. William thanked him and repaired to his room where he rested on the bed and thought over his frenzied activity of the day, trying hard to place names on the faces which swam into his view. It had been an enjoyable day, a wonderful start to his existence in the city of Durham, which he was now prepared to say was the foremost city in the realm for friendliness and entertainment. When he put this proposition to his employer at the table, he was greeted with a smile and a request for all his activities.

"I am glad" said Mr Allcot "That you have found such agreeable entertainment on this day. Perhaps you will work the harder because of it next week." The amused smile belied the words but his employer went on to say, "Make the most of your new acquaintances, they sound to be worthy folk but I shall be introducing you to some people in higher circles before long. They may not be so entertaining but likely to be of more use to you in your career." William smiled and thanked his employer but he wondered if he could enjoy himself half as much in such exalted company when he had made such good and easy friendships in the course of a single afternoon.

That friendship was pursued the following weekend. They had agreed to rendez-vous on the river bank where they had first met and William astonished Sculley by turning up on Gaynor.

"She really needs the exercise," he explained "and she can manage us both with ease. Climb up behind me and we shall explore some of your Weardale countryside, if you would be good enough to direct me."

With great enthusiasm Sculley scrambled aboard the patient Gaynor and he guided William across country, past Old Durham and, after fording a stream, climbing to reach the venerable looking Neville's Cross. Sculley recounted the tale of the great battle, fought here many years ago but still remembered when the army of the Scottish King David was roundly defeated and the King himself was captured and held for ransom. He laughed.

"A big amount of money was agreed but they never paid that ransom, those canny Scots, so his captors were put to a lot of expense in keeping him for nothing."

He told how, as children, he and his friends used to run nine times around the cross and then listen with an ear to the ground, when they were supposed to hear the sounds of the battle. "We told each other that we could so hear it but I do not think any one of us really did so."

Sculley was delighted with his novel form of transport. As he explained, it allowed them to reach places normally too distant for even the most enthusiastic walker especially given the shortening hours of daylight. He was intent now on taking William to a deep and narrow ravine through which flowed the Browney Beck, not, as he explained to seek out his butterflies but to enjoy the plentiful birdlife, which dwelt in this seldom frequented valley. His plan met with success, as they encountered many different species: Dippers bobbed in the beck, two Goosanders flew noisily away and they watched a Ring Ouzel, a bird which William had seen but rarely before. There was a companionable silence as they rode back in the late afternoon, broken only by plans to make another expedition on the following Sunday. William ascertained how he could contact his friend, should some development prevent him from going, and learnt the whereabouts of his master, Mr Cleaver, on Silver Street, which meant of course that he could carry his friend to the very door as he passed by on his way to Mr Allcot's residence. He supposed aloud that he should have guessed this would be where all the silversmiths were established but was corrected by Sculley who told him that the street's name was really connected to the existence there of a Royal Mint in olden days. Doubtless Mr Cleaver, and indeed another silversmith, had decided to profit by the name and set up their establishments in the street. Not for the first time that day, William had been made conscious of the long history of this city, a history of which its inhabitants were clearly proud and which was remembered by all classes of society. He was beginning to form a strong affection for the town and its people.

He had of course only consorted with a particular class of the inhabitants as yet; members of the poorer artisans and quite a distance socially from his employer and his clients. This omission was to be rectified soon. Mr Allcot informed him that they would have company on the following Thursday morning for dinner at eleven o'clock. A certain Mr Armstrong would be coming along with his wife and daughter. It would be in the nature of a social occasion of course but there was a small matter of business to attend to and Mr Allcot begged that William would entertain the ladies whilst he and Armstrong withdrew to the office for a few minutes.

"Armstrong has business interests in your part of Yorkshire, William, and I shall take the opportunity to hand him a letter for your uncle which I am sure his agent, Stanhope, will see delivered for me." William reddened instantly. He felt sure that this was a mild reproach for his own failure to write to his uncle and he made instant confession.

"You do right to remind me, Sir, of my duty to my uncle. It is unforgivable of me not to have written myself but I have been so taken up with all the newness of things and time has sped past me. Perhaps Mr Stanhope would also undertake to carry my letter too?"

"I'm sure he will my boy and gladly. He is always looking for contacts in that part of the world to further George Armstrong's business interests." This was said with a knowing sort of smile and gave William some clue as to the character of the man he would meet later that week.

As the date drew nearer, William was conscious of an increasing feeling of tension and anxiety. This was strange. From his boyhood he had been fairly self-confident about meetings with other people, regardless of their position in society. It had been perhaps a confidence based upon a limited number of contacts in a context of familiarity and with a personal background of security. Even his encounter with the Scottish Queen and her courtiers had been managed, he thought, without loss of his own dignity and with the feeling that he had held his own. But that had been an adventure, thrust upon him by immediate circumstances and without time to ponder on the enormity of a country lad holding discourse with his immeasurable superiors. The impending social engagement, however, was of a different order. He could not say why this was the case but he had the decided feeling that this meeting would impinge upon his position here in Durham, in his employment with Mr Allcot and with his professional future. He had to perform well in the presence of Mr Armstrong, to show himself in the best possible light, and equally he would have to comport himself properly towards the ladies and not disgrace himself with gauche behaviour or manners.

It seemed that he was an open book to the wise and sympathetic Mr Allcot who raised the subject after their next evening meal together.

"T'will not be such a fearsome ordeal as you imagine, William," he said with a smile. Startled to have his thoughts so accurately interpreted, Willam looked up and asked if his anxiety had been so very obvious.

"Yes, my boy, it has been so ever since I mentioned the engagement to you. Let me put you at better ease by describing our Thursday night guests. Armstrong is a rich man, very rich. He is a merchant, concerned with many aspects of the woollen trade in all of which he seems to prosper. But t'was not always so with him. Very humble beginnings in the far north of Northumbria and I believe he has connection with the notorious border reivers of that name. You will find him to be blunt, loud and cheerful; an easy dinner companion. The ladies are of a rather different strain. His wife comes from a quite highborn family and is all-knowing in the arts of polite behaviour, correct dress and such matters of importance in society. But she is withal a kindly person and would do nothing to make a young stranger ill at ease. The daughter is perhaps more nice in her behaviour and opinions, but then t'is better I leave you to appraise her worth for yourself."

William felt better as a result of this briefing. Mr Armstrong sounded a bit intimidating but with a lively personality. Hopefully he would be able to just relax and listen without having to participate too much in the conversation, thus avoiding making any serious breaches of etiquette which would upset the ladies. Then he remembered that he was to spend some time with those same ladies whilst the business between the two men was conducted. He sighed inwardly and thought he could only do his best. Meanwhile he attended to the task of completing the letter to his uncle.

When the day dawned it was clear that this was to be a complete day's holiday. Much of the preparation had been completed earlier in the week: cook had been busy with purchase of foods and then the necessary baking, Peters had been concerned with the cleaning of the plate and glassware and ensuring that the rooms ands furniture were all clean, wine had been decanted into jugs from the barrels and the Brabant had been liberally spiced with honey and cloves then left to stand overnight. Breakfast was taken very early and after its clearance the table was arrayed for the repast. It was set for five places and William realised that the Armstrongs would be the only guests. A white linen cloth was spread and napkins of similar material were placed with a silver spoon alongside silver plates. There were elaborately wrought Venetian glasses and a porcelain bowl for the fingers in each place. William stared in wonder at this evidence of the opulence of his master. Normally their meals were served in clean yet simple style but now the best of the house's finery was to be employed. William bethought him that he too must look his best and retired to his room for a further wash and to change into his best clothes. In comparison with many folk he had seen in the city, his own clothing was subdued and, he suspected, markedly out of fashion. His doublet was of a dark green colour and his sleeves were of white the armhole joints being concealed by tightly rolled pickadils in black and yellow. He was pleased that he had kept abreast of fashion in that his codpiece was small, neat and undistinguished in a tan colour which matched his hose. His shoes were simply cut from leather but he at least sported silver buckles and silver buttons at his sleeves. He felt reasonably confident that he would not be letting down his uncle in sartorial appearance. Mr Allcot, when he appeared, was attired in a splendid plum-coloured doublet with sleeves of a lavender shade.

The guests arrived promptly at eleven o'clock and were ushered in by Peters, stiff and solemn to the point of pomposity. Introductions were made and they all accepted a small glass of hippocrass accompanied by little sweet-meats. Conversation was general but rather one-sided as Mr Armstrong lived up perfectly, as William thought, to Mr Allcot's description. He was certainly loud but he was also clearly good-natured and seemed to take a great interest in his new acquaintance, asking William many questions about his home and surrounding countryside. The ladies retained a suitably modest silence, having carefully taken in William and his appearance, Mrs Armstrong with a gentle smile, the daughter with a slightly supercilious smirk. It was a pity about that smirk, thought William, as it spoilt a very pretty face so he refused to take any note of it and concentrated on listening to her father. Before long they moved into the dining room and William was careful to see to the chairs of the ladies, receiving a smile and word of thanks from Mrs Armstrong and a curt nod from her daughter. Her name was Katherine and she seemed to William to think rather too much of herself.

It was a magnificent feast and, despite his concerns about his social short-comings, William thoroughly enjoyed himself. The fresh baked bread was delicious and there were plates of wildfowl, pheasant and chicken with red meats represented by beef and pork. To accompany these dishes were plates of onions, garlic and leeks along with cucumbers, cabbage and white beets. Mr Allcot offered wine and Peters served glasses of sack to the men, whilst Mrs Armstrong and Katherine drank a glass of Brabant.

"T'is a respectable Rhenish wine, Elizabeth," said Mr Allcot, "and if you find it wanting then I can but place the blame upon your husband, for he it was who procured the barrel for me."

"Aye, and ye'll note that I was careful not to choose it myself today," intervened Mr Armstrong to general amusement. William was eating steadily and with great pleasure. The Robinsons of Worton ate very well as a rule but never did he remember a meal like this with such variety and choice. When the sweet courses were brought to the table, his face glowed in anticipation. There was a magnificent apple pie, a Marchpane of blended almonds and sage whilst the pièce de résistance proved to be a Florentine covered in a special pastry and baked in a deep pewter bowl, the only piece of non-precious metal which William could detect on the table and excused as such by its prodigious size. Inevitably, William's enthusiasm for his food was noted and remarked upon. In fact, he became the butt of a good deal of humorous teasing from all sides but, such was his feeling of joie de vivre and relaxation (doubtless helped by the generous drafts of sack poured for him), that he accepted it all with smiling good humour and was even prompted to counter-attack his master when asked if he had noticed any serious omission in the bill of fare. "Why yes sir," he replied. "A pigeon pie would have been just the thing to fill up the odd corner!" He went on to explain to the Armstrongs that at Worton they had a large dovecote which provided eggs for those who had a taste for them and every once in a while a cull of birds produced enough meat to furnish a deeply satisfying pie. Mr Allcot apologised to the company for his lapse in this regard and suggested that in the absence of pigeons, perhaps a couple of dead magpies lying in the trap outside could be pressed into service. They were declined with thanks.

The moment which William had once dreaded now arrived. The attorney and merchant apologised to the rest of the company and, filling up their glasses, retired to the study. William was left to entertain the ladies but he was now confident that he could do so without difficulty. Mrs Armstrong was delightful and easy to converse with. Katherine was still holding herself a little aloof but she was certainly a very beautiful girl and he was determined to make further attempts to gain her interest. He was asked how he had been spending his time in Durham, apart from his working hours, and he recounted his adventures with Sculley beginning with their meeting at the jousting on the river. Mrs Armstrong smiled and nodded throughout his account but Katherine's lip curled somewhat as he described his companions.

"You will find such gentle company as this to be a better form of entertainment an' you are able to achieve it," she said loftily.

Annoyed, her mother said quickly, "I am sure we can arrange that without difficulty, William would be a welcome guest at many a table in Durham."

"Perhaps," continued her daughter relentlessly, "but we must needs present him in more fashionable attire if he is to be a success."

William was nettled but enquired with good humour how his dress should be improved.

"Why, a peascod-bellied doublet to begin and we must cleanse you of this dowdy green hue to which you cling. Green is so seriously out of fashion these days."

"You astonish me," rejoined William, "Just a few weeks ago I was in the company of a lady of the highest rank who used the colour green for much of her dress and at all times of the day."

Katherine laughed and enquired sarcastically, "The highest rank indeed; and who might that have been?"

"Oh, t'was the Lady Mary, Queen of Scotland," he shot back and could have bitten off his tongue. In the momentary stunned silence he had time to reflect upon the stupidity of that admission. What a fool he was to have been led to rise to her goading. In a few weeks time he might be engaged upon a hazardous exploit on that lady's behalf, an exploit which would cost him his life if his part in it was discovered.

The silence and the awkward moment were broken by the return of the older men but he was to learn that his lapse was not forgotten and the subject was pursued.

"Mr Allcot," exclaimed Mrs Armstrong. "You are remiss in not informing us of the distinguished connections of Mr Robinson."

Mr Allcot looked at her in enquiry.

"Yes, I refer to his acquaintanceship with the Queen of Scotland, no less."

Mr Allcot switched his astonished gaze to William and said

"Come now, you were speaking in jest I doubt not?"

"No sir," he said quietly, "although the word acquaintanceship is in the nature of a jest. The truth is that I suffered an accident in the woods near Nappa Hall and her Majesty was kind enough to help me. She bade my Lord Herries carry me back to Bolton Castle, where she cared for me and engaged the physician to set my broken arm. It has mended well and I am deeply in the Queen's debt."

The explanation having been given and accepted, William was now plied with questions from the men as to who he saw at the castle, and from the women as to what exactly the Queen had been wearing. He answered both to the best of his ability but heartily wished that the subject of the conversation would change. One compensating factor was that the hitherto dismissive Katherine was now hanging on his words. He found that very satisfactory for she was indeed beautiful.

The party broke up with effusive thanks from the guests who all left in good humour, but not before Mr Armstrong had accepted the letters he was to bear to Yorkshire. He said a pleasant 'goodbye' to William and asked that they might meet some time for a discussion on the prospects in Wensleydale for trade and manufacture. William replied that he would be delighted to help if he could and it was decided that a return dinner date be fixed in a month's time at the residence of the Armstrongs.

When the guests had departed, Mr Allcot looked at William thoughtfully and said that it seemed that his encounter with the Scottish Queen had been fortunate for him.

"I believe she saved my life Sir," he replied quietly but, wanting to close the subject, he continued hurriedly "Mr Allcot, Sir, I do thank you for the fine dinner. Your guests were exactly as you described them and I enjoyed their company and conversation until I fear that your liberal dispensation of sack caused me to speak too much and too loudly. I do regret my intemperate behaviour and hope I have not spoiled the occasion for you. If you will excuse me I should like to retire to my room to recover my proper senses."

"Have no fear, William. Your presence at the table was enjoyed by us all. Now off you go for a rest and I will not expect you for supper unless I hear from Peters."

Thus dismissing William, Mr Allcot gazed thoughtfully at his retreating back. He knew that William had not been excessive in either speech or behaviour, but it was obvious that he bitterly regretted revealing the story of his meeting with the Scottish Queen. There was something else to this matter, he knew beyond doubt, but he also knew that he could not enquire. Perhaps the information would be freely given at some date in the future. Meanwhile he knew better than to pursue the subject.

....

Lord Herries was an extremely worried man. The weather through which he was travelling was atrocious; heavy ice-cold sleet was driving directly into his face, propelled by the strong and bitter wind as he headed north. It had saturated all his clothes, penetrating even through his innermost layer, which made his recurrent contact with the saddle a miserable experience. The horse too was suffering. He suspected it had picked up a small stone in its hoof, making it slightly lame, but, concerned as he was for its condition, he was not going to dismount now.

Having passed somewhat reluctantly through Aldbrough without stopping, he had subsequently missed his way in the general murk and found himself at a cottager's hovel in the forest, miles from his route. Redirected by the good occupier, who had been rewarded to his surprise with a small coin, Herries was now within striking distance of Ripon, his original goal. From here he knew he could make it back to the castle in half a day's ride and time was of the essence.

For it was not the adverse weather and darkness which caused the noble Lord such anxiety; it was the intelligence he brought back from Westminster. That was of supreme importance, so much so that he was convinced it was a matter of life or death for his sovereign lady. This was why he had ridden virtually non-stop from London for the last four days. As he struggled on in the miserable conditions, he rehearsed in his mind the plan which had been decided upon. He could see no way of improving it and it must serve, for the crisis which he had feared was upon them.

For once he was grateful for his royal mistress's propensity for seeking to attract the opposite sex. Hitherto destructive, her loose morals, the root cause of her present danger, might well now be the saving of her. His idea to bring about this salvation depended upon the degree of infatuation of a young Yorkshire lad for his wayward sovereign. He felt sure that the spell she had cast over the boy was strong enough to impel him into action. It might well be an action which could cost him his life but Lord Herries was ruthless enough to discount this as being of little importance in the situation they now faced.

He was pulled out of his reverie by a faint noise which he recognised as the blowing of a horn. It was repeated twice and, although he could see no lights as yet, he guessed he was nearing his goal. In this he was correct, for it had been the Wakeman of Ripon who had sounded the nine o'clock curfew and before long he was enquiring of the watch where he might find accommodation. The inn at the sign of the Black Bull was opened to his knocking and, his horse being taken away by an ostler, he was soon luxuriating before a blazing fire with a plate of stewed meat and a flagon of wine. The hastily prepared bed was warm and comfortable. As he gave himself up to sleep, his last waking thought was that he must make an early start and go, not to the castle, but directly to Worton to call upon William Robinson, in the fervent hope that the boy had returned from Durham.

He had, but it had been late on the previous night and so it was Joseph who greeted Lord Herries at the door, William being still abed. Herries was glad of the opportunity to speak alone with the uncle.

"Good Master Robinson, I have imposed o'er much upon your time and hospitality of late and yet I come again with a request for your help and understanding. Ye will be aware that it is your nephew who commands our attention and I call now to see him and ask that he makes good his promise of help. I would however also seek your permission to 'borrow' the lad for an evening's work. For, certes, he is a lad of great sense and I doubt not that ye have a pride in him. But he is a man of honour to boot and would repay the debt he believes he owes to my sovereign lady, Queen Mary of Scotland. We have found a way in which this can be done, with no dishonour to himself or his house but with a small, and I say again, a small risk of danger. Now, ye'll forgive me if I cannot make you privy to the details just now. T'would be best if you know nothing of the affair at all; but if the night's work be successful then t'will be rewarded with the grateful thanks of a Queen."

"Aye my Lord, he is a lad of exceeding good sense and with a proper regard to honourable conduct. He is full grown and able to make his own decisions but I would yet ask for a certain reassurance from him before I accede to your request."

Herries acknowledged this and William was sent for.

When he entered he was greeted precipitately by Herries who said to him

"Tonight, William, it must be tonight or we are lost."

"How so my Lord?"

"Because the Queen is to be moved directly; to Stafford I believe although my spies were uncertain of that. Once there, we shall have no great hope of achieving our goal."

Joseph Robinson now interrupted:

"William, I am told by my Lord Herries that you are to assist him in some secret enterprise this night. I would like your assurance that you will not be involved in foul play or violence against a person. Can I have your word on that my boy?"

"Aye uncle, I can do so. My Lord Herries will attest that it was a stipulation which I myself made when first we talked on the matter. I have to go uncle. It is a matter of honour."

Joseph nodded. "So I understand William and I cannot deny you the fulfilment of your obligation. I do not think t'is beyond my wit to guess at the nature of the deed you will attempt tonight. Lord Herries has hinted that there may be some danger and I agree. Whatever the outcome of your venture, there will be a search for local accomplices. I think it essential that you remain closeted here in the house until it is time to leave under cover of darkness. When your work in this matter is completed you should then return directly to Durham. As nobody saw you arrive last night then you will not have been here. I leave to you to devise an explanation for your master, Mr Allcot. Herries smiled appreciatively and complimented Joseph on his sound thinking.

"Now, William, we meet as planned. I myself will inform your friend of the arrangement and instruct him to attend you here at nine o'clock. The hunting party has long been arranged, My Lord Fleming, who has been lying low in Northallerton, will join us too at the appointed time, which is one hour after midnight. Be guided by this; t'is set aright and will strike so keep it close."

He set down a large oval object on the table. It had an elaborately pierced cover and William realised that he was looking at a travelling clock, of which he had heard but never seen.

"Now I leave you to make contact with your friend." Herries saluted both men and left without another word.

It was well after nine as William sat on the back of Gaynor in the darkness of the yard, fretting because Kit was late and wondering what had gone awry. The wind was still quite strong but the rain had stopped and through the torn clouds there were glimpses of moonlight. Eventually, however, not one, but two horses materialised out of the gloom. It was Kit and he was accompanied by Bess. William was furious.

"What do you mean by this Kit?" he asked angrily. "You know we agreed to keep her out of this."

"I had no choice Will. She threatened to reveal all to father unless I allowed her to come."

"Aye, so I did, and with you I stay if you are bent upon this foolish outing. But I do give you an improvement to your plan."

William groaned.

"And what might that be Bess?" he enquired sourly.

"Why, I shall play the Scottish Lady you fool! Instead of you riding off alone, I shall ride with you and if I am seen so much the better. In the dark a farmer's daughter might pass for a Queen."

William had to admit that it would be a potent addition to the deception, but he shook his head.

"No Bess. There may be some danger and I cannot bear to think of you being caught and punished."

"Nonsense Will," she replied, "I am your safeguard. Should we be stopped, we shall be eloping together to Durham! We would have nought to do with others, especially foreign Queens."

William gasped at the effrontery of the suggestion but he had to laugh and they all joined in the merriment.

"But come you two. We are late and must hurry." So saying he led the way down the dale towards Walburn.

Mercifully the rain had stopped completely, although the swollen becks and rivers testified to the vast amount of water which had fallen from the skies. Further north it had been even worse and somewhere on the banks of the river Wear a waterlogged old tree stump had been wrenched away from its entanglement in the bankside vegetation to be swirled and bumped along the bottom, coming to rest eventually in a broader and deeper pool near the city of Durham. Meanwhile, the sky was beginning to clear and more and more moonlight was filtering through the clouds so that their journey was becoming comparatively easy. There was still a stiff breeze and it was cold but the only real impediments to their travel were the occasional swollen streams which they had to cross. They made good time, however, and arrived with some twenty minutes to spare. Walburn Hall was silent and almost totally blacked out. Only a few lighted sconces were mounted on the battlements and within the courtyard. Of the watch there was neither sight nor sound. William was wondering how he would be contacted when a footstep startled him and the Scottish Lords appeared from within the ruins of the cottages opposite the Hall, leading a horse for each of them and a spare one for the Queen. Herries was inclined to be angry at the inclusion of yet another party to the plot.

"What does that wench here?" he demanded roughly.

William explained the rationale for the presence of Bess and was rewarded with a grim smile.

"An she be not caught t'will be well but have ye thought of the fate of the lassie if she be taken?"

The story of the elopement was explained to him and he could not restrain a laugh.

"To be sure there are resourceful folk in this dale," he said. "Just be sure William that you yourself are not somehow trapped in this young maid's subterfuge!"

At that moment a dim light appeared on the first floor of the Hall. It came from the mullioned window to the right of the main gate and they realised that this must be the chamber of the Queen.

"Her bodily escape is the worst of the matter," said Herries. "Sir Francis swears that she be able to squeeze through yonder window and slip down to a waiting horse. But I doubt me that the opening be large enough." Nonetheless, he enrolled Kit to help him urge the spare horse silently against the wall and beneath the window. As Kit glanced up, he realised that the width of the window was clearly going to be a major problem. What a tragedy it would be if the enterprise should fail because of Sir Francis's miscalculation as to the girth of his royal guest. He could not suppress a grin at the thought but it was temporarily dismissed as Herries whispered in his ear.

"I have kept back a detail laddie. Know ye of the gentleman Sir Aubrey Waite?"

"Aye my Lord, he has a house at Cotterdale, where he sometimes resides."

"Well he is there now and expects us this night, or early morn I suppose t'will be. We are to rest awhile with him before pressing on."

Fleming nudged his arm and they looked up to see that one of the windows had opened silently and knotted sheets were being pushed out. The horse was hastily manoeuvred beneath the window and, as they watched, a begowned leg was thrust through. More of the body appeared but then there was a pause and a muffled curse before everything was withdrawn. Then an arm appeared, followed by a shoulder and a head, the latter only just squeezing through the narrow gap. Once again, however, progress was halted and, after some ineffectual writhing, all disappeared again. They were then startled as an object fell from the window to the ground. It was a hat and it was followed by a green shawl, well remembered by William. There came then at intervals a series of skirts, underskirts and corselets all making their descent into a pile on the ground until a female figure, clad in shift alone, managed to squeeze between the mullions. There was a flash of white thigh as her gracious Majesty made an undignified and decidedly unregal descent down the sheets onto the back of the waiting horse. Within seconds, however, she had slipped off onto the ground and commenced re-dressing before the embarrassed gaze of William. The noble Scottish Lords had deferentially averted their gazes but Bess watched scandalised and looking rather angry, whilst Kit was convulsed with laughter.

At length the clothing was all in place again and the lady remounted her steed looking more like the regal figure they had known. Looking round the waiting company, she fixed her gaze upon Bess.

"You are to play my part girl?" she whispered.

"Aye my Lady, I shall."

"Then best wear this," said the Queen and with that she placed her hat on Bess's head. "Now my Lords, let us away."

Kit made to lead them away and it was not a moment too soon. Indeed, the timing could not have been better for, as the "Ho there! Who passes?" rang out in the night, William and Bess wheeled their horses noisily around to distract attention from the real escapees and made off rapidly towards Downholme. The alarm having been raised, the household was soon astir and Lord Scrope ordered an immediate search of the building. Knocking at the locked door of the Queen's chamber yielded no result so that, despite the protests of Sir Francis, it was ordered to be broken down. This accomplished, they found a terrified maid, bound and gagged who, when released and questioned, could only point mutely at the window. The watchman, who had raised the alarm, was questioned minutely and gave a confused picture of events. At first he had thought there was a large party outside the walls but then it seemed that only two remained, and they galloped off to the north.

"But two?" Lord Scrope demanded, "and what manner of person could you distinguish?"

"A man and a woman, my Lord," was the answer, "and the woman had on a hat such as I have seen worn by the Queen."

Lord Scrope cursed and assembled his men-at-arms in the courtyard.

"It seems the fugitives have ridden north," he said. "They must be caught, but without harm to them, and then brought back to the Castle at Bolton. Now, away and make haste to catch them."

The party of nine men clattered out through the gate and sped along the track to Downholme. The pursuit was on. To cover all eventualities, however, Lord Scrope despatched a messenger to raise the alarm at Bolton Castle and instructed him to continue on to Nappa Hall and inform the household there, currently in the charge of young Thomas Metcalfe. Kit, meanwhile, had led his party silently down towards Leyburn and before the entrance to the village had turned right along the ridge running westwards, thus avoiding any habitation. The track led along the edge of this ridge and Kit advised caution because of the severe drop into the valley below. It was a timely warning for, just before the path led down towards the hamlet of Preston, the Queen's horse was startled by an owl which flew overhead screeching. The animal reared and nearly threw its rider but, excellent horsewoman as she was, she controlled it with a struggle and calmed it down. The party now descended carefully to the valley below, Kit taking them on a little used path, which bypassed all the small hamlets and made for the river. Here the way lay along the banks of the river Ure, passing within half a mile or so of the walls of Bolton Castle, unseen in the dark but its threatening presence felt by all. Lord Herries permitted himself a small smile as they passed this point of greatest danger. He was sure that Lord Scrope would not credit them with taking the bold route of skirting his own stronghold in their bid to escape.

As it was, no light was seen, no challenge was heard and Kit led them on up the dale.

William and Bess had galloped down the track to Downholme and passed through the village with much deliberate noise and disturbance. No lights were lit and nobody stirred, but it was certain that their passage had been heard. They climbed the hill to the moor edge and there rested the horses whilst listening for sounds of pursuit. They heard none but William urged Bess on at a canter, passing by the little cottages at Huddes Well and thence to the descent through Sleegill to the wooden bridge over the Swale. The noise they made as they crossed the bridge and headed past the green and up the cobbled hill was sufficient to attract the attention of the Watch and there were calls for them to identify themselves. They ignored these of course and continued on up the hill, circling round to take the track towards Gilling. They rested the horses again at the top of Richmond Hill and this time they could discern definite sounds of pursuit. Voices were heard calling to the Watch and William decided that enough had been done to mislead the chasing band. It was time to make their own escape and, leaving the Queen's hat in the road as a final incentive to the pursuers, he led Bess onto an overgrown track which turned down the east side of Richmond town and headed towards the River Swale. At one point they stopped and remained motionless and silent as they listened to the sound of galloping hooves and the clattering of arms from the pursuing group. The party breasted the rise and swept on without pause towards Gilling leaving a relieved pair of youngsters grinning in self-congratulation. Then they continued winding down the valley side, passing the sad remains of the once lovely Easby Abbey, formerly the splendid home of the White Canons but these last thirty years a desecrated ruin thanks to the attentions of old King Henry. Here, they were to part company, William heading east, then north toward Durham and a new life, whilst Bess sought the river crossing at the bridge of Catterick and thence the long ride home.

They dismounted for a brief respite from the saddle and William enquired earnestly of his friend if she was confident about making the rest of her journey alone. She cheerfully reassured him and, knowing of her great resourcefulness, he did not press the point but seized her by the shoulders and, giving her a hug, he congratulated her upon her performance that night.

"We fooled them Bess, we really led them astray and all thanks to your help and of course the hat!"

They laughed together and then grew solemn as William said that she and Kit must keep their adventure a complete secret, from friends and parents. They should be safe from the inevitable rage of the authorities as there was nothing to connect them at all with the escape. His own meeting with Mary would be remembered of course and might lead to enquiry as to his whereabouts, so he feared that he would have to stay away from the dale for some considerable time.

"But be assured I will return when I can," he said and, quickly kissing her on the cheek, he mounted Gaynor and, with a shouted farewell, he galloped back up the hill.

Kit meanwhile was leading his party up from the river and, crossing the road from Redmire to Carperby, he made for higher ground. When Herries enquired as to the reason for this, he was told that their original track, although heading in exactly the right direction, passed within a few yards of Nappa Hall.

"Home of the Metcalfes, my Lord, and no friends to you or your Queen. We must keep well clear of them."

Herries nodded his agreement. He had of course met Sir Christopher and his unpleasant son and was thankful that he had happened upon such a knowledgeable guide. The hours and the miles passed without incident until the weary party made their way into the little valley of Cotterdale and thence to the abode of Sir Anthony Waite. This gentleman, a noted recusant, kept this dwelling to which he could retire out of the public eye. He had been expecting them and welcomed them effusively with refreshment and a warming fire. Herries, by now confident of the success of his plan, allowed that they might spend some hours in sleep before setting off in daylight to tackle the difficult moorland path to Appleby. He was sure that they would not be looked for in this direction and his confidence was infectious to the extent that, lulled by the warmth and the food, they all fell gratefully onto the prepared couches and slept soundly. Before being overcome by sleep, Kit marvelled at the way he was being treated as an equal in this company but he reasoned that extreme circumstances could make for strange, if transient, bedfellows.

Kit and his company woke warm and refreshed. Lord Herries had permitted them a good long sleep and their host insisted upon providing them with a hearty breakfast of good nourishing food including a hot broth. Having consumed this gratefully, they thanked their host profusely and made ready to set off to find the drover's road over the fells to Appleby. It was then that Mary made an awful discovery. She communicated the news of her loss to Herries, who was shaken but not despondent.

"It cannot be helped now ma'am and we must hope that its discovery, if made at all, will be too late to affect the issue of our escape."

It was not.

Tiny Watkin was up early. Being the smallest and least useful of the litter, he was encouraged to forage as best he may in order to supplement the family larder. He had become expert at 'walling' for rabbits and he was bound now for a favourite hunting spot on top of the ridge running west from Leyburn. Here, some dry stone walls came down to the very edge of the cliff and at one ungated gap there was a face of the wall through which rabbits could enter or leave with some ease. Such was the space between the big stones that rabbits could move freely within the wall often reappearing yards from their point of entry. The little black animals he was hunting were descendents of escapees from Jervaulx Abbey, where they had been bred by the monks for their larders.

He had already spied one, no two of them, entering the wall a few yards away and he guessed where they would emerge. He was right but even so the first to pop out took him by surprise and he missed it. The second was not so fortunate and a blow from Tiny's cudgel broke its neck so that it died instantly. He rolled the little corpse into his sack and gazed around for another victim. There were none but just a few yards away there was a great disturbance of the ground as though several horses had milled around and on the grass there lay a lump of material. He picked it up and marvelled at the smooth and soft texture of the green shawl which he had found. This was a better find even than the rabbit. He would take it home immediately. Jabber Watkin was in no doubt as to what to do with the shawl.

"Get it taken to Bolton Castle as quick as ye might boy! T'would be a hanging matter if we kept such a thing as belonged to the fine lady up there. Lord Scrope might even reward ye for findin' it. An he does, ye mun bring it all back here now!"

The horses filed away up the track onto the high moor with Kit planning to keep them to the old way which ran along the edge of the Mallerstang vale. It was the murky light that was their undoing. They quite failed to see the party which lay in ambush for them until it was too late to evade capture. The horsemen hastily assembled from Bolton and Nappa Hall were under the command of young Thomas Metcalfe, who was revelling in the important task assigned to him. He had certainly guessed correctly as to the route which the fugitives would take and he had chosen his place of ambush well. A dip in the ground, where a moorland stream tumbled over the rim and down into the valley had hidden the horses until the travellers were almost upon them. As they were being surrounded Lord Herries made as if to run for freedom but he was restrained by Fleming, who said

"T'would be of no avail, my Lord. We must stay by our Queen and render what service we can."

But Kit was made of sterner, if wilder stuff and, seizing the bridle of Queen Mary's horse, he turned his own steed to plunge down the steep hillside towards the valley floor.

A quarrel weighs about one quarter of a pound and when fired from a good crossbow can penetrate armour at fifty paces. Kit wore no armour and the bolt took him in the neck fracturing the cervical vertebrae and killing him instantly. Queen Mary had leapt from her horse and cradled the boy in her arms so that she became besmirched with the blood flowing from the severed carotid artery. Rough hands hauled her to her feet causing her to let fall the lifeless body.

"I fear I must interrupt your grieving my Lady. My Lord Scrope must needs have words with you," sneered the triumphant Thomas Metcalfe.

Queen Mary looked him steadily in the eye and said coldly,

"Take away your vile hands from my person you upstart lout. I shall indeed speak to My Lord Scrope, who will doubtless be interested to learn how you committed murder and put to risk the life of his royal guest."

But Thomas Metcalfe was not to be dissuaded from his purpose by any brave words. He was in command and the situation was entirely under his control. He relished it and issued his orders with a tone of great authority.

"Keep the royal Lady close," he instructed his men with an ironic inflexion on the honorific, "And make these two secure," he said indicating the Scottish nobles. Herries and Fleming were outraged to be placed on their horses with their hands tied together in front of them like common felons but there was no appeal. Finally, Thomas pointed to the body of Kit.

"Sling that carrion over the horse and we shall lead it to its owner. I know well who that is and he will answer for it." With that, the sorry cavalcade set off on the long road back to Nappa Hall and in the minds of the three captured fugitives the spectre of the consequences of their failure loomed before them.

Chapter 4: The Move

Cecil divined that the extreme reaction of his monarch to the news of the attempted escape was born as much out of fear as annoyance. Whatever the cause, the effect was dramatic to say the least. Elizabeth marched up and down the chamber declaiming loudly and occasionally rounding upon her advisor, as if to lay the blame for the event upon his shoulders. He was not too worried; the lady would calm down in due course and in the meantime he assembled his own thoughts concerning the matter. Rather more quickly than he had supposed, the Queen ceased her tirade and sat down abruptly, motioning to Cecil to attend her.

"Were there conspirators from our country?" she enquired.

"Yes, your Majesty, I fear so."

Cecil knew how grave a concern this aspect of the matter was to her. Her tenure of the throne, so miraculously won against all the odds, was still fragile and her northern territories were least supportive, a large element of Catholic sentiment still remaining in this region.

"What families then?"

The question was asked in some trepidation, weighted with the possibility of the discovery of some hitherto unsuspected disaffection.

"None of quality, your Majesty. A peasant farm lad was discovered with the party and killed at that time. T'would have been better had he been caught and questioned."

"So no-one has been apprehended?"

"The father of the boy is in York jail, ma'am. We are questioning him but I fear he knows naught."

"Make sure t'is so Cecil. Take whatever means necessary to get the truth."

Cecil assured his Queen that this was being done but that he was convinced that the lad had been suborned by the Scottish Lords, probably for financial gain.

"Then he received his deserts," said Elizabeth grimly. "And who was responsible for their recapture?"

"A local family, supporters of my Lord Scrope, your Majesty. Metcalfe is the name."

A flicker of interest crossed the face of the Queen. "I know that name, but wherefrom I remember not." And then remembrance came with a shock. It had been whilst her sister Mary had been on the throne. On one of the rare occasions when she had visited Elizabeth she had boasted of the support she had in that city, recounting the story that a clan from the Dales had attended her judges in York. There had been three hundred of them and all mounted on white horses, or what passed for white in those parts. They had probably been grey. And the name had been Metcalfe. Staunch supporters of her Catholic sister!

Elizabeth supplied Cecil with this information and he smiled reassuringly.

"Aye Ma'am; t'was so in those days but marriages and your own succession have produced the change in faith. Do not be concerned your Majesty, there are none so keen as the newly converted."

The Queen laughed at this cynical assessment.

"It may be so, Cecil, but I would have you watch this family close. I have no liking for their reputation, nor their propensity for demonstrating their power."

Cecil nodded his agreement but he had already investigated Sir Christopher and his family thoroughly and found nothing to concern him. He changed the subject.

"In the matter of Queen Mary Ma'am, I am concerned that she be stricter confined."

"Remember of whom you speak, Cecil. This is a Queen, a royal personage and she must be treated with respect!"

Cecil knew well of his Queen's feelings about her loyalty to fellow monarchs, and more particularly the legitimacy of their power. He suspected inwardly that this solidarity was a manifestation of her own feeling of insecurity. He was quick to amplify his thoughts.

"T'is her very royalty that is the problem Ma'am. I think you know well my fears about her danger as a focus for foreign intervention but that may be the least cause of our fears. The greater danger lies at home. Your Majesty knows as well as myself that there is great disaffection amongst certain families who resent the loss of their traditional faith. These are the very people who may exaggerate her spurious claims to your throne to raise a rebellion. Therefore I would request that she be confined more strictly within the centre of your Majesty's realm rather than at the outer fringes, where control and management are more difficult."

"You go to the very core, Cecil, to remind me of the weakness of my tenure of this land. Yet you speak naught but the truth. Find a suitable place and have it so arranged."

Tutbury Castle was chosen, home of the Earl of Shrewsbury.

....

It was a day in early January, a cheerless day with the remnants of a small snowfall clinging still to shaded parts of the streets and a bitter wind coursing along those same streets, which kept them empty of all except those on necessary business. In the study William and Mr Allcot worked silently, the former bent over his work and writing notes for future discussion. Occasionally Mr Allcot would glance up to study his companion and contemplate their changed relationship. It had been Christmas Eve when William had returned unexpectedly from Worton. He had been exhausted and somewhat dishevelled, whilst Gaynor had been lathered with dried sweat and had clearly been put to hard work. The boy had excused himself to retire to his room after a brief explanation, that he had been compelled to return early from Worton, and expressing the hope that he would not discommode his master's arrangements for the Christmas festival. Mr Allcot informed him with a smile that there were no plans for any celebration other than that of Holy Communion on the morrow, to which he invited William to accompany him. They had gone together and Mr Allcot had been surprised and slightly disconcerted to have his natural curiosity left unsatisfied as to the circumstances of William's early return. William had evaded his questions with vague answers but assured his master that his uncle was well and there was no problem in their relationship. He nonetheless had the air of a man with something weighty on his mind. In the cathedral he had sat quietly and seemed deeply pre-occupied. Afterwards, he had excused himself from the social gathering which always followed the service and made his way back to the house, where Mr Allcot found him later working on some papers.

And that had been the formula ever since his return; a dedication to his work, which was admirable, but with a reserve which had not been present before and which had a noticeable effect upon the atmosphere in the house. In the few months during which William had been working with him, Mr Allcot had conceived a strong affection for the boy, admiring his quick mind and willingness to learn. His friendly, open character and intelligent conversation had been larded with just the right amount of deference towards his master and at no time had Mr Allcot regretted his admitting the young man to his after supper discussions. William had never taken advantage of this familiarity. But now his speech appeared guarded as though there was something he simply must not accidentally reveal. In addition, there had been a noticeable increase in his interest in the outside world as though he was awaiting news of some import. As he pondered over the possible reasons for this change in his protégé's behaviour there was a distraction as Peters knocked and entered the room bearing a letter.

"The Carrier said t'was urgent, Sir," he said, apologising for his unaccustomed intrusion into the sanctum and Mr Allcot opened the missive then and there to reveal another letter enclosed inside. He glanced at the superscription and handed it to William.

"For you my boy. It may be that it is this message which is urgent."

They each broke off to read their letters and Allcot discovered that he had been correct. Joseph Robinson craved his pardon for imposing upon his friend but asked that he deal sympathetically with his nephew, who would be the recipient of very bad news in his letter. 'He will be much disturbed and I am sure he would do well to ask for your guidance,' he wrote .'I hope sincerely that he does so.' Mr Allcot glanced across the room and was concerned to see the shocked and horrified expression on William's face, which had drained of colour entirely. He waited until the letter was lowered and a grief-stricken countenance turned towards him.

"Your uncle thinks you may have something to tell me and that I may be of help. I would like to think that you will allow me to do so, if it is in my power."

There was no mistaking the tone of friendly sympathy in his voice, which was not lost upon William and it had an immediate effect upon him.

"Thank you Sir," he replied in a shaking voice. "There has been a disaster and I am responsible for it. I have ruined the lives of some who have been very dear to me and caused pain and suffering which cannot be assuaged. I know not what I should do, nor whether I should stay here or return home. It has been my foolish pride in fulfilling my word of honour that has brought about this terrible thing and I know I can never be forgiven."

There was a hint of moisture on his cheeks which underlined the heartfelt confession and Mr Allcot made haste to draw him out as to the reason for his distress. He listened to the full story, as far as William had known it, without comment but clearly became very concerned when he heard the latest news from Joseph Robinson. The Queen had been recaptured, but worse, his friend Kit had been mercilessly slain, his father taken off to York in chains and his mother going with him clinging to him in the cart which took them away. Bess had been given a roof at Worton Hall and his uncle was employing her as a housemaid to ease the burden on the ageing Hannah, the only good thing in a catalogue of ill tidings.

William raised a face suffused with a tragic expression.

"Mr Fawcett knew naught of the affair. He will not be able to tell them anything and he will suffer for it, I know. And Kit, poor Kit! Bess, who knows all, will ne'er forgive me for the loss of her dear brother. I must go back and try to comfort her! I must go to York and tell them that it was I who was responsible for the attempted escape and they will release her father!"

Mr Allcot raised a hand. "Hold hard now William. Impetuosity will not be a help at this moment. Your motives do you credit but let us consider the logic of the situation. Your young friend Kit is sadly beyond recall. T'will be altogether too late to prevent the mischief inflicted upon the worthy Mr Fawcett. By now he will have been persuaded to confess to something he did not do and will have been hanged, or they will have been forced to accept his words as true and he will be released. His suffering will probably be at an end in either case. You can, of course, go to York and confess yourself to the sheriff. He will be glad to hang you too. Perhaps you might think it the moral thing to do but I do question that moral responsibility which you are so anxious to assume. T'was not your scheme; you merely sought to discharge a moral obligation. Which moral obligation weighs heaviest then? No, your sacrifice, albeit noble, would serve no one but would distress many: your uncle, your little friend Bess, mayhap even the Scottish Queen (although not, I warrant, the Lord Herries) and in addition, dare I say it, myself."

William looked up and could not forbear to smile at that last remark. It was an affirmation, if it were needed, of the regard in which the kindly old man held him.

"Your uncle goes on to say in his letter to me that he thinks you should lie low in Durham for the present time. It seems that questions were asked of the villagers who all swore that you had gone off to London in September to become a lawyer and you had not been seen in the village since. To London indeed! As if there were not a sufficiency of good legal minds in the North to give you the necessary training! Well, t'will serve to muddy the waters and put them off your scent if they be actively seeking you, the which I doubt. So, yes, lie low boy and keep out of public sight. I know t'will be a trial to your uncle and yourself that ye cannot visit Worton for a good while but it is for the best that you keep out of sight and out of mind."

And so the decision to do nothing was made and in time William became reconciled to it. Later letters from Worton told of subsequent events. Mr Fawcett had been released from York jail but was brought back a broken man by his sorrowing wife. Unable to work the farm, he was dispossessed by the owners, who were the Metcalfe family, and he returned to his parish of Aysgarth, where family took him in and cared for him. Further enquiry in the matter had ceased and it was widely assumed that Kit had been suborned by the promise of Scottish gold to take part in the escape plot. There was still the mystery surrounding the couple who had been reported as galloping away from Walburn Hall in the direction of Richmond and there were some who continued to hold an interest in that matter. Young Thomas Metcalfe in particular was forward in questioning local folk as to the whereabouts of William Robinson on that eventful night. Bess continued to work at the Hall, which she enjoyed, but there were two other major developments. The Lords Herries and Fleming had been despatched home to Scotland and an uncertain future, whilst Mary had been moved to Tutbury Castle. Her future too a matter of great uncertainty.

Winter gave way to spring at last. Wet and windy for a large part but with some welcome bright days. The spring flowers took advantage of the longer daylight and the warmth to raise their cheerful heads above the regenerating grasses. Birds sang and the first butterflies appeared, notably the 'Orange Corners' as Sculley called them. The danger from exposure as a member of the escape plot having lessened, William felt able to resume his country expeditions with his friend and also to resume his contacts with the younger folk of the city on a Sunday morning. He continued to work and learn, and in this latter respect made his first appearance before the judges in a case of disputed property ownership. He merely acted as Mr Allcot's assistant but was introduced to the judges who, upon better acquaintance, were not the crusty old tyrants they appeared to be in court. He had been glad to experience court procedure and was fascinated by the presentation and rebuttal of argument. To a point it was enjoyable, although some lengthy points of trivial discussion did leave him rather bored.

There were social events too and the long promised return engagement at the house of the Armstrongs took place. It was an exceedingly pleasant occasion, friendly and of great interest as Mr Armstrong pressed William for information about Wensleydale. He was a merchant who had made a great deal of money from the export of wool, which was of course plentifully available from the large sheepwalks of both Northumbrian and Yorkshire dales. He bought at several centres, including Richmond, but now he was looking for a change in business. As he explained to his guests, and William in particular, his need now was for cloth rather than the bulky basic material of wool. The cost of carriage was high and the demand on the continent was now for cloth or knitted garments. What he sought was an industry in the dales, which could provide him with processed material. His agents already purchased the produce of the individual families, who carried out weaving as an alternative to farming, when times were bad, but could they be organised into a collective bulk supplier such as was happening elsewhere in the country?

Furthermore, he wished to become what he described as a clothier, an entrepreneur who could control all the processes of producing cloth suitable and ready for the making up of garments, from the spinning of yarn to the dyeing and fulling of cloth. Were there any fulling mills in Wensleydale and, if not, was there a possibility of setting them up? Knitted wear was in demand too now and he would like to encourage this activity by setting up a continual market for locally-knitted goods. William explained that there was, indeed, a thriving cottage industry in the production of yarn and cloth but, whilst he was certainly no expert in the field, he thought that all this produce was taken up by the clothing industry in Ripon and York with some buyers even coming from Wakefield and Bradford. He thought Mr Armstrong would find it a very competitive market. This intelligence clearly disappointed his inquisitor but William had been thinking along another line.

"You say, Sir, that there is some demand for knitted goods?" he enquired.

"Aye, that is so both in foreign parts and at home," was the reply.

"Well then something might be achieved in that way," said William.

He went on to describe the prodigious skill and speed possessed by local women in the knitting of jerkins for wear over their fustian tunics in very cold weather and stockings for their men folk to wear under their cockers, which were knee-length boots. Could there be an outlet for this work he wondered? Armstrong pondered for a moment in silence before saying

"Aye, there might indeed. Let me think some on't and I shall speak to ye again on the matter."

William was glad that something positive might have come out of their conversation but further discussion was prohibited by the ladies. They had other subjects to air and the gentlemen had to give way. It was strange that on this occasion Katherine regarded him with so much more interest and her initial condescension had been replaced by something more akin to respect or at least a suggestion that he was an equal in the company. He wondered if that was on account of the attitude of her father towards him or because of his association with the Scottish Queen. He suspected the latter and this was born out by a later remark she made to the effect that she understood that Mary was no longer living in the Scrope castle.

"You will doubtless miss her company," she said with just a hint of her former sarcasm but William was not to be drawn and explained that his continuing sojourn in Durham prevented him from spending any time in Wensleydale, even to be with his uncle at Worton.

He was then pressed to describe his home and this loosened his tongue as he extolled the virtues of life in the dale and the delights of Worton Hall and the surrounding countryside. Questioned further it became clear to them that the Robinsons were affluent, well possessed of land which rendered them a good and steady income. William was at pains to tell them that this was in large part due to his uncle's careful investments and skilful employment of his profits. He called for the aid of Mr Allcot to substantiate that claim, which he did with enthusiasm.

"T's true, I have acted for Joseph Robinson for many years now and been impressed by his canny judgement and sound investments. His best investment however is like to be his nephew and ward, young William here. He has done well by the boy in preparing him for life, as William I know does acknowledge. T'is pleasant to see when care such as his is appreciated by the recipient."

William was embarrassed by this fulsome praise and his discomfiture was increased when he noticed an exchange of what could only be described as 'significant' glances between mother and daughter. Mr Armstrong noticed too, rolled his eyes towards heaven and then grinned at William and winked.

"D'ye hunt my lad?" he enquired of William, who shook his head and said that he had merely trapped rabbits as a boy. "Well now ye might have some sense of what it feels like to be the quarry!" He laughed uproariously at his own witticism and the ladies, after looking momentarily shamefaced, joined in the merriment. Mr Allcot laughed too, as he had missed nothing of the interchange, and eventually William was able to laugh as well. All awkwardness had been punctured by the humour and the evening continued in this happy fashion.

At one stage Katherine was commanded to fetch her cittern and she then sang to her own accompaniment on this neat little string instrument, which looked a little like the lutes William had seen played in York. Her voice was pleasant enough and the company pressed for more but she demurred and insisted that they all participated in a part song. No musician himself, William nevertheless enjoyed this pastime and the feeling of being a performer in a communal project. Things started to get a little out of hand, when Armstrong launched into a series of border ballads and humorous songs, which became bawdier as he went along. The momentary expressions of disapproval on the part of the ladies gave way to grins and then chortles of mirth at some of the more outrageous items and eventually it was with real sorrow that William realised that the party was drawing to a close. Amidst the exchange of thanks and pleasant goodbyes there was a meeting of eyes which sent a thrill down the spine of William. So intent was he upon the warmth of that smiling expression that he failed to notice the predatory expression on the face of the mother.

As the weather improved and temperatures increased it was natural that the Sunday activities on the river bank near Old Elvet should be resumed. William was pleased that this was so, as he enjoyed the friendly banter and light-hearted pursuits of the largely younger element of the city who gathered there. It bothered him not a bit that they were also representatives of the poorer classes of apprentices, farm workers and the like. If anything, he was more comfortable in their company than in the more rarified circles in which he was compelled to move by virtue of his occupation and his association with Mr Allcot. His expeditions into the country with Sculley were also resumed and as the days grew longer some evening trips were accomplished. All this energetic activity was an excellent counterbalance to the enforced sedentary occupation which he had espoused and he remained fit and healthy, retaining his customary zest for life. All this was approved of by his employer, although there had been a noticeable decline in the after supper conversations, which was a matter for some regret. There were, however, some evening social occasions to which William was taken along by Mr Allcot who, truth to tell, was enjoying showing off his new assistant.

This was noticed by his friends and acquaintances, who were amused by the proprietorial air he affected in relation to the boy. The Armstrong family were often present at these affairs and so William encountered the lovely Katherine on a fairly regular basis. It seemed to him that there was a conspiracy on the part of the older members of the party to encourage the degree of social contact between them, so much so that he began to feel as though he was being gently shepherded, not to say driven. He was not too happy about this. Whilst it was nice to feel that the Armstrong family thought him to be a suitable companion for their daughter, and whilst he was definitely attracted to the girl herself, he did not relish the feeling of being herded towards an inevitable conclusion. To be fair to the girl, she too appeared to be annoyed by the often unsubtle arrangements to throw them together. Despite this, she nevertheless gave the impression of enjoying his company, although there was also a slight reserve as though she could not quite determine whether she regarded him as being in an equal in social position or not. Certainly he had made a place in local society and his behaviour in these circles was impeccable but she recoiled in some distaste from his associations with the lower classes, as exemplified by the apprentices, and labourers who frequented the Sunday recreations by the river. This was brought to a head one day, when William issued an invitation.

The warm weather had seen a resumption of the river jousting which William had witnessed on the first weekend of his arrival in Durham. At the first of these gladiatorial contests William had watched as, once again, the mighty Jed had devastated the rest of the field and precipitated them all into the water. Disembarking from his skiff, he spotted William amongst the watching crowd and made a bee line for him.

"Now young Master Robinson, have you gained sufficient courage yet to meet me on the water?" The jibe was sufficient to sting William into a response.

"Nay Jed, I have never lacked the courage, merely the skill. But, lest ye think it be the case, I shall be happy to take you on next Sunday." He was committed now and there had been a good many onlookers who had overheard the challenge and response. There were not a few who hoped that the newcomer, who looked to be a strong and fit young man, might be the one to topple the swaggering Jed and a few bets were taken on the outcome of the match. The word got around that there was to be something of a grudge competition next Sunday, which distressed William when he was made aware of it. There was no grudge as far as he was concerned and for him it was not a life or death matter whether he triumphed or not but he could see how that might be the case for Jed. It would be essential for a man of his character to retain his pre-eminence amongst his peers and, like a stag in spring, he would want to see off the opposition, real or imagined.

Remarkably, intelligence of this proposed encounter had reached the ears of some even of the upper echelons of Durham society and William was chaffed about it. He responded to a jovial remark by Mr Armstrong by issuing the invitation.

"You must come along Sir and see the sport. Perhaps the ladies would come too and be amused by the sight of me being battered with a straw sack until I fall into the water. That is the likely result but t'is good entertainment and usually causes much merriment." The party agreed that, given good weather, it would be a pleasant diversion and arrangements were made to take a picnic down to the Old Elvet on that day.

It was a good day as far as the weather was concerned; sunny with blue skies, if a little windy, but that wind served to enliven the crowd at the river and behaviour was good-humoured if boisterous. Boisterous enough, indeed, to make the Armstrong ladies feel slightly ill-at-ease. Katherine recoiled from the crowd of rough, often ill-clad, youths who thronged around them and, as she spotted William in their midst clearly enjoying their camaraderie, those doubts as to the his suitability as a companion resurfaced. Armstrong himself gazed around him with interest and a look of happy reminiscence on his features. He must have enjoyed a similar environment and company as a boy. Was there a look of mild regret on his face? It would not have been surprising. William had joined the party for a while to explain that the jousting event was to take place very soon. He had secured the services of a young boy to row him into battle and arranged to hire a skiff for the purpose. Armstrong noted that he was certainly not dressed in his best and was clearly prepared for an inevitable soaking. He smiled and, patting him on the back, enquired if William was a good swimmer.

"Aye, Sir, I have done some swimming in the river at home but I will benefit from the practice I shall likely get today!"

With that he set off to take his place on the bankside as did all the other competitors. They had all provided themselves with sacks and there was a great show of feeling the contents to ensure that no rocks had inadvertently found their way amongst the straw. Then, with much shouting of encouragement from the spectators and good-natured threats and insults between the combatants, the flotilla of little boats thrust off from the bank.

There was no nicety of an official start, no rules were called and no standing on any ceremony whatsoever. Hostilities erupted immediately. Bags swirled in the air and were brought crashing down on opponents, boats were manoeuvred, hopefully to the advantage of their occupants, and the scene of frantic activity was accompanied by a tumult of noise from the banks. Sacks sprang apart at seams leaking straw into the air, for it to be whirled away in the powerful wind and distributed over the watching throng and Katherine looked down with distaste upon the fragments which clung to her shawl and which looked none too clean. She shuddered to think of the possible sources of some of the straw and the identity of the accompanying debris which landed on her. The first victims fell into the river and swam to the bank, where they were pulled ashore by the jeering onlookers. For some the contest ended when their sacks burst completely and all the straw was lost thus depriving them of a weapon. They simply had to retire. There was soon just a hard core remaining and, of these, William was one. He had just despatched an opponent, when he was assaulted from behind and nearly knocked off his feet. He turned to see that his friend Sculley had delivered the blow and urged his oarsman to turn the boat to meet him. His intention was frustrated by Jed, whose boat appeared alongside him. They exchanged blows, largely fending off each other's attempts to 'unhorse' his opponent but eventually Jed won the battle. By feinting a blow to the head and then ducking under William's riposte he aimed a mighty blow at his adversary's legs and William lost his balance. A quick recovery of his sack and Jed completed the coup with a blow to the head which saw William propelled over the side.

Jed was triumphant, but his victory had been won at fatal cost. During the intense encounter, Sculley had worked his way behind Jed and, at the very moment when he relaxed as his vanquished foe entered the water, Sculley launched his own attack. So well co-ordinated was it that he was able to capitalise on Jed's lack of readiness. The erstwhile champion of the river teetered on his feet, whilst his grip on the sack was lost as he waved his arms about striving to keep his balance. He was not allowed to recover as Sculley delivered a smashing blow to the back of his head and he was precipitated forward, striking the gunnnel heavily on the forehead before splashing overboard.

There was a gigantic roar from the crowd to acknowledge Sculley as the last man standing and therefore the winner of the contest. Despite his evident popularity in the community, there was also an undoubted element of satisfaction in the toppling of the swaggering Jed and almost as a man the audience turned to jeer at him in his discomfiture. He was not to be seen. A strange silence fell upon the crowd as they gazed at the surface of the river and William, who had been treading water during the final encounter, recalled the mighty blow which Jed has sustained on the edge of the gunnel before he fell into the water. Without any further thought he turned and dived at the spot where he fancied Jed had submerged. Visibility was poor; the frenzied activity of the combatants had raised clouds of mud from the bottom and William peered about him helplessly as he kicked his way down to the river bed. Suddenly he saw movement, a shape could be seen struggling in frenzied manner and he made his way towards it. Moving closer the shape became dimly recognisable as Jed who was fighting a losing battle against the weight of a wooden log, which somehow held him prisoner. Swimming as quickly as he could, William approached the tableau and saw the despairing look in Jed's eye as the last bubbles of air escaped from his lips. As he reached the log, he saw that a projection had snagged the back of the man's shirt, penetrating the material and holding him fast. The situation was clearly desperate and expediency brought the solution to William's mind. Turning over the now inert body he ripped the shirt until the projecting spur of log became free. Then, grasping Jed around the waist, he kicked his way laboriously upwards. As their heads broke water there was no shortage of willing hands to haul them ashore but the contorted blue visage and lack of breathing on the part of Jed caused the spectators to shake their heads and lament the tragic loss of such a fine young man.

William, however, refused to accept the finality of the situation and heaved the body of his erstwhile foe across a pile of sacks. He pumped Jed's back regularly and fiercely until he was rewarded by a gush of water which issued from the mouth and then a long, shuddering, indrawn breath of air. This was followed by a prolonged bout of coughing which sounded quite alarming but was welcome evidence of a return to life. William's position was now usurped by a host of motherly souls who rushed up to bring recuperative help by stripping the lad of his wet clothes and wrapping him up in an amazing collection of garments peculiar to both sexes and in conflicting colours. Too weak to object, Jed resigned himself to these ministrations and eventually lay back with a sheepish grin to enjoy the attention he was receiving. Having established that all was now well, William gave him a cheery wave and sought out his guests, the Armstrong family. Mr Armstrong was all praise and hearty congratulation, slapping him on the back repeatedly so that water flew out of his shirt in all directions. His defeat in the jousting contest had been more than offset by the prompt and successful rescue he had carried out. The ladies too were full of praise but kept their distance from his saturated and, it must be said, evil-smelling garments. Katherine's emotions had run through a bewildering series of changes. There had been the distaste she had felt at his association with what she thought of as the rabble, then the excitement of the jousting had gripped her attention only to be spoiled by the defeat of her champion. Horror at the supposed death of the young man had been superseded by relief when he recovered and, just now, her revulsion as William approached in his bedraggled condition had been dissipated by the realisation that he was the hero of the hour and the object of much acclaim by the entire crowd. On balance she decided that perhaps he was a worthy companion for a young lady of her position in society. If only he would clean himself up quickly and become more presentable.

That evening at supper there were more congratulations from Mr Allcot, who had heard of the affair from Peters. That worthy had heard the story, by now slightly embellished of course, from a group of folk gossiping in the street. He was asked if it were not true that the hero was actually dwelling in the same house as himself and he left the scene wrapped in a slight glow of reflected glory after he had amplified the details of William's background for the chattering crowd. Mr Allcot had praised William for his presence of mind and quick reaction but he had had one minor criticism.

"Thy notion of 'lying low' is not one with which I would agree!"

He said it with a smile but they both knew that the attention he had received might prove to be unwelcome. And so it proved. Nine times out of ten the event would have been forgotten in a few days and been replaced by some other interesting tale but on this occasion the story was repeated in more exalted circles and even the names were remembered. Mr Allcot was of course well known in the city and now the name of his new assistant had risen to a temporary prominence. Again, it would be most likely that the interest would not be lasting but as it happened there was one listener who remembered the name of William Robinson in a different context and, when he eventually returned to London, he took the story with him.

It was in early July that Mr Allcot received his invitation to the Palace at Bishop Auckland. It was quite a surprise as, although he had met the Prince Bishop of Durham on several formal occasions, there had been no social connection and now My Lord Bishop was inviting him to take drinks in the forenoon of Tuesday next. He found the occasion pleasant enough and there was one other guest who was introduced to him as Sir Francis Knollys, who he knew to be the vice chamberlain to Queen Elizabeth. During conversation, the Bishop recalled the adventure on the river bank in which his assistant had featured and Mr Allcot was alerted to the real reason for this meeting when Knollys enquired if William had been in his employ for long. The wily old man determined to adopt an attitude of frank and enthusiastic response.

"Aye Sir Francis, since last September when he came to me from Worton in Yorkshire. He is the nephew and ward of a valued client of mine, Joseph Robinson of Worton Hall in Wensleydale, who begged me to take him on as an articled assistant. In truth he has been a wondrous help and, not only lessened the burden on an old man, but provided companionship and intelligent conversation. His uncle has done well by the boy to see him properly educated and now he seeks to find him a career, in the which he should prosper for he is quite dedicated to his work and takes none of the holiday I would allow him."

"Does he not then return to his home and his uncle betimes?" enquired the knight.

"He does not and yet I do confess to ye that there is another attraction for him in this city other than his work and my company." This was said with a smile and was picked up by the bishop who enquired as to the identity of the other attraction and when he heard it was Katherine Armstrong he chuckled.

"I fear ye have the right of it Sir. Any man would be condemned to take second place in competition with that young beauty!"

But Sir Francis was not to be so easily diverted and he pressed Mr Allcot again. "But he would surely have spent the Christmas festival at his own home?"

"Not so, Sir Francis, not so. He and I celebrated the Christmas rites in the cathedral. A splendid service my Lord Bishop, and mayhap you remember we were in attendance?"

"That is so, Mr Allcot, I recall it well but by his evident preoccupation I fear that your young companion had more thought for his other 'attraction' rather than for any words which I uttered from the pulpit!"

They all laughed and the conversation turned to more general matters to the well-disguised relief of Mr Allcot. It appeared that Sir Francis had been convinced by the alibi he had wrought for William and which had been achieved without the telling of any real falsehood and in this he was proved to be right for some two months later Knollys confided to Cecil that he had eliminated the young Robinson boy from his list of suspected conspirators in the failed escape plot of the Scottish Queen.

But the event had been a terrible shock to William and Mr Allcot. It was clear from the line of questioning that William had indeed been under some suspicion. Not knowing how effective the alibi had proved to be, it seemed best that the process of 'lying low' be enforced with greater care and furthermore that a return to Worton in the near future was out of the question. Not only would his appearance there be a reminder of his association with the Scottish Queen but it would run counter to the assertion that William never took the holidays due to him but remained happily in Durham. And to some extent this latter was true. At Worton, letters were received by Joseph Robinson from his legal advisor in Durham and from his nephew. Mr Allcot wrote to the effect that for personal reasons it was advisable for his assistant to remain in Durham for the time being. William's letters, which were thought more liable to interception, simply said that his work was hard but enjoyable, that there was no time available, alas, for him to return to Worton during the summer, but that he would miss his uncle's company and his beautiful home. He even hinted that there were plenty of enjoyable distractions for him in his new home city and Joseph was able to guess at what one of those distractions might be.

In terms of his inability to return to Wensleydale, William had very mixed feelings. It was true that he badly missed the leafy serenity of the dale, the familiar neighbourhood and his uncle's company. But he knew that things would never be the same after the escapade at Walburn Hall. Kit was gone, the Fawcett family dispersed, although Bess was apparently still living and working at Worton Hall. And that was a huge problem. He did not know how he could face the accusations of that girl, whose life he had ruined and whose brother had been killed as a result of his actions. This factor alone was enough to persuade him that return to Worton was impossible regardless of any risk to his own person. His shame at the results of his prideful behaviour outweighed any feelings of fear of exposure.

And, let us be truthful, the distraction about which the Prince Bishop and Mr Allcot had joked was real enough. At each of their fairly frequent meetings William was struck more and more by the beauty and elegance of Katherine Armstrong. She was friendly enough and yet there was always the suspicion that she harboured a feeling of superiority to him, which manifested itself in an occasional aloofness although that expression of disdain which he had noticed on their first meeting had never been repeated. All this made him strive harder to win her approval but never in a ridiculous fashion so that his general demeanour met with the approval of both maid and mother. Certainly the ladies were glad to converse with him and were sufficiently impressed by the acuity of mind and chivalrous behaviour to be entertained and pleased by his attentions. And, as to that, his attentions were rarely allowed to be confined to Katherine alone. When they were, however, it was purely a matter of conversation, sometimes serious, sometimes in much lighter or even frivolous fashion but never was there any physical contact. William hoped that this would not continue to be the case indefinitely.

Meanwhile he worked hard and enjoyed much of his leisure time in the company of Sculley. The two lads, mounted on the patient Gaynor, became a regular and well recognised sight as they departed the city for their Sunday excursions into the country often returning late in the evening and not always in the tidiest of conditions. Perhaps the old pastimes enjoyed with Kit and Bess had been replaced by a more adult behaviour but there were still trees and crags to be climbed in the search for nests, still thickets to be penetrated and pools to be examined in the quest for life forms of interest. Sculley learnt much about birds from his friend and William began to learn about the butterflies of the region. In the absence of any recognised classification they made up many of their own names including the 'Colour Sergeant', 'Copper Spot', 'Speckly Blue' and 'Ermine Blue'. Theirs was not the pastime of the chase but of identification and observation and in the process they became familiar with great tracts of the surrounding countryside. William found there to be a subtle difference between these more northerly dales and those south of the Stainmore Pass. The climate seemed to be just that little bit harsher and the effect on vegetation was noticeable. Trees tended to be more stunted and the growing season shorter. On the plus side he found growing in the high hills some plants which he had never seen before. With the Bird's Eye Primrose he was familiar but the low growing springtime Gentians were new to him and of such a brilliant blue as to fill him with wondering astonishment.

Thus the summer sped by, William's employer becoming more and more pleased with his assistant and more reliant upon his help, whilst his uncle Joseph, although missing the boy a great deal, was heartened by the regular reports he received from Mr Allcot about his continued good progress and happiness. William too wrote, perhaps not as frequently as he should, but always in cheerful manner and never failing to thank his uncle for the opportunity which he had been given and the continued financial support which he received. In Wensleydale the great drama of the attempted escape had receded into the background, especially now that the Scottish Queen was no longer housed in the area. Only the most closely engaged in the event retained any lingering thought about the matter, the Fawcetts of course and the young Metcalfe, whose service to the English Queen had been little recognised, let alone rewarded. The ambitions of the Metcalfe clan still burned strong but their influence in royal circles had diminished since the days of Queen Mary. Perhaps that was the root cause of the problem. Perhaps it was necessary to make sure that his loyalty to the new Queen was recognised and valued. Thomas yearned to achieve that restoration of royal regard which had once been manifested by the appointment of his grandfather and father as High Sherrifs of Yorkshire. His father, he knew, was spending lavishly in order to maintain a position in society but this he suspected was unsustainable and in any case non-productive. Some deed of note was required and Thomas searched for the answer. His part in the foiling of the escape from Walburn might be built upon. There were still questions to be answered in this affair. Sir Francis Lascelles was clearly under suspicion as having been privy to the attempt but no overt accusation had been made and there was certainly no proof of his complicity. The question of the unidentified riders who had led the pursuit astray had never been resolved. It must have been someone with local knowledge and the young Robinson lad had been his favourite candidate for suspicion. But it seemed that he had been absent at that time studying the law, in London as it was first thought but now known to be in Durham. Thomas still wondered if William's involvement could have been possible and could be proved to be so. He was intelligent enough to realise that the wish was father to the thought but that wish was very strong. He had, of course, conducted his own enquiries, somewhat forcefully, amongst the local inhabitants but nobody had any knowledge of William Robinson being seen at Worton after he had departed for London (as they believed) in September.

He had thought to interrogate the sister of the slain Fawcett boy but had received a sharp rebuff from Joseph Robinson, who refused to let him in the house and called shame upon a man who sought to pester the sister of a boy he had murdered. The incident made no improvement to the already sour relations between the two families. Thus Thomas reluctantly and temporarily abandoned his attempts to implicate William although the memory of the intervention of Queen Mary on his behalf still rankled and indeed provided a motive for the suspected assistance he might have rendered. It seemed then that the danger to William was diminishing and both Joseph and William were entertaining hopes that they might be reunited for a short time at the following Christmas festival. Those hopes were to be dashed in a dramatic and deadly fashion.

The summer passed into autumn in a pleasant but largely uneventful fashion. William saw much of Katherine and there was a noticeable warming in their relationship but despite several rather half hearted attempts on his part the physical side of the their mutual attraction did not seem able to develop. William's attempts were half hearted, not because of a lack of desire to prosecute them, but because it seemed clear to him that they were doomed to failure before he began. The constant chaperoning of the couple, which was insisted upon by Mrs Armstrong, did not help but William was convinced that this monitoring of their social contact could have been evaded, at least temporarily, had Katherine only possessed the will. Apparently she had not. Furthermore those physical contacts which did occur through politeness and formality, the offering of an arm or hand to assist or safeguard, were indeed merely formal or polite. Any pressing of that hand or arm was dealt with by a firm breaking of the contact, which was done without irritation or annoyance but was nonetheless a clear enough indication that any form of intimate touch was not welcome.

In the absence of this encouragement one might wonder why William continued in his pursuit of the young lady but she was good company in that she conversed well, was highly intelligent and certainly seemed to be better disposed towards him than at the time of their first meetings. And of course, above all she was very beautiful. Small and slightly built, she nevertheless had a superb figure and a delightful countenance. Her dark, black hair framed a face of delightful proportions with dark brown eyes and a delicate mouth which, when opened, revealed small but regular white teeth. When she smiled her face became irradiated and her eyes sparkled. William could sink readily into their depths and want for nothing more. When she intimated her disapproval, the curl of her lip and scorn in her eyes was devastating. Her character was summed up in her face. At times convivial, interesting and interested in her companion, at times cruelly dismissive and hurtful, but never boring; a fascinating and brightly glowing candle around which William's moth-like wings beat incessantly.

Leisure time was still divided between his association with the Armstrongs and his continuing strong friendship with Sculley who he met either to undertake an expedition into the country or simply to enjoy the company of all their other friends amongst the young people of the city. William's well-developed qualities of adapting manners and language to fit in with the current company helped to make him an accepted participant in any gathering, whatever the degree of living they represented. There was one noticeable difference about these latter gatherings however. Jed, whilst having acknowledged his debt to William for saving his life, exhibited none of the enthusiasm for his company one might have expected. Indeed he had cut himself off from most of that crowd which had formerly looked up to him as leader of the pack. He felt he had lost face, not merely because he had been in beaten in that jousting event but because he was beholden to his rival for his very existence. Certainly he was not treated to the adulation which had once been his, other than from a small group of his most devoted followers who tended to be the small minded and most antisocial of the young men in the crowd. The activities of this breakaway set became more and more distasteful and William was not dismayed by being excluded from them. One particular event served to exemplify the differences in behaviour that had separated the youth of the city into two camps.

It was on a sunny Sunday morning in September, when William was accompanying the Armstrong ladies on a stroll by the riverside. A loud disturbance made up of shouts of excitement and the barking of dogs was coming from the neighbouring field, where a large crowd was gathering. Katherine expressed a desire to investigate and they approached to find a scene that sickened William to his stomach. A large pit had been dug in which a badger was held to a post by restraining leathers around his hind legs. Meanwhile several dogs were being urged to attack the poor beast, which defended itself as best it could. It was a good defence too, as his powerful jaws did immense damage to any dog which came within their range but the odds were loaded against him. The dogs were numerous and, hampered by the ties on his back legs, the badger sustained many serious bites. Blood was flowing copiously from both the trapped wild beast and the dogs, several of which were limping badly from their injuries but if they tried to escape from the action they were picked up by their keepers and thrown back into the fray. At each renewed assault there were loud cried of encouragement whilst the assembled throng looked on in horrified fascination. William caught sight of Sculley who was visibly distressed by the affair but clearly felt unable to intervene. Indeed, had he done so, he would have met with a violent response from the chief perpetrators who were very obviously highly worked up by the excitement and the sight of blood.

To his astonishment William found that his arm was being squeezed forcefully by the young lady who hung upon it. Glancing up at Katherine, he saw that her face was flushed and little beads of perspiration stood upon her upper lip. Much as he regretted the cause for this unexpected intimacy, he took advantage of the situation and returned the pressure. Then, greatly daring, he removed her hand and put his arm around her waist. Without invitation she pressed her body close and he was overwhelmed by the consciousness of her shape being thrust upon him and the scent she wore which made his head whirl. How long he held her thus he could not tell but eventually things came to an end with the death of the poor badger, whose body was riven apart by the victorious dogs. The excitement over, William and his party of ladies moved on, Mrs Armstrong loud in her condemnation of the behaviour of those young men and Katherine silent as she sought to recover her composure. The strong physical contact had been broken and was not resumed but the awareness of what had happened remained with both of them.

Chapter 5: Rebellion

Mary was livid with fury as she bounced about in the uncomfortable carriage which conveyed her back to Tutbury Castle. With hardly any warning, she had been compelled to pack and move from the comfortable house in Wingfield, where she had spent much of the summer, and was now being taken to the damp and unpleasant castle where she could expect a stricter confinement. But her fury was less due to her present discomfort than the collapse of her schemes.

In September of 1569 Elizabeth had been given cause for concern when she discovered that her kinsman and premier nobleman, Lord Norfolk, was entertaining plans to marry her unwelcome guest, the Scottish Queen. She was also aware of the closeness between Norfolk and the northern earls, who were known to chafe under the imposition of the new Anglican faith and whose independent behaviour was facilitated by the remoteness of their power bases from the English court. Acutely aware of the dangers this presented, she peremptorily forbade the marriage, as a result of which Norfolk left court in a dudgeon. He did not, however, break contact with his northern friends who had in fact been long conspiring to replace their current monarch with the Catholic Mary, suitably wedded to a prominent nobleman close to the royal line.

Faced with the Queen's displeasure and decisive action against his proposal of marriage, Norfolk developed a severe case of cold feet and counselled his fellow conspirators to abandon their plans. He wrote to the Queen begging for a pardon and was persuaded by Cecil to return to court where he would be leniently treated. In fact he was intercepted by Sir Francis Knollys and Sir Henry Neville who conducted him to the Tower. When news of this reached the northern earls they arranged to meet at Northumberland's house in Topcliffe which they did on October 11th to discuss their future. Northumberland's reluctance to commit himself to outright rebellion was overcome by Westmorland and his party. Meanwhile the Lord President of the Council of the North, Lord Sussex, had been expressly commanded by the Queen to look out for signs of revolt. He made light of the current rumours about the situation, obtained assurances of loyalty from Northumberland and Westmorland

and advised the Queen not to worry. Nonetheless he fortified the city of York, Hull, Knaresborough and Pomfret. But the Queen had other informants and asked Sussex to order the earls to return to court, which Sussex communicated on 30th October. When they made excuses not to attend, Sussex finally demanded that they come to York by the morning of November 5th.

On November 4th the tocsin rang in the town of Topcliffe to declare rebellion.

....

Rumours had been circulating around the city for some days. They concerned the activities of several members of the nobility and gentry who were known to be unhappy with the present regime in London and who still resented the imposition of a new faith at the expense of their own deeply-held loyalty to the Roman Church. There was talk of serious protest, even to the point of outright rebellion and this was made the more credible when news arrived from nearby Brancepeth that the castle, seat of Lord Westmorland, was become a meeting place for other members of the nobility who were accompanied by men at arms. Opinion was greatly divided amongst the citizens. There were many who welcomed the news; people who had never accepted the new version of Christianity, which had been thrust upon them; people who would not be too upset to see Elizabeth replaced by the Scottish Queen, who had been so cruelly imprisoned in England and who was known to be a staunch follower of the true faith. The idea that a group of Lords, and moreover Lords of their own region, might rebel against the Queen and her Protestant, southern-dominated, government was entirely pleasing to them.

Of those who were less enthusiastic about the news, there were few whose actual concern was the preservation of the new Anglican Church. They were God-fearing enough, to be sure, but the form their worship took was of little account to them. The deity they worshipped remained the same and their faith remained a simple one, whatever extra layers of dogma were superimposed upon it by the prevailing ecclesiastical rulers. No, it was not religious change they feared, but the interruption of what had become a peaceful and settled lifestyle. Apart from the physical dangers which accompanied armed rebellion, the thinking people were frightened of the general effects of the turmoil which would inevitably accompany an insurrection and the repercussions which would follow quite regardless of the outcome. This was the main topic of conversation around the supper table at the Allcot household on the evening of Saturday 14th November, when even the ladies had been constrained to remain at table for the discussion after the meal. All were agreed that, unless the affair fizzled out through lack of resolve or support, there would be serious effects upon the lives of all citizens. Mr Allcot was deeply concerned about the suppression of civil law under the martial conditions that would prevail. The sword becomes mightier than the pen, at least temporarily, when a state of war exists and many a miscarriage of justice can occur without guarantee of it being righted when peace returns. 'To the victor belongs the spoils' is a truism which frequently becomes all too practical a reality regardless of ethical considerations.

Mr Armstrong's concern was primarily the effect on trade. Inevitably, the general wealth of the realm would be damaged, the more so of course in areas where battles were fought and the losers were stripped of their possessions. These were not necessarily recycled, for war is always wasteful: goods and crops would be destroyed, buildings razed, and the brunt would be borne by the long-suffering peasant whose livelihood would be lost and therefore even his miniscule purchasing power would vanish along with that of many others of higher degree. This would be a major blow to the merchants whose markets were being reduced. In short, trade would suffer badly; nor would it make a quick recovery. William noted that, in assessing his likely misfortune, Armstrong seemed able to overlook the greater suffering of the aforementioned peasant who had no means to live, nor hope to recover even his meagre place in the world.

Talk turned to the possibility of the rebels raising the standard of the Scottish Queen and Allcot was quick to point out the irreversible nature of such a move. Rebellious protest could be forgiven, with suitable restitution made of course, but plans to unseat a ruling monarch were treason and could never be forgiven. If unsuccessful such a rising would result in death for all involved. Mr Allcot turned upon William and spoke earnestly to him.

"I know, lad, that ye have had dealings with the lady and perhaps harbour some regard for her, but I would counsel ye not to take sides in this matter. Remain unswayed by appeals to rally to her banner especially as it be my judgement that her cause is already lost."

"I thank 'e Sir for the advice, which accords well with my own thinking. I feel no obligation to support the lady for any debt of honour I might have had has been totally redeemed in blood."

The Armstrongs were quite mystified by this dramatic declaration but perceived that it was a matter known to Mr Allcot but not to be shared and so the subject was not pursued. As might be imagined however the air of mystery which surrounded these remarks did nothing to lessen the interest of the ladies in this young man, who appeared to have had an important part to play in the saga of the Scottish Queen's adventures in England. The conversation took on a lighter tone and soon there was laughter in place of frowns and serious contemplation. The party broke up in good spirits and the expectation of a pleasant meeting again on the morrow in the cathedral, followed by an expedition to the country if the weather held.

Sunday, 15th November dawned fine and bright but there had been a keen overnight frost. This combination of winter-bright sunshine and sharp frost had tempted the populace into their gayest warm clothing, overlaid in the case of those more fortunate, with furs, hats and gloves. There was no lingering outside the cathedral as people hurried in to the illusory impression of warmth which the candlelight in the building suggested. The press of bodies which the unusually large congregation had produced soon made the illusion a reality. The Prince Bishop was away at this time and the service was to be conducted by a lesser ecclesiast. It had barely begun when there was a disturbance at the doors. Into the cathedral swept a large body of men, all armed and all purposeful of mien. The leaders, clearly marked out as men of noble birth by their dress and bearing, marched up to the altar, whilst men-at-arms were stationed at intervals along the nave and at the doors. The buzz of comment and query in the congregation was stilled when one of the leaders, a stocky, dark featured and dark haired man, turned to face them and held up an imperious hand enjoining silence. He was recognised as Charles Neville, Earl of Westmorland. He addressed them in loud tones that rang through the uncomfortable silence.

"Y'ell remain seated," he gestured at the surrounding men at arms and continued, "Nobody will leave; ye'll hold yer tongues and not interrupt until our business here is completed."

With that, he turned to his companions and nodded at which some seized hold of the altar table and, to horrified gasps from the congregation, overturned it roughly, spilling the communion plate, the sacrament and the great new bible to the floor. One gentleman in the group trampled the book, tearing pages and breaking the spine. There was a cry from the cleric who had been officiating:

"For shame, my Lords, this is the house of God!"

"T'was indeed so once and will be returned to His service even now!" Westmorland's reply was accompanied by fervent shouts of support from the large company of knights and men of quality who attended him. A tall young man was being hustled along the nave. He clutched a bag which rattled and clanged as he proceeded and he was followed by two men bearing some wooden apparatus which was bulky and clearly very heavy. There were murmurs as the function of this wooden contrivance became apparent. It was unfolded to reveal a portable altar, but one such as had not been seen for many years. Complete with triptych, which bore blatantly Marian images, it was being set about with all the paraphernalia necessary for the celebration of Mass. The tall young man now reappeared from the vestry clad in his priestly robes and the new service began.

It was a strange and forbidding atmosphere that pervaded the great cathedral. The congregation was largely composed of regulars who came principally as a matter of form and did not perhaps attend to the words of the services with as much concentration as would have been desirable. Now, the older ones found themselves struggling to recall half-remembered responses and procedures under the watchful gaze of armed men, whilst many of the younger worshippers, including Katherine and William, were completely at a loss and felt deeply uncomfortable. The invading throng of lords, knights and gentlemen participated joyously in the service, which they clearly saw as something more than a religious ceremony. It was a declaration of change and a new order to come, which was made abundantly clear after the conclusion of the Mass when Neville again harangued his captive audience with the news that he was preparing to march south, rescue Mary, Queen of Scotland from her prison at Tutbury and set her on the English throne. Elizabeth and her heretical government would be deposed and severely dealt with for their misdeeds. Few doubted the meaning of that grim threat but, Neville assured, the general population, including all present here, would remain unaffected and allowed to continue their lives as before, providing, of course, that they all returned to the true faith.

Perhaps Charles Neville experienced his first intimation of ultimate failure from the profound silence which greeted his speech; no cries of protest but then no calls of acclaim or celebration, just a stunned and uneasy quiet which must have chilled his heart. In the days of preparatory plotting for this rising there had been a bland assumption that the vast majority of ordinary people would gladly support his cause and be happy to reject the new, imposed religion. In this, his first confrontation with a local populace, he must have been disappointed by their lack of enthusiasm. He really needed to carry them with him. The days of powerful barons commanding unquestioning obedience from tenants and serfs were ended centuries ago. The newly-emerging middle classes of merchants, yeoman farmers and lettered professionals were serious forces to be reckoned with and a temporary show of military force, such as he had just staged, would not be enough to sustain his cause. A positive and meaningful act, such as the proclamation of Mary as Queen was necessary and the sooner the better.

But, in terms of rallying support, Neville was a disaster. It seemed that, as Earl of Westmorland, he was so far above lesser mortals as to be unable, or certainly unwilling, to communicate with them. The way in which he abruptly signalled that the congregation might now leave was contemptuous. His overbearing attitude won him no friends and not a few enemies. Some people streamed out of the cathedral in relief but others remained in the nave discussing the amazing train of events.

William was discussing the situation with Mr Allcot and some legal acquaintances when a familiar voice rang out across the cathedral.

"Young Robinson, William I say!"

He turned, startled, to find Sir Francis Lascelles striding towards him. In his surcoat and helmet William had failed to recognise him amongst the crowd of knights but now there was no disguising the slightly portly and bluff figure who hastened towards him. It was with a great dread that William awaited this highly public meeting with this link from a past from which he was desperate to distance himself.

"William, my lad, t'is good to see thee here! How goes it with 'ee my boy?

The jovial greeting was loud enough to turn many heads in the vicinity all of them clearly prepared to listen attentively to the coming conversation.

"Why, thank'ee Sir Francis, I am well enough and happily employed here in Durham. T'is pleasant to see you here too, Sir, but in strange circumstances."

"Aye, so it may seem but this has been a marvellous time for me; a momentous decision and a cause dear to my heart. I was at Markenfield Hall, staying with my cousin Thomas, when the summons came. A goodly assembly of knights and gentlemen gathered there and what a brave sight we made as we rode from that lovely house, crossed the moat and made for Ripon where we met with more of our kind and persuasion. We have marched together now for several days and some say in the wrong direction!"

He laughed heartily for a moment but became more serious.

"Aye, we should be engaged in the business of securing the Lady Mary from her prison and for that we need the support of all our friends. So what say 'ee lad? Wilt saddle up and ride with us? I know you have a high regard for the lady and even mayhap a duty."

So there it was. A highly public association of himself with the rebel party had just been witnessed by a sizable number of citizens of Durham. His connection with the Scottish Queen had been loudly proclaimed and there was a clear assumption that he was in sympathy with their aims and would likely join them in their endeavours.

This, he reasoned, was not a time to prevaricate or dissemble. He must take a risk and act decisively.

"Alas no, Sir Francis. I am bound here in service to my master here, Mr Allcot, but even were he to give permission for me to ride off with you I cannot do so. I have a high regard for you, Sir, and indeed happy memories of your kindnesses to me over many years but I fear I cannot ally myself to your cause. I am yet loyal to my Queen and my country and as for the duty to which you refer t'was discharged in full with an unhappy result if you recall."

Mr Allcot had been watching this exchange with growing concern. William's clear statement of opposition to the rebellion was bad enough but it had been delivered in a firm and carrying voice. This was all against his advice to take no side but William had taken a calculated risk and it seemed to have paid off. After a startled silence, Sir Francis smiled and then chuckled.

"Bravely said lad, and I doubt not your good heart. 'Tis plain that we must disagree on some matters, some indeed dear to my heart, but such disagreement will not stand between us – my hand on't."

William accepted the proffered hand in astonishment but as he looked into the elderly knight's eyes he saw nothing but friendliness, perhaps overlaid with a touch of nostalgia. He made haste to introduce Mr Allcot, describing his position as the premier attorney in the city, and Sir Francis made pleasant conversation declaring that if things went badly for him he might stand in need of a good legal representative. He finally remarked

"Methinks you have an excellent pupil here, Sir."

"I know that to be true," was the response and William glowed a little.

The knight took his leave but turned back to say quietly to William "There are things in the past which were perhaps better forgotten for your sake. Be at ease in your mind that I shall reveal nought." He smiled and moved quickly away to rejoin his companions.

William heaved a sigh of relief and turning to Mr Allcot he saw an expression of amused admiration upon his face. The attorney grabbed his arm and whisked him out of the cathedral.

"By God, my boy, but that was well done. I confess I thought you to be lost but ye knew the gentleman well enough to risk all and now I warrant ye to be safe in the eyes of the Queen and her government. Many here heard the full discourse, your voice was pitched aright to achieve that, and t'was recognised as a bold and challenging declaration. It was a speech which invited instant retribution as all could see, but you escaped that and are now marked as a Queen's man, loyal even to the risk of death!"

The occupation of Durham by the rebel forces was to continue some days and Mass was heard in the cathedral throughout this time. Westmorland and Northumberland had retired to Brancepeth for a while but not before a proclamation had been read in the market place, which sought to persuade folk that their hostility was directed not against the Queen so much as her advisors who by their "crafty dealing have overthrown the Catholic religion, abused the Queen, dishonoured the realm and seek to destroy the nobility." The proclamation declared their intent to restore the ancient customs and liberties by force if necessary and it was followed by attempts to rally people to take up arms with them. This was only partly successful and, when a few days later a party of new recruits was marched away to Brancepeth, it was noted to be largely composed of malcontents and ne'r do wells. William was saddened to learn from Sculley that Jed had been a member of that party: the temptation to regain face and influence had been too great. Furthermore, there had been suggestions that the rebel host was to be joined and supported by the reivers of Tynedale and Liddesdale. Everyone knew of their propensity for acquiring plunder given half a chance and so there must have been an element of expectation amongst these new recruits of bettering their lot in terms of material gain at the expense of innocent citizens who stood in their way.

On November 20th, the rebel army marched south from Durham and tension lessened within the city. There followed a period of intense speculation as to what was happening in the rest of the country and various pieces of news, often conflicting, provided material for debate and predictions of possible outcomes. This speculation came to an end on November 30th when rebel army returned to Brancepeth. Sir Francis Lascelles came to Durham and sought out Mr Allcot and William. He had a sorry tale to tell.

There had been an abortive attempt to ride upon Tutbury to rescue the Scottish Queen. Intelligence had been received that the southern army was moving against them and outnumbered them to a considerable degree. The rebels had decided then to retreat northwards and this was the beginning of the end. A futile action had been taken against Sir George Bowes in Barnard Castle, which had indeed fallen after a siege, but that had achieved nothing of any real value. The rebel party was now at Brancepeth and was disintegrating. Northumberland and Westmorland were fleeing to Scotland, whilst others, like himself, were remaining to await their fate. He had come immediately to Durham to consult with Mr Allcot, as to what might be attempted in his defence.

....

Once again Mary was suffering the discomfort and indignity of a forced change of dwelling. This time there had been a decided impression of panic amongst her keepers and she knew why. Despite the reduction of her entourage at the orders of Queen Elizabeth, she was kept well informed as to the activities of her supporters. She knew that the rebellion was to occur and she understood that it had been prematurely raised as a result of the weakness of Norfolk, the nobleman who had planned to marry her and set her on the English throne. She had been prepared to go through with that alliance in order to achieve her objective for she had no doubt that she could rid herself of the old fool when the time was ripe. Now it was manifestly unlikely to happen. Norfolk was in the Tower and few escaped from that predicament. Besides, the English Queen was now privy to this plan and would certainly see that it came to nought. But there would be other ways of securing her liberty and seizing the throne. The current rebellion was her best hope at the moment and, if that failed, there was always the strong possibility of outside support from both France and, more importantly, Philip of Spain.

Meanwhile she was being buffeted about in a coach which traversed the bumpy road from Tutbury to Coventry in the early hours of a bitterly cold morning. There had been a marked absence of deference in their handling of her departure. Sir Francis Knollys had been abrupt with her and, despite her protests, she had been bundled into this coach with little warning and even less in the way of provision for her comfort. Her effects and retinue would follow in due course, they said, but her own departure could not be delayed. She knew why of course and it was a matter of keen disappointment to her. She had been living in the hope and expectation of a dramatic rescue from her imprisonment at Tutbury but it seemed that secrecy had not been sufficiently well maintained and she suspected the handiwork of her great bête noir, Cecil and his spies, in this hasty removal. Well, there was one who would go to the block if, no when, she corrected herself, she ascended the English throne. She comforted herself with thoughts of his downfall as she endured the miserable journey.

If rage and disappointment were the prime emotions of Queen Mary, it was with equal rage but also real apprehension that Queen Elizabeth viewed the situation. The defiance and indeed outright rebellion of the northern earls was bad enough but at least their intentions were now out in the open. What was really worrying was the lack of support her Lord President of the Council of the North was receiving. He had written to the government complaining of the poor response to his call to arms and had declared himself unable to do anything other than hold the city of York for the Queen. He urgently needed help as the north was incapable of providing for its own defence. This assessment had infuriated Elizabeth. Not only had it been the northern earls who had rebelled but the north countrymen were refusing to support their legitimate monarch. Well, they would suffer for it. In the meantime it was necessary to mobilise the southern armies and despatch them to the aid of her loyal officers in York and Hull, Knaresborough and Pomfret. Lord Clinton and the Earl of Warwick were in charge of this but it was a slow process and Sussex was kept immobile in York. Well, at least she had scotched the plans of the rebels to liberate Mary. She had been moved but at night, in order to prevent her being seen by the populace who might have responded sympathetically to her treatment. Elizabeth was only too well aware of the magnetic personality of that highly dangerous woman. It must have been at this time that the thought of permanent removal of this focus of revolt crossed the mind of the English Queen. The spectre of religious uprising had finally come to be a reality with Mary as the acknowledged figurehead. The only good news was that, according to the intelligence received from Cecil's spies, the rebels too had experienced little joy in rallying recruits to their cause. It seemed that nobody wanted to fight on either side.

....

Sir Francis had been closeted with Mr Allcot for the major part of an hour and William had sat fidgeting in the office, shuffling papers meaninglessly backwards and forwards. When the study door finally opened and the two men emerged, each was smiling but, whilst one smile was clearly meant to be encouraging, confident and offering comfort, the other showed apprehension and doubt. The departure of their visitor was not protracted. Sir Francis took William's hand and wished him well, repeating his assurance made in the cathedral several days earlier that he would not reveal the part played by either of them in the attempted escape.

"T'would serve me not at all in my present case," he admitted with a wry smile. Turning to Mr Allcot, he grasped his hand and said, "I believe I leave my life in your hands, Sir, and I believe too that I can do so with confidence and trust in your good offices to me. I thank you for your time and patience." He was seen out by the servant leaving the two men of law to regard each other gravely.

"But what can be salvaged from his predicament?" asked William.

"Little enough perhaps," replied the advocate, "but we can try. At worst he will lose his head but we can take some action to save his family from penury by the prompt and careful movement of his assets, although about his land we can do nothing. If it is seized, then so be it. It is also necessary to establish that his immediate family knew nothing of his plans to join the rebellion, nor assisted him in any way. At best we may convince Cecil and his investigators that Sir Francis was indeed a mere peripheral participant in the plot. He has affirmed that his interest was in the freedom for himself to practice his old religion and declares that he harboured no wish to see our Queen deposed in favour of Mary. The plan to release that lady from her imprisonment was completely unknown to him and, when revealed, it prompted him to doubt the validity of the whole enterprise in which he had become embroiled. When, at last, it dawned upon his simple mind that the objective of the chief rebels was no less than overthrowing his monarch, he was appalled and rejected the idea of this treasonable act, at which time he approached me for guidance."

He smiled as he observed the expression on William's face. "Yes, my boy, we both know that the timing was not quite like that but we must do what we can for our client. It is necessary now for me to make haste in writing several letters and making copies of the deposition made by Sir Francis. I will need your help, William, for time is of great importance."

William was glad to assist and, studying the deposition made by Sir Francis which he was to copy, he was once again compelled to admire the skill and thought processes of his mentor, Mr Allcot. It was clear that most of the words had been put into the mouth of the man, who was indubitably pleading for his life, and he emerged as a simple minded eccentric who pined for the old days and the comfort of the religion he had been taught as a boy. Some sort of nebulous wish to establish a sort of local enclave, where Roman Catholicism could be practised with the blessing of Queen Elizabeth, was advanced as his motive for joining the rising. That was reprehensible, as he now realised, but his thoughts had never strayed into the realm of threats to the Queen's person or authority. That was indeed unthinkable.

As he studied the text, William was impressed by the careful way in which the idea of imbecility or mental incompetence had been avoided and yet an air of simple-mindedness had been conveyed, which contained nothing of hostility to the crown but rather a belief that the establishment of his foolish, utopian scheme would help to diminish the tension between believers in the old religion and those who followed the new church. Sir Francis may have been dismayed to see himself portrayed as a good hearted man of poor intellect but better this than be suspected of being a determined rebel, bent upon the overthrow and removal of his legitimate monarch. Meanwhile Mr Allcot was writing to his many contacts within the judiciary and indeed to members of the state administration including one letter addressed directly to Sir William Cecil. Although he was not privy to the contents of that letter, William could guess at the difficulty of its composition.

To say that the overall mood in Durham was sombre would be an understatement. Expectations for the future ranged from vague apprehension to downright fear. There were some, a few only, who actually left the area taking what they could and accepting losses in so doing in order to escape what they foresaw as inevitable retribution. Most, however, remained either through inertia or a feeling that they had too much invested in their home city to desert it on the hazard of possible penalties levied by the State. The problem was of course that, whilst the good citizens of Durham could not be held responsible for the initial revolt, they had passively accepted the new status quo by continuing to attend the popish ceremonies conducted in the cathedral. There had been no popular revulsion at this imposition and indeed it had been received with no small enthusiasm by certain elements of the populace and people realised that there would be no shortage of reports to a vengeful state from those wishing to ingratiate themselves with the authorities. As usual, it was the higher elements of society who worried most about the inevitable recrimination, whilst, also as usual, it was the poor and powerless lower classes who were destined to bear the greater burden of the retribution when it came. And come it did.

Chapter 6: The Aftermath

The suffering of the northern people began with the depredations of the southern army under the leadership of Lord Clinton and the Earl of Warwick. Because of the flight of the rebels to the border country this great body of men had been left masters of a field which they had not actually contested. The traditional reward for soldiery was, of course, the opportunity to plunder, primarily the defeated opposing army, but also to some extent the surrounding countryside. In the absence of a defeated foe it was the country folk who bore the entire weight of the despoliation.

Across the entire region between Doncaster and Newcastle the southern army drove away cattle, seized goods, lands and leases, imposing a reign of terror and severe hardship on the northern populace. From his base in York, the Earl of Sussex had tried hard to stop this indiscriminate plunder by issuing proclamations against it, but to little avail. Only the sheriffs or their officers were empowered to distrain goods but this weighed little in the minds of the foot soldiers whose ambitions were to accumulate as much loot as they could carry. They were not to be denied and the ravages they inflicted upon the poor inhabitants of Yorkshire and Durham were barely curtailed by their leaders. As they were mainly looting the poor, the very meanest living inhabitants, their returns were concomitantly poor in terms of material goods. Coin and valuable artefacts were rare but livestock was abundant and was mercilessly pillaged. The soldiers enjoyed a period of feasting on fresh meat that had no previous parallel in their lives, whilst the peasants and smallholders were reduced to the merest pittance of existence. Those who resisted were peremptorily slain but not a few, who conceded their animals, died anyway of starvation during the following winter. And perhaps their leaders were not too unhappy about the situation, as they knew full well that all this was tacitly endorsed by an administration which saw a need to totally cow this potentially rebellious corner of the realm. It was Sir Thomas Gargrave of Pomfret who had the task of carrying out the official forfeitures and he was concerned that much would be lost through this unlicensed looting. Nevertheless, he amassed so much in the way of livestock that it became a severe embarrassment to him, there being insufficient food to keep them alive. Many died through being driven or starved and the wastage was appalling. He had wished to sell some of the stock to lighten the load but the Queen was insistent that all be gathered and kept.

The infamous 'harrying of the north' carried out by the Norman King William was perhaps a much worse visitation upon the region, principally because the loss of life was greater but the effect of the seizures upon an already poverty-stricken land was cruel in the extreme. If Queen Elizabeth and her ministers were less bloodthirsty than King William, there were nonetheless some five hundred rebels executed by the beginning of February in 1570. These were mainly of the poorer sort and their deaths were designed to over-awe the people and administer an unforgettable message that an attempt to unseat a monarch would be met by the severest of punitive measures. And yet, ironically, it was the members of the gentry who had exhorted or even compelled their tenants to join the rising, who, to an extent, escaped the wrath of the government. It was this lack of justice and persecution of the poor that Mr Allcot had foreseen. True, huge fines and confiscation of land were imposed upon the gentry. Sir Francis Lascelles was one who suffered in such a way. His fortunes were severely curtailed and he lost much land but at least he kept his head, as did many of the local gentry. Not all of course; there were those who had declared themselves to be implacably hostile to the monarchy and such a stance allowed of no reprieve. They had to die and to do so publicly. After the shortest of trials they were executed in various centres of the north such as York, Carlisle and Durham.

The last such event was that carried out at Durham and was of great importance because the principal candidate for the executioner's axe was to be Northumberland, one of the prime movers of the rebellion. He had sought refuge with the border reivers of Liddesdale and placed his trust in them, surely the most untrustworthy of allies. They had betrayed him and some of his followers to Moray, Regent of Scotland and, after the latter's assassination, he had been eventually returned to meet his fate in England. To under-line the significance of this matter, the worthies of Durham were required to attend and witness the despatch of the rebels. An elaborate 'ceremony' had been devised and the spectacle was to be witnessed on Gallows Hill. A scaffold had been erected and seating arranged for the dignitaries and eminent citizens whose attendance had been demanded. Few excuses were accepted and even the common people were required to witness the event, all shops and busi-nesses having been closed down for the day.

Mr Allcot with other senior advocates had been called to attend the brief trial of all the accused. There had been no possibility of averting the death penalty; no protests of innocence were heeded and all calls for clemency were dismissed.

A thoroughly depressed Mr Allcot joined William and the Armstrongs in their allotted seats. The whole of the city seemed to be present and all looked subdued. There was no exhibition of revelry or high spirits as so often accompanied public executions. Everyone there knew someone who was to die. Friends, acquaintances and relatives would appear before them and be despatched within the full panoply of the law and church. For the Prince Bishop himself was presiding in the role of final confessor. Apart from the clergy and judiciary there were many state officials present and the whole arena was surrounded by armed men. No risk was being taken and, within the crowd, agents had been placed to detect any signs of dissent or support for the rebels.

By virtue of his status as a major peer of the realm, it was Northumberland who mounted the scaffold first. As was customary, he was allowed a final speech to the assembled throng and, as was customary for him, he was direct, unrepentant and full of scorn for the triumphant apparatus of the State which he faced. He made it clear that he found the proscription of the Roman Catholic faith unacceptable and he was proud to accept martyrdom in the name of that religion. His address was received in silence but it was the respectful silence accorded to a man of principle. When he had finished, the Prince Bishop stepped forward to give a final blessing but was angrily rebuffed:

"No my Lord, no sanctifying of this judicial murder if you please and especially at your hands."

The Bishop allowed a few seconds silence to pass before saying "My son, you go to meet Almighty God, as shall we all in our turn. Will you not accept a commendation of your soul to Him from whoever's hands? It is with a sincere concern for your life hereafter that I ask."

For a few seconds Northumberland gazed into his eyes and, seeming to be reassured by what he saw there, he nodded briefly and bowed his head. The final exchange between them was not heard but, as he lowered his head to the block, there appeared to be a calmness about the man which had not been there before.

The executioner stepped forward with his axe. He had received from Northumberland the coin for carrying out his duty to the best of his ability and also his forgiveness for the taking of his life. He was not the big, strong, heavily muscled man one might have expected, but he was skilled, very skilled. One blow sufficed to sever the head completely and neatly, whereupon a collective sigh arose from the arena. It was not the sound of a triumphant acclaim of justice being done, nor indeed a sound of resentment or disapproval. It had been a sigh of acceptance of the inevitable, a recognition of the ending of a great man's life regardless of any political dimension.

One by one the condemned gentry mounted the scaffold and it seemed that Northumberland had set the standard for their conduct. None rebuffed the Bishop's final offices. A few made speeches, mostly brief. One incident excited the sympathy of the crowd when a local squire touched his hands to his lips and offered them to the section of the crowd which held his family. Each death was met with dignity and each was received in almost total silence. The State would have no grounds for the further persecution of the citizens of Durham.

Matters changed when the lower class prisoners were paraded for death. Not for them the noble courtesy of the axe; the hangman's noose awaited them all. They took their turn and waited in line as they were 'turned off' six at a time. The numbers were such as to make a long afternoon of it and the liquor, which had found its way into the lower class enclosures began to make its presence known. As the victims appeared, there was much shouting and ribaldry with boos and jeers accorded to some whilst a few had a sympathetic reception. Recognition of many was recorded in the form of ghoulish jests, some of them so witty as to elicit grim smiles or even laughter from the prisoners themselves. It was, in fact, the normal behaviour to be expected at a public execution.

It seemed to William and the company he was with that it would go on for ever. The decapitations had been received with a calm acceptance which had been helped by the demeanour and conduct of the condemned but the callous despatch of dozens of peasants and working class citizens was utterly repellent. Some merely protested volubly, some thrashed about in vain attempts to escape restraint, some wept, some cursed but some accepted their fate stoically. There was, in fact, no great swell of sympathy for these unfortunates. True, some could be said to have been the victims of their masters' insistence upon joining the rebel cause but a great many had joined the rising voluntarily. A few had done so as a matter of religious conviction but most had done so in the hope of personal gain – largely of course in terms of loot. Such a one was Jed, who with many others had gladly joined the bands of border reivers who had seized upon this opportunity to despoil the English countryside. It would have been difficult to detect a religious element in the motivation of these northern brigands, nor indeed was there any sympathy for the ultimate fate of their temporary English guests, who were turned over to the English state authorities, when it became expedient to do so. The betrayal of Northumberland was the most dramatic instance of their treachery but the rank and file suffered similar treatment.

And here was Jed, stripped to torn shirt and long red undergarment, with bruised face and other signs of rough treatment. He had clearly put up a fight before, and maybe even after his capture, for his hands were tied behind him and he was being pushed relentlessly forward by the pressure of a pike in the small of his back. There were shouts of recognition and encouragement from some of his old cronies and William realised that Katherine too had recognised him. Glancing at her face, he noted again how pallid was her countenance, as indeed it had been throughout the afternoon. He had worried that she might have fainted away at the sight of so much blood and suffering but this was not so. Rather had she exhibited a sort of internal excitement revealed only by a certain rigidity of the body and the very slightest trembling of the limbs. Her facial expression remained fixed with only a glittering of the eyes to suggest mental engagement with the unfolding events. To William's astonishment this state of excitement grew steadily as each struggling form stretched its rope to the limit and kicked helplessly for a while. His astonishment increased at her reaction to the death of Jed. Launched into space, he fought desperately at the end of the rope. His legs, indeed his whole body, jerked violently, providing great sport for the common element in the crowd. What was more, as sometimes happens in such a case, the violent motions coupled with the stricture around the neck caused the wildly pumping heart to direct the blood to the lower parts of the body. To the vast amusement of the crowd, the dying man produced a huge erection, which the loose undergarment did little to conceal. The watching men cheered him for what they took to be Jed's last defiant gesture to the life he was quitting.

How long this would have continued is uncertain because a slight young figure forced his way through the crowd and its surrounding soldiery. It was

Sculley and, with stricken expression, he rushed toward the gallows and, leaping up, he seized the legs of the tormented man, jerking them down with such force as to break his neck. There was a silence broken only by the shout of a man at arms who rushed forwards and hurled Sculley to the ground. But, as he menaced the lad with his sword, a low growl went up from the crowd and he thought the better of it. Indeed his expression softened and, laying down his weapon, he offered a hand to the lad and pulled him back to his feet, sending him back to his companions.

Throughout the duration of Jed's final agonies, William had been aware of Katherine's fingers digging more and more fiercely into his arm. He was sure that, even through the fabric of his tunic, the flesh would be bruised but it was her face which claimed his full attention. The pallor was almost deathly but the eyes sparkled with a frightening intensity. Her bloodless lips were open revealing a row of small, white, even teeth but these too were parted slightly giving a glimpse of pink tongue pressing behind them. There were beads of sweat forming on her upper lip which, running down over her chin, fell into her robe, running down between her breasts. She clung tightly to him as the last few men were hung but this it must be said was carried out amid a general feeling of anticlimax after the dramatic spectacle of Jed's departure. It was a sad thought for William, that these last few prisoners choked out their miserable lives to the complete indifference of the spectators; lives doubtless precious to themselves but of no apparent interest to anyone else.

The spectators were now allowed to disperse, mostly to their homes but some to relief provided by the local taverns. The Armstrongs, together with Mr Allcot and indeed many other prominent citizens, had been invited to a reception in the castle, where they were to meet Lord Clinton, the Queen's Marshal. This invitation was, of course, in the nature of a command. No opportunity was being lost to remind everyone of the re-imposition of royal power and also that they remained under scrutiny. Katherine suddenly spoke out loudly –

"Home, I need to go home!" and Mrs Armstrong, perceiving for the first time her daughter's deathly visage urged her husband to take them there quickly.

"We cannot do so," he said grimly. "No excuse will be tolerated for our failure to attend." Grasping William by the shoulder he spoke urgently to him. "See her safe home for me, my boy. We shall be most grateful if you would do us this service." William glanced at Mrs Armstrong, who nodded her assent. Wordlessly and impetuously Katherine tore herself away from their company with William hastening to catch up with her. He did so, took her arm and glanced back to see the relief on the faces of her parents.

Not a word was spoken by Katherine as they hurried through the streets of the city, although William kept up a steady stream of encouraging remarks. They reached the Armstrong home and entered noisily, sweeping past the astonished maid.

"I must go to my room," said Katherine vehemently. "I must go to my room and I must not be disturbed. Mr Robinson here will see me safely up the stair but then I must be left entirely alone." She mounted the stair rapidly, making a nonsense of the necessity of William's assistance and, entering the salon, she bade him sit and wait whist she went into her room. As he sat anxiously on the gilded chair, William was very troubled on her account. She had clearly sustained some major reaction to the terrible scenes she had beheld and he worried about her state of mind and her general well being. After a short while there was a cry from her room.

"William, come quickly!" and he rushed through the door not knowing what to expect. What he saw paralysed him completely. She was standing by the bed, naked and with her breasts heaving in a great tide of passion.

"Take me William, now," she gasped out, her voice distorted with passion. "Take me, now I say. For God's sake, if you are a man, you must take me at once!" and she rushed at him clawing at his clothes. The frenzy which followed left William's mind reeling as he found himself trying to meet the demands of this woman, possessed as she was by a violent need for sexual release. If his mind worked at all during this tumultuous coupling, it was to register total surprise at the complete reversal in her attitude towards intimacy with him and when all was over and they lay exhausted and drenched with sweat he reflected that, whilst it had been a realisation of something which he had long yearned for, it had not happened at all as he had envisaged it and he was disappointed at the lack of tenderness and gentleness, with which he had hoped to imbue their first love making. He was not given much time for further consideration of the situation because he received a fierce nudge and an instruction to get up and get dressed. "Quickly now, you must go. Do not delay, go quietly and above all do not presume to remind me of this, when we meet again."

William dressed himself and sought to find suitable words to say as he left but could not do so. It did not seem to matter however as Katherine had turned her face to the wall and ignored him, choosing not to witness his departure. He was able to leave the house without disturbing any of the servants and made his way, almost blindly, through the streets until he reached the Allcot house. He entered and, with only the briefest of acknowledgments to Peters, made his way up to his room where he collapsed onto the bed. The feeling of physical gratification having now passed away completely, he thought about what had happened and analysed the facts.

Quite obviously the effects of the mass executions, the bloodletting and the hangings, instead, as he had thought, of shocking her into a state of horror and terror, had acted as an aphrodisiac of the most powerful kind on the girl. So, manifestly, this was the reason for her extreme behaviour but it was leaving a rather sour taste in his mouth. The more he thought about it, the more he realised that he had been used shamelessly. There had been no feelings of love in her demands upon him, which were entirely selfish, and when she had been satisfied he had been dismissed almost like a servant. Exactly like a servant he realised with anger and a feeling of humiliation. Nor did she want to talk about it at a later date. It had been an event which did not happen and certainly she was not interested in how he had felt, and what sort of an experience it had been for him. But there was confusion in these thoughts for Katherine was a truly beautiful girl and he had enjoyed her body, being totally carried away by the extreme physicality of their union. Even now there was the kindling of a desire to experience that again. He shook that thought out of his mind and thought about the other events of the day, which had been naturally overshadowed by his bedding of Katherine.

The punitive measures taken against the rebels were, of course, expected and there had been an air of inevitability about this which had increased over the intervening months. But, when it came down to it, the reality of the deaths was shocking and mind jolting to William. Important though the characters who led the rebellion undoubtedly were, it was the killing of the lower orders which had had the greater effect upon him. To be sure there had been those who fully deserved their fate but he was also sure that there were many who had been sacrificed to appease the anger of the monarch, or at least to simply make an impression upon the minds of everyone in what was seen as the restive north; a political necessity in fact, which he could understand even if he hated it. He was reminded of the presentiment of Mr Allcot who had preached the likelihood of injustice and hardship. What had been particularly hard had been the sight of former companions from his leisure times being hung. Jed was a particular case in point but there had been others he had recognised, some of whom he suspected had recognised him as they went to the gallows. It was in this contemplation of recent events that the idea formed in his mind of using the legal skills he hoped to acquire in helping the least well off and relatively helpless people in the community. He wasn't quite sure how this could be achieved, nor how effective he could be, but he vowed to try.

And so life slowly returned to something like normality in Durham although the scars would be felt throughout the community for years to come. The Allcot practice was kept busy by the abnormal number of requests for help from families which had been penalised by the State. Minor debts and obligations were being called in to bolster deeply wounded estates and it seemed that many had come on the recommendation of Sir Francis. Work sometimes spread over into what had been traditionally leisure time but the will to socialise returned and a flurry of activity occurred to dispel the gloom which had accompanied the purging of the city. William took less pleasure in this than before. He was still very uncertain as to his feelings about Katherine. The unfeeling way in which she had treated him in merely gratifying her lust still rankled and yet there was this undeniable physical attraction which had actually strengthened as a result of their passionate encounter.

The heavy workload was a useful distraction from a slowly deteriorating pleasure in his existence in Durham. He still made excursions into the countryside but this was now a lonely pastime. Katherine simply did not wish to venture into the country; metropolitan life was her metier; she knew the city well in terms of both its intricate layout and the people who dwelt therein – or at least the people who mattered. She was not one to waste her time on those who had no wealth or no connections, unless mayhap they had qualities of wit or entertainment value which gained for them access to the charmed circle of the elite. This was the circle to which he too belonged, William realised, and he was not wholly happy about that.

For some time he had been conscious of an artificiality in their conduct and a lack of purpose in their lifestyle, which consisted of a high degree of repetitious behaviour. Relationships were often shallow and fragile because of the lack of a sound basis.

What disturbed and saddened William greatly was the fact that his membership of the higher ranks in the city had alienated him from other friends. Whenever he tried to join the Sunday morning jollifications by the river, he was rebuffed, gently and always very politely, but rebuffed nonetheless. Nobody seemed to want to spend time with him and to his great dismay this extended to his old friend Sculley. He observed with growing sorrow the number of excuses, each more feeble than the last, as to why he could not partake of an expedition into the country and in the end William tackled him directly as to the real reason. It seemed that a slight unease as to the social position of William relative to themselves had grown as it became clear to them as to the connections he had with the rich and powerful. He was a person of consequence whilst they were certainly not. This feeling had crystallised irreversibly on the day of the executions, when it was noted that William sat amongst those who, ensconced within their protected enclave, were seemingly impervious to the wrath of the State by virtue of their power and position. This illogical view angered William, who pointed out that far more highly placed people than himself had met their deaths that day and the common people, who had been hung, were, as far as he could tell, plainly guilty of being in open rebellion against their monarch. But Sculley was not to be persuaded by this argument; he maintained that there was a gulf between them that could not be bridged. In vain William reminded him of the good times they had had together, days of happy exploration in the countryside and the companionship and healthy rivalry on the Sundays by the river. Sculley acknowledged the memories with a wistful sigh but told him that his early participations in the leisure activities of the common folk were regarded as an intrusion, tainted by condescension. It appeared that the barely concealed disdain of the Armstrong ladies on their visit to the river bank had been noted and resented and, like it or not, William was undisputedly linked to these people.

He was terribly saddened by this loss of such a large section of his acquaintances and he perceived that, either by accident or clever design, the vengeful state had driven a wedge between the classes in the city which would prevent an easy relationship between them for decades to come. Looking back upon his earlier experiences, he now realised that the signs had been there all the time. Even Mr Allcot, the fairest-minded man he had ever known, whilst not condemning his association with Sculley, had not been enthusiastic and indeed had made haste to introduce him to his own circle of friends, who were of course all members of the higher echelons of society. Unused to the strong class divisions in a big city and the prejudice against crossing the borders, William had quite failed to appreciate that they existed but was now painfully aware that they had probably always done so and that the current situation was just an exacerbation of pre-existing class loyalties. He still took Gaynor out for long rides on his own, for of course she needed the exercise, and he continued to enjoy the lovely surroundings of the Wear valley. His pleasure in life, however, had diminished and, as always, he sought to lose himself in his work and legal education, to such an extent that Mr Allcot was moved to complain faintly that he could not cope with the constant demands upon his time. He did not however look too displeased at this but did seem to become preoccupied with some matter which clearly weighed upon his mind. He did not, however, share this with William.

And so matters remained until a letter arrived for William from his uncle. He had business in Durham and Mr Allcot had invited him to stay with them for a few days. Mr Allcot enlarged upon the matter by admitting that this had been arranged some time previously. His uncle wished to consult him on a legal issue and had accepted an invitation to stay awhile in order to enjoy a short break in the city and partake of the social life there.

"We shall of course have a dinner to celebrate the arrival of my old and valued client. I dare say there will be persons to whom you would like him to be introduced." He smiled conspiratorially as he said this and William dutifully returned the smile but it brought to a head a worry that had been plaguing him, the introduction of his uncle to Katherine Armstrong. This now seemed to be less of a pleasurable anticipation than it had once been. He simply did not wish to give any indication to his uncle that he had designs of a permanent nature regarding this girl, largely because he did not yet know his own mind in the matter. A complicating factor was that Mr and Mrs Armstrong were more and more inclined to assume that an understanding had been reached between them. They had long ago agreed between themselves that a union between William and their daughter would be highly suitable and several broad hints had been dropped as to the acceptability of an approach by William. He had fended them off with declarations about his need to work hard and make his place in the world before settling down and this seemed to satisfy them for the moment but this situation of expectancy still persisted.

Despite this misgiving, William looked forward in eager anticipation of his uncle's visit. Quite apart from the gratitude which he felt for the care and expense which had been lavished upon him, he was very fond indeed of this open minded, vigorous, yet gentle man who had supplied him with the love and guidance that his deceased father had been unable to give. Part of the driving force which kept him so hard at work was the desire to repay his uncle's faith in him by excelling at his chosen profession and linked with that was a horror letting him down in any other way, such as a misguided alliance. Perhaps, if he could summon up the courage, he would reveal all his thoughts and feelings to the man who would be sure to give him sound and well thought out advice. In the meantime there were preparations to be made for the impending visit and he entered into them with a happy spirit which pleased his employer, who had been concerned at the depression which had surrounded his pupil over the last few weeks.

Their travel-stained visitor arrived in mid morning of the day appointed, having broken his journey at a tavern in Piercebridge. After effusive welcomes from his hosts, he was shown to his room by an immaculate Peters, who put on an impressive show of solemnity and style to honour the occasion, much to the amusement of Mr Allcot and William. Peters was relieved of the demeaning job of stabling Joseph's horse by William who was glad to reacquaint himself with the animal, which he had not seen for a considerable time. It was nice to think that the beast had actually remembered him although that may have been just fancy. Before long Joseph descended refreshed and relaxed. They all entered the dining room, which had been set with a splendid cold table, and it was pleasant to see Joseph fall to and eat heartily. Mr Allcot took his usual sparse helping and William ate hardly anything at all such was his excitement. The wine was passed around generously and talk was general at first, touching mainly on the state of the country in the aftermath of the rebellion.

Joseph Robinson was able to report that, happily enough, the upper reaches of Wensleydale had been untouched by the tide of destruction and looting which had so troubled the lower valleys. He was able to assure William that there were no deleterious changes at Worton but this opened the floodgates of William's curiosity and he plied his uncle with questions. Yes, he was told, all were well at the Hall.

"The aged Hannah still imagines herself to be in charge but in reality t'is Bess, who keeps the household running sweetly."

It was time to pose the question to which the answer was dreaded.

"How is Bess uncle, and does she hate me for the misfortune I brought upon her and her family?"

"Why no, my boy, there is no hate at all for you, just a fond remembrance. Yes she is bitter, but that bitterness, which she shares with her poor mother, is directed at the Metcalfe clan and in particular at young Thomas, who has pursued and harried them. You will know that they were evicted from Cuebeck? The father lingered for a while in Aysgarth but died, most likely from a broken heart rather than the wounds from his torture in York. The mother lives on in Aysgarth with relatives and little is seen of her. But Bess – well now there is a true jewel! She tackles all the work in the Hall and despite the interference from Hannah she gets it all done in fine style and with no trouble. She is all attention and kindness to me and I feel well cosseted in my home!"

"As to that, uncle, she is doubtless trying to repay your kindness in taking her in with kindnesses of her own." William smiled and wished he could see Bess at that very moment to thank her for her forgiveness.

Joseph turned to Mr Allcot and brought him back into the conversation with a light hearted enquiry, "Well Allcot, how is the boy shaping?"

"I have one serious complaint; he is working me too hard. His thirst for knowledge is insatiable and he learns quickly, but more of that later. Can we now reveal the purpose of your visit?"

"Indeed it is time to explain," said Joseph. "William, my boy, I have come to consult with Mr Allcot for the purpose of drawing up adoption papers for yourself; I want to make you my legal son and heir. No!" he raised a hand to stifle William's reply, "you know I am otherwise childless but I have for many years regarded you as my son and I have rejoiced in the fancy that you have a reciprocal feeling for me. I believe the whole village are aware of this but that may not be enough. You know that the Metcalfe has cast envious eyes on Worton Hall, thinking it to be his by family right, and I am sure that after my death he will pursue every means of discrediting you as my heir, even resorting to force of arms to acquire his fancied right to the property. Mr Allcot agrees with me that this adoption would protect you by establishing you in the eyes of the law as my son and my undisputed and rightful heir. So I have come to see that done, that is if you have no objection?"

There was a pause and an intense silence until William spoke softly.

"I remember my father of course. I remember the good times as a little boy when I worked with him and for him and was proud and glad to do so and I will never forget the sacrifice he made in bringing me to you and returning alone to Walburn. But, loving father though he was, he could never have done for me the things you have done. You not only raised me in comfort and with affection but you gave me that priceless gift, an education, which I am now old enough to appreciate fully. Why should I object to being your son? You have been more than a father to me and I accept the honour in all humility."

He rose and approached Joseph who rose too and they clasped each other in a powerful embrace, which bade fair to linger on until a discrete cough from Mr Allcot caused them to disengage with broad smiles. William reflected that this was probably the first time that he had expressed his love for this generous man, who had given him so much in life. He was sorry for it and felt guilty that it had taken him until now to make his uncle aware of his feelings. He was wrong of course. By a thousand little things he had observed over the years, Joseph Robinson was certain of his foster son's devotion to him. But now Mr Allcot took centre stage.

"Yes, gentlemen, I stand firmly behind my opinion that this move is a sound one, the more especially in view of the ambitions of your neighbour. It is not a matter to be entered into lightly and I have advised Mr Robinson of this but he assures me that he has no doubts about the matter and regards it as a very desirable relationship to achieve. If I may say, and, knowing you both as I do, I agree wholeheartedly. Well then, that is settled, and I have the papers already drawn up for you both to study. They are simple enough and a few minutes will suffice. But now gentlemen I have another matter to raise. It is a proposition which will come as a surprise to you, William, but not to your uncle, whom I have made acquainted with my thoughts. It concerns your progress as my pupil here, William."

Falling from the depths of elation to anxiety, not to say fear, William wondered how he had transgressed. He thought he had applied himself to his work well enough. Perhaps it was his unresolved relationship with Katherine which was an issue or his late involvement with felons who had met public deaths on Gallows Hill. "Has my work been unsatisfactory sir?" he enquired.

"As to that," was the reply, "I have the serious complaint that you push me too hard. I cannot keep abreast of your insatiable demand for knowledge and I am beset with questions, with requests for opinions and in short, Sir, it is too much for me at my time of life and with my limited powers of prolonged concentration." The smile which had gradually appeared on the old, lined face transformed into a positive grin as he recounted examples of Williams importunate demands to an amused Joseph.

"T'is my lifestyle you destroy sirrah! Before your arrival I lived the quiet life, doing only so much as to keep me amused but see how you have prodded me into actions and cases simply because you wished to learn how they are conducted. I tell you it is more than I can support but I have a remedy for't if you will hear me.

William, you will recall my disgust when you told me that it had been assumed that you had gone to London to study law. 'As if there were not good lawyers enough in the North' I pointed out irritably. Well t'is true we have good lawyers and I have tried to be of that number but, in truth, if an advocate really wishes to succeed, to reach the very top of his profession, then he must go to London to complete his studies. I count you as one who has the ability to do this. The experiences to be gained there, the level of legal ability and the opportunities for advancement are far greater in London than here in this principality. So, therefore, I propose to seek a position for you at Temple Inn, if you have no objection."

For the second time William was reduced to an astonished silence. It was tremendously exciting to contemplate the idea of living and working in London; to be at the very centre of things, to mix with the best legal brains in the realm. But other considerations dragged him back to reality.

"Sir that is a generous thought but it cannot be. I am articled to you Mr Allcot and I will be pleased to complete the agreed term in your service. I will not break that contract. And then there is the expense. How am I to ask my uncle to support me from his own pocket in what must be the most expensive of all places in the country? I am truly grateful for your confidence in me and flattered that you seem to hold my worth in such high esteem but you can see that it is impossible."

Mr Allcot nodded and said "Yes, I foresaw your response which is quite what one would have expected from you and it does you credit, but yet I must persist in my argument. As to the expense I can remove your doubt. I have already been in touch with a colleague in London and negotiated a place for you, starting next year in the summer, when his current apprentice should have completed his term. Upon my recommendation he will take you on and pay a small retainer, not much in truth but enough for you to live modestly, very modestly in fact. T'is indeed a costly business living in the capital city and there will be little enough to spare for entertainment and amusement but that might be all for the best eh? As for myself you must know that as I am advancing in years so I am decreasing in energy. I have a mind to retire from the scene and enjoy some peace, quiet and a well deserve rest. Your departure would assist me greatly in achieving that objective."

William looked at his uncle, who smiled and nodded.

"A golden opportunity William, not to be missed I am sure."

"It must be rare," said William, "that a young man should have two such kindly and thoughtful benefactors. T'is true that I would wish to go to London, if that be not too much of a burden for you in being alone. But if I do so, then I swear to do all I can to justify your faith in me," and he stepped forward to embrace a thoroughly embarrassed Mr Allcot.

"Well, well now, there is work to do. You must read the adoption papers and, if satisfied put your names to them. We shall have Peters to do the office of witnessing your signatures, which will do much to increase his self importance and then we might get decent, mayhap even cheerful, service at dinner. After that William, I would suggest that you write immediately to your prospective employer accepting his offer. T'would be wrong to hazard your future by risking another beating you to the place."

And so it was all done and there was leisure now for William to conduct his uncle on a short tour of the city. It was necessarily short for there was to be a dinner party which would be attended by the Armstrongs and several others of their group.

It was a happy occasion. The guests were soon apprised of the reasons for the celebration and William was congratulated by all on his good fortune. There was a moment when Katherine had said distinctly that she too would quite like the idea of living in London and eyes had swivelled to William to see how he would respond but they were disappointed by his noncommittal nod and smile. He had been pressured into responding to the congratulations by making a small speech and this he did, acknowledging his great good fortune. He asked the company to drink a toast to his two great benefactors, which they did in hearty fashion and with sympathetic laughter as he stumbled over the introduction of Joseph starting to refer to him as 'uncle' and hurriedly correction to 'father'. It was a very cheerful evening and conversation flourished in the relaxed atmosphere. William introduced Mr Armstrong to Joseph, as a man more conversant with the business affairs of the dale than himself, and the two were soon deep in the discussion about the potential for development. It seemed that there might be opportunities of the kind which Armstrong sought and Joseph promised to look into matters when he returned.

Meanwhile he had been studying the young lady of whom William had written and who he suspected might be figuring largely in his new son's future plans. He was certainly struck by her beauty and admired her deft handling of the social scene in which she was involved. Clearly a talented young lady, she effortlessly related to the other members of the group, many of whom were her seniors by far. He watched for the evidence of the sort of relationship which existed between William and herself and was a little puzzled by what he saw. Whenever she spoke to him or of him she evinced a marked proprietorial air although he struggled to detect any warmth in this. On William's part there seemed to be a certain unease, almost nervousness, and he once or twice caught an expression which he fancied he had seen on the face of a rabbit confronted by a stoat but that was soon supplanted with a smile and dutiful attendance. If, however, he had harboured plans of a permanent relationship then he had quite failed to take advantage of the current situation and sought Joseph's approval to make a proposition. Ah well, a lack of haste was a good thing after all!

The dinner party came to an end as did the visit of Joseph to Durham. He parted from William with affectionate embrace and from Mr Allcot with expressions of mutual regard and good will. The Allcot household returned to its usual routine and the days passed smoothly and uneventfully. That is until a letter arrived from Worton. Joseph Robinson, as good as his word, had been investigating the commercial possibilities of upper Wensleydale and had found what he thought might be a splendid opportunity for Mr Armstrong. He was extending an invitation to the whole Armstrong family to visit him at Worton Hall and of course it would be very nice if William could attend too. Anxious to visit his home again, William sought permission to take a few days' break from his work and Mr Allcot agreed readily enough. The Armstrongs were delighted to accept and a date was set for late June, which delighted William as the dale would be at its best at that time.

The preparations for the journey involved two separate coaches, one to Richmond and then the mail coach from Richmond to Lancaster. The timing of this plus the distance to be travelled enforced a break in the journey at Richmond. William made arrangements for the Armstrongs, although he intended to accompany the coaches on Gaynor. He looked forward to the exercise of this long ride but the real purpose was to return Gaynor to her home stable. Of late he had felt guilty about the lack of time he had spent with the mare and in anticipation of his removal to London, her return to Worton would be timely. They were fortunate with the weather and good time was made to Richmond, where they alighted and repaired to the Bishop Blaize Inn, at which rooms had been prepared for them. There was just time for the ladies to take a stroll around the castle walls and admire the view down to the Swale before returning to the inn for an evening meal. It was plain but very filling and almost immediately thereafter the ladies retired to bed feeling the need for a good rest after the tiring journey in an ill-sprung coach over roads which had been in a bad state of repair. William and Mr Armstrong however strolled into the taproom, where the latter was agreeably surprised to encounter acquaintances who were in the wool trade. They were of course commercial competitors but there was still a friendliness based upon mutual respect and conversation flowed, in proportion to the amount of ale that also flowed from the vast casks kept by the landlord. The talk became too technical for William who excused himself and went to see that Gaynor was well accommodated. The horse was delighted to see him in these new and strange surroundings and gave a whinny of pleasure at his arrival. William spent time talking softly to her and gently stroking her neck and scratching her back, which she loved. Then he retired to bed to ready himself for the final leg of a journey which he knew would fraught with emotional undercurrents.

It was indeed an emotional experience to travel the well-remembered route. There was the sad spectacle of the abandoned Walburn village, now become overgrown with nettle and thistle, the mean little houses broken down by robbers of the stone they once yielded. Of the mill there was a better memorial, for it had been worked for some time after the death of the remainder of the village, but that too was now deserted and forlorn. Walburn Hall too had suffered in that the once well-tended gardens appeared neglected and, although clearly inhabited, there was a distinct lack of activity and an air of gloom about the place. William smiled as he passed beneath the window from which the intrepid Mary had descended and scandalised her would-be rescuers by appearing in a state of extreme undress. But then his mood became more sombre as he recalled that this had been the last time he had seen and spoken to his great friend Kit who had been destined to meet his violent end on the hills of Mallerstang.

But the air of depression could not last in this glorious June sunshine and he revelled in the sights and sounds of the day, hoping that the Armstrongs were suitably impressed by the lovely dale through which they travelled. Leyburn and then Wensley were reached and here there was a change of horses but little time for a stretch of the legs, for this was the mail and time was of the essence. There were no further stops, except a brief pause at Aysgarth to set a passenger down, and then they were on the final short leg of the journey to Worton. It was a homecoming for William that raised his spirits with every long mile, and they were long because he disciplined himself to continue to ride behind the coach instead of galloping ahead to the Hall.

Alerted by the rattling of the coach and a loudly blown horn, two figures came to stand side by side at the door of the Hall. As William dismounted, Bess came rushing forward and flung her arms around him, dispelling at once any lingering fears he might have had about his reception from her. All was obviously forgiven. He held her at arms length and appraised her carefully.

"By Heaven, Bess, but you look bonnier than ever – but no longer a young lass. I must mind my manners." But they grinned at each other as though no time had passed at all and William teased her about the weight she had put on, whilst she affected to pick some grey hairs from his aging head. Bess became serious for a moment.

"If I am built up somewhat, t'is your uncle, I'm sorry I mean your father, to whom I owe my thanks for his care and kindness. I am taken on in service as a housemaid but in truth he treats me as a daughter. But come now, we must make the guests welcome."

The Armstrongs had been greeted by Joseph and a farmhand summoned to assist with the mound of baggage that naturally accompanied the ladies. But there were wines and sweetmeats, too, for their host. William embraced his stepfather warmly whilst Bess showed the guests to their rooms, all of course sparkling with the cleanliness of white linen sheets and dressers adorned with jars of fresh flowers.

The two Robinsons caught up on each other's news and William mentioned his pleased surprise at seeing Bess so well looking and so grown up.

"Aye, she has blossomed and recovered well from the blows which fate had dealt her. I hope I have provided well for her but, certes, she has been a boon to this household. T'is not just the work she accomplishes you understand, but the youthfulness and happy spirit, which she has somehow recovered and now bestows upon us here in the Hall."

William felt a twinge of guilt as he realised that his own prolonged absence, although enforced, had deprived this lonely man of the company he might have provided and he resolved to improve his attendance at Worton as much as possible. He could see, however, that this would be difficult once he had taken up residence in London.

The programme Joseph had devised was to allow his guests time to recover from their journey and then to entertain them to drinks in the garden before sitting down to a meal. There would be no business conducted that day. It was late afternoon when the party finally assembled in the small but pretty garden at the rear of the Hall. They sat at tables which looked over the valley and William pointed out the grimly fortified tower of Nappa Hall, home of the Metcalfes and just a mile or so away from them. In between Nappa and Worton stood the old mill, situated on the bank of the Ure where a sudden steep gradient in the river bed provided a good race. At this point, Joseph astonished William by revealing that the prospective business partner he had arranged to visit Mr Armstrong at the Hall on the morrow was none other than Sir Christopher Metcalfe himself.

"How can that be?" wondered William aloud. "This is a man with whom you have been at severe odds for as long as I have been here. You have told me of his hatred of you on account of your possession of this very property, which he regards as belonging to his family. Can we deal with such a man?"

Joseph smiled. "You forget my boy that it is not you or I who will deal with him but Mr Armstrong, with whom he has no quarrel. And he will in any case swallow his pride as I believe him to be in need of an extra income."

He turned to Mr Armstrong and explained that the Metcalfes had always aspired to assume a role in society at a level which they could ill afford. Much money had been spent upon keeping up appearances, a habit begun under the family leadership of old Sir Thomas, a man with great ambition to be a person of note. Indeed, he had achieved this to large extent by becoming High Sheriff of the county. He became one of the king's commissioners and was knighted by him in 1525. But there had always been a tendency to live beyond their means, continued by the present Sir Christopher. He too became High Sheriff of Yorkshire and when attending the judges at York he appeared with a retinue of three hundred of his kinsmen, all of whom bearing the name of Metcalfe and all of whom were splendidly mounted upon the grey horses which were widely bred in the dale at that time. This extravagant behaviour not only faintly amused many of his neighbours but also imposed a strain upon the estate that it could not support. Altogether Joseph felt that there might even be a certain eagerness to find an extra source of income, which would bode well for a satisfactory agreement. He confessed to having risked discovery and his neighbour's wrath by conducting a covert examination of the mill, which he found to be in reasonable condition structurally, although it would need to be gutted and fitted out with the necessary equipment for its new purpose. There would be men enough to operate the mill and a ready supply of wool from the dale. The provision of the crude cloth for fulling was perhaps more problematical but this industry had been adopted by the inhabitants of other dales, with similar geographic locations.

Mr Armstrong was cheered by this intelligence and expressed his eager anticipation of the meeting. Meanwhile, the ladies were exclaiming at the beauty and peacefulness of the scene but enquired if it was not depressingly quiet at times and especially in the winter months? Joseph smiled and told them that life on a farm was always busy and that village events and pastimes helped pass the time. Mrs Armstrong nodded, but appeared unimpressed by this assertion and enquired about the nearest big towns and how far away they were. Richmond and Lancaster were cited and the Armstrong ladies exchanged significant glances. Richmond they had sampled without being overly impressed, Lancaster they knew not at all and both were half a lifetime away. Katherine, in particular, looked thoughtful.

Throughout this time, Bess had busied herself with the dispensation of glasses of cordial for the ladies and sack for the men. She disappeared into the kitchen and emerged with the sweetmeats which had been brought from Durham, attractively arranged on a large platter and which were consumed with the appreciation of all. The remainder of the afternoon passed pleasantly, with Joseph giving his guests a guided tour of the house and farm before strolling around the little village. It was clear to both William and Joseph, that, although the ladies were mildly interested in the rural scene, they were not impressed with the farm environment. They had shied away from the large byres with their bovine inhabitants and had stepped with great care about the yards. Alas, this had not been sufficient to prevent the besmirching of their fashionable footwear. They lost no time in repairing to their rooms in order to deal with the damage and prepare for supper.

The room had been set with great care. Both the large refectory table and dresser had been polished until the wood gleamed and in the light of the prodigiously large candles, the cutlery shone and the glassware twinkled. Despite the proximity of mid-summer, the illumination was necessary for the weather had deteriorated with darkening skies, affording little light to penetrate the small, mullioned windows. The table had been covered with a damask cloth, an inheritance from the Metcalfe family, which was a great credit to their taste. Its laundry and pressing had produced a perfect foil for the delights to be heaped upon it. There was only a little in the way of silver for Joseph had not aspired to such luxury but there were spoons which had also been inherited from his wife's family. The trenchers and flagons were all of pewter and the table embellishments were of rustic type but worthy of interest. The centrepiece was a condiment bearer fashioned from the horned skull of a ram, its glass eyes peering from the carefully preserved wool of the face. Cleverly carved wooden bowls held sauces and herbs, whilst on the dresser stood a wooden platter magnificently carved with a woodland motif and which bore a heavy load of cheeses of both local and imported origin. There were baskets upon the table which held bread, freshly baked that afternoon by a lady of the village.

There had been great pride in undertaking that commission for all the village knew that the young master was at home and was entertaining his intended bride. Whilst not making their presence too obvious, several village folk had found it necessary to conduct business in the streets whilst the visiting ladies had conducted their short tour of Worton, and some had been fortunate enough to be in the vicinity of the Hall when the party descended from the coach. The travelling clothes had been duly noted and not a scrap of lace had been overlooked in the afternoon dresses worn by the Armstrong ladies, so there was much to exercise the thoughts and tongues of the local womenfolk and indeed, to a lesser extent, the men folk.

William too had supplied food for discussion in his dress, bearing and evident maturity. There was a general feeling of satisfaction in seeing him returned to his home and in good health and with a charming young guest who was clearly destined to become his wife e'er long.

The visitors exclaimed with pleasure at the lovely setting of the room but William's pleasure in their remarks was destroyed utterly when Katherine laughed and said,

"Your little serving maid had acquitted herself well in preparing your table except in one respect. Her lack of mathematical skill is shown by the setting of sixth place, unless of course she feels that a servant can sit at table with her betters." And again she laughed, whilst William felt the blood rising to his face. With a total lack of expression, Bess stepped forward and said quietly to Joseph

"I am sorry for the mistake sir, I shall of course take my meal in the kitchen after I have served you here."

William's angry protest was forestalled by Joseph, who raised a restraining hand and spoke gently to Bess, thanking her for all her efforts. And her efforts were praiseworthy indeed. There was a pottage to commence proceedings, which consisted of a beef stew, liberally supported with cereal and root extracts, and this was followed by delicious fresh young lamb cutlets. A redcurrant sauce had been made to accompany this dish, which was quite new to their guests.

But the real novelty came with the next dish, which was a plate of small crustaceans, boiled to a bright red and with their shells already cracked but cleverly put together again to preserve their original appearance. Mr Armstrong exclaimed that, but for their diminutive scale, he would have thought them to be lobsters but Joseph smiled and explained that they were crawfish, a local delicacy from nearby rivers and streams. "We are indebted to our neighbour, Sir Christopher, for the introduction of this creature," he said. "He brought them up from the south country many years ago and they have prospered in our waters. Whilst delightful to the palate, this is not a dish which can be eaten elegantly I fear. They have to be dismembered to reach the juicy meat and the butter sauce in which they are cooked will make a sorry mess of dainty clothes unless you take care to guard against it". An extra supply of napkins had been made available to deal with this butter sauce as it dripped from the jointed shellfish and the company armed themselves with these as they cautiously attempted to eat. Expressions of pleased astonishment replaced the doubt and apprehension on the faces of the guests and they needed no bidding to empty the plate. Joseph apologised for the lack of replenishment, saying that they were not so plentiful as to allow of unlimited quantities. But there were other delights to come. Pies appeared with their crusty ramparts guarding chicken, goose and pigeon breast. To accompany these dishes was a salad of lettuce, borage, watercress and dandelion leaves. William was reminded by his guests of his complaint at Mr Allcot's table about the lack of pigeon pie and he blushed at the recollection of his intemperate remarks during that evening as a result of the wine he had imbibed so freely.

Yes it had been a superb meal and clearly both Bess and Hannah had been very busy in the days before they had arrived at the Hall. But it had not been enjoyable. As he sat eating, without tasting, the fruit gelatine which he normally relished so greatly, William was still seething over the remarks made by Katherine concerning Bess. He had been looking forward to her company at the meal as an opportunity to catch up on her news and chat about old times but this possibility had been destroyed now and would be impossible whenever the Armstrongs were present. He felt aggrieved by what he saw as Katherine's lack of tact, but in truth that young lady had struck a deliberate blow. She had observed with irritation the familiarity which existed between William and the young girl, who seemed to be treated as a member of the family. The attention she received was at the expense of that which she thought her due as a guest and important player in the future of William. She took her revenge by imposing upon Bess to fetch and carry at every opportunity whilst not deigning to acknowledge her presence in any other way. Conversation was not too prolonged as the travel-weary guests looked for an early night to fully recover. William comforted himself with the thought that he would have an opportunity to talk to Bess on the morrow and he too retired to a sleep which he badly needed.

But Bess was not visible on the following morning; indeed she was not to be found in the house at all. In a brief aside Joseph explained to him that he had given permission for Bess to walk into Aysgarth to see her mother. Breakfast was served by Hannah, who seemed pleased at the opportunity to wait upon the company and lingered in the room until she had to be dismissed by an amused Joseph. He smiled at the company and explained that Hannah seldom got the chance to 'appear in public' nowadays and was obviously relishing every moment. The few pleasantries which William had been able to exchange with her had been the cause of raised eyebrows and, once again, he was made aware of the disapproval with which his association with people of lower classes aroused in the Armstrongs' eyes. He refused to be influenced by this, however, and persisted in his conversation, making it plain by his dialogue that Hannah was regarded as an old friend of his childhood days. She, of course, was thrilled by this recognition but the air of disapproval did not abate and eventually William arose from the table in a thoroughly bad mood and excused himself, announcing his intention of going into the village to conduct some private business.

It was not a complete fabrication as he wanted to reacquaint himself with the local folk. He started at the farm and spoke to the hands some of whom he had not seen for two years or so. There was much to learn as to their current circumstances, new arrivals in the families and so on, and his visit was quietly appreciated by the men, many of whom had been present when he first arrived at Worton and watched him grow up. Next he strolled round the village speaking to anyone he met and gradually allowing the atmosphere and the familiar sights to soothe his angry mood. Finally, he saddled and mounted Gaynor, trotting around the locality to renew, with some nostalgia, his acquaintance with his old haunts. So many of them were associated with memories of Kit and a sadness supplanted his anger and irritation as he relived old times in his mind. Suddenly he realised that he had ridden without thought to Cuebec farm. He reined in and looked on as a woman crossed the yard carrying a pail. He did not recognise her, did not even know the names of the new tenants, so he turned Gaynor and descended the hill to Worton. He had promised Joseph that he would be present for the arrival of their business guest and he also hoped that Bess might have returned so that they could talk. There was damage to repair there, he thought.

Bess was not there but Joseph was relieved to see his return. He was not unnerved by this appointment with a representative, indeed the leader, of the clan that had exhibited constant enmity towards him, but he welcomed the moral support of his adopted son, for whose quick thinking he had a great respect. Yet again, William raised this issue with him and expressed surprise that Sir Christopher had been invited into the house which he coveted, thinking that the visit might elicit an outburst of accusation and threats. Joseph, however, reiterated his point that the Robinsons were only acting as a medium for the introduction of a potential business partner and in any case he felt Sir Christopher was mellowing in old age and less of a threat to them.

"It is the son Thomas, who bears the malice now. Perhaps inculcated by the parent but enlarged upon and no secret made of it. But Sir Christopher I fear not."

Nevertheless the air of expectancy had a touch of nervousness about it as the hour for the meeting drew near. Almost exactly upon the appointed hour, Sir Christopher clattered into the yard on his horse. He was entirely unattended, a surprise given his love of display, and he was unarmed. Both conditions were a subtle compliment, announcing that he had no fear of foul play on the part of his host and this was not lost on the two Robinsons. He dismounted and Joseph went forward to greet his visitor with outstretched hand.

"A good few years since I last set foot in Worton Hall, which, as you know, I think of as my own." This was said with a slight smile and no element of aggression.

"You are welcome, Sir Christopher," said Joseph in reply. "May I present my son William?"

Sir Christopher gave a short laugh.

"Aye, we met several years ago under different circumstances and you bore different relationship to Mr Robinson. I congratulate you on your adoption, of which I have heard, and which appears to have slammed the door of Worton Hall firmly in my face. I own that I had been scheming to wrest possession from you if you tried to inherit as a nephew of doubtful origin, as it seemed. However, my case is lost and I must accept this with as good a grace as I can muster." He smiled somewhat grimly as he said this and stepped forward with hand extended which William took in some surprise and relief.

"Sir, I thank you for your direct and honest delivery, something I always admire," said William.

"Aye, but there is yet one in my family who fain would see you dispossessed. My son bears no love for you and I caution you against him. Keep a watchful eye upon him and present him with no opportunity to be at open odds with you. But then, from what I hear of your progress in the legal world, you should be able to outmatch his clumsy attempts to best you."

He was actually smiling broadly as he said this and William had the strange and yet powerful suspicion that there was an element of pleasure at the prospect of seeing his awkward son thwarted.

"Now what business might we have in common Mr Robinson? You were circumspect in your note." The switch in conversation was abrupt.

"It is not I, Sir Christopher, but my guest here, Mr Armstrong of Durham who seeks to do business with you."

The introductions were made and Sir Christopher contrived to pay compliments to the ladies, being noticeably impressed by Katherine. He glanced at William and gave a knowing smile. A tray of drinks was brought in by Hannah and William guessed that Bess had not wanted to be present when the hated Metcalfe was in the house, hence her visit to Aysgarth.

Excusing themselves the men folk retired to the library, where, after a brief explanation of his own small part in the matter, Joseph left the two principals to their discussion and rejoined the party in the garden. William expressed his complete astonishment at the attitude of Sir Christopher and his apparent willingness to concede defeat in the matter of the ownership of Worton Hall. He had conveyed the impression of being a man prepared come to terms with the situation and his neighbour, which was a pleasant thought. Joseph agreed by but repeated the caution about Thomas.

"There was a real malice in his attempts to link you with the escape plot. It was a personal vendetta against you that continued long after any reasonable hope of incriminating you had disappeared. He hounded Bess and her family but only in the hope of finding evidence of your involvement. It is difficult to understand."

"I think I understand it well enough," replied William. "It dates from our encounter in the forest when Queen Mary not only thwarted his desire to further cripple me but made it clear that she considered him to be lying in his accusations against me. He was made to look foolish in the eyes of the assembled hunting party and so for that I shall never be forgiven."

"Aye, well, even so he makes a bad enemy and one who I believe would stoop to any means of damaging you. You would do well to follow the advice of his father."

Joseph too had perceived the pleasure Sir Christopher took in the idea that his son might be defeated in his malicious aims. He told William of several unsavoury deeds Thomas had been linked with, and how his father was, it seemed, not able to keep him in check. "It is the inheritance which keeps him loyal and that is all. He too has developed a taste for the costly life and will not risk losing the family fortune, depleted though it may be."

There came the sound of voices as the two men emerged from the library, each manifestly in high good humour. Sir Christopher approached Joseph with the words

"By God, Sir, but your friend is a shrewd enough fellow! He would persuade me to dip my hand into the Metcalfe purse to the tune of a thousand or more on the idea of a fulling mill. T'is a tidy sum but the figures he supplies show it may be a rewarding investment, with a good income resulting from it. T'is worthy of thought and I am obliged to you Robinson for the introduction." Sir Christopher declined the offer of refreshment and, after making his farewells all round, he took his leave with the air of a man who was not displeased with his morning's work.

Bess was still absent and so it was Hannah who provided a simple cold snack. The main meal would again be supper, the last dining occasion for the visitors who were to return to Durham on the morrow, and Bess was to return in time for its preparation. She did so at mid afternoon and, as soon as he knew she had arrived, William made his way to the kitchen. He desperately needed to talk to her. Looking up as he entered, Bess could tell by his expression that his mind was engaged with serious thought and she stopped work to face him. His first task was to apologise to her for causing the death of her brother and father and he asked if she could ever forgive him for that. A tear formed in her eye but she declared firmly enough

"Forgive you? Oh there is nothing to forgive on your part William. We all three took part in that adventure willingly and all accepted the danger. But there is one who I will never forgive. The young Metcalfe took Kit's life, when I am sure it might have been spared. But there is no mercy in him and no remorse for that deed. He pestered me many times, seeking to implicate both you and I in the escape but I avoided all his traps and it may be that he is now convinced we had no part in it."

"That was well done Bess, and I thank you for your words but I shall never be able to forgive myself for involving you in my escapade with such disastrous results for yourself and your family." He asked about her family and learnt that her father had died shortly after his release from York prison. He had been ill-used but the real cause of his death had been some terrible disease that he had brought from there. A rapid debilitation coupled with a loss of desire to live had seen him pass quickly away. Her mother, stricken by the loss of both husband and son, had been evicted by the Metcalfe landlord and went to live with her sister and family in Aysgarth, where she now dwelt quietly but harbouring a great hatred for the Metcalfe clan.

William commiserated with her but then moved on to his second disagreeable task.

"I must apologise too Bess for the rudeness of Katherine. The only excuse I can offer on her behalf is that she is unaware of our long association. She does not see you as I do, a true friend and a connection to a happy past. But even that is a poor explanation of her bad behaviour."

Bess smiled.

"Oh William, you really must understand what passes through the mind of a girl when her affianced man pays attention to another woman, no matter what her station!"

"You anticipate more than you should Bess," replied William with a frown. "There is no such understanding between us yet, although I do confess to having thought about it."

Bess laughed aloud. "I have watched her carefully and I do not think you will have much say in the matter. I believe your destiny is no longer in your own hands. Now, run off back to your guests and let me get on with my work."

William left her then, happy in the knowledge that she bore him no grudge over the death of her family but annoyed that, yet again, people were making assumptions about himself and Katherine. Perhaps that was silly and their marriage would eventually take place, if he could sort out his thoughts on the matter properly. But it was infuriating that other people should be so confident in their appraisal of the situation when he wasn't so himself.

There was a certain coolness in the air when he rejoined the party but Katherine soon launched into the attack.

"All is well in the kitchen I trust?"

"Yes indeed, Bess is even now preparing the meal for this evening." William kept his tone neutral sensing the impending scene.

"I am astonished at your familiarity with the servants William," came the continuation, "but, if I remind myself of your association with some of the lower characters of Durham, one of whom danced upon the gallows for us, then I should not be too surprised."

Joseph Robinson intervened.

"The situation is perhaps not quite as you imagine it my dear," he explained. "Bess is more of a companion for me than a servant and we are indebted to her for reasons which I cannot divulge as yet."

"Indeed," Katherine smiled frostily but it was clear that the real status of the girl had not changed in her mind and she made that abundantly clear throughout her remaining time at Worton. Various demands, poorly disguised as requests, were made; nothing too demeaning but each one a reminder of the relative status of the two young ladies. Mr Armstrong was oblivious to this byplay but his wife smiled appreciatively at each of her daughter's sallies, whilst Joseph and William were both piqued but unable to intervene. Bess completed all her assignments without question and showed no sign of resentment. In fact she even managed a conspiratorial grin when she caught a sympathetic glance from William.

Why was life so difficult for him? He was unable to suppress his natural friendliness toward people, no matter what their particular station in society might be and yet such crossing of class borders was frowned upon by most of his friends, including even that most reasonable minded of men, Mr Allcot. He had quickly learnt not to try to mix those friends who came from different poles of society but even the very knowledge that they existed seemed to upset them all. He resented the fact that he had to adopt one class only in which to move thus losing valuable friendships and contacts which were unacceptable to that class. He recalled with pleasure the friendships he had made whilst at school, when class barriers had not appeared to exist, although he supposed that only certain classes were able to attend such schools. But no, the question of class difference had never been raised at any time even in discussions about one's way of life. People were people, with different backgrounds and pursuits; just human beings who were either friendly or unfriendly. Such was the simplicity of schoolboy philosophy and it was sad to have had to leave it all behind. But that was not all! There was this general assumption from all around that he and Katherine were sure to be married, when he had made no such proposal and was now in doubt about his feelings. Mr and Mrs Armstrong treated him as a prospective son-in-law, whilst Katherine herself acted as if he were promised to her and behaved as though it was only a matter of her choosing the time and place. Well that may be so; she was beautiful and his blood raced as he remembered that one passionate sexual encounter they had shared but there was that in her character that he did not much like. He consoled himself with the thought that time was on his side in as much as he faced a lengthy sojourn in London which would afford him the opportunity of thinking things through for himself, far from the cloying atmosphere of Durham society.

The supper was a most enjoyable occasion, largely because everyone contributed to the good humour which prevailed. Katherine clearly recovered her good spirits and had forgotten her displeasure at Williams's attentions to Bess. The latter waited on table as before but remained in the background as much as possible. Mr Armstrong chatted enthusiastically about the business deal he had proposed to Sir Christopher and explained that he would undertake to purchase a certain minimum amount of fulled cloth each year at a fixed price for a period of five years with options to renew the contract thereafter. This would justify the expense of repairing and converting the mill to its new purpose. It was anticipated that three years profit on the production would repay the financial outlay after which the income would be appreciable. He had refused the offer of a partnership in the new venture for, as he had explained to Sir Christopher, he was a dealer who traded in commodities with a vast network of contacts and trading options and whilst he was good at this business of trading he had no head for the running of factories or mills. He further explained that he did not wish to be tied down to such a long-term operation and valued the freedom to move on after the agreed period if he so wished.

Talk shifted to William's approaching period of work in London, which it was thought might be another three years or more. Katherine was enthusiastic about this prospect and prevailed upon her father to promise that they would all visit him whilst he was living there. William was unsure as to whether she was anxious to see him or simply to realise her ambition to visit the capital city with all its social attractions but he acquiesced to the idea readily enough and promised to send details of suitable lodgings and entertainments. There was said to be a number of acting companies who played to enthusiastic audiences, although whether or no this was a suitable pastime for the ladies was a matter of doubt. He would investigate and report back to them all. It was true that this was an exciting prospect for him and William found himself dwelling more and more upon the possibilities that would be open to him. To be sure his chief devotion would be to his studies but there was the thrill of being at the centre of the realm and close to government and the court activities. There should be spectacle enough and much culture to imbibe. He went to sleep that night looking forward to travelling back to Durham and taking up his duties again with Mr Allcot; he was determined to give his full worth to that good man before leaving his employ.

William fulfilled that determination and worked hard, doing his best to relieve his old colleague of as much work as he could and being allowed to handle many cases on his own, which delighted him, as he realised it was providing him with a wealth of experience, which would be of great value to his next sponsor in London. Apart from the work, which kept him busy but contented, he enjoyed too the improved relationship with Katherine. There was certainly an increased warmth in her behaviour towards him, a more romantic air about their time together, but there was no reference to their one and only sexual encounter, and no encouragement of any sexual advance, other than an embrace and a kiss, which could be exciting enough for William. He was content with this arrangement and so it seemed was Katherine and indeed her parents. It was clear that all three members of the Armstrong family were marking time until he should have completed his studies in London. They reasoned that marriage would be out of the question on his very small income and there was therefore no mention of it at this time.

Happily there was time this year for a visit to Worton at Christmas and William spent four pleasant and relaxing days with Joseph, who was more like a friend now than a father. It was so very nice to be able to talk freely together, to discover their common interests and to make plans for the future. William supposed that, after he had completed his contract with the London attorney, he would be expected to remain and work in London. He would much prefer to return to Yorkshire, or at least the north of Britain, but it might be long before a suitable opportunity presented itself. Perhaps Mr Allcot would consider a partnership? Durham was not so far away from Worton and it was after all Katherine's home town. He might just sound out the old man during the months which remained in his employ. Slightly uncertain the future might be, but all the possibilities were pleasant. Life was very satisfying.

Chapter 7: Fate

The spring was transmuting into early summer, foliage of that bright, fresh green which can only be seen at that time was abundant not only in the trees of the forests but also within the city walls. Durham had regained its atmosphere of composure and stability after the traumatic events of the previous year. Life was very pleasant for William at that time, almost at a level to counteract his eager anticipation of the transition to the London environment. Work had been interesting but not too arduous, the gentle and genteel tenor of life in the Allcot household had continued as before and there had been a continuation of that warmth in Katherine's attitude towards him. There had been strolls for just the two of them in the warm May sunshine with animated conversation and an atmosphere varying from high spirits to quiet companionship. There had been the occasional hint of romance too, a warm embrace and a kiss; no further than that, for William was conscious of the continued interdiction upon pursuit or even mention of their passionate intimacy on that incredible day in the January of last year. He was agreeably surprised at this change and reflected upon the possibility that Bess had been correct in her diagnosis of a touch of jealousy being the cause of her unpleasant behaviour at Worton.

He smiled to himself. A wise head on very young shoulders, he thought and a fine friend to boot. He was glad to think of her living in Worton Hall and looking after his father. That too was a lovely warming thought. His own father, in name and not just custom, a recognition of the love that bound them, the obligations he had, and the duty he owed. But preoccupation with the changes to come was growing. He had read, at Mr Allcot's urging, the latest pamphlets and broadsheets to emerge from London so as to familiarise himself with the major topics of political and social interest. He had been warned of the likelihood that he would be mixing with persons of high rank and political influence and certainly did not wish to appear in their eyes as an ill-informed, not to say ignorant, country clown. Beyond that, however, was the desire to be able to participate and hold his own in meaningful conversation, so as to become even better informed. There were reports too of judgements in important legal cases and these he discussed at length with Mr Allcot.

He soon realised that he had a lot to learn in order to fit himself for practice in the big city.

It seemed then that all was well in his world, solutions to his personal problems were emerging and his future prospects looked bright and exciting. It is strange that, at such propitious times, fate often contrives to step in and upset everything. Fate presented itself on this occasion in the form of a letter, addressed in uncertain hand and sent by carrier from Wensley. William felt a thin stab of apprehension as he took the letter into his hand and the contents, when he read them, fully justified his fear. It was devastating news. It had been written by Bess, who was sorry to inform him that Joseph had been struck down with a palsy. It was not, she thought, an immediate threat to life but extremely incapacitating. There was much that he could not do to help himself. She and Hannah were coping with the situation and the top hand, Walter, had taken over management of the farm but she knew that Joseph would very much like to see him if he could get leave to visit. He showed the letter to Mr Allcot, who commiserated with him and said that he should leave without delay to investigate the severity of the problem and reassure his father as best he could. There was no delay in his departure. Throwing some clothes and things together, he rushed out and tried to obtain a seat in the coach for Richmond but was too late. He regretted now that he had left Gaynor at Worton as he could have ridden throughout the night in order to arrive as quickly as possible, and as the thought struck him he walked on to the livery stable.

Here, he was lucky enough to hire a steed for the journey but had to part with a good deal of money as a surety, when he explained how far he was going and how long he would be away. He lost no more time and rode quickly south.

There was a brief respite for horse and rider at Piercebridge but William was in a fever to reach his destination as quickly as possible and so he pushed on to Richmond, where he found the Bishop Blaize open and welcoming. There was time for a hasty meal and the horse was tied in the yard with a feedbag and water. It was near to an hour before he was able to resume his journey and he begrudged every minute despite having fed well and rested whilst doing so. He paid his tally and inspected the horse, which seemed in good enough shape to continue. It was dark, of course, by now but William was on home ground and, although he could not make great speed, he was able to maintain a steady enough gait to eat up the miles.

It was the early hours of the next day, before sunrise, when he arrived at the Hall and knocked on the door. Nobody heard, or at least nobody stirred, so he walked around to the back and tried to gauge where Bess would be sleeping. Having made his choice he threw a handful of gravel at the window and repeated this until a head appeared and an angry voice demanded to know his business. It was Hannah and it took a while to convince her as to who he was and to persuade her to descend and open the door. She did so, complaining loudly about his interruption of her night's sleep and informing him with relish that there was no bed ready for him at this hour. William was too tired to bandy words, so he merely sank into a chair and commanded the old lady to fetch him a flagon of ale, which she brought with ill grace, and he drank with appreciation. He shooed Hannah off back to her bed and settled down to await the morning and the proper arousal of the household.

Not surprisingly he fell asleep in the chair and a startled Bess discovered him there. Endeavouring to cover him with a blanket, she only succeeded in awakening him and was immediately blasted with a barrage of questions. How was Joseph? Had there been any change in his condition? Had he been seen by the doctor? When could he see him? How was Bess managing to cope with the situation? Gradually Bess was able to calm his agitation. Yes, Joseph was alright. There had been little change except for a slight improvement in his ability to move one arm. The doctor had seen him and pronounced that this was a cerebral injury and there was the possibility of some further improvement but he would never regain all his lost control and sensation. The mind was still active, almost doubly so to compensate for the physical disability, and he had made a remarkable adjustment to his current situation. Bess and Hannah were coping quite well with his care but there was no doubt that he would be delighted to see William home again. They would be preparing his breakfast soon and it would be nice if he could take it up for him. Meanwhile he should relax and take a bite himself. She would get Walter to see to the horse, which William had left tethered to a railing at the front of the house.

Bad though the situation was, William was relieved that there had been no deterioration in his father's condition. He was stable and apparently there had been a slight improvement. Please God there would be more to come. He fretted and paced about the downstairs rooms until Bess appeared with a tray which bore a bowl of gruel with a spoon and a glass of some sort of cordial. She handed it to William and instructed him:

"You will need to spoon the food for him, he has not yet mastered enough control for that, and of course you must help him to drink. You will find he can talk well enough and indeed you may have difficulty in finding the opportunity to feed him as he does so! There may be other bodily needs which he will require and you must call me to assist if that is the case."

William was horrified. It was not until this moment that all the implications of a paralysis sank into his consciousness. In that instant a series of images flashed through his mind and he looked again at this capable girl who was dealing with everything as though it was just a normal matter. He seized her hand.

"Thank you, Bess, I feel sure I can deal with things myself but if I am in trouble I will call for you." He smiled, released her hand and took up the tray.

He knew well the way to Joseph's room of course and, knocking gently, he waited a second or two and then entered. He had thought he was prepared for this moment but it was still a shock. The figure in the bed looked shrunken and the features were strange. There was no strength in the muscles on the left of the face, which produced a flat, dead appearance. The mouth sagged at this side and the eye remained fixedly open. But, shocking though this was, William was rewarded with an instant smile, when Joseph recognised him in the doorway. The smile lit up his eyes and extended to the face, where it appeared, albeit one-sidedly, as an unmistakeable reaction of joy at the sight of his son. William strove hard to maintain what he thought was a calm and yet sympathetic demeanour. He was determined not to allow any sign of the shock he had experienced to appear in his expression. He approached the bed.

"Now father," he said cheerfully, "you have a new sickbed attendant to see to you this morning and I am here to see that we have you up and about as quick as may be."

Joseph spoke with just a slight slurring of his words.

"Ah, my boy, what a great joy it is to see you here. And that itself is enough. We are both experienced enough in the ways of the world to know that this affliction will not go away. I dare say, and I certainly hope, that some improvement might be achieved. In fact I have already travelled a little way down this road and have a real optimism about further progress. But you must not worry unduly on my behalf. I am so well cosseted by Bess, and even Hannah, that I would find a full recovery difficult to bear!"

They both smiled at this lie and William put down the tray and went forward to embrace his father, as he had been longing to do from the moment he had entered the room. He was immediately struck by the lack of physical response to his embrace, a facility which was simply not there any more, but the emotion in his father's eyes told the whole story of the meaning of this encounter. William tore himself away and resumed his cheerful manner.

"I fear you are to be subjected to a difficult examination of your patience father," he said with an assumed gravity. "I prevailed upon your better-practised nurse to relinquish to me the responsibility for administering your morning nourishment and it is likely that I will not be quite as adept as she in this business. So if you will pardon my lack of expertise, we should commence."

He half filled the spoon from the bowl of gruel and poised it well above his patient's mouth. Not too dramatically so, not farcically so but with just that slight exaggeration which made a slight joke of the event. It was enough to override any little awkwardness which might have been felt on either side as the two engaged in these unusual roles for father and son.

William maintained a steady monologue as the process continued, relating the news of the city, amusing anecdotes and more seriously the condition of the populace as they struggled to overcome the greatly depressed state in which they had been left by the loss of so much material wealth. Many peasants had left the area and migrated south, where it was felt, there were better opportunities for employment and a hopefully better life. Some succeeded but others returned, having failed, and the whole countryside was in a state of constant flux as people looked for a solution to their desperate state. There had already been a few sad cases of people starving to death as a result of the loss of all their stock and grain reserves. Mr Allcot had vouchsafed his opinion that the land would recover its strength in time but the overall effect would last for many years to come and there was much hardship to be endured before that happened.

The breakfast completed, Joseph asked if Bess might be sent for.

"I need to have a proper discourse with you my boy and interviews with some of the men so I must needs be tidy. So Bess will shave me and help in my ablutions. No," he waved aside Williams protestations, "I know you would be able and willing to undertake that task yourself but, at the risk of damaging any pride you might have in to your prowess as a barber, I have to say that she is really very good at this. I am shaved and powdered every day in expert fashion and I doubt me that you could do as well! Now, pander to an old invalid and send up the girl. I shall see you again later."

William descended, relayed the request to Bess and went off outside to stroll around the farm. He wandered around, noting again the well-remembered buildings, with their childhood hiding places and little adventures. He saw them all with new eyes. He looked at the stock and stared at the sheep, which studded the adjoining fields. The thought which had been ever-present at the back of his mind grew and matured so that, when the time came for his next meeting with Joseph, he was resolved as to his intentions.

Joseph opened the discussion with a resume of his condition as he saw it. He described without any trace of self pity the limitations which he must now endure. He dismissed any fanciful hopes of recovery except in the most minute and trivial particulars.

"I shall remain, my boy, much as you see me at this moment, physically useless but blessed with a functioning mind – if indeed that be a blessing under the circumstances. It is beyond doubt that I shall need help. True, Bess and Hannah are coping well at the moment, but I feel I shall have to hire a manservant who can deal with the more trying physical tasks which I present to my carers. So much for the situation within the house. The farm too will need some proper attention. Walter has handled things fairly well to date but he lacks both confidence and, to be frank, intelligence. I shall seek a skilled person to manage the day-to-day affairs for me, whilst I shall hope to have some role to play in decision making and policy. I may have to ask for your help William in securing such people as I need."

"Yes father," William answered, "I will of course help you but the solution to most of these problems is actually quite simply achieved."

Joseph looked at him with some concern. Was the boy incapable of seeing the difficulties which lay ahead? It was disappointing that he was taking things so lightly. He had expected a greater maturity of thought from the young man.

William smiled.

"I see in your eyes the suspicion that I am not viewing the situation with the seriousness which it deserves. You are relying on me to think hard about the problem and I am doing so. In fact, I have already done so and come up with a solution which satisfies my own mind and I hope will do the same for your own. There will be no need to hire a seneschal or body servant. I shall fulfil both roles myself, for I am coming home."

Joseph sighed and said

"Oh, it is so pleasing to hear your generous proposal, what I should have expected of you, but it is of course quite impossible. You can only remain here for a short while before you leave for London and opportunities to return will be of necessity few and far between with little enough time to be here. No William, we must be practical."

William shook his head firmly. "No father, you misunderstand. I shall return to Durham to complete my short term of contract which remains with Mr Allcot but then I come home for good. There will be no going to London. There will be work enough here for the both of us. I can and will take over the running of the farm but I lack the knowledge and experience. You have both and you must share them with me. There is much for me to learn, much to understand and I will need help from yourself and the hands. But I am a quick learner, strong of limb and very willing to work. As to yourself, it will be my pleasure to care for you and see to your needs. A lifetime of care and responsibility on your part deserves no less from me. It will be a privilege to serve you for a change."

As William had been speaking, tears had rolled, unchecked perforce, down the cheeks of the man propped up against his pillows. He spoke now in a choked voice.

"I cannot allow you to make such a sacrifice. It is your destiny to go on to London and succeed in this profession you have chosen and at which you are excelling. But I do thank you for the offer, which has moved me as nothing else has done."

"I fear that you do not yet understand me father. You talk of sacrifice and I tell you that there will be none. I have been compelled to evaluate my life and my ambitions over the last few hours and everything has become crystal clear to me in even that short time. My experiences in Durham have convinced me that city life is not for me. During all that time I have sorely missed the peace, the quiet, the integrity of country living, where subterfuge, pretension and extravagance play no part. If that is true of Durham, then how much more so would it be of London? I am fortunate to have had the opportunity of making the comparison. Few boys have been given the opportunities that you have placed before me and I own that I might have progressed and become that lawyer, whom you expected to evolve, and I would have played my part in the busy city scheme of things, perhaps to some degree of success. But, interesting though the learning process has been, fascinating as the contest of legal arguments have been to me, I never was able to feel myself completely at home. Here I am at home, not only physically but assuredly so in my mind. I hope you will forgive me for giving up the course upon which you set me with such hope, but I feel I can fulfil my own destiny here, whilst being of use to your dear self in the process. And the training I have received may yet prove of value, even here in the remote dales. I am sure there are lesser mortals who cannot afford the fees of city advocates and yet stand in need of such advice. Perhaps I can provide that for them."

William paused for breath and there was a silence as Joseph regarded this boy who he had taken to be his son and who now spoke in such assured manner and with such conviction.

"Are we then agreed father?" the question was put with a smile but a challenging one.

"Yes," came the whispered reply, "I am content and I hope that you will remain so after this momentous decision. Thank you my boy. Now I must sleep a little, or at least pretend to, whilst I mull over these developments and formulate new plans."

He smiled wearily and closed his eyes leaving William to make a quiet withdrawal.

Downstairs, he asked Bess to make him up a pack of food for he was determined to return with all speed to Durham and the difficult interviews he faced there. Difficult they would be indeed, but they would not become easier by delay and he wanted to deal with them promptly and resolutely. As he set off on the return journey, it was in an incredibly different frame of mind. Whilst he had travelled to Worton in whirl of apprehension, speculation, and indecision, he rode now with a mind totally at peace. Not everything had been resolved but he was confident that all would be, and all would be for the best, whatever decisions were reached.

The first of these interviews was accomplished immediately he returned to the Allcot residence. Mr Allcot was anxious to hear the news of his old friend Joseph Robinson and he listened sympathetically as he received the description of his sad state. It was much as he had feared and he went on to enquire as to the suitability of his carers and their degree of dedication to him. William swallowed hard and delivered his unwelcome message.

"It is that subject about which I wish to speak now and I regret that I shall certainly incur your grave displeasure. I am determined to give up my ambitions as far as the law is concerned and devote myself to the care of my father and the running of his farm and business affairs. You will doubtless berate me for the great wastage of time and effort in my studies with you, but I must tell you that I not only feel it my duty to assume this task for my father, but I feel deep within me that it is actually the place on this earth where I will be most happy. I am a country boy sir, whatever layers of city gloss you have tried so hard to lay upon me! But I do not wish to give the impression that I am not grateful for all you have tried to do for me. Your teachings, your sound advice and above all your great kindness to me will never be forgotten. It is sad that you have had such an ill-deserving student and one who has let you down so badly."

Mr Allcot regarded him steadily for a long moment.

"You will note William that I do not insult you by asking if you have really thought this through. I know that you will have done so. Other means of caring adequately for your father could have been found, I am sure, but without your saying it, I know that you sincerely wish to be personally involved. Nor do I think that it is a grossly exaggerated and unnecessary sense of duty and repayment of debts, which impels you to this decision, although I am sure that there is an element of this in your thinking. So I do not try to dissuade you. Only you can know how valid your reasons are and how sensible is the course which you wish to take. As to your preference of country to city I cannot comment. It is the exact opposite of my own inclination as you probably are aware. I have difficulty in discerning the difference between one end of a sheep and the other, but each to his own. What I will say, however, is that you value too lightly your ability to argue and prosecute a legal case, to reach to the nub of a dispute and to reach sensible opinions on such matters. I fear the profession is losing a potentially valuable member but that does not mean that you have let me down. I have watched and enjoyed your progress and admired the hard work you have put into it. To that extent you have repaid me and now, as always, you are being true to yourself – a way of ensuring that you will never deceive others. One more thing. Training and knowledge gained is never wasted. All knowledge, however irrelevant it might seem at the present time, may yet assume an important role in your armoury. Now, you will want to take your leave of this place as quickly as is practically possible. No, I will hear no protests about fulfilling a contract. You have contributed much to this practice and I am grateful for it. I send you off with Godspeed and a sincere wish that all goes well for you."

It was all William could do to express his thanks to this generous-hearted man without breaking down but he did succeed.

"Just repay me by looking after yourself and your father, who I hope will be the recipient of my kindest wishes for his welfare from your lips. I shall write to him in due course. Now I believe you may have a more difficult interview to conduct. I wonder how a certain young person will feel about leading the life of a country lady, rather than being a dazzling star on the London social scene!"

William grimaced. "Yes sir, I have grave misgivings about the next few hours. I do not expect to emerge without some discomfort."

In fact it was Mr Armstrong to whom he first applied.

"Sir," he said," I believe you have been aware of my interest in and high regard for your lovely daughter, Katherine. I come now to seek your permission to ask her to marry me but before you answer I must explain to you my new circumstances."

He went on to outline his plans for the future, which were of course nothing less than the assumption of his role as heir to the Worton estate and his intention to manage it in the place of his father. Mr Armstrong laughed.

"I see no diminution in your prospects as a son-in-law," he said. "A country squire in Yorkshire is a perfectly acceptable alternative to a begowned figure in the distant city of London. But what think you of your chances, when the minx finds she will not go to London after all?"

"I worry about it a good deal," admitted William. "I do know she had her heart set upon living in the capital city, with all it has to offer a lady of taste and fashion. It would not surprise me if she turned me down."

Armstrong laughed again. "Fear not, my lad. She will be as happy lording it over her neighbours and being a leader of fashion rather than a follower. She will accept. Now be off with you and catch her before she leaves to harangue the tradesmen of the town this morning."

So William went off for what he knew would be the most painful of his three interviews of the day, his misgivings slightly allayed by his prospective father-in-law's summing up of the character of his daughter.

The Queen looks contented, thought Seton, the childhood friend who had voluntarily shared her imprisonment and acted as lady-in-waiting. But, knowing her as she did, Mary Seton realised that this was a superficial assessment, which might satisfy her jailors but did not fool her most intimate friends. Perhaps 'jailors' was too harsh an expression for the kindly Earl of Shrewsbury and his domineering wife Bess, both of whom had been greatly concerned over the Scottish Queen's health and spared no effort or expense to bring her back to a reasonable state of fitness. Seton could not help but wonder how much of their concern was a genuine fondness for her mistress and how much could be attributed to the fear of the consequences should they lose their charge through death. Queen Elizabeth would be furious should that happen and she be exposed to whispers and allegations that she had disposed of her troublesome Scottish guest by assassination. Be that as it may, her beloved Queen Mary was much recovered from the effects of that dreadful journey from Bolton to Tutbury, which latter place was far from comfortable and conducive to an improvement of health, and Seton was bound to admit that the relationship between Bess and her mistress was one of great friendliness. That she had quickly won the affections of the Earl himself was, of course, only to be expected. He had merely joined the long line of men who had succumbed to her bewitching smile and slightly coquettish behaviour. But Seton was surprised to discover that those same attributes of charm and open friendliness had won over the indomitable Bess of Hardwick too and for this she was glad, as she would rather have Bess as a friend than an enemy.

There had been many forced removals and uncomfortable journeys over the past few months and several different places of confinement but now, with the defeat of the rebels, it seemed to Queen Elizabeth that the dangers to herself were lessening and she became more amenable to allowing a certain freedom to the movements of the Shrewsburys and their charge. And that was how they were now situated at Chatsworth, a most beautiful manor house in lovely surroundings. The Countess had taken Mary to a small lake, surrounded by dense shrubbery and across a stone bridge to reach the island in the middle. Here there was a tower from which could be seen a superb view of the surrounding countryside, through which flowed the River Derwent with the wild hills beyond. Mary had exclaimed at the beauty of the location and Bess had promised that she should use this as her retreat.

So here she sat in the sunshine with an expression of contentment which all could see. Only Seton knew of the superficiality of that expression. Mary would never be content until she was out of the clutches of Elizabeth and restored to her native Scotland, preferably on the throne.

....

"John, Joseph, where are you?" William called again and again as he walked through the house and into the farmyard. His question was answered as he saw Walter chasing the two imps out of the hay barn and across the yard towards him. The boys were shrieking in fear (or was it mock fear?) and Walter was swinging his leather belt, a ferocious expression on his face which was certainly assumed and bade fair to break down into laughter. The little lads rushed to their father's side and clung on to his legs for protection from their pursuer, who pulled up short, fighting to retain his fierce scowl.

"Well now, what's all this? What have you been doing to make Walter so angry with you?" He strove to keep a fierce expression to match that of Walter.

"We were just sliding father," said John and Joseph echoed his brother:

"Sliding was all, nothing broken."

William looked up interrogatively at Walter who explained.

"Aye slidin' alreet; from't top of't stack an' pullin' down all't hay from top edge. A right pile of it there be on't barn floor, and all to sweep up and put back agin."

William gazed down at the boys who were squirming under this accusation and looking up at their father to gauge his reaction to this heinous sin.

"Well then, that's a good half of an hour's work for Walter that you two have caused. We shall have to set you on make good the loss of time. What shall we say Walter, a spell of mucking out in the main byre tomorrow morning? "

"Aye, so as they're up early an' not slow me down."

"Right, that's it then boys. Now into the house with you and quickly. Your mother is wanting you cleaned up and dressed tidily because we have a visitor."

He patted their backsides lovingly and sent them off indoors. Then he turned to Walter again, clearly wanting a description of their activities.

Walter was now all smiles and chortled as he related the story.

"Aye, t'little beggars 'ad climmed up t'ladder an' were playin' on t'op oft' stack when young Joe fell off. 'Ee shouted loud eneaff but t'were just shock an' when he started a'laffin, John pulled some 'ay loose and pushed it ower to make a cushion to land on. Then ower 'ee goes and they took turns one after t'other climmin' up and slidin' down. Each time they did that another girt swirl of 'ay comes down with 'em. Well, when I sees what's goin'on, I gives a girt shout and rushes in with me breeches belt a' swingin'. The little divilkins dashes to t' side of t' barn and tries to creep out behind the row of 'ayracks leanin' aginst wall. So, ah swings me belt across t' handles of 't rakes and it makes a reet good din an' freetens little imps to death. Ah reckon t'will be a long time afore they plays that game agin!"

The men laughed together at the thought of the panic engendered by Walter's carefully placed blows with the belt but William said,

"See to it that they do a goodly spell in the byre tomorrow morning, Walter. I have to make good my word to see them punished properly."

With that he wandered round the corner into the garden, where sat Joseph in his padded chair. It had not taken William long to devise a system of poles which could be easily fixed to the chair as a temporary measure and which enabled he and Walter to move chair and occupant downstairs to the library or, as in this case, outside on a fine morning. It had transformed Joseph's life and he enjoyed simply sitting in the open air taking in the sights and sounds of the countryside. Over the twelve years or so since he had been struck down by the paralysis there had been little improvement in his condition. Apart from a slight movement of the fingers of his left hand, all his limbs were useless. His speech was still slightly slurred, although that had improved a good deal. His hearing was acute and had perhaps actually grown better since the onset of his affliction – perhaps as a compensatory measure. Locked in his immovable world, he might have become an irate and troublesome old man. That he had not done so was, he knew, entirely due to his adopted son, his lovely daughter-in-law and their lively family of three.

These last were a complete joy to him and had been brought into contact with him at every feasible opportunity so that his handicaps were no longer noticed by them, except in as much as they knew they had to bring things to him, hold them for him and manipulate them where necessary. Their relationship to him was natural and beneficial to both sides. He could talk their language but did not continually talk down to them. There was much he could impart in the ways of the world, which little people longed to learn, and his determination to treat them as little adults bore fruit in the attention that they paid to him. Then, of course, there were the endless hours in which he listened to their adventures, commenting now and then but not criticising and just occasionally dropping in a correction of fact or imparting a bit of knowledge to amplify what they were discussing. The children took up a good deal of his waking time but there was time spent too with his son and daughter. Certainly the meals were taken together, the chair could be moved into the dining hall or even the kitchen and conversation was easy and natural. At no time was he made to feel that he was a burden upon them, although he knew of course that he was. There was time during the mid morning to enjoy a beverage together and talk over with William the business of the farm, its management and the progress of stock and crops. Occasionally there was need to discuss the other properties, which produced further income for the Robinson family.

When he had taken up permanent residence at the Hall, some twelve years ago, William had been astonished to discover just how much property his father had acquired over the years. He had, of course, inherited a good deal of wealth from his wife's family, which, added to his own possessions, had produced a splendid basis for a comfortable living, but he had not stopped there. Careful investments in property over the years had resulted in a small empire, not all in one place as was the case with most estates, but dotted about the county in small parcels of land, some let out to farming tenants but also some sites let out to commercial enterprise in the form of warehouses and workplaces. All paid rents and it had been Joseph's habit to set off on a circuit of his properties twice a year, riding round and calling on each tenant to collect his rents but also to pass the time of day and enquire as to the welfare of each family. His was a kindly landlord and, on smaller farms in particular, help was often extended where it was needed and concessions were made in terms of rentals. Now, of course, it was not possible for him to make the rounds; the one occasion when William had tried to take him by carriage proving to be a disaster. It had simply been too difficult for him to manage and so he had now entrusted this role to his son.

William had quickly taken to this new duty and enjoyed his periodic visits to the farms, getting to know the families and taking over his father's benign management of his properties. His character was such as to make it easy for him to adopt the same caring and generous dealings with the tenants so that they felt no difference in their circumstances and rejoiced in the knowledge that the young man was of the same calibre as his father. All the details of the land holdings and the tenants had to be talked over with Joseph of course, but there was time too for Joseph to simply close his eyes and doze in the sunshine or the solitude of the study, his mind replaying the events of the day or events much further in the past, of which he was the only one to remember.

William was making for the study, where he was planning to do some preliminary reading from his notes before the arrival of their luncheon guest, when he glanced through the open kitchen door. The sight that greeted him was his little daughter, Martha, whose deathly pallor would have been alarming had not further scrutiny revealed that she was covered in flour from finger to elbow and chin to hairline. The bits in between were shielded by her little fustian apron, which also bore the powdery evidence that she had been 'helping' her mother. William stepped into the room and saw his wife leaning over the kitchen table, relentlessly kneading the dough for the day's baking. Since the death of the aged Hannah, some years ago, Bess had run the household on her own, declaring that she needed nobody's help for such a simple job. Stepping silently up behind her, he grabbed her around the waist, twirled her round and planted a kiss on her mouth, which was open in surprise. Stepping back and taking in her flour covered arms he laughed and said:

"Nay, Bess my love. That't worse than the bairn for getting clarted up. I ought to strip you naked and run the yard pump over you but I fear I do not have the time to warm you up again this morning. More important things to do."

He dodged the flailing rolling pin and skipped happily out of the kitchen, only half hearing the torrent of abuse which was aimed at him.

William entered the study, closed the door and picked up the sheaf of notes he was to study. But instead he gazed sightlessly out of the window and marvelled at his happiness and the road he had travelled in order to reach it. His mind flipped back to that decisive day when, having spoken to Mr Armstrong and been encouraged by his words, he had tracked down Katherine to her salon. It seemed that his attendance was not entirely unexpected for certain preparations had been made. Clearly the visit to the city had been delayed although the necessary accoutrements were to hand. The hat, the gloves, the sunshade were deployed about the room rather like a stage setting. It was a statement about the social position, elegance and lifestyle of the owner, who raised a cool, enquiring face towards him. William bowed, somewhat unexpectedly given their usual informality. He felt however that this occasion definitely merited a formal approach. He began.

"Katherine, my dear, I have been speaking to your father and I sought his permission to ask you to marry me. I am pleased to say that he raised no objections. I do hope you will be able to say yes and so make me a happy man."

There was not a flicker of change in the girl's composure and she replied in even, if slightly lofty, tone,

"Ah William, I was beginning to doubt your constancy but then I reminded myself of the difficult decisions which you have had to make. I was sure that eventually you would come to a sensible way of thinking and I am delighted that you have done so. My answer is 'yes', I will marry you gladly and am even prepared to wait for a year or so until you have built up your social and financial standing in London to the point where you can properly house us and maintain us in our rightful station. No, no my dear," she continued, raising a hand to suppress his attempt to speak. "This is one sacrifice which I shall be happy to make in order to make our alliance begin on a firm footing."

There was a short but extremely uncomfortable silence as William tried to find the right words to explain the true situation. He was reduced to stammering.

"Er, er, Katherine, my love, I fear you do not understand the position. I have indeed come to a sensible decision but not that which you describe. I must needs take care of my father, who, because of his condition, is in desperate need of help.

What better way of doing that than by moving in to Worton Hall and taking over the running of the farm and property. As soon as we have celebrated our marriage here in Durham, I shall take you off to Wensleydale and install you in the Hall. It is a beautiful house but may, I dare say, benefit from improvement and modernisation and you shall have the major role in the planning of this. For my part I am content to forego the legal career which was planned for me in London. I shall find it no hardship to live in the north country rather than the southern capital."

Katherine stood. The glacial expression on her face was highlighted by two spots of colour on her cheeks and her eyes glittered in fury.

"You would find it no hardship?" she hissed. "And what about me? You do not consider my feelings on the matter. Do you really expect to be able to bury me in the uncivilised, raw countryside of Wensleydale, where no decent town exists, where there is no fashionable society and no conversation? Or must I learn to discuss the merits of different sheep, the intricacies of farrowing piglets, the uses to which manure can be put? You may feel able to forego the city life but I can not. I will not. Nor do I wish to share my home with a young strumpet who would gladly give herself to you when your inclination so runs. Unless you see reason and revise this senseless plan of yours you must consider our engagement at an end."

William experienced an incredible gamut of emotions as this tirade progressed. There was discomfort and to spare at her extreme reaction to his proposition. There was chagrin at his completely inaccurate assessment of her likely acceptance of the change in circumstances and finally there was anger at her totally unjustified allusions to Bess as an immoral creature of no account other than as a threat to the sanctity of her marriage. With that, of course, was the insinuation that he was likely to have called upon the sexual services of Bess in a moment of boredom with his legitimate wife. He paused for a moment to collect himself before answering.

"Thank you, Katherine, for your plain speech and honest reply. I can see now that I have totally misjudged you and that I was wrong to suppose that being married to me would be enough of itself to render you happy. You must have known that I cannot 'revise my plan' as you put it. My duty to my father is paramount. I accept your refusal and will intimate the circumstances to your father immediately. I bid you goodbye."

Saying thus, he bowed again, turned on his heel and left without a backward glance, leaving Katherine nettled and disappointed that he had not put up more of a fight. It was almost as though he was glad of the opportunity to escape from his attachment to her. In that she was absolutely right. With each word spoken, William had felt an increasing feeling of relief, of salvation and the loss of a heavy load. All his misgivings about the character of his intended bride had been amply justified in the space of a few moments. How easy it was now to see that it had been pure physical attraction which had kept him in pursuit of this self-centred and uncaring woman and that a permanent relationship would have been disastrous.

It was necessary for him to conceal his good spirits from Mr Armstrong, when he called in upon him to give the news. He managed to look like a devastated suitor, whose dreams had been shattered, and Armstrong was duly sympathetic. He was also clearly disappointed and his expression boded ill for his daughter in their forthcoming interview. William contemplated her probable discomfiture with equanimity; he thought he couldn't care less what a bad time her father gave her. He strode off through the streets of Durham with a decided spring in his step and had to restrain himself once again, as he entered the house of Mr Allcot. He cannot have succeeded in his objective however for, when he eventually took his leave of the attorney, the old man laid a hand on his arm and said with a smile how relieved he was to discern that William would survive his disappointment. This had had the effect of increasing his good humour to the extent that he was actually singing as he rode Gaynor out of the city gates and headed home.

The homecoming had been rather strange. He had related the turn of events to Bess and his father as they greeted him and provided a glass of sack for his refreshment. Both were sympathetic but neither could understand the matter of fact way in which he was accepting the situation. In fact they were almost scandalised when he called for a good supper to celebrate his return, hinting that they might sing a few songs for self entertainment. Individually he explained the situation to them. In the study, he told the full story, including his feelings at the time, to Joseph who nodded his head and congratulated William upon a lucky escape.

"It seems to me that you were expected to marry the lass for the social station each would confer upon the other. I suppose that is how things work in the big cities, where influence is all important. Here we are more fortunate, I think. I can tell you that Anne and I married for love, pure and simple. We knew we were meant for each other and we knew we were meant to stay together forever. Sadly that was not to be. No," he raised a hand, "no, don't concern yourself. I can talk about it now, with sadness of course but also with gratitude for the years we did have together. Anne's parents were of the Metcalfe clan and thought their family to be above me in rank. Her uncle was a knight and lived at Nappa, whilst I was a simple yeoman farmer with a smallholding at Thornton Rust. I still own that farm," he said with a smile. "But Anne was the apple of their eye and prevailed upon her parents to accept me into their family. We lived happily at Thornton Rust and Anne did not seem to mind the step down in her living conditions. But I did! I worked as hard as I could to improve our lot and in some measure I succeeded. Then her parents died of some fever which seemed to have sprung from their cattle. It was not sudden; they lingered for over a year and Anne nursed them all the time. I confess I was worried for her own health but she was untainted, thanks be to God. Well, we moved here to the Hall and I worked the farm as best I could, although there was plenty of money from Anne's inheritance.

That was when the first mutterings started amongst the rest of the Metcalfes. T'was all legally sound, however, and they could do naught to change things. Then we lost a child, stillborn, but Anne was desperate for a family so another was conceived. I lost both at once." There was at last a hint of a tear in his eye but Joseph rallied and continued. "After Anne passed away the property became mine but the Metcalfes were outraged, claiming that the Hall should revert to their ownership. There was talk of eviction, threats of physical violence and even recourse to law. It was then that I took legal advice by contacting a celebrated attorney in Durham. Mr Allcot no less! He arranged a hearing before local magistrates and the subject was aired and decided in my favour in a very public manner. This drew the teeth of the Metcalfe clan, although, even now, they still hanker after reclaiming their ownership of Worton Hall. That is why I took the step of making you my son and indisputable heir."

William shook his head.

"A sad story father, and I had heard some of this but not the detail."

"I tell you it my boy because I want to emphasise to you the value of marrying for reasons of the heart and not the pocket. We were no happier with the wealth of Anne's parents than we had been as we struggled a little, up at Thornton Rust. We worked together and there was all to live for. Find someone who will happily work with you and live for you as we did for each other."

There were real tears now; coursing down the frozen face but William did not turn away. He seized his father's hand.

"I do hope to take the place of that child, the child which you and Anne could never have," he said with all the intensity he could muster.

"You have," was the reply, "you already have. Now leave me to my memories for a while."

So dismissed, William had gone in search of Bess and found her in the kitchen. She placed a hand upon his arm and said how sorry she was that he had lost his fiancée in this way. William thanked her but reassured her that he was not at all upset by the outcome.

"Do you believe in a protective God?" he asked Bess.

She gazed at him silently, remembering that no protective God had intervened for her poor father. Perhaps William realised the trend of her thinking for he went on quickly, "Well I, at least, have been protected by some power from making the greatest possible mistake of my life. I confess to you Bess that I was overcome by her beauty, but I was to discover that it was a beauty which did not penetrate to her nature. There were many examples of a meanness of spirit which I glossed o'er and ignored. To my shame I did not see beyond the pretty face. The worst thing of all was her rudeness to you, when the Armstrongs stayed here with us. It was that which set my doubts to form and I began to wonder a little if I was doing the right thing. This rejection has given me release from a tortured fear about my future. I am now a free man and I revel in't."

"Not free for long, I'll warrant," said Bess with a laugh. "The local girls will never leave you at peace now, mark me!"

William looked into that happy and guileless face and all the memories of their past lives as children came flooding back to him. He tore his gaze away and repeated his demand for a good table to be spread so that they could all celebrate his good fortune.

"And we shall eat together," he declared. "None of this running off to the kitchen my girl! My father and I need you with us."

It had been inevitable of course. When two young people of similar mind work together and for each other, there will always be an increasing closeness to reinforce the existing affinity between them. They had neither of them been aware of this on a conscious level but some set of circumstances, which would bring realisation, was bound to occur eventually. It had been the calving of the brindle cow that had brought things to a head. It was clearly a difficult business for her and she was suffering badly. William had consulted Joseph, who opined that the problem might well be a bad positioning of the calf.

"You may have to help her yourself, my boy." He proceeded to give more detailed instructions and William set forth, with many misgivings, to play physician to his bovine charge. He was equipped with a length of rope, a saucer of goose fat and a bucket of water. After a good half of an hour, Bess made bold to peep into the byre to see what progress had been made. It was all too clear that nothing had been accomplished. William was totally besmirched in blood, the animal was lowing softly but piteously and there was no sign of a calf. The midwife looked up from his labours.

"I just cannot unravel the position of this calf," he admitted. "It is certainly wrongly placed but I have not been able to turn it."

"Let me see," ordered Bess, who stepped forward despite William's protests. Smearing her arm with goose fat, she introduced it into the cow and a frown of concentration suffused her features as she explored the confused tangle of body and legs. "T'is here!" she suddenly announced. "The head is here and t'is twisted. I cannot move it but perhaps you will have the strength."

Under her guidance William tried again and found the head for himself. There seemed to be a leg wrapped around it and after a good deal of manipulation the head became free and he was able to rotate the small body to its correct position. Now the matter became much simpler but speed was of the essence, if the life of the calf was to be saved. They took it in turns to pull, whilst the cow did her part with regular contractions. The actual birth came very suddenly. The calf dropped into the straw and Bess seized a handful to wipe the little creature's muzzle and clear away the mucous.

"T's alive!" she exclaimed excitedly. "Look, t'is breathing now."

The mother now took an interest in her offspring and a rough tongue supplanted Bess's ministrations. She nudged it and with a little bleating noise it stood up, only to fall over again. The mother repeated her attempt to raise the infant to its feet and this time it stood, albeit in a somewhat wobbly fashion. And then the age old miracle repeated itself. Without instruction, the calf sought and found the teats. The young couple watched the magic moment in silence for a while and then William turned to Bess and said

"Oh, well done Bess, I would never have managed without you."

And he kissed her. It was the sort of kiss you give to a sister or your mother, a familiar but chaste salute; an appreciation of the bonding that takes place with achievement through combined effort. But there was a tenderness too, and as they broke away they each looked into the other's eyes and then kissed again. This was not the same sort of kiss. It was filled with an emotion, the intensity of which grew by the second until it became passionate. They parted eventually and then, with a start, William drew away.

"Oh Bess, I am sorry," he gasped. "I must not, I cannot – -"

Bess smiled a little bleakly.

"Yes, of course William. I understand. You and I are on separate levels and we do not, and never can, belong together like that. You must seek a bride from your own place in society and not be misallied with a country wench such as myself. So do not be upset; I do understand."

"No, you do not understand!" William smilingly replied. "My hesitation was born of an entirely different fear. You see, I was frightened that you would consider me to be acting like a man who, balked of his prime objective, was looking round for a distraction, a substitute for the woman he secretly still desired even after she had spurned him. But that is not so Bess. You are no plaything, no object of momentary attraction. You are the girl who has grown up with me, has been in my heart all the while, although I did not know it. But now I know it! I can only hope that you might come to feel the same way about me."

Her eyes were brimming with tears but she smiled up through them as she gazed into his face.

"Oh, William!" she sighed. "Did you but know how oft I have thought and dreamed of this moment. Is it really true? Do you really want to be allied to a simple country lass such as myself, when you could have your choice of women, of far better standing, intelligence and education?"

William laughed in response.

"I have not prospered by associating with that particular class of female, you must allow, and in my present condition there isn't one who would not recoil from me in horror and loathing!" and they giggled together like children who had come across an unexpected and wholly delightful treat.

They kissed again and this time it was full of the deep tenderness, which each of them felt for the other. They broke again and William spoke of immediate action.

"I must seek the permission of my father to marry. I do not think there will be any opposition, once I make my choice known to him. But I do think that perhaps we might improve our appearance before we approach him." And he gestured to the soiled and dishevelled clothes they wore and the blood and mucous which was liberally distributed about their bodies. Bess agreed with a laugh and they left the byre hand in hand leaving behind a cow, which had taken no notice whatsoever of this important development, totally preoccupied, as she was, with her new infant.

William emerged with a small start from the reverie into which he had sunk as he recalled that day and the emotions aroused; emotions that were still aroused with the same intensity after their ten years of marriage. Yes, it was ten years he realised with shock and he ought to do something to mark the occasion – could he but remember the actual date of their wedding. But it had been a wonderful day he remembered. The ceremony had taken place in the church at Aysgarth and had been attended by a good many folk of the area. Mrs Fawcett had been present and was pleased to be a centre of attention in her role as mother of the bride but she had declined to invitation to come back to Worton Hall, where a wedding breakfast had been laid. It had been the bride herself who had organised the refreshment but there had been no shortage of volunteers amongst the ladies of the village to help out with the baking and cooking. The event had been exactly what any native of the Dales could have wanted from such an occasion. There was no real formality; it was all friendly, casual and jovial but without matters getting out of hand. Amongst it all sat Joseph in his chair, attired in his very best and brightest clothes, with a recognisable smile permanently adorning his face. Nobody could be in any doubt as to his approval of the match his son had made. The villagers, who were nearly all able to attend, were delighted that son of the manor had chosen one of their own to be his wife. It cemented the already close tie between manor and village. Formality was acquired for the short time it took to propose the health of bride and groom and it was maintained during the short speech which Joseph made, expressing his happiness at the union. The toasts were loud, the flagons clinked together and a happy tumult broke out which persisted until the tables were moved aside and the two local fiddlers struck up with lively jigs and reels. After a while there were figures to be found slumped in their chairs, some snoring loudly, others beating a feeble time to the music, which they were too exhausted to take advantage of by dancing. There were those however who seemed to have inexhaustible energy and who pranced up and down the floor, not missing a single dance. It was a continuous festival of fun and music in which everyone was absorbed so it was relatively easy for William and Bess to slip unobtrusively out of the room and ascend the stairs to their bridal bed.

It had been a satisfyingly productive bed. The firstborn, John, had been the image of his father everybody said, although even with the eye of faith, William had not been able to see this. Joseph, closer to his mother in looks, an opinion which even William could agree with, was also close to her in his manner. Much quieter than his elder brother, whom he adored, little Joseph was a follower, a disciple and a faithful conspirator in the various deeds of mischief into which John led him. From a very early age, the two of them led their parents a merry dance, with escapade after escapade threatening to turn them prematurely grey. But whilst there was plenty of mischief there was never any viciousness or gratuitous violence, no meanness or lack of respect where it was required. They were beloved of all in the village, even the victims of their misdeeds. Walter, the old farm hand, would have nothing bad said of them, although he made a great show of the nuisance they were to him and the trouble they put him to. And all this was due to the inherent charm they possessed. The way in which they could switch from being potential menaces to attentive and polite youngsters in the presence of their elders captivated the community and the solemn face and large blue eyes of Joseph in particular were enough to melt the heart of any woman in the village.

The diminutive Martha was almost a carbon copy of her mother in every way. Serious of expression, until something particularly funny occurred, when she would erupt into uncontrollable laughter, she was, despite her tender age a conscientious little girl, who strove hard to please her mother even to the extent of anticipating her wishes, with the occasional disastrous result. The broken vessels on the rubbish tip behind the Hall attested to that. All had gone as well as it could possibly have done with this family until the tragic time when the miscarriage had occurred and the life of Bess herself had hung in the balance. William had been terrified that she might die and, even after her eventual recovery to full health, he was all solicitude until she firmly forbade him to fuss around her any longer. She was embarrassed by it she said and she could not stand his interference in her work, which she was now perfectly able to carry out, without his constant unwanted attentions. Nonetheless, she was clearly pleased when he took her in his arms one night and told her that their inability to have more children was of no account to him in comparison to the blessing of her return to good health.

"The way matters were going," he said jokingly," I don't think my sanity would have survived another of your children."

"My children indeed!" she retorted. "Everyone knows where the devilment comes from, and it is not me."

Despite this devilry, however, they were a happy and harmonious family. William was always touched to his soul when he covertly watched them squatting around their grandfather's chair, listening to some exciting tale of yesteryear or drinking in some words of wisdom which he might impart. The muscles of the face may not have been capable of showing expression but

William could tell from the glow of the eyes how much Joseph enjoyed these little sessions.

Once again William returned to the reality of the day with something of a start. He had been clutching those notes, made years ago at the office of Mr Allcot, but not a word had he read. He had intended to brush up on his knowledge of the laws of common land before his guest arrived to discuss this very matter. Those notes were all he had now to guide him after the passing of his old mentor some two years ago but he could well remember the words and arguments of that fine man, whose clear, logical thinking, and almost saintly moral attitudes had so impressed him. He smiled as he thought how appalled the attorney would have been at the use of the word 'saintly' in connection with himself. Now it was too late to consult Mr Allcot and too late to consult his notes.

The sound of an arriving horseman alerted him to the arrival of his guest and he hastened into the yard to greet him. It was George Calvert who had been invited to take dinner with them. He was a young man who farmed at the hamlet of Appersett, beyond Hawes. William had liked this man ever since they first met, when George had put in some work at Worton before acquiring his own small farm. Now, it seemed, his livelihood was being threatened because the sheep he ran had been turned off their grazing at Abbotside. Traditionally this had been land with common grazing but his animals had been driven off by his powerful neighbours, who had curtly informed him that they had assumed ownership of the fells and needed all the land for their own use. William had promised to help George mount a legal defence against this act and today they were to lay their plans.

....

As the Robinsons were sitting down to their simple dinner at Worton, another meal, rather more lavish, was being consumed in Sheffield Castle, where Mary was being entertained by the Earl of Shrewsbury and his Countess, Bess. This was not a particularly special event, not a celebration of any sort but just one of the occasional gestures made by the jailors towards their captive, which was characteristic of the relationship which had formed between them. The Earl was a kindly man by disposition and he was sympathetic to Mary's position. He had, on several occasions, petitioned the Queen for improvements to her living conditions and even dipped his hand into his own purse when these petitions had not met with success. He was, however, totally loyal to his own Queen and had proved to be a reliable and vigilant warder, a fact which had not gone unnoticed by Elizabeth.

Bess of Hardwick, his wife and the dominant half of their marriage, had also succumbed to the charm of Mary and had shown great concern for her health and wellbeing. In fact the two women had become close companions, each with a respect for the other's strength of character, and each with a propensity for enjoying the gossip and tales of intrigue emanating from the royal court at Westminster. They could often be found working together at their embroidery and chatting as they did so. There had been much to discuss recently. The return of the seagoing adventurer, Francis Drake, from his circumnavigation, had excited a lot of attention and had produced endless topics springing from his exploits and discoveries. He had just been knighted for his services to the crown, some of which could bear little scrutiny in terms of their legality. But the state had benefited both strategically and financially, which excused all moral transgressions. Apart from that excitement however, there was the delicious scandal over the Queen's behaviour over the Duke d'Alençon, her French suitor. Every detail, every little scrap of gossip, which could be obtained from sources at court, were rehearsed gleefully at Sheffield Castle, as the ladies plied their needles.

It was said that Elizabeth had made a complete fool of herself over the affair. She was clearly flattered by the courtly attentions of the young Alençon, so much her junior in years, and behaved at court like a moonstruck teenager. But that was not all. There were also wild rumours about her relationship with Jehan de Simier, Alençon's best friend and a courtier of great wit and charm. Scandalous tales of secret assignations and nighttime encounters were circulating and all this was manna to the imaginations of Mary and Bess. The latter was moved to elaborate upon this character assassination of Elizabeth to declare that it was well known that she had given birth to at least one child fathered by the Earl of Leicester. If Mary doubted the authenticity of this particular rumour, she willingly suspended her disbelief in the pleasure of sharing the low opinion of Queen Elizabeth with her new friend and confidante.

The Earl and Countess were genuinely concerned over the health of their permanent guest, which was certainly not good. She was troubled with persistent and painful arthritis, almost certainly a legacy of cold and damp journeys by coach and the constantly damp apartments at Tutbury. There had been other, more serious episodes of illness, infections which caused respiratory distress and therefore matters of even greater concern for her hosts. Bess had been a model of care and concern, taking charge of the nursing and summoning of doctors when they were required. In addition, they had contrived to prevail upon Elizabeth to allow Mary to stay at Buxton in order to take the waters there on several occasions, and this seemed to have had a marked beneficial effect. They were, of course, partly motivated by the dread of Elizabeth's reaction should Mary die whilst in their charge, and this risk of mortality was almost certainly the reason why Elizabeth allowed these visits. She too was concerned about the possibility of the death of her prisoner and the certainty, in that event, of the accusations of assassination, which would ensue.

But Queen Elizabeth was under no illusion as to the true feelings of her prisoner. She was well aware of the hopes and threats which her Scottish rival possessed. Mary's protestations of sisterly love had been revealed to be the sham they were at the time when the Ridolfi plot had been exposed and Norfolk had gone to the block. Mary's complicity and willingness to see Elizabeth assassinated were plain enough. There had been pressure on Queen Elizabeth at that time to have Mary executed as well as Norfolk. There was evidence enough, her advisors told her, that as long as Mary lived she would form a focus for rebellion and even foreign intervention. Elizabeth knew this to be true but she, more than anyone, was afraid of the Catholic reaction to Mary's execution. She was painfully aware of the large body of Catholic support for Mary within her own country but the spectre of a combined invasion by France and Spain was the possibility she feared most. That would certainly bring the Catholic extremists out in support and she would be overwhelmed. No, the time would eventually come when it would be possible to eliminate the threat Mary posed for once and all. She must be patient.

There was another factor. Elizabeth had a great respect for the sanctity of royal title and her own position was not dissimilar to that of the Scottish Queen. The execution of a prince of any realm was repugnant to her and there would rightly be a surge of distaste and revulsion across the whole of Europe. So Mary had to be contained safely and the reliable Earl of Shrewsbury carried out this task faithfully and effectively.

Shrewsbury, however, confident as he was in his ability to hold his prisoner close, would have been horrified to learn of the clandestine correspondence which went on between Mary and her Catholic supporters. Under their very noses the plotting continued and plans were being laid with Mary's full assent to the necessary removal of her English cousin.

Chapter 8: Dales Lawyer

William watched as George Calvert, his late dinner guest, rode away up the road towards Hawes. It had been a pleasant occasion and George had been an ideal guest, enjoying the company of the Robinson family with all the uproar that generally accompanied a family meal at Worton Hall. Immediately after eating however, the men had retired to the study, there to discuss the problem with which William had been asked to help. He had agreed to do so and was now pondering the possible consequences. Over the last ten years or so he had acquired something of a reputation as a man learned in the way of law and prepared to help his less well-off neighbours. This had usually amounted to assisting the illiterate elderly in the construction and writing of their wills. He had advised them as to the correct way to phrase their instructions and pointed out pitfalls. He had even carefully questioned some of their decisions and occasionally managed to change a testator's mind, when he was made to see the error of his intentions. William liked to think that he had quite often prevented a family feud over an inequality of legacies or incautious description of a family member. This secular portion of the document had been easy for him but he had had to acquire a facility in the phrasing of the actual testament. True, there were several models for the testator to adopt in the way he commended his soul to God but these people were all individuals and often preferred their own wording and certainly were firm in their instructions regarding interment. William often reflected upon the fact that, for these people, the approach of death was one of the most important events in their lives. All the customs and ceremonies had to be properly conducted, all the rites celebrated in due form and any failure to do so would reflect badly on the entire family. He considered it a privilege to be asked to assist in his limited way and, on their part, they were pleased to have the guidance of a man experienced in the law, who yet did not charge for his services.

There were other little ways in which he could help; resolution of boundary differences and mediation in minor disputes. His reputation as a fair and honest man had become widespread and he was known to many as the Dales Lawyer. It had simply amused him at first but he became aware of the fact that Bess and Joseph were inordinately proud of this unofficial standing, so he had changed his mind about trying to suppress his title. But now this reputation was leading him into deep water. George was asking him to act for him before the magistrates. That was bad enough, but the subject of his complaint made things very difficult indeed.

George Calvert was a husbandman who held a small farm by copyhold and eked out a living with the help of his wife, who also had two small children to look after. He was a hard worker and, at lambing time, he had been engaged by the Robinsons to help out at Worton, which he did gladly to earn money to buy what was not produced on his little holding. His wife worked hard indoors, spinning thread which was taken to the market at Wensley for sale to a weaver. It was a long trip, as their farm was situated at Appersett beyond Hawes, but recently Queen Elizabeth had granted a market charter to Askrigg and this was going to make a huge difference to the upper reaches of the Dale. As was customary, George ran his sheep on the slopes of Abbotside Common. This was an excellent summer pasture and produced a tender and herb-flavoured meat for those who could afford to buy and eat. Most farmers, however, kept their sheep for the production of that great cash crop, wool, and many of the animals never left that pasture until they died. But this summer the sheep had been turned off. A gang of armed men had enforced the clearance of the animals belonging to the local farmers and resistance had been futile and dangerous. One protesting farmer had received a sword cut to his arm, which looked likely to cause its loss. The rest had been frightened into submission by this callous act. To rub salt into the wound, their sheep had been replaced by others belonging to a nearby landowner, Metcalfe of Nappa Hall. They were told that he now held sole right to the grazing on Abbotside by grant from King James of Scotland, after his coronation and assumption of power. This seemed to be incontrovertible but George had nonetheless approached William to ask if anything could be done.

William had researched the history and found that the land had been granted to the Earl of Lennox by King Henry VIII after it had been wrested from the ownership of the Abbot of Jervaulx. Ownership was therefore uncontestable, but the rights of the farmers might yet be preserved. The Abbot had granted the privilege of grazing to a certain number of farmers in the locality but restricted to certain areas of the fells. There was, alas, no documentation to prove this that William had been able to discover but he had another potential weapon in his armoury, which he was about to explore.

The ride up the dale on the following morning was wet and miserable. He hoped it would be worthwhile but at least the foul weather more or less ensured that his quarry would be at home; and so it was. He found old Harry Thwaites crouched over the little fire in his cottage at Hanging Lunns. When he introduced himself as the son of Joseph Robinson of Worton Hall, the old man welcomed him in with enthusiasm. William had been told by Joseph that Harry had once worked at Worton, so he was not surprised when he found he had to listen to tales of Harry's experiences there, and what good employers Mr Robinson and his lovely young wife had been. That had, of course, been many years ago, when even then he had been getting on a bit in years, but he remembered the times well and indeed retained an excellent memory of all things past. This gave William his opportunity to bring up the subject he wished to discuss and soon he was listening to what he really wanted to hear.

"Aye, farmers 'as allus run sheep on't Abbotside. T'wer t'auld Abbot frae Jervy that sad as 'ow they could. And t'Abbot afore 'im said so an' all. Mi father told me as 'ow, when 'e were a lad, folk used t'fell fer't sheep and 'ad done frae way back fer as long as could be remembered. Then old King 'Arry took t'land off the Abbots and gie it to some Scottish earl – Lennox it wer'. But 'e nivver changed owt and t' farmers went on running their sheep like before. Neabody said owt about it."

William thanked his host and was pressed to take a glass of small beer, an invitation which would have been difficult to refuse without causing offence. He thanked Harry again as he accepted the glass and that worthy said he was very welcome.

"Tha sees ah reckon ah knows a bit about thee young man," he said with a smile. "Ah've heeard tell tha's a grand lad fer 'elpin' folk out an' ah'm thinkin' this is about that Metcalfe turnin' sheep off t'fell."

William confessed that this was correct and asked if Harry would be willing to swear to what he had told him before a magistrate.

"Aye, ah would," he replied. "But not ift' magistrate is that same Metcalfe!"

William assured him that the case would have to be heard by a magistrate who was not personally involved in the matter and Harry declared he would be glad to testify as to what he knew of the history of the grazing on Abbotside.

It was about ten days later that William bade farewell to his wife and family in order to spend a brief time in Northallerton. He made the children promise to be good and helpful to their mother whilst he was away, the distribution of little gifts upon his return being contingent on a good report from Bess. The boys promised readily enough whilst little Martha just nodded solemnly. William knew that nothing would prevent her from helping her mother and that this assistance was always a mixed blessing. He arrived in the late afternoon and put up at the coaching inn on the main street. A brief walk around the town, with which he was not familiar, allowed him the opportunity to make several purchases with which he was quite pleased. Returning to his accommodation, he unloaded his packages and then partook of an excellent meal before deciding on an early night in preparation for his morning appointment. This was with a Mr Gervaise Tennant whom he knew to be a magistrate and who lived at a splendid country house just outside the town. William was received pleasantly by Mr Tennant and commenced by thanking him for granting him this appointment and then going on to introduce himself, as the son of Joseph Robinson of Worton. There was a smile and an airy wave of the hand from Mr Tennant.

"I have indeed met Mr Robinson but I know ye well enough too, by repute at least," he said. William was surprised to say the least.

"I cannot think, Sir, how you might have heard of me," he said.

"Why from your mentor and former principal," replied Mr Tennant. "Mr Allcot, God rest his soul, was an acquaintance of mine for many years, until his sad demise, and he spoke of you fondly and with a rare praise indeed for your abilities and character. No, do not be embarrassed! He spoke of your defects as well! He was disappointed that you were unable to fulfil what he thought was your great potential in the legal profession."

"Yes, Mr Tennant, it was a matter of regret and some shame to me that I did not repay his kind interest in me by following the path he had mapped out." William looked intensely into the face of the magistrate and continued: "It was my father, Sir. I could not simply abandon him to the care of others when it was within my power to return home and look after him. And too, I was not so set upon a life in the big city. A country home and country pursuits have always been my preference."

Mr Tennent nodded. "Aye Sir, so it may be, but I perceive a certain self sacrifice in your action, say what ye may. But now, Sir, to the purpose of your visit."

William explained how he was acting for a group of small farmers all of whom had been deprived of grazing on their traditional grounds and how he was anxious to put the case before a magistrate. When Tennent asked why he could not go before the local magistrate, William explained that that individual would be defending against the suit and therefore not be able to sit. Tennent nodded again but pointed out that, whilst he was agreeable to hear the case, it would have to be presented in Northallerton, a long way for the plaintiffs to travel. When William asked if he might not represent them all, Mr Tennant shook his head and said that each plaintiff needed to be present in order to give verbal evidence.

"But what about a test case sir?" William enquired. If I could establish the rights of just one farmer, would that not act as a precedent for judgement in the other cases?"

Mr Tennent conceded that this might be so, although there was no guarantee that all the circumstances were exactly the same and so a general judgement could not be made. William had to be satisfied with that and agreed to await notification of a sitting of the bench at which he could state his case. The Metcalfes would be similarly informed and invited to defend their position. William was offered refreshment, which he took gratefully in the form of a glass of canary wine, and then excused himself as he left for the long ride home. The cordiality of the final exchange of civilities left William with the feeling that his arguments would be sympathetically heard.

The long ride home was in fact a pleasant one. The weather was kind now and the familiar scenery unrolled before him, whilst he savoured the experience of riding his new mount, Belle. Poor, faithful, old Gaynor had been finally laid to rest few weeks ago and he had purchased this splendid looking mare shortly afterwards at a fair in Askrigg. Sad though he was to lose Gaynor, he much appreciated this young and powerful animal, which responded energetically to his demands. He anticipated another long and happy association with this successor to his old mount. As he rode, he was making plans to convey his client and their chief witness to the sitting in Northallerton and he decided to allow no expense to stand in his way. His greatest concern, of course, was the fact that he would be opposing the Metcalfes of Nappa, with whom relations were always at a low level. Win or lose, he would be incurring their further enmity and this at a time when he had hoped for a cooling of the feud between them. He could well believe that his appearance on behalf of George Calvert would be construed as a thinly disguised personal attack upon the Metcalfe family and he felt that there would be a danger of some sort of retaliatory move. Well, he could do nothing about that. Best to put it out of his mind.

William was pleased to return home and be greeted by his assembled family. In addition to their pleasure in seeing him safe home, there was a certain air of expectancy, which he studiously ignored, until a little prompting came from young Joseph.

"Father, did you have time to find any presents?" was the cautious query.

"Oh dear!" said William sadly and watched their faces fall. "I'm sorry," he continued mournfully, "but I must have left them outside, in my saddle bags."

There was a cheer and a rush towards the door but William called them back and bade them await the proper time. They obeyed of course but it was clear that the 'proper time' could not be long delayed and soon they were standing in line as the gifts were handed out to be eagerly unwrapped.

For John there was a beautifully carved wooden horse, nicely coloured and equipped with saddle and reins. For Joseph there was a cap of velvet and with a large feather to enliven it, whilst Martha received a new apron with brightly coloured stitching, only a little too long. Bess declared that she could shorten it to exactly the correct length and then let it out again as the girl grew. For his wife William had brought gloves and she remonstrated with him vociferously at this huge extravagance:

"And when will I be wanting to wear expensive gloves like these?" she enquired, but her eyes were shining as she tried them on and admired the fact that they were gauntleted and bore beautiful embroidery upon the backs and cuffs. She pulled down his head to kiss him on the cheek and whisper "Thank you my dear, darling husband."

....

Harry Thwaites could not believe his good fortune. It had been the most wonderful experience in his long life, a life, which admittedly had not been not overly blessed with wonderful experiences. First of all, there had been the adventure of travelling down through the dale to Northallerton, a town of which he had heard but never seen. The first part of the journey had been taken in the inexpressible luxury of a coach, a vehicle which had often splashed him as it dashed by, but which now cosseted him in leather upholstery and a padded backrest. And the speed at which they travelled was breathtaking! The scenery flashed past so quickly that he found difficulty in identifying landmarks that he should have known instantly. The further they went, the less familiar became the countryside through which they passed and Richmond, when they reached it, looked frighteningly large and busy, although he remembered that he had visited this town once as a young man.

The second part of this momentous journey had to be undertaken by carriers' cart, not nearly so sumptuous but still a delight to one who travelled everywhere by foot. There was much to see and admire. The ample evidence of arable farming was of great interest to a farm worker who saw little of this sort of agriculture in the higher reaches of the dale. The size of some of the fields, for instance, was almost beyond belief. But the climax was their arrival at Northallerton which, late in the afternoon though it was, astonished him by the multitude of large modern-looking buildings, bustling throngs upon the streets, and several carriages transporting the gentry along the wide thoroughfare, which at evening was lit by torches burning in sconces attached to the walls of streetside houses. There was more to come. Never in his wildest dreams could Harry have ever imagined that he might be sleeping in a smart coaching inn. The room, admittedly not of the best and situated at the rear of the building in an attic, had a proper bed with good mattress stuffed with feathers and not straw. He wondered greatly at such lavish treatment as was being afforded him, but he had been repeatedly assured by both Mr Robinson and Mr Calvert that his role on the morrow would be of the utmost importance. His testimony would be crucial to their case. The result of this build up was not, as might have been expected, a tongue-tied and confused babbling before the bench, but a virtuoso performance, marred only by the necessary interruptions from the magistrates, requesting a translation of his all but incomprehensible dialect. Harry held forth at length until their worships had to beg him to desist. But there was evidence of humour in their mild irritation and Harry certainly proved his worth. Despite vigorous opposition from Thomas Metcalfe, his testimony convinced the bench of the existence of a right from time immemorial, which empowered the farmers to use the land at Abbotside. Details of the restrictions upon this use had to be hammered out and there was much cavilling from Thomas but eventually all was decided and there was no doubt that William had triumphed.

There was no doubt, however, that his misgivings about the reaction of

Thomas Metcalfe were fully realised. It was in the street outside the court that the confrontation occurred. A furious Thomas accosted William with a tirade of abuse. The gist of his remarks was that William would regret siding with the farmers in a bid to disgrace and humiliate the Metcalfe family. There would be no peace for the Robinsons in future because of this personal attack, which was nothing more than an attempt to achieve revenge for the fully-justified beating he had been given at their last meeting, so many years ago. It was in vain that William protested that his intention had only been to see justice done to those who were not strong enough to obtain it for themselves. His explanation was dismissed with a sneer to the effect that everyone knew the farmers could not afford any sort of payment to their representative, that there must have been some deeper motivation for him taking on the task, and that he, Thomas, knew exactly what that was: a desire to bring financial harm to the Metcalfes. He was advised to look to his safety in the street as Thomas could not guarantee that some overzealous sympathiser might not do him severe bodily harm.

"Further," he continued menacingly, "Y'ell find it a long ride home and any mishap may befall you on the road."

"If 't should be so," replied William, "there are many witnesses here as to the probable author of such a mishap, so you had best hope that I return home without harm."

William pushed away through the small knot of people who had stopped to hear the altercation and, accompanied by George and Harry, he made his way back to the inn. It was time to go home.

Upon his return to Worton, William had appraised Bess and Joseph of the satisfactory outcome of the hearing before the magistrates but he had also passed on the threats made by Thomas Metcalfe. Joseph had been dismissive of these as mere symptoms of frustration and annoyance, not to be taken seriously in fact, but William was not too sure and he bade Bess keep a cautious eye out for herself and the children.

"You surely would not think him capable of harming the family?" enquired Joseph.

"Aye father, I do believe he could stoop to such action. He truly is a vindictive man with no scruples. We must take care."

But William was wrong. The resentment and sense of injury had not been lessened; it was just that Thomas, no fool, had realised that his incautiously-uttered threats in Northallerton had indeed been overheard by many and that any covert reprisal was out of the question for the time being. Dammit, there was even the possibility that a totally accidental mishap to the Robinsons might be attributed in some way to him. He cursed himself for failing to put a bridle on his tongue and resolved to bide his time.

And so the expected attack by the Metcalfes did not materialise. All remained quiet and the only unexpected event was a very pleasant one. It was in the early summer that a deputation appeared in the yard at Worton. There were five men, only two of which William knew, one of them being George Calvert. They were leading a calf, a beautiful and sturdy little animal of red with white markings.

"Now then, George, what's all this?" enquired William.

George introduced all his companions and said "Mr Robinson these 'ere be all the men who have benefited from your action in facing up to the Metcalfe. We want to show our gratitude for keepin' us on our farms, which we would surely 'ave lost," and he pulled the calf forward.

"George," said William, "I did tell you that I would not accept any payment for that little service which I performed. I meant it and I stick to it."

"Aye you did right enough. An' that's why this 'ere calf is not for you."

William blinked in astonishment.

"No Sir, we knew as 'ow ye'd refuse it, so't little beast is for your bairns. We reckoned that it was mebbe time that t'lads 'ad a proper job on't farm, wi' summat of ther' own to leeak after," chimed in one of the men, who William had not known. He shook his head and smiled.

"By God men, but you are crafty devils. You knew well that I cannot refuse a gift for my children; but you shall make it yourselves. Now I shall find them to receive this calf from your hands but in the meantime we must all have a glass of beer to celebrate this event."

He went into the kitchen to seek Bess and round up his family. The flagons of beer were poured and they all assembled in the yard, whilst Joseph was moved so that he could watch from the window. The boys were made to stand in front of him whilst William explained what was happening. They were wide-eyed and silent until little Joseph spoke.

"You mean it is not your calf, and not grandfather's calf but all ours?" he asked in disbelief.

"Yes that's right, all yours to look after, to feed and water and to make sure it stays well. Now what do you say to that?"

William was not sure what impelled the children to their action but he was never to be prouder of them. John it was who stepped forward and going up to each man in turn he thanked him and shook his hand. Joseph, always quick to copy, followed close behind and was voluble in his thanks. Bess had been whispering in Martha's ear and the little girl stepped forward in font of the group and made a little curtsy. It was all so lovely. William glanced across to the window and saw Joseph smiling as best he could with his twisted features and then he turned to see Bess, her eyes brimming with tears. The small ceremony over, Walter, who had magically appeared and had naturally claimed his glass of beer, was asked to accompany the boys as they led away the calf to find a suitable place in the byre.

William chatted to the farmers for a while and received their assurance that there had been no more interference with their flocks on the moor. Perhaps he had misjudged the Metcalfes after all and there would be an acceptance of the situation. He somehow doubted this, but again time proved him wrong.

The summer months drifted by without incident and winter led them through into another year and another summer of peace and prosperity. The whole farm prospered but nothing more so than a beautiful young red heifer, which was totally spoilt by her joint masters. The boys had taken well to their responsibilities and were seeking fresh charges for their care. They had been given a pet lamb after the death of its mother and had poultry to look after too. Walter was moved to say that they were no longer quite the nuisances they used to be. Martha too was becoming a real help to her mother in the housework and there was an air of contentment in the household that comes from honest employment, well done. The following winter was hard and very cold. It took a great toll of life in the dale both amongst livestock and the elderly and infirm. As always, William was often engaged in assisting the terminally ill and the bereaved in terms of the will-making and dispensation of bequests. His reputation, already good, rose steadily and it culminated in a request during the summer of 1585, that he attend the residence of an old acquaintance.

It was to Walburn Hall that he was bidden and, as he rode past the remnants of the old village of Walburn, he was amazed and saddened at the extent of the desolation of his former home place. Not a single house remained whole. Many had been completely flattened and most had lost at least some of their stone, robbed out for construction in neighbouring villages. His father's old mill was in a sorry state and yet he felt that it could still be reconstructed if anybody had the will and the money. He was met by an elderly retainer, who conducted him to a ground floor room at the rear of the property. It had probably been a small withdrawing room at one time but was now converted into a bedroom. Sir Francis was seated in a chair beside the bed and made no move to rise as William entered.

He apologised for this and said that his health did not permit him to stir very much but he greeted his visitor effusively and bade him sit and take some refreshment. It being hot and close, William gratefully accepted a glass of beer, brought by the servant, and then enquired further as to the state of Sir Francis's health.

"'Tis poor indeed, I fear. Truth to say I shall not last for much above the year end and yet there is work to be done."

When asked about the nature of this work, he announced that it would involve William himself, that is if would take on the commission.

"You understand that this is a professional contract which I ask you to undertake and for which I will pay you handsomely; indeed you must name your own price."

"But why me, Sir Francis?" enquired the mystified William. Surely there are other, more qualified attorneys and nearer to hand too. I fear you place too high a value on my abilities." The elderly knight smiled and replied,

"Aye, that may be so William, but none that I can trust as well and none that are better suited to perform this task. There was but one other I could have called upon and he, alas, is long dead."

William began to see why he was being involved and his guesses were confirmed a moment later. Sir Francis went on to explain, that, as a measure to avoid total despoliation of the estate by the Queen's commissioners after the abortive rising, he had gifted by deed several parcels of land to various near relations, who were not likely to fall under the scrutiny of the inspectors. Most of these had now passed on by inheritance into the various families and he was content that this was so. However, there was one quite large estate which he had gifted to his wife and she had leased it to her brother, a simple and inoffensive man who had been grateful and had managed the land well. With the recent death of his wife, he had re-inherited this gift and was now anxious to dispose of it in the form of a gift to his brother-in-law, free from attachment and duties. Sir Francis was terrified that the Queen's ministers would learn of this land, which they might think should have been confiscated in the first place, and demand that it be yielded up to the crown.

"I do not want them to have it!" he declared vehemently. "I want it to remain in the possession of poor old Roger, who would be devastated if it were taken from him. He knows nought of all this, nor does any man alive except yourself and I beg you to undertake the task of delivering it up to him safely."

William nodded sympathetically, his mind whirling. He sought to explain the difficulties.

"There must be a notary involved Sir Francis, one who is capable of recording the deed of transfer of the property. It cannot be otherwise and so we must seek one who is discreet and sympathetic. If we find such a one then your wishes can be carried out."

"Aye, I feared another must be involved but I know of nobody in that area of Staffordshire, where the property lies. I had hoped that you could guide me in that matter too."

"Then that is my first task, Sir Francis. I will enquire amongst my legal contacts to see if a personal recommendation can be obtained. Until then we can do no more."

It was arranged that William would notify Sir Francis, if he had any success in this search, after which more detailed plans could be laid. There was time for a little chat and a few reminiscences before William noticed that the old man was flagging. He took his leave, with a promise to set about his enquiries immediately.

He was very lucky and discovered through his recent contacts in Northallerton that there was a very reliable and discreet attorney in Tamworth, the nearest big town to Hoarfield Hall, home of the brother-in-law of Sir Francis Lascelles. He had visited Walburn again and agreed to undertake the commission, not so much for the money, although that was generous indeed, but for the memory of past kindnesses and a feeling of nostalgia for the old days. Sir Francis wrote a letter of introduction and an authority for him to act. He then penned a letter to the Staffordshire attorney, a Mr Gresham, warning him of the arrival of his representative. Then it was a matter of urging William to make the journey as soon as possible. He wanted to know that his wishes had been satisfactorily carried out before he died, an event that he knew to be imminent. Although it was by now early December, the weather had not yet become severe and so William agreed, a trifle reluctantly, to set off on his mission as soon as he could arrange to be away from home for the necessary time involved. He hoped it would be completed quickly and in time for him to be at home for Christmas with the family.

·······························

He had lost count of the number of times he had cursed his own soft nature. It would have been far better to have waited until the New Year before undertaking this journey south. Sir Francis had been very persuasive, citing his deteriorating health as the reason for haste and so he had weakly given in and now here he was, on the eve of the Christmas day, far, far from home. It would be another two days at least before he could expect to reach Worton, and more if this appalling weather continued. There had been snowfalls of only a moderate degree, but driven by winds, which had produced sizeable drifts. He had attempted to get away on the previous day only to have to give up because of the constant blockages on the road. Perversely, a thaw had set in during the evening which raised the spectre of flooded roads on the morrow. During the early hours of the morning, however, there had been a drop in temperature and a frost, so he had made a good start, setting off from Tamworth in pitch darkness. The frost had been a boon as it solidified the treacherous slushy road and allowed Belle to pick her way with care but with little speed. As the light dawned and the sun rose, he made better time and began to enjoy the ride through the frosted landscape. Near Wychnor he had to ford the infant River Trent, the level of which was fortunately low but the banks were lined with sheets of ice, which he splintered noisily as he ploughed through them. He had done his best to keep his legs dry by hauling them up before him, but of course they had suffered to some extent. As Belle galloped on, the heat of her body soon made him feel comfortable again and he patted her neck gratefully. Just a few miles beyond the ford he came across a strange tableau. The large blot against the snowy background resolved itself into a coach surrounded by a group of armed men on horses. A tall man, thin despite his ample clothing and cloak, was striding restlessly up and down, pausing occasionally to peer at the activity in front of the coach. As he neared the scene, William could see that the nearer of the two horses, which had been harnessed to the coach, was being attended by the driver and it was clearly in some pain. Attempts to get it to walk were completely unsuccessful, the animal being incapable of putting any weight on its left foot.

William reined in and enquired as to the problem, asking if he could help.

"This fool of a coachman tells me the horse cannot continue on and we have a desperate need to make progress on our journey. I tell him he should drive the idle creature on with the whip but he refuses."

"'Tis the leg, my Lord. I believe it be broke and the horse is finished," put in the harassed-looking coachman. But William had been eying the horse and its foreleg, watching its behaviour closely.

"My Lord," he intervened quickly, "I have some knowledge of animal husbandry and in particular of horses. May I take a look at the leg?"

"By all means, sir, take the leg off and re-set it, if t'will serve the nag better."

Clearly his Lordship had no confidence in the efficacy of a strange traveller when it came to curing his horse's malaise. William patted the distressed animal and took up its leg. There was no wincing or plunging as he handled it and no evidence of fracture as he manipulated it. Turning over the hoof, he cleared away the packed snow and ice to reveal what he had all along suspected. Just visible was the edge of a sharp stone which had become wedged in the soft part of the hoof.

Letting the leg down gently he felt about in his pack and came out with a folded cloth, which, when unrolled, revealed a row of metal instruments. He selected a long thin spike and, picking up the hoof again, he worked as gently as possible to free the stone. The horse suffered but it seemed to sense that it was in good hands for it hardly moved and William was able to complete the removal at the first attempt. With the horse once more on four legs, he patted her neck, spoke a few calming words into her ear and then led her gently forward. She stumbled a little but picked up her gait and walked quietly and steadily behind him. William wheeled her round and led her back to the coachman with a smile.

"Give her a gentle run until the next town my man," he said.

"My Lord," he turned towards the visibly cheered nobleman, who had been conversing with the passenger inside the coach, "she will pull you on to the next stables but, once there, you must change her for a fitter horse. She has a bruised hoof from the stone which she had picked up and t 'would be a cruelty to make her work further. I wish you a safe onward journey, my Lord," and he bowed before turning away.

"Hold, Sir," called his Lordship. "I must express my thanks for your timely and expert intervention in our mishap. We are grateful indeed and my Lady wishes to express her thanks too." He gestured towards the open window of the carriage, in which could be seen the face of a woman, who beckoned towards him.

"Sir, you are not a knight in shining armour but you have rendered the service of one such. You have saved a lady in poor health from a tedious wait in the cold and I do thank you."

There was a humorous lilt in her voice and William would have recognised it anywhere. Gazing into the carriage window he was shocked to see the same well-remembered features but lined with age and stress. The hair contained strands of grey and yet there was still the indomitable spirit shining through the ravages which time had wrought.

"It is always a great pleasure to serve your Majesty," said William bowing low.

"You know me then, Sir?" came the reply after the briefest catch of breath.

"Aye, my Lady, I had the good fortune to meet with you many years ago and I firmly believe that on that occasion you saved my life. Then you had me cared for and my injury treated."

The smile radiated her features. She was obviously thinking hard and then,

"William!" she cried. "I have it right do I not? William.... er, no, I forget me the full name."

"Robinson, your Majesty, and I have not forgotten," he said with a smile.

"There was another meeting I believe, which did not end so well," said Queen Mary a little sadly. "But t 'were best not to mention that here and in this company. Tell me William; are you then a married man now?"

"Aye, my Lady, these twelve years."

"And with a family?"

"To be sure ma'am: two boys and a girl."

"And is she named Mary?" The question was put with a grin.

"No, my Lady, I fear not. She is called Martha," William admitted with a matching grin.

"Well, however she may be called I'll warrant she will be beautiful and sprightly, if she favours her father. Now, Sir, will you take a little keepsake for her from a grateful Queen? 'T would please me if you say yes." And she leant back into the coach to take something from her hair. It was a pin, a long pin used to hold back the long tumbling tresses and it had a large green stone mounted on the head. It was an emerald, William felt sure, and he demurred.

"Ma'am, that is too much, I cannot -"

"But you can, and you will, or risk displeasing me entirely."

William took the proffered pin, bowed again deeply and muttered his confused thanks.

"I fear we shall not meet again, William, but I shall treasure your memory as I do that of all those who have helped me. Now farewell, Sir," and she sank back into the gloom of the coach interior. It was a timely withdrawal as the accompanying party of armed guards had been re-assembled and the escorting nobleman was impatient to be on the move. William watched as the coach rumbled away, slowly he was glad to note, and shook his head sadly as the cavalcade passed out of sight.

He, too, knew that he would never see that charismatic lady again.

It was a pensive William, who continued on his way. True, it had been wonderful to have met the Scottish Queen again and in such strange circumstances. It was gratifying that she had remembered his name, well part of it at least. But he had been struck forcibly by the evidence of her premature ageing. He almost wished the encounter had not taken place as he would have preferred to remember her as she had been at Bolton Castle, youthful, lively and coquettish. But that was silly. Here he was on his way home after a satisfactory discharge of his mission. The business had gone smoothly and he had left behind a relieved and grateful Mr Markham, the new titular owner of Hoarfield Hall. He had been worried about his continued tenure of the property ever since the death of his sister and to actually have the property gifted to him was more than he could ever have hoped for. His gratitude was expressed in a letter, which William carried now, to Sir Francis. He was indeed a member of that same family who inhabited Markham Hall near Ripon and from where the gentlemen had ridden out proudly to join the northern earls in their rebellion. But this Mr Markham was as far away in connection with that family as he was geographically and had not fallen under the scrutiny of the Queen's commissioners in their attempts to exact full retribution from those involved in the failed rising. William was confident that he would remain beyond the scope of the Queen's revenge. Meanwhile he was now riding away from an encounter which he had started to foolishly regret, bearing away a lovely gift for his little Martha, who he knew would treasure it, the more especially when she learnt the full story. But that would not be yet awhile.

His thoughts were now directed towards his family and the plans he had for them. It was time that the boys went to school. Up to now they had been tutored at home by himself and Joseph, but both agreed they were not competent to take the boys' education further. He had in mind his old school in York for John, who was a very bright boy with an enquiring mind. With little Joseph he was not so sure. It was strange how his own characteristics and propensities had been polarised in his two sons. His own ability to understand and enjoy academic work was very noticeable in John, who, he thought, had a far better brain than himself. Joseph was entirely different. Whilst not a dullard, he had no inclination for theoretical work and was completely engrossed with nature in all its forms in a 'hands on' manner. It was he who spent most time on the farm with the animals, who followed Walter around and learnt from him the practical lore of farm work. He was soon able to turn his hand to most tasks which arose and which his physique would allow. And that physique was improving all the time; he grew in stature as he did in dexterity. His love of the countryside and its wild animals was responsible for the occasional truancy and William remembered his own forays away from the mill, when he should have been on hand to help his father. No, perhaps a formal education would not be suitable for little Joseph. He decided to consult his father on this point. Martha would be simply the future mistress of a house. She had no other aspirations and she would be very good at it. Her playing in the kitchen had progressed to real usefulness and Bess was often glad of her help now rather than being distracted by it!

As for Bess, he wished she would seek some mature help in the work about the house but she would not. Pride perhaps in her ability to manage alone, or the feeling that things would only be done properly if she did them herself. But the Hall was such a large house and with two men (one an invalid) and three children to cope with, there was little enough spare time for her. He would try again to persuade her to take on a woman from the village for at least some of the drudgery such as the washing and cleaning. He knew she would not give up the dairy work, the baking and the cooking. And he must spend more time with her. There would be no more riding off for days away from home on some other person's errands, however remunerative they might be. He made that resolve here and now, as he hunched forward in the saddle. The snow was falling again and he needed to find shelter for the night. He wished it might have been his own bed to which he was going.

It took another two full days for him to reach Worton. The weather had prevented any short passage through Wharfedale and over the Bishopsdale pass. It had to be the long way round, through the lowlands of Ripon and then Bedale and even then travel was often difficult, especially as he made his way updale. It was two days after the Christmas festival, therefore, when he rode out through Aysgarth on the last short leg of his journey and the lights of Worton village were a joy to his eyes.

He dismounted stiffly in the yard and entered the Hall enjoying the warmth that greeted him; not just the warmth of the building, but the greeting from his wife, who enveloped him in a fierce embrace. Not the worrying sort, she had nonetheless been concerned about his delayed return, knowing how foul the weather had been. The children were abed and they had time for each other, as Bess made him a warm beverage, which he sipped gratefully. He listened to the account of the Christmas celebrations, at which he had been sorely missed, and renewed his vow not to be absent on other such occasions. Then it was his turn to impart his news. Bess accused him of jesting when he started to recount his meeting with Queen Mary but he finished the tale and then said he would furnish the proof. He groped about in his pocket, sneezed violently and then produced the pin. Bess handled it wonderingly.

"William, my love, is that a real emerald?" she enquired.

"Aye, it truly is," he said, "and a wonderful coming of age present for our little girl," and he sneezed again. Bess needed no more encouragement.

"T'is bed for you my man!" she declared forcefully and he was ushered up the stairs for that rest which he had craved these long days in the saddle.

"I must be up betimes," he murmured before sleep claimed him. "I must visit Sir Francis with the good news."

"We shall see about that," rejoined his wife, who was not going to let go of her man again so quickly.

The following morning found William deep in the cold that had been threatening on the previous night. He was made to stay in his bed and hot stones were placed about his feet, whilst he fretted about the need to deliver that letter to Sir Francis. Bess dismissed that impatiently.

"Sir Francis can wait," she said. But Sir Francis couldn't wait. He died the next day.

Chapter 9: A Time to Be Born and A Time To Die

William had stepped back from the graveside in the Aysgarth churchyard to receive the condolences of the mourners who filed past him. The bright, low light of the January sun shone straight into his eyes and he had to shift his position in order to see that faces of those to whom he spoke. The very brightness and mild weather, which had tempted out small bunches of very early snowdrops under the trees, was ill-suited to the sombre occasion. It was ironic too that, having survived the virulent infection which had characterised the bitter early months of the previous year, poor Joseph should have died during such a pleasant spell of winter weather. But there it was. The coffin which housed that paralysed body with its able mind was even now being covered with the first shovel loads of soil. Watching in tearful silence were the three children, with Bess holding tightly to Martha's hand. The end had been mercifully quick; another sudden palsy had shut off the mind and bodily death followed just a few short hours later. There had been no time for preparation but then, thought William, how does one prepare for the loss of such a guardian, parent, friend and advisor? There had been that time last January when Joseph had suffered with them all from the virulent disease which he, William, had brought back from Staffordshire. With symptoms like an ordinary cold to begin with, there had developed a period of burning temperature, aching limbs and a head that throbbed incessantly. They had all succumbed to this in turn, John being the worst affected and taking the longest time to recover. Bess and Martha had shrugged it off comparatively quickly, whilst William and young Joseph had spent two days or so confined to their beds. The old man had contracted this illness too, comparatively mildly, although it was difficult to tell how much he had suffered, given his restricted powers of communication.

All had recovered, although there was some concern that John's lungs might have been left in a weakened state. The good summer had seen everyone make a full recovery, however, and John had been sent off to school in York in September. At Christmas time he had enlivened the occasion with accounts of his experiences at Archbishop Holgate's School and William had reminisced himself, scandalising his family with tales of his misdeeds. And now, so soon after his return to York, here was John at home again to pay his respects to a much-loved grandfather. Like the other two children, he was clearly badly affected by this death.

And this had not been their only loss. Just a month before Christmas, Walter had been found dead in the barn. It seemed he had been trying to lift a large bale and it had been too much for his aging heart. This too had been a major shock to the family. Walter had been an institution at Worton and had been present when William first came to live there. Everyone missed his slightly cantankerous manner, relieved by a rough good humour. It was fortunate that there was a ready supply of fit young men in the area, anxious to fill his position on the farm.

Now the last few people were passing William by with a handshake and a few words of condolence. Looking past them, he was astonished to see the figure of Sir Christopher Metcalfe waiting in the background. As soon as he was able to detach himself, William strode forward to greet him.

"Sir Christopher, 't was kind of you to come today and I do appreciate your attendance."

Sir Christopher proffered his hand.

"Joseph Robinson was a man respected by all, not least myself," he said. "Methinks you have only to remember how many attended the service today to gauge his place in the affections of the community. Despite his enforced physical withdrawal from the village life in recent years, he was nevertheless well remembered and will be much missed, more particularly by yourself and family of course. I do offer my sincere condolences."

William was warmed by this unexpected appearance and extension of sympathy from a man he had hitherto regarded as an enemy. He felt that this olive branch should be seized without fail.

"Sir Christopher," he said quietly, "you will be riding through Worton on your way to Nappa. Would you do us the honour of calling for a little refreshment? My wife has prepared a cold table and I would be glad if you could eat with us."

There was only the slightest hesitation before Sir Christopher smiled and accepted the invitation.

"I thank you, Sir, and I will be pleased to call upon you. I have one, short engagement to fill in Aysgarth before I can attend you but that should take no more than a half hour. Until then, Sir." He nodded and stepped away.

William found his way to Bess's side and laid an arm upon her shoulder. He told her of the invitation to Sir Christopher and his acceptance and, predictably, she tore herself away from him, gathered the children to her, and declared

"We must be off immediately to get everything ready." William laughed at her. "As if everything was not perfect before we left!" he chided. But no, they had to leave now and hurry on back to the Hall. Meanwhile Bess in turn chided her husband.

"Why then did you invite that Metcalfe into our home? We have no love for them and no obligations."

"Bess, my love, he came to the funeral. He spoke well of Joseph and offered what I believe to be sincere condolences. I think we should repay his courtesy with our own."

Bess looked doubtful but remained silent and William remembered that this was the family that had taken the life of her brother. He was hoping to be able to convince her that the son was not like the father, but was he sure himself?

There were of course other guests at this funeral feast and, as is always the case at these events, a gathering which started out in sombre mood soon transmuted into a lively and good-natured affair. Tales were told of past times, usually with a humorous content, and few could remain solemn, especially as the liberally provided liquid refreshment loosened tongues and increased the volume of the conversations, even if it did not improve them. There was a decided lull in the conversation when it was seen that Sir Christopher Metcalfe had entered the house, but when he was met by William Robinson and ushered by him to the table of fare, talk resumed at a renewed level of volume, and there was much looking over shoulders and shaking of heads. Clearly the Metcalfe was not the most popular guest under the Robinson roof that day. People were standing in the entrance hall, lounging against the walls and milling around the dining room tables. The few seats were occupied by ladies and Willam, after helping to serve his new guest, suggested that they retire to his study, where there were chairs and relative peace and quiet. Sir Christopher accepted gratefully and, as they settled themselves comfortably in the peaceful room, William was complimented upon his consideration.

"I do not stand as well as I did," admitted the knight. "The years have left me with a hip that plays the very devil if overtaxed and knees which have grown tired of supporting me."

William sympathised and admitted that, although he was by no means handicapped as yet, there had been signs that his joints were not as healthy as they should be at his stage in life. He described the deterioration that had occurred in this respect after his journey last winter, which had resulted in his illness. Aching limbs seemed to recur whenever he was slightly low in health. He was asked about his family and Sir Christopher nodded approvingly, when he heard that John was attending school in York.

"A wise decision William." He paused. "I beg your pardon, may I be so familiar?"

"I would welcome that, Sir," was the reply.

"Well, as I say, in these days a good education is of much greater importance than hitherto. It can open many doors quite apart from imbuing a life with interests, which would not otherwise have been possible. And it is your old school which he attends?"

"Yes, Sir Christopher, I was pleased to be able to install him in that institution, which did so much for me. I believe it will be very good for him."

"I think you to be right and I would hope that he derives a greater benefit from his education than you did yourself. I understand that you made a great sacrifice in terminating a promising career so irrevocably."

"I believe it was nothing less than my duty Sir." William felt uncomfortable at the turn of the conversation, hoping it could be changed. But his guest continued,

"Oh indeed, Sir, it was your duty. What is remarkable is the fact that you did not shirk that duty. I wonder how many young men in your position, with the world at your feet it might be said, would have given up all, as you did. Furthermore, unless I am mistaken, you gave up rather more than a career when you abandoned the city and let a certain member of that society slip away from you."

William grinned.

"Sir Christopher," he said, "I am sure you must be aware that, now and then, fate can give a person the chance to reverse an unfortunate decision. It was thus with me."

Sir Christopher laughed loudly.

"Too precious for ye was she? For certes, I found the mother to be shrewish and that is always an indication eh? The father was shrewd enough, too shrewd for me. I declined his offer." His tone changed then as he said, "I would touch upon another subject, the grazing on Abbotside common. You did us some financial harm there, you know."

"Yes, Sir," admitted William. "I guessed 't would be so but I had to defend the rightful beneficiaries of that common land. There was no personal feeling 'gainst you in my action."

"Aye, William, I know that to be true. I have been able to form an opinion of you without being actually in your company. A man's actions over time can reveal much more of his character than can his conversation. I was sure that there was no malice in your decision to bring that case against us. I would that I could convince my son of that truth. The fact is that he is obsessed with an unreasoning hatred against you. I admit this freely and warn you against him. I have been able to restrain him from any foolish actions 'till now but how long I shall be able to do so I know not."

Much had become clear to William during that short speech. He sought to confirm the conclusions he had drawn from it.

"Sir, there were some hard words spoken in Northallerton on that day. Threats were uttered, which put me on my guard. When nothing resulted from those threats I reached the conclusion that Thomas had seen the truth of the matter and moderated his opinions of me. I see now that I was mistaken and that it is you I have to thank for my trouble-free existence since then. I do thank you and give you my word that I will do nothing to provoke any further reason for his displeasure in me."

"Always excepting circumstances when he is doing mischief to a defenceless peasant eh?"

William sighed and said with a weak smile "Just so, Sir Christopher, just so."

Conversation changed to matters of more general interest and the subject of Mary Queen of Scots came up.

"You will know perhaps that she is guilty of treason in attempting the assassination of our own Queen? Well, that is the end of her. The Queen will be unable to preserve her life now, the Commons will insist upon an execution."

William nodded sagely, although his mind circled in sympathy with this tragic figure who had been born into a time when she had come inevitably into conflict with her English cousin. He listened as Sir Christopher told how the Scottish Queen's chain of communication with conspirators who were resolved to assassinate Queen Elizabeth and put Mary on the English throne had been cleverly suborned by Sir Francis Walsingham. He had come into possession of a letter in which she endorsed such a course of action. There was no defence to that. She was being held at Fotheringay and it was rumoured that the warrant for her execution had already been drawn up, but that Elizabeth was loath to sign it.

Sir Christopher took his leave after thanking his hostess for the meal, and William was left to ponder the fate of the vivacious young woman whom he had once idolised, but who was, in fact, just one Queen too many.

....

Mary looked and felt every inch a Queen as she entered the Great Hall at Fotheringay. But the awaiting throng were not her adoring subjects; they had come to see her die, and she was determined to die well. The spectators could not but admire her poise and regal bearing and, whilst there were many who had passionately wished for this day, there were none who did not admire her steadfast composure. Feelings ran from hate to sad sympathy, but in every heart there was respect. Mary took her place on the black cushioned chair and listened dispassionately as Robert Beale, the clerk of the court, read out the death warrant. She glanced around at the expectant throng. Before her stood her late jailor, Sir Amyas Paulet and beside him the Earl Marshall of England, The Earl of Shrewsbury, that same, kindly old man who had been her custodian for so many years. There were tears in his eyes and Mary was touched that there was one sympathiser amongst her final audience. To the side stood Cecil, Lord Burleigh. His countenance was sombre but not gloating, she noticed. His had been a dispassionate war against her; he had been an implacable opponent but he had evinced no viciousness or hatred. For him it had been a game of chess, which he had won, and he was even now planning his next stratagem in his endless task of protecting his Queen.

At his side and almost in his shadow, as he had been throughout, thought Mary, stood Walsingham. It was he who was the author of her destruction; he had been the instrument Cecil had used to bring her to this state. Mary grimaced inwardly, as she recalled her pleasure at learning of the arrangements which had been made to smuggle her correspondence in and out of Chartley. She had thought it an excellent idea for the letters to be concealed in the beer barrels, which were delivered to her by the brewer from Burton. It *was* an excellent idea; it was Walsingham's. Clearly he had intercepted her most secret messages and broken the ciphers in which they were written. It had been her own hand that had condemned poor young Babington to his appalling death last year.

There was a brief silence and then she was approached by the executioner and his assistant, who begged her forgiveness for what they were about to do. She did so and, in her answer, embraced the whole world in her forgiveness. It was a world which she thought had conspired against her and she announced her willingness to leave it. Her grieving assistants, Jane Kennedy and Elizabeth Curle, stepped forward to help her out of her gown. It a was a magnificently embroidered garment of black satin and, when it was removed, Mary stood revealed in her crimson, velvet petticoats which concealed blue stockings and fine Spanish shoes. A camisole of fine Scottish plaid, which had been made the previous night by her devoted ladies, covered her from waist to throat. The blindfold was placed over her eyes and she was led to the cushion where she was to kneel. She laid her head upon the block; the Earl of Shrewsbury raised his baton and the axe fell. It was a poor stroke, which certainly hit Mary's head but quite failed to despatch her. A groan arose from the crowd and the flustered executioner delivered another blow, which once more was ineffective. For a third time he raised his axe and this time, when it fell, the head rolled away from the body. With a triumphant cry the executioner seized the chestnut hair and hoisted it aloft with the words "God save Queen Elizabeth!" To everybody's horror, the wig detached itself from the head, which fell and rolled away off the platform and onto the floor.

·······························

Bess expelled a long sigh of contentment. She was shelling peas, which may not be a prime activity for engendering contentment, but she was sitting in the garden, with the hot sun falling on her back, the scent of garden flowers on the air and, lost somewhere in the blue sky, was a skylark, which by the continuous joyful song it was giving to the world, must be experiencing a similar feeling of contentment. However, whilst these sensations were all delightful, it was principally a mental happiness that had evoked that sigh, for Bess had been thinking about her family and how fortunate she was to have them. In an era when nearly a quarter of all bairns died before their tenth birthdays, she had raised three lovely children to maturity. Silly to call them children, she thought, when they were all taller than she, but that was how she still thought of them. True there had been that miscarriage and she felt again a pang as she recalled the double blow of the loss of a little daughter and the news that there were to be no more children. This latter fact no longer troubled her. The three had been enough she thought, for her at any rate, and William seemed to be equally resigned to the situation.

William, that lovely husband who looked after her so well and gave so much affection. Perhaps the burning passion was no longer there, although there were occasional moments, she thought with an inward smile, but the love was undiminished. William was happy too she believed. Certainly he had about him the air of a contented man. He kept himself busy, far busier than a man of his means needed to do, but it was this full occupation that produced his contentment. There was the work on the farm and although Joseph saw to most of that and supervised the work of the hired men, William lent a hand when things were very busy, the lambing and shearing of sheep, and the harvesting of the hay and small amount of cereal crops, which William had decided to grow. His greatest interest however was in his attempts to improve the flock, which he did by obtaining the services of the best rams he could find in the district. He was quite prepared to travel for miles if he heard of an animal with a good reputation. It was still the fleece, which was of the greatest importance. Wool far exceeded the demand for meat and produced by far the greatest revenue for the farm and so, of course, that was what he bred for. It was a measure of his thoroughness, thought Bess, that he weighed many samples of the fleeces, which had been shorn each year, noted them in his book and the parentage of the animals that had yielded them. This had been going on for years and the Worton flocks had established a great reputation in the county.

William's involvement with the legal problems of the local people still continued, indeed the word local was a trifle strained in view of the huge area in which he had helped. The officials at the consistory courts always recognised his handiwork and were able to grant probate without any delay in those cases where he had drawn up wills. The story of his stand against the

Metcalfes had circulated widely so that now even the threat of him bringing a case before the bench was usually enough to persuade heavy-handed land-owners to reconsider their attempts to appropriate that which was not really theirs. More and more, he was called upon to mediate in disputes, so that they never reached the courts. His reputation for wisdom and fairness grew to the extent that the advice he handed down was regarded as a sort of pronouncement of Solomon and all parties usually accepted it. Yes, William was happy, she was sure and she was glad of it. There were times when she regretted her own comparative lack of intellect and she recalled how he looked forward to the homecoming of John, when father and son could immerse themselves in deep conversations, to the exclusion of all others and had to be brought down to earth, when the meal was served or some other matter had to be discussed.

They were all so proud of John and his achievements but none more so than William. Bess remembered well that day, when John had returned from school bearing a letter from the headmaster. It was a letter which poured the highest praise upon the work and ability of their son and his teacher strongly advocated that John should be sent to university to complete the training of an excellent mind. There was no question that this advice be followed and a place was secured at Oxford for the grateful boy. It was exactly what John had hoped for and he promised all the family that, if given this opportunity, he would not let them down. Bess was saddened a little by the realisation that she was losing her son's presence at home for another long spell but she suppressed that feeling with the knowledge that both he and his father were so delighted with this course of action.

It was strange how her husband's major attributes and preoccupations were polarised in his two sons. Academic achievement was certainly not the goal of their younger son. Joseph was a real son of the soil. He loved his work on the farm, enjoyed all the activities associated with the animals and in his spare time still sought to escape into the country in order to observe the creatures of the wild. He was so like his father in this respect, thought Bess, and that was why there was such a close affinity between them. They would sit together in the evening talking over the prospects for the farm and these were conversations in which she could happily join. Her early life at Cuebeck had not been forgotten, when she was expected to perform many tasks to help out, some of them involving quite heavy work. She did not forget the things she had learnt and believed that this hard upbringing had made her healthy and fit enough to undertake all the household chores she now undertook. Although William had often asked, she refused to countenance the addition of another woman from the village into her kitchen. True the work could be hard but she had the now welcome assistance of Martha, who was quite capable of dealing with the washing and scrubbing and other energetic tasks, thus taking the load off her mother. Bess enjoyed the dairy work, cooking and all the myriad little household chores so that an outside helper was simply not required.

Yes, they all seemed to be happy in their various ways and it had become noticeable that certain other people had been contributing to that happiness of late. Joseph had been seeing a good deal of young Rosie Goodman from the village. She was a pretty thing but practical and hard working for all that. She needed to be. Her family were one of the poorest in the village for her father was a chronic invalid and her two other sisters were also weakly. Rosie and her mother had to work hard in order to make a living for all the family. Bess had often thought that if she did need to employ a girl to work in the house then Rosie would be the ideal candidate. She was certainly a nice natured lass and maybe, Bess thought, she would be alright as a daughter in law but she didn't know what William would think about that. Anyway there was plenty of time for that and there would probably be other girls who were better matches for her Joseph – no bad catch for any woman she thought with motherly pride.

John seemed not to have time for affairs of the heart, so engrossed was he with his studies. She worried a little that he had no outdoor pursuits and led a very sedentary lifestyle but then he had certainly been left with a bad chest after his illness a few years ago, so perhaps he was wise to cosset himself. No matrimonial prospects from that branch then; which left Martha. Bess smiled as she thought of the boy they called 'Martha's Shadow'. This was Robert Calvert, son of the George Calvert who William had helped in his case against the Metcalfes. George had often been hired to work at Worton during busy times such as lambing, shearing or haymaking but his place had been taken, in recent years, by Robert. When he was not working in the fields Robert followed Martha around seeking to help her in any way possible, just so long as he could be with her. Martha did not seem to be upset or annoyed by this attention but it caused a great deal of amusement to the rest of the family. Both William and Joseph thought highly of the lad as a worker and Joseph declared that he had never seen anyone who could shear as quickly as Robert. Nor did his skills stop there, for he was an excellent thatcher and could be relied upon to finish a haystack in such a way as to protect it from any weather the dales winter could throw against it.

And that was where they all were right now, in the hayfield; William and Joseph, Robert and two other casual labourers who had been hired to bring in the hay before the weather broke. They had been blessed with a fine spell which had allowed the grass to be turned and then, when dried, built into small haycocks. Now it was time to bring it all together in the big stack, which was being constructed near the barn. Two horses were harnessed to the wooden sled onto which the cocks were piled and dragged to the waiting men with their pitchforks. Robert and Joseph awaited their arrival on top of the stack and distributed the hay evenly and neatly.

Bess recalled with a start that it was time she broke off from her preparations for the evening meal and helped Martha to assemble the refreshments for the hot and weary haymakers. She went indoors to the kitchen to find that Martha was already placing pastries, bread and baked cakes into a basket. Bess filled a large pitcher with beer, collected some tankards and the two women sallied forth into the field where they were greeted with acclaim by the hungry men. They sat or lay about on the grass eating with relish but it was the beer that was in the greatest demand and Martha had to make a trip back into the house to replenish the pitcher. And this period of rest, short though it may be, was a relaxing time for all of them. This was the time for small talk, for snippets of news from further up or further down the dale to be relayed, for a bit of leg pulling, largely at the expense of Robert and Martha. But it could not last long; they had to resume work quickly. The sky was beginning to acquire a sort of hardness, which betokened the advent of sultrier and eventually stormy weather. With her practiced eye, Bess could see that it would take all of the remaining day to bring in the crop and that it was likely to be a late meal that night. That being the case, she and Martha took away the empty tankards, basket and pitcher, back to the kitchen and, after the washing and putting away was completed, they both attired themselves in appropriate working clothes and went outside to seize rakes and help in the clearing of the ground. This was real community work, carried out in a community spirit and with a tremendous feeling of achievement and satisfaction when all was completed. No wonder they all were happy.

How quickly things could change! Christmas was approaching, John would be home from Oxford soon, making this a time of happy anticipation in normal circumstances but the house was pervaded by an awkward, miserable, atmosphere. Bess thought back to the carefree summer days and regretted her complacency. Not that any other attitude would have made any difference to the situation now. The even tenor of life at Worton had been shattered three days ago, when Martha had approached Bess with her news. She had been very matter of fact about it, had exhibited no signs of excitement, worry or remorse. In fact so off hand had been her opening remarks that it took Bess a while to realise what she was hearing.

"I've missed twice now mother so I suppose it must be going to happen. Well, it should be a June baby so that will be nice won't it?"

Bess's mind was numbed with shock. Shock as the import of Martha's words sank in and shock at her own failure to have realised what was happening to her daughter. How could she, an experienced mother, have been unable to read the signs before now? But in honesty, even now, looking back, she could not think of any hint she might have picked up on. She eventually found some words;

"Oh Martha, what will your father say? How do you feel now, are you well? You must take much better care of yourself now. What are we going to do?"

Martha seized upon the last question.

"Well mother, that will not be too difficult a decision. Robert and I shall be married and we will go to live at his father's house in Appersett. Robert has already asked his parents if this could be done and there will be a place for us."

"But what will your father say?"

The repetition of the question was an indication of the turmoil in Bess's mind. She really knew quite well what William was likely to say and this was simply a prevarication as she sought to focus her thinking along relevant lines.

"I think father will be happy for us," said Martha, more in hope than certainty. "In any case we shall have to marry, for the child's sake as well as our own, and that is that."

There it was. In that short statement, any idea of preventing the birth had been ruled out and Bess was glad of it. She was beginning to think clearly now and sorting out ideas in her own mind.

"Well, from what you say, the Calvert family know all about it and are happy for the wedding to go ahead?"

"Yes, Robert's mother seemed to be very pleased and his father said very little but I think he accepts the situation."

"Aye, well he might," said Bess a trifle grimly. "A good catch for a poor husbandman. Now advent is upon us, there is no time for even a special licence and so the wedding will have to wait until Christmas is over. We can announce the contract but you must wait for the reading of the three banns before the marriage can take place. Well, that will give us time to plan the day and for us to make a dress. T'will have to be made, as you will never get into my old wedding gown. Anyway it is dyed blue now, but perhaps you would not mind! It may have to be larger than you would have wanted for decency's sake. We must see the vicar in Aysgarth and arrange a date. There won't be much in the way of flowers. I shall have to give the house a good clean to be ready for the wedding breakfast."

It was a jumbled outpouring of thought; there was no stopping Bess now and Martha was glad to let her run on. She had the feeling that the more her mother made plans, the more support she would give her daughter when the time came for the interview with her father. Despite her apparent sang froid, this was an event, to which Martha was not looking forward with any confidence.

Whilst each of them had been afraid of an angry reception of Martha's news, they were both totally unprepared for William's actual reaction. Always a reasonable man, who tempered his remarks with moderation and forethought, William fell into a towering rage. It was frightening and the more impressive because it was the first time anyone had seen him exhibit this sort of temper. He was furious with Bess for allowing this to happen to his daughter. Despite the unfairness of this, Bess did not object as it had the effect of diluting his anger with his daughter and that was terrible enough. How could she let down her parents, indeed the whole family, like this? Where had been her self control? Had she just thought of nothing but her own carnal pleasure, with no regard for any consequences? And what of the evil youth who had enticed her into this misdeed? He deserved a horsewhipping at the very least. He had thought better of George Calvert than to allow his son to fornicate with, and totally undo, the daughter of his friend and benefactor. Well, Robert Calvert would be held to account for his actions. There would be no escape for him and he would be marched to the altar by force of arms if necessary.

"There will be no need for that, father," Martha cut in, greatly daring.

"Robert has asked me to marry him as soon as possible and he says he will provide for me."

"Aye, he will that," snarled William. "Not a half penny piece will he see from me, if that was his plan. So, you mun lie in the bed you have made for yourselves!"

William sent his daughter away to her room, to which she willingly escaped.

William paced up and down, loud in his denunciation of the youth who had ravished and impregnated his daughter and equally loud in his condemnation of his daughter's loose behaviour and lack of common sense. When Bess tried to pacify him, she too came under fire for her lack of proper supervision of the girl and a failure to educate her properly as to the risks involved in sexual activity.

Exasperated, she told him that John would be home soon and would celebrate his birthday. Astonished, he paused in his diatribe and enquired what bearing that could possibly have on this dreadful situation.

"Perhaps you might also remember that we celebrated our twentieth wedding anniversary this year?" Bess continued heatedly.

"True," snapped William, "and again I ask what bearing does that have on the subject which is vexing us so?"

"Being a man, you will not remember the date of our anniversary, I suppose."

This was said with something like a sneer and William rose to it.

"T'is in May, the twenty second, and you must own that I did not forget it."

"No, dear husband you did not; but I ask you, the great reckoner in our family, to do the sums and then tell me if the world views us in worse or better case than our daughter and her lover."

There was a brief silence and then William blustered on about there being no similarity. It was a matter of betrayed trust, taking advantage of an innocent young girl, and so on, and Bess smiled.

"Yes, you will know about taking advantage of an innocent young girl of course."

Infuriated, William stomped off into his study and shut himself in but Bess thought she might have scored a telling point.

The next two days were fraught with studious avoidances, icy silences and a general feeling of subdued anger and misery. But then John came home. He was immediately aware of an atmosphere in the house and was soon left in no doubt as to the reason for this. William, with none of the wisdom of angels, rushed in to point a quivering finger at Martha and declare.

"Your little sister is in the family way; what think you of that?"

John stooped, embraced Martha and planted a kiss upon her forehead.

"Well done, little sister," he said, "I wish you all joy of your little one."

Turning quickly, he said to William:

"Father I need to talk to you urgently, ladies will you excuse us? And he ushered his father into the study. Bess stared at the closed study door and wondered what other terrible blow might be in store for them. The door remained obstinately closed and voices could be dimly heard but they did not seem to be raised in anger. Mother and daughter sank into chairs and anxiously awaited the outcome of this interview. It was a long vigil but when the door did eventually open, it was John who burst upon the waiting scene with congratulations for Martha and questions about the wedding and if it would take place before he had to return to Oxford. He was all good cheer and enthusiasm, which raised their spirits and served to eclipse the slow and subdued reappearance of William at the study door.

Bess stole a glance in his direction and he appeared thoughtful and perhaps just a trifle shaken. In a steady voice however, he summoned Martha to join him in the study and she went, dutifully but fearfully. Joseph came in at that point and the brothers greeted each other affectionately. There was much to discuss, not the least the eventual arrival of a niece or nephew for them both. Joseph admitted that he had been upset by his father's reaction and expressed the hope that he would calm down and accept the situation.

"The milk has been spilt alright but we mun just mop it up and carry on."

John was happy to hear this opinion from his younger brother and felt that, with a united front, they would surely prevail upon their father to moderate his attitude. With that he engaged them both in conversation about his experiences at Oxford and brought a smile to their lips now and again with humorous stories, but Bess's eyes kept wandering to that closed door. In the event she did not have long to wait for the door opened and the two came out together, William looking sheepishly pleased and Martha smiling through tears. Nothing was announced to the waiting couple, but now the atmosphere had been quite magically changed and it was possible to talk openly and cheerfully about the forthcoming marriage. Plans were discussed, and at one point John artfully brought his father into the conversation by appealing to him on a point of law regarding marriages within the period of Advent. The evening finished cheerfully but with William remaining subdued and rather quiet. At least he had lost that seething rage, which he had exhibited for the last few days.

Suddenly William arose and announced that he needed to retire as he was very tired. He turned to Bess and she saw that he was seeking her company. She complied readily and, leaving the three younger ones to chat, they climbed the stairs together. Bess had the decided feeling that there would be much talking to do before they fell asleep.

....

As Bess regarded the group which stood at the church door, she felt that the strange swings in the weather matched her wildly conflicting emotions. Just as the showers of rain, driven by a sharp wind, gave way suddenly to flashes of weak sunshine, so her feelings changed from sadness to joy. She looked around at her accompanying family. Her husband, smiling now, as he gazed affectionately at his daughter; John, standing just a little apart, but also looking happy for his sister, and Joseph beaming around at everyone, as he stood close to Rosie, not a member of the family yet, but soon to be so. That had been another major development. Joseph, probably inspired by the recent events, had approached his father and cautiously enquired how he would feel about a marriage between Rosie and himself. He realised they were both young, he said, but he was convinced that Rosie was the girl for him and she would make a grand partner in life.

To his utter and complete astonishment, William had been enthusiastic. He seemed almost eager in his encouragement and proposed that, when married, they should continue to live at the Hall. Now that Martha was leaving home, there would not only be plenty of room but Bess would welcome some help in the absence of her daughter. Joseph was even more mystified, when his father hinted that he and Rosie would in time be able to take over the Hall, after the departure from this life of his parents.

"But John, father, John is the elder and he will surely inherit Worton Hall?"

"No my boy," was the unexpected reply, "John does not choose to live here at Worton. He has plans to remain at Oxford and make his living there. You must ask him about it before he leaves."

Bess, who had witnessed this exchange, knew why her husband was behaving in this fashion. He had told her all, that night after John's return and the great rapprochement between himself and Martha. The sensitive and perspicacious John had instantly summed up the situation, as he had walked through the door, and knew that something drastic needed to be done to reverse his father's feelings about this pregnancy. He knew what would accomplish this, although he had not planned to reveal the details of his own situation so soon. However, he realised it had to be tackled at some time and this seemed to be an opportune moment to distract his father's rage with another problem, a counter irritant as it were. Accordingly, he had abruptly marched his father into the study and, taking advantage of William's surprise, had asked him to reconsider his attitude to Martha's pregnancy, especially in the light of what he was about to hear.

"Father, you are going to acquire a grandchild and you should be glad. You should be glad because this might be the only grandchild you are going to have. I fear that I shall be letting you down in this respect because I will never marry and never produce an heir for your beloved Worton Hall. I had not wanted to broach this subject yet, but there is no good time to tell you and now is perhaps the most opportune moment."

William stammered his incomprehension and John continued, "I have to admit to you father that I have no feeling of attraction towards women. I can of course like them as people, as characters and friends but, as to what passes between man and woman naturally, well, I cannot participate in that sort of relationship. Indeed I am repelled by the very thought. I can only express my extreme sorrow in disappointing you in this way and I hope you will not love me the less because of my inclinations."

William sank into a chair, speechless and stricken.

"Now, my dear father, do not despair. You have another son, a vigorous son and one who possesses all the right inclinations to help perpetuate your empire! He is the one upon whom you should build your hopes. I would prefer to make my home and my living in Oxford. I can tell you that, conditionally upon a satisfactory completion of my course, I have actually been offered a place at the University to lecture. The church was a consideration for me at one time but I much prefer the idea of an academic career. I gladly leave the calling of farming to my younger brother and I know he will revel in it. In the meantime, you have a daughter who is bringing you the gift of a grandchild. That must be a consolation to you now and I urge you, Sir, to accept it with a good grace, indeed with pleasure."

And John's stratagem had worked, but clearly at some cost. William's mind was now totally refocused and he was encouraging any moves to propagate the Robinson family but as to his relationship with his eldest son, Bess was unsure how things stood between them. It had been a devastating blow for them both but William especially had been hard hit. Certainly there was no outright animosity, but there was a little distance between them now, which she hoped would disappear as time brought a greater understanding and tolerance.

Joseph on the other hand looked supremely happy as he stood next to his intended bride. Rosie too was smiling but looking just a little uncertain. Bess thought it must be difficult for her to suddenly become a part of an alien society. These were people who she had long regarded as her superiors in class, wealth and just about anything else. But she was making a good try and had already endeared herself to Bess by working hard at the Hall to prepare the wedding breakfast. Martha had, perhaps understandably, proved to be a broken reed on this, her wedding day, and had not only spent her time in her room fussing about her appearance but had laid claim to her mother's time too. Bess had tried to divide her attention between kitchen and bedroom but eventually left everything in Rosie's hands; and capable hands they had turned out to be.

Now they were all together on the threshold of the church, where they had been joined by George Calvert and his wife Joan. Robert's younger brother, Edward, stood at his side, allegedly to give support but looking in need of it himself. Martha appeared radiant with happiness. She wore the long russet coloured dress, which Bess had made over the Christmas period. She wore silk slippers, a wedding present from her elder brother, and in her hair was a chaplet of mistletoe and hellebores cleverly woven together. The ceremonies had been duly completed; William had formally given away his daughter and Robert, his face scrubbed painfully clean, had been handed the dowry which, given his family circumstances, was a welcome foundation for their resources. The ring had then been blessed by the vicar and Robert had placed it upon three successive fingers of Martha's hand, thus protecting her from demons, before leaving it on the third finger of her left hand. These little customs, followed to the letter, were now all done and it was time to enter the church for the sermon and blessing. As she turned to go in a powerful gust of wind seized the bride's dress, which threatened to balloon up over her head, but the thickness of the material and a restraining hand kept it in place. It also imperilled the floral chaplet in her hair, but this too remained safely in place. It was securely fastened by a large pin, at the head of which was a brightly gleaming emerald.

Chapter 10: The Lawgiver

There was a low mist, hugging the valley floor as William rode out of Worton. By the time he had climbed the hill to Cuebeck, however, he was in bright sunshine and, looking back up the dale, he could see the brightly-lit flanks of Great Shunner and the other fells. Across the other side of the river the pele tower of Nappa Hall could just be seen poking through the grey curtain of mist, a grim reminder of days gone past, when men had to fortify against the marauding Scot or die. William knew that it had been built over a hundred and fifty years ago, by a Thomas Metcalfe who was grandson to James Metcalfe, the original owner of the estate. This land had been a gift from Sir Richard Scrope of Bolton Castle, under whom he had fought at Agincourt. Legend had it that the original farm had been destroyed by a Scottish band and this had been the impetus which had driven Thomas to build his fortified home. William shook his head as he mused over the enmity which had existed between Robinsons of Worton and the Metcalfes of Nappa for the last two generations. He could understand the family's distress at the loss of their ancestral home. Worton Hall had been the place where James Metcalfe had lived before he was given the Nappa estate but through marriage and inheritance the ownership had passed into the hands of the Robinsons.

The late Sir Christopher had come to accept this fact and indeed had developed a respect for his father, Joseph, and to some extent himself. But the son, Thomas, had remained an implacable foe of the Robinsons and most particularly William. His enmity had been kept in check by his father and William had dreaded the day when Sir Christopher was no longer around to restrain him. He feared that an unbridled Thomas would find every means to prosecute his feud even more violently but events had taken a surprising turn when Thomas died first, leaving Sir Christopher and his grandson, also called Thomas, who would be his heir. In fact the inheritance was not long delayed for within a year of his son's death, Sir Christopher also passed away.

The death of Thomas had evoked a few unchristian remarks from Bess, who had never forgiven him for the killing of her brother and William too had had to admit that he was relieved to see the end of his relentless foe. Now the estate was in the hands of the young Thomas, who was proving to have inherited the family propensity for living beyond his means. There were many stories of his wild behaviour but he had caused no trouble for the Robinsons of Worton. William had met him at the funeral of his father, for he had wished to pay his respects to Sir Christopher, who had softened his approach and even warned him of his son's deep hatred and the possible mischief he might have caused. There had been little said between the new knight of Nappa and himself on this occasion but William had been unimpressed by the young man and he tended to dismiss him as a ne'er-do-well, lightweight character. At least it seemed that the bitter feud was now at an end.

With no small degree of self satisfaction, William contrasted his neighbour with his son Joseph, a hard working young man, dedicated to the successful running of the Worton estate and now happily married and settled. Now there was a satisfactory outcome! His choice of wife, Rosie, had been absolutely right for him, as he had predicted. But not only right for Joseph; the whole household had benefited from her cheerful and hard working presence. Even Bess, when pressed, had been forced to admit that her arrival at Worton had been a godsend, coming as it did at the time when Martha left home. She and Rosie had become firm friends and, to add to that delight, there were now two lively young boys running about the house and farm and it appeared that there would be another infant coming along soon. That would mean another christening. He was riding past the Aysgarth church as this thought occurred to him and he mused over the many family events which had been witnessed there. The latest had been rather sad. It had been the funeral of Mrs Fawcett, mother of his wife, but something of a stranger to them. Bess had visited her from time to time but was never received with enthusiasm. Terribly embittered by the loss of her husband, and son, the old lady had blamed William, Bess and Thomas Metcalfe in equal measure for this tragedy and had shunned their company. When she eventually died, however, it was William and Bess who accompanied her to the grave with only one other Fawcett relative to augment the mourners. Small wonder then that Bess had tempered her grief with the feeling that her departure was a relief to all.

The sunshine was swallowing up all the mist now and it was going to be a lovely day. William was grateful for that, as it was a long ride to Richmond. He had set off very early but not too early for Bess to fuss around him and ensure that he had sufficient provisions to sustain him along the way, adequate clothing for all weathers and all he required for his overnight stay. He had always enjoyed riding and the journey down dale was a great joy to him, passing as it did through the lovely countryside bathed in the early summer sunshine. Besides the beautiful scene there was much to think upon, notably the correspondence which he had been having with his eldest son John. That young man was firmly established in a teaching position at Oxford University and completely immersed in his work. He was mixing with an exciting mixture of academics and people of note in politics and trade so that he lived an interesting and busy life.

Not so busy, however, that he could not find time to write to his family and, in particular, his father. A few months ago he had passed on the intelligence that a group of merchants were banding together to form a company dedicated to exploiting the potential profits to be had from the East Indian trade. They had been impressed by the huge success of the Dutch and Portuguese in this area and saw no reason why they should not follow suit. John had written to say that he was aware of one merchant who was desperate to be included in this venture, but who was not in possession of sufficient funds to subscribe and was therefore looking for a backer. Would his father be interested? John enquired. William had made a few enquiries and then plunged into the investment to a considerable sum so that, although his name did not appear on the original deed of subscription, he was nonetheless the financial power behind one who was so listed. He smiled to himself as he realised that he, who had never even seen the sea in his life, was now the partial owner of an ocean-going ship destined to sail into exotic waters. The investment was an exciting one and, whilst it was certainly a risk, there was a promise of huge profits should all go well.

It was especially pleasing that this business had been carried out through the medium of his son. It had brought them closer together, a welcome development for William, who was trying hard to repair their relationship. John's announcement a few years ago of his aversion to the opposite sex and therefore his inability to provide issue for the Robinson family had upset both his parents but in particular his father, who somehow blamed himself for this unwelcome and bewildering news. His total lack of understanding had been obvious and his inability to communicate fully with John had opened up a rift between them, which he was now trying to close. The truth was that John had not changed at all. He was the same intelligent, warm-hearted boy who had left home for Oxford and there was no outward sign of his different sexual orientation. As this realisation had slowly dawned upon William, he had bitterly regretted his initial alienation from his son and now strove to mend some fences. The boy was to come home for a short spell later in the summer and he looked forward to resuming their long discourses, of which he had been so fond.

William checked his horse suddenly. He was approaching the bridge at Hestholme and it looked to be in a parlous condition. The northern parapet had collapsed and there was a huge crack in the road surface right on the crest of the bridge. Fortunately there was little water in the Bishopdale beck and it was a simple matter for the horse to wade through and scramble up the bank but the matter ought to be attended to. It occurred to him that, if his suspicions about today's meeting were correct, he might well be the one responsible for seeing to its repair.

The meeting in Richmond was the second one to which he had been bidden this year by Gervaise Tennant of Northallerton. Since his appearance before the Magistrates several years ago, when he had upheld the right of his neighbouring farmers to graze their sheep on Abbotside, the two had met again several times and become good friends. It was a friendship that had survived the difficulties of the many miles between them and, over the years, there had been a few meetings here in Richmond to which he had been invited for convivial meals and discussions with a group of influential men, largely but not exclusively from the legal profession. These meetings had been presided over by a James Cotterel, Alderman of Richmond, and a man with a huge reputation as a successful lawyer until his move to York, where he became a judicial examiner for the Council of the North. He was also a Justice of the Peace and had actually chaired the bench before which William and George Calvert had appeared.

William had been flattered to be included in this company, and the more so because in recent years his opinion had often been sought about matters in the higher reaches of Wensleydale. He surmised that this was because, after the death of Sir Christopher Metcalfe, there was no Magistrate who could be said to properly represent the people of the upper dale. His son Thomas, who might have been expected to assume this mantle, had been too ill to officiate and the grandson, also Thomas, was thought to be too young and irresponsible to be considered. On the last occasion when they had met in Richmond there had been present a Mr Justice Humphries, a judge of whom William had heard but never met. Once again the subject of the constitution of the bench arose and in particular the under-representation of the sparsely populated and remote parts of the higher dales. William was astonished to be asked if he would consider being nominated for this position but, whilst thanking them for the compliment, he explained that he had no qualification and little experience. Humphries had picked him up on the latter point.

"That is not my evaluation Mr Robinson!" he exclaimed. "Perhaps not a university qualification, but a great deal of experience and from a variety of sources. Although you never appeared before me, you had a very good reference from that excellent old advocate, Mr Allcot of Durham. He sang your praises continually and confided in me that the profession had lost a potential star when you declined to continue your studies. In addition, I had heard of you in very favourable terms from my late friend James Cotterel, who sadly died just a few years ago. Well now, you have been dabbling in legal matters for some years from the security and comfort of your own home. Perhaps it is time you came out from that shelter and accepted a fuller responsibility in the wider community."

William realised that there was no animosity in this last remark; it was merely a way to prod his conscience into considering the proposition seriously. He declared that he would indeed be proud to occupy such a prestigious position and would thoroughly enjoy the work, in which, he admitted, he had a great interest but he expressed his doubts as to his suitability from the social point of view.

"I have no pedigree, gentlemen. I come from working stock with no gentlemanly status. Any small degree of success in my life has been entirely due to the influence and efforts of my adoptive father and the care he has lavished upon my education and, even in that matter, I failed to carry out his wishes for me. My formal training was cut short for personal reasons. Therefore without qualification or family position I cannot be seriously considered as a candidate."

Humphries had grunted in disagreement. "You are mistaken, Sir. In recent times our gracious Queen Elizabeth has considered it important to broaden her regional government with what she calls 'new men' to balance the traditional knights of the shires with sound and honest citizens of lower orders. You may be a better candidate than you give yourself credit for."

That had been some six months ago and now here he was again travelling to Richmond on business, whose nature had not been specified by his friend Gervaise Tennant. William was now urging his horse up the last rise before entering the town of Leyburn. He had left Wensley behind, as indeed had progress. Once the capital of the Dale, it had never recovered from the devastating plague which had hit it at the time when Walburn village had been wiped out. Now it had been overtaken by the town he was approaching, both in terms of population and importance. As the road neared the entrance to the town, William glanced left at the limestone escarpment behind which lay rich grazing land. He smiled as he recalled that people were now referring to this feature as Leyburn Shawl and wondered if this name, born of a growing tradition about a certain royal escapade, would remain a permanent part of local, geographical nomenclature.

With this reminder of his past, his thoughts returned full circle to his own family. He and Bess had both decided to keep all knowledge of their involvement with the Scottish Queen from their children. True it was a long time ago and Mary was gone from the scene but Elizabeth and her councillors were still wary of any hint of religious dissent and sympathy with the Roman Catholic cause. Even though it was now ten years since the defeat of the Spanish Armada and the removal of the direct threat from that country, there was still a certain nervousness about the intentions of Catholic Europe. It was not a time to let slip the information that a supporter of Queen Mary, and a conspirator in her plans to escape, still dwelt in the Yorkshire Dales. The presentation of the emerald pin to his daughter for her wedding had been a small problem. Naturally Martha was thrilled and very anxious to know from whence it had come but she was to be disappointed. William had merely smiled mysteriously and admitted that there was a romantic story behind the existence of the jewel in their family but said that he was not, as yet, at liberty to reveal it to anyone. He did say, however, that it was Martha's by right, a gift for her and of which he had been the custodian until the coming of the proper time and he promised that, as soon as it was safe to do so, he would inform them all of the interesting history of the emerald pin.

Martha had been satisfied with that explanation, as indeed she had been satisfied with her enforced marriage. In truth, it was the marriage she would have hoped for, even if it had been thrust upon her much sooner than she had planned. In a way William had fulfilled his threat to withhold financial largess from his daughter and son in law. He was of the opinion that they should work hard to establish themselves and it was an opinion that was shared by most, if not all, of his contemporaries. A man engaged in farming had to work hard to survive in this hard environment and the fact that William had been lucky enough to avoid this necessity in his younger days did not alter his views. In fact he had found ways in which to assist the young couple without having to give handouts. Small contracts at very good rates were offered to Robert and several deals at advantageous terms were conducted. Robert was well aware of what was going on and, whilst not turning down any of these opportunities, he was just a little resentful of this patronising treatment at the hands of his father-in-law. Martha, when she became aware of his attitude, begged him to restrain this feeling and accept the favours gratefully and without protest.

"T'is my father saying 'sorry' to me my love," she explained. "He regrets his extreme reaction to our news and wishes some of his words unspoken. He wants to be forgiven."

And so good relations were maintained, which was just as well for William doted upon the two little girls the couple had produced. Anne was tall and slender with the blond looks and blue eyes of her father, whilst Elizabeth was also fair of hair, short and quite stoutly built but with a wonderful friendly smile, which reflected the lovely outgoing nature of the child. Martha imposed a strict rationing upon her father's attempts to spoil the girls but he often found a way around her restrictions. They were still living with Robert's parents and space was at a premium but they all seemed to get along very well.

William's devotion to his young grand daughters did not detract from his fondness for Joseph's two boys, William and John. They were not quiet and self controlled little boys. They did not always behave in the manner required by their parents and grandparents. They were not tidy and seldom remained clean; moreover they were noisy and boisterous so that the Hall often rang with their shouts of joy, triumph, disappointment and rage. But they were not undisciplined; both Joseph and Rosie shared the task of keeping them in line and they were successful. Joseph's sphere of influence was most usually the farmyard, whilst Rosie imposed the rules of the house. Both William and Bess forbore from interfering and this was not difficult to do because, despite their often rowdy behaviour, the lads could be instantly brought to disciplined obedience. They were often given free rein to play as they willed but the moment of truth, when either parent decided that enough was enough, was immediately recognised and it was also realised that appeal would be to no avail.

Furthermore, their life was not only play and disruption. There were regular tasks to perform every morning and evening. These were jobs around the farm; the feeding of poultry and collection of eggs, the feeding of stock kept in the byres and occasional mucking out and cleaning jobs. In the house they were exempt from labour; this was not yet an age when the male sex was expected to perform household duties. But they were expected to follow certain rules. The breakage of pots and dishes was always accompanied by penalty. Damage to furniture was also punished. Grandfather's study was inviolable; dire punishment followed any transgression of that law.

But the noise and the activity was a breath of fresh air to William, who not only tolerated it but sometimes actively subscribed to it. Bess was astounded on one occasion to find her husband on all fours, rolling apples at a row of ale bottles masquerading as ninepins; and this upon her immaculately polished hall floor! She was scathing in her condemnation of his foolishness, although they had a good laugh about it during the ensuing evening. No, there was no favouritism dividing the grandchildren and the cousins were all good friends.

As for William's relationship with his second son, Joseph, he was often put in mind of that other Joseph, his uncle and then father. They got along together very well because each knew where his field of endeavour began and ended. Joseph ran the farm. That was beyond doubt. William might be invited to express an opinion but it had always been clear that Joseph was a natural farmer, who knew almost instinctively how a job should be tackled and when. He bowed to no man including his father except in one respect; and that was policy. Joseph simply did not have the head for figures and calculation which his father enjoyed. He was quite able to accept the older man's decisions on buying and selling, choice of animals and crops for the ensuing year. His skill was a purely practical one and William knew that the farm would always be in safe hands just as long as Joseph was at the helm. Their discussions were always pleasant and of interest. William was glad that the position had been made clear as to the inheritance of the Hall and farm. He was sure that it would be the best arrangement. Whilst puzzled at his brother's lack of interest in this regard, Joseph was the better encouraged in his efforts to make the business prosper; for it was to be his one day and that was the limit of his ambition.

Reflecting as he did upon his good fortune in all aspects of life, it is not surprising that William entered the town of Richmond in high good humour.

He was looking forward to dining with his friend Gervaise and was even daring to anticipate an exciting development in his life. Would it be for good or ill? He had just been congratulating himself upon his happy existence; he did not want that to change but it might. He had made excellent time in his journey and, after stabling his horse, he found the leisure to stroll around the town. Although not a market day, there was a bustling throng and much evidence of prosperity in terms of new shops and dwelling houses. He wandered a trifle aimlessly through the narrower streets that surrounded the castle keep and came upon it suddenly, finding to his surprise that there was no impediment to his entering the main courtyard. It had a forlorn appearance, with tufts of whin bushes growing unchecked and the curtain walls in some disrepair. The massive keep itself was sound but clearly uninhabited and William marvelled that such a huge defensive fortress had lost its importance to the extent that this utter neglect suggested. He supposed it was a reflection of the townsfolk's feeling of security, especially after the crucial English victory at Flodden, that the castle and town walls had all been allowed to fall into decay.

He completed his tour of the ruined castle and then returned to the Black Lion and his meeting with Gervaise.

William reflected for perhaps the hundredth time upon the vagaries of the northern weather. The beautiful summer's day had turned nasty and wet yesterday afternoon as dark clouds blew in from the west. The rain had poured down, rattling on the slates of the inn and giving him cause for thanks that he did not have to make the return journey that day. It was, however, little better on the morn and after bidding his friend, Tennant, a good journey home, he headed out into the dreary weather for the long ride to Worton. Dreary the weather may have been, but his spirits were high enough, as he relived the events of the previous afternoon and evening. They had dined well in their usual comradely atmosphere and there had been much conversation both serious and jovial to accompany the meal. William always enjoyed these engagements with a man whose speech was by turns incisively germane or devastatingly amusing, even mischievously so. It was certainly never dull. But throughout their discourse, William had felt that something was being held back and once or twice Gervaise had made a move to open the little satchel which lay on the table at his side but then changed his mind and embarked upon another topic of conversation. Whether or no he was being deliberately toyed with, William could not tell but eventually Gervaise brought his prevarication to an end, untied the satchel and produced from therein a scroll which he handed over with a smile.

"I am charged to deliver this document to you William," he said, the smile broadening. "If you will excuse me from the table for a moment, I enjoin you to read it in my absence," and he rose, a trifle unsteadily, and made for the chimney place, where he passed water noisily.

As soon as he was handed the scroll William knew exactly what was in it. Even so he could not restrain a feeling of excitement as he opened the document and, with slightly trembling fingers, unrolled it on the table. And there was the author's name, in large elaborate lettering, over which some clerk had laboured and applied his considerable skill: Elizabeth the First. His eye travelled to the bottom of the document and there was her signature and alongside the royal seal. He read every word of the superscription with a feeling of incredible pride that such a document should have been sent to him.

'Elizabeth the First, by the grace of God of the realm of England, Queen. To Our trusty and well beloved William Robinson of Worton, Greeting.

We, having been made abundantly aware of your loyalty, and reposing especial trust and confidence in your knowledge and good conduct, do by these presents constitute and appoint you Justice of the Peace in Our County of Yorkshire from the twentieth day of July in the year of our Lord fifteen hundred and ninety nine.

You are therefore carefully and diligently to discharge your duties in this office according to the laws of the land now in force or such laws as may be passed by Us from time to time in Council and We hereby command all constables and chief constables to obey and carry out your orders and directions.

Given at Our court at Westminster this day, the eighteenth of April in the forty second year of Our reign. By her Majesty's command.' And there followed the signatures of the court officials, under which was that of the Queen along with the seal.

William sat transfixed by this royal signature until a low voice said gently
"T'is what you wanted William, is it not?"

"Aye Sir, it is indeed and I doubt me not that I have yourself to thank for this honour being bestowed upon me." William took his hand and shook it warmly.

"Nonsense man, it is recognition of worth and I congratulate you. May I see the full document?"

William handed the scroll across the table and Gervaise studied it thoroughly.

He gestured to the wording 'having been made abundantly aware of your loyalty' and smiled.

"I think we both know to what this alludes, do we not? If I heard the story once from old Allcot I must have heard it a dozen times. You stood forward and declared your allegiance to the Queen at a time when this might well have proved fatal. You can be assured that this deed did not go unreported to Cecil by his spies and such information is never lost, but noted carefully and filed away for future use, even now some years after his death. You see the signature at the bottom of the scroll? That is Sir John Puckering, the Lord Chancellor. It is he who makes these appointments, not Her Majesty, and they are always based upon the best intelligence. If consolation is needed, then you should know that the Queen always has to approve the choices and would doubtless enquire into the circumstances of your selection."

It is true that, for William, a little of the gloss had disappeared from the moment, as he realised that it was not the Queen herself who had picked his name from the candidates but he quickly appreciated that this could not really have been expected. Whoever had picked it, she had approved it and that was all that mattered. William had listened intently as Gervaise expounded on the duties and responsibilities of his office. He had known about the responsibility for the upkeep of roads and bridges in his area, the regulation of inns and alehouses, the monitoring of travelling players and the upkeep of jails in the area. He knew a good deal about the administration of justice including the magistrate's responsibility for deciding on paternity cases but there were certain duties about which he knew little or nothing. Just last year there had been a new statute concerning the new laws for dealing with the poor and William was grateful to Gervaise for providing him with notes on its requirements. As he understood it, he was to appoint an overseer for the poor in his district who would be responsible for raising the contribution for poor relief, fixed at a maximum of 2d per parish and even to consider the desirability of creating a poorhouse in the upper dales area. He thought this latter unlikely to be necessary. His duties could largely be carried out as an individual magistrate but attendance at the quarter sessions was also necessary. Gervaise had indicated that the necessity for him to attend the bench at Northallerton would be reduced as much as possible but there would be some occasions when it would be unavoidable.

All in all there was a good deal of responsibility upon his shoulders now but William was not afraid of this. He would have officers to undertake the various works he called for and the running of the farm from day to day was no longer a matter for him, with Joseph in total command of the situation, and he had determined to take Bess with him to Northallerton when he attended bench meetings leaving the capable Rosie to look after the Hall. It was time his wife was able to enjoy a little leisure and the thrill of investigating the shops in the big towns. Whilst musing on the pleasures of being accompanied by Bess on his judicial visits, he suddenly found himself confronted by a rushing stream. He was at Hestholme again and the bridge which he had declined to use on the previous day had now disappeared apart from a few crumbled remains of stone on either bank. He congratulated himself on his cautious decision but meanwhile he was faced with the daunting prospect of fording the rushing waters of the Bishopdale Beck. Only a brief inspection of the stream was necessary to convince him of the danger of that procedure. The waters, swollen by the recent heavy rain, were sweeping by at a tremendous speed. They would doubtless recede again within a day or so but he had to get home and this meant a long diversion up to West Burton, where there was another, and hopefully sound, bridge. There was nothing for it but to turn back, which he did, cursing the weather and the ruined bridge. And then, with a grin, he realised that it was now his responsibility to see to the repair, or more realistically the complete reconstruction, of that very bridge.

Oh well, he had to commence duty somewhere!

....

Death

"Nay, should I lie down I have a persuasion that I shall never rise!"

Queen Elizabeth expressed this explanation for her behaviour to her ladies in waiting and her actions complemented her words, as she alternately walked stiffly about her chamber or sat passively in her chair. She sat for long periods in silence, her mind given wholly to meditation, and refused to engage in conversation. She continued to refuse the medication which had been prescribed for her and which was urged upon her by her physicians, her women and visiting members of the Council, giving the explanation that she was beyond its help. For Queen Elizabeth knew that she was about to die. Was this not, after all, her climacteric year, her seventieth, in which, according to ancient lore, great changes could be expected? And so she sat in silent contemplation, preparing herself for this final event in her life. Just a few weeks before she had parted with the ring which symbolised her marriage to England. It had become so deeply embedded in the flesh of her finger that it had to be filed off, there being no other way to detach it. When, at this time, the Lord Admiral had asked her about the succession, she had mentioned no name but had replied enigmatically,

"My throne hath been the throne of kings: neither ought any other than my next heir to succeed me."

This circumlocution had been widely interpreted as referring to James, the King of Scotland and daughter of her former royal adversary, Mary Queen of Scots. As a result of this, many of the members of her nobility had become involved in secret communication with the Scottish King, seeking to win his favour against the day when he should succeed. When this became known to the Queen it had saddened her, as had the news of the death of one of her favourite friends, the Countess of Nottingham. The one person to whom she spoke and to whom she listened at length, was the Archbishop of Canterbury, John Whitgift, her ardent supporter for the whole of the thirty years since he had been appointed. Elizabeth seemed to find great consolation in his words and it was whilst she conversed with him that the deputation from the Council arrived. The party consisted of Sir Robert Cecil, son of her late and much-lamented advisor William Lord Burghley, Sir Thomas Egerton, Keeper of the Great Seal and the Lord High Admiral, Charles Howard, Earl of Nottingham. With their arrival, Whitgift excused himself, bidding his monarch be of good cheer and leaving the field to the ministers.

It was Nottingham who asked, in the name of the Council, what her mind was in the matter of the succession and she replied

"I have said that my throne was the throne of kings, and I would not that any base should succeed me."

But Robert Cecil needed complete clarification and asked her what these words meant. The answer which came was:

"I will that a king succeed me, and who but my kinsman the King of Scots."

The long wait for the expression of the Queen's will in this respect was now over to the relief of the deputation and indeed the whole Council, when the news was relayed to them. A few days later Elizabeth did lie down on her bed and, true to her word, she never rose again, dying on 24th March, 1603. A messenger, Sir Robert Carey, rode post haste to Scotland with the news and, on the streets of London, there burned bonfires that night to celebrate the beginning of a new age.

....

Joseph was cold, wet and bone weary as he gratefully entered the warmth of the house, after removing his boots at the door. The wrath of either his wife or his mother, had he failed to do this, would have been too terrible to endure and, as he had inspected those boots, he had been forced to admit that, on this occasion at least, they would have been fully justified in being angry. The land was in a poor state as a result of the regular night frosts followed by the daylight thaws, which produced treacherous conditions up on the fell tops. And that was where he had been all day helping Ned the shepherd to monitor and assist, where necessary, the sheep which were struggling to bring their lambs into this cruel world. It had been a foul winter, with endless snowfalls, some bitter frosts, then rain and finally, even now in April, more frosts and sleet to threaten the new generation of the flock. They had had losses already and Joseph feared there would be more unless the weather relented. But it showed no signs of doing so and it was quite possible that it could continue for some weeks longer. He sighed as he realised that this sort of winter was the price one paid in the dales for the verdant river meadows, the lush grass and the never-failing streams. Less practically there were also the lovely spring flowers and even a busy farmer could appreciate those, when he had the leisure.

Joseph padded into the warm kitchen, where the women folk were preparing the evening meal and he accepted a glass of spiced wine to warm him through. He reported to the ladies that the boys were still out there on the fells and might remain so for some time and then submerged himself in the heady beverage and fell into a reverie. He really was very grateful for the whole-hearted support of his sons in this difficult time. Perhaps that was silly. They were always a good support to him at any time and were both now well able to run the farm in his absence. He and Rosie were proud of them and Joseph was delighted that they were both bent on being farmers. The problem of course was that only the eldest, William, would inherit the Hall and some provision would have to be made for John. The matter was likely to become more pressing in that Rosie had told him she had detected the faint ringing of wedding bells in the air and Joseph himself had not been unaware of the time his younger son, John, had been spending with Gladys Telfit, daughter of a farmer from West Witton. Large though the Hall was, the arrival of another family would place a strain on their living space and it would be far better if John could find another place to farm. He had mentioned this problem to his father and William had nodded, smiled a little mysteriously and told him to wait awhile before trying to solve the matter. He gave the impression that there was some solution just around the corner and it was only a matter of time before he could reveal it. In the meantime he would divulge nothing further.

In fact he had relatively little conversation with his father about their over-all financial position. This was not because William was secretive; he would have been quite ready to discuss any matter pertaining to the family possessions but he knew that Joseph was not desperately interested. Joseph admitted this to himself. His abiding interest was the farm and its welfare and he would converse with his father for ever on that topic. Whenever John came home from Oxford, he and his father would indulge in long conversations on general philosophy, economic matters and politics to all of which Joseph listened with only half an ear, if indeed he listened at all. He freely acknowledged that their talks were on a different plane to his own understanding and he was content that it be so. Two academic minds were quite sufficient in one family, he considered, and he was content to converse on more down to earth matters and leave philosophising to others.

His father was a continual source of surprise to Joseph, however, for there were times when he opened up and revealed information which he had kept very close to his chest. A prime example of this had been at the party following his neice, Elizabeth's, wedding last year to John Alderson of Askrigg. Martha and Robert had been glad to accept the offer of Worton Hall for the wedding breakfast and it had been a splendid meeting of family and friends, lasting well on into the night for some. It had been during those latter hours of the celebration that Martha had pressed her father to tell the story of the emerald hair pin which had been given to her on her own wedding day. She had wanted to pass it on to Elizabeth but felt she could not do so until an explanation for its existence in the family had been given.

William had thought for a little while and then turned to Bess.

"I think we might venture to explain now my love," he said with a smile. "The old Queen has now been dead these twelve years or so and her successor would surely take no exception to the small part we played in his mother's life, even if he should ever hear of it, the which is doubtful. T'is ancient history now and no longer of any account in the world."

The listening family were now agog with amazement at hearing references to no less than three members of royalty who seemed to be associated with this family heirloom and they settled down eagerly to hear William's account. If there was initial disbelief, it soon disappeared as the story unfolded and was vouched for by Bess. The family looked at the older couple with new eyes as they learnt of their adventurous involvement in the attempted escape of the Scottish Queen; they began to appreciate the reason for the alienation of Robinsons and Metcalfes as they saw the bitterness on the face of Bess, when she recalled her older brother Kit and his violent death at the hands of Thomas. Then there was the episode of the exile to Durham, where William lay low until he was forced to take a stand of loyalty to Queen Elizabeth in the face of the rebel forces in the cathedral. John was particularly impressed by this part of the story and resolved to press his father for more detail at a later date. William finished his tale with the return to Worton in order to take over the farm from his uncle Joseph and his subsequent marriage to Bess and the family sat silently for a while, digesting this mass of new information. It was Martha who broke the silence.

"Yes, but the pin father. How did you come by the emerald pin and why did you tell me it was a gift for me, when I was not even thought of at that time?"

And so William explained about the incredible coincidence, when he came across Queen Mary's coach with the disabled horse.

"I knew her immediately I heard her voice from within the coach, but I was amazed that she had remembered me. She enquired after me as to whether I was married and had family and it was when I described my lovely little daughter to her that she brought out the pin and gave it to me to hold in safe keeping until you were ready for it. I think I chose a good time," he said, smiling at Robert and Martha, as they sat together on the settle. There was a slight pause and then Martha spoke.

"Thank you father for upholding that trust. I can now value the pin even more than I have done and yet I would be pleased, if you do not object, to pass it on to Elizabeth. I know she will value it and pass it on in her turn to her own family."

William assured her that this was exactly what he had hoped might happen and, with that matter disposed of, conversation flowed around the discoveries that had been made. John and Joseph remembered the illness which had laid the family low after their father's return from Stafford and other little bits and pieces of memory were fitted into the picture which had been revealed to them. In particular, an explanation had been provided for the continual animosity between the Metcalfes of Nappa and the Robinsons of Worton and this was something which worried Joseph more than a little.

It was true that the virulent hatred had disappeared with the death of Thomas; true too that Sir Christopher had become an agreeable neighbour; but the young Sir Thomas was an unknown quantity in this respect. He must have been subjected to a constant attitude of animosity for the Robinson family from his father and, whilst there had admittedly been no manifestation of this feeling in his behaviour so far, he had acquired a dreadful reputation for wildness and irresponsibility. Joseph now thought of him as a potential menace to the continued peaceful existence they enjoyed, the more so because of something which had happened some three or four years ago. William had lent some money to Sir Thomas.

It was not often that Joseph presumed to question his father's financial arrangements but on this occasion he had spoken out. There had been a coincidence, an unfortunate one to Joseph's mind, when a large dividend had come into his father's hands, as a result of the successful return of some trading ship or other, and at the same time it became known that Sir Thomas was seeking a loan of a thousand pounds. The security offered was a mortgage upon an estate in Raydale, beyond Semerwater. William and Joseph had taken the time to ride up the dale and look at the property and William recalled that he and Kit had once visited this little side valley on one of their youthful expeditions. It had been a thriving farm at that time but now it was empty and desolate. Raydale House itself was in reasonable repair but some of the outbuildings were in need of attention. The tenancy of the estate had been granted to Sir Thomas by the new monarch, King James, in appreciation for the welcome and support accorded him by the Metcalfe family on his accession to the throne. There had actually been much amusement and shaking of heads amongst the dales folk at the behaviour of the Metcalfe clan on this occasion. It seemed to them like a blatant currying of favour as the assembled Metcalfe family had ridden north to greet him and assure him of their loyalty. The new king had been invited to lodge at Nappa on his protracted progress into England, in order to indulge his well-known passion for hunting. The invitation had been declined but not forgotten and after rewarding those supporters who had been quicker off the mark than the Metcalfes, their turn had eventually come with the award of this lease in 1609. It was a signal honour, of which Sir Thomas was very proud but his immediate requirement was for money rather than the kudos of farming a royal estate. He had inherited all of the propensities of his family for living beyond his means; he was desperate for ready money, hence his willingness to immediately mortgage his prestigious lease.

With nobody present, William and Joseph were able to look around at leisure and formed the opinion that with just a little work the place could be transformed into a good working farm. Joseph had assured himself that this was an eminently reasonable thing to consider. The valley was beautifully sheltered, with good grazing, and the house well situated under the shelter of a limestone cliff. He could well have been happy in a place like this, had it not been for his inheritance of Worton Hall, which was of course far superior. No, his worry was not the value of the security but the reliability of the mortgagee and he had expressed his doubts on this subject. William had glossed over this aspect of the deal. As he said, failure to repay on the part of Sir Thomas would result in the acquisition of a splendid farm by the Robinson family and in the mean time the interest on the loan would be a useful one hundred pounds per year. The presentiment of trouble, which Joseph had experienced at this time, had now been augmented by the failure of Sir Thomas to pay any interest over the last three years. His father had once again played down the difficulty and assured Joseph that all would be resolved in a satisfactory manner when the time came. Joseph wished that John were here to discuss the matter with his father, for he felt that William would take much more notice of his elder brother's opinion than of his own. Just recently he had been apprised of reasons for the strong antipathy between the two houses and this had re-awakened his fears. But then he shrugged his shoulders. He could surely trust his worldly-wise father to continue to navigate their family fortune in a satisfactory fashion. He had a superb record after all!

The daydreaming was interrupted by noises in the entrance hall as the boys clattered in and shed their boots in accordance with the strict disciplinary code of the ladies of the house. That noise had also served to rouse William from his study and he emerged to join the rest of the family. All this coincided with the announcement that the meal was ready and there was barely time for the younger men to splash some water over their dirty hands and faces before sitting down to the welcome repast. It was not the smartest of dinner parties but it was a contented one, redolent with the feeling of satisfaction born of achievement. There would probably have been a good deal to talk about after the meal had it not been for the fact that then working men were simply too exhausted and opted to retire early to their beds. It was an ending not dissimilar to many other endings of the day in the working life of the farm.

································

It had been three years now since Joseph had admitted to himself his misgivings about his father's deal with Sir Thomas and his fears had turned out to have been justified. The redemption date for the mortgage had long passed and not a penny piece had been received from the Metcalfe purse. Six years interest owed and there had been no offer to redeem the property by a return of the capital lent. It was a bad situation and Joseph hoped that his father was going to do something about it. But not all the happenings of those three years had been bad. There had been a family wedding and simultaneously a solution to a family problem.

Rosie had been quite right in her predictions of a romance between her second son and his sweetheart from West Witton. John had married Gladys Telfit at the end of the last year, 1616, to the great pleasure of both families. Joseph was a little surprised that his younger son had been so willing to delay his marriage for so long, but when the great news was revealed by William he understood perfectly. The farmer at Thornton Aiskew, in Thornton Rust, had relinquished his tenancy, as William had long ago known was a possibility. Being the kind of landlord he was, he had placed no pressure upon old George Slade to quit his holding but he had hinted to John that it could well come about soon and that, when it did, the farm was to be given to him and his new wife. There was of course great joy throughout the family that a suitable home and living had been provided for the young couple but for William it had an even greater significance, for this was the hereditary family home of the Robinsons. He knew that it was here that his own father, John, and his uncle, Joseph, had been born. He did not know for sure but he believed that his grandfather, who he had never known, had also been born here and so it was traditional Robinson territory and, whilst it had remained in the ownership of the family, it was at last going to be inhabited and farmed by Robinsons. Compared to Worton Hall the land of Thornton Aiskew was of small moment but it was the history of it that compelled this strong feeling of completion. It was probably only at this moment of satisfaction that William fully appreciated the feelings of hereditary deprivation which the Metcalfes had experienced over the loss of Worton Hall.

Chapter 11: The Siege

This was the final insult, which could not be overlooked. William's patience had been wearing thin now for the best part of the year. He had applied to Sir Thomas Metcalfe repeatedly for the payment of the outstanding loan together with the interest, all unpaid as yet, and his efforts had met with no success. If his letters had received any acknowledgements at all, they had been casual to the point of being dismissive. Their general tenor had been that it was not convenient for the loan to be repaid at this time and the last appeal had been met with a blank refusal to pay. It was suggested that Mr Robinson apply again in two years time, when the matter might be considered anew. The implication that his financial affairs were of no moment compared to those of the lofty Knight of Nappa incensed William and caused him to put into action a plan to force the issue for once and all. He called Joseph into his study to discuss the matter.

Joseph was relieved that his father was at last going to take decisive action in recovering his money and, although surprised by his scheme, he was a willing supporter of the plan. In essence it was to take over the property on the grounds that had been forfeit through lack of redemption, but to do so in such a way as to present no doubt about the finality of the move. He wanted Joseph and Rosie to take up residence in Raydale House, conduct repairs and make the farm work again. He was at pains to assure his son that this would be a temporary expedient and that his eventual reinstatement as manager and heir of Worton would not be long delayed.

William pointed out that, with the completion of shearing, this would be a suitable time to hand over the running of the farm to young William, which would be an excellent trial for him. In the meantime, everyone in the family would assist him in the task of rebuilding and restocking the farm at Raydale. Whether or not the family would retain ownership of the lease was immaterial. It would be easier to sell again if the estate was made profitable. To Joseph, this was a challenge he would enjoy meeting and a welcome change from the routine of managing Worton, fulfilling though that task might be. They decided to make another trip to Raydale together and assess more accurately what would need to be done. In the meantime, William would inform

Sir Thomas officially of his proposal to effect the take over.

They had made this exploration and returned with definite plans for improvements, which were studied and costed when the crucial visit was made. It was heralded by a clattering of hooves in the courtyard and then a furious pounding on the door, which when opened revealed an angry looking Sir Thomas Metcalfe, who demanded to see Mr William Robinson immediately. He was received by William in his study and invited to take a seat, a courtesy which was ignored.

"I do not stay long in your house Robinson," was the opening sally. "I come merely to warn you against further trespass on my land at Raydale. It has been reported to me that you have been there making free with my property, taking measurements and generally conducting yourself as being the owner. I tell you, Sir, that this must stop and you must abandon any foolish plan to appropriate a property which is mine by right of a royal lease."

"You are mistaken, Sir Thomas. The property is no longer yours; you have lost that lease by default. Even at this stage, however, I am prepared to give up my right to its ownership if you were to make immediate repayment of the loan and the interest due to me, the which has been unpaid these last seven years. I go further and would consider any part payment by instalment, providing it is regularly honoured, until the debt is cleared."

The knight nearly exploded with rage.

"How dare you, Sir! The noble house of Metcalfe is not accustomed to bargaining with tradesmen and other lower orders. If I am in your debt, it will be discharged at my convenience and I brook no more interference with my property."

"I am sorry you cannot be persuaded to see reason, Sir Thomas." William's resolve was only heightened by this further insult. "My action in assuming the lease of Raydale is taken out of consideration for you, as being the least embarrassing course of action. I cannot think that the noble family of Metcalfe would be pleased if I took you to Court of Chancery, where debtors receive little consideration; far better that I simply take Raydale in complete cancellation of your financial liability."

"Be damned to your consideration, Sir! I leave you with the warning that if you or any of your agents set foot on my property I shall see that they are evicted with whatever force is necessary and that includes force of arms, Sir, force of arms!"

Manifestly enraged, the knight swept out of the room, let himself out of the house and galloped off in the direction of Nappa. William had followed him into the courtyard and watched his departure with a grim smile. Unsettling though this meeting had been, he was glad it had happened. Everything was now in the open, the gloves were off and if his resolve was to be tested then so be it. But of course it was not simply a matter of his own resolve; his son and daughter in law had to be considered and so Joseph was summoned to a meeting in the study, where he received an account of the confrontation. He tended to dismiss the threats of violence as being uttered in the heat of the moment, not to be followed up by serious action but William demurred.

"I think if you had witnessed his behaviour and heard the tones in which his threats were made, you might be more concerned. I agree that it would be foolish in the extreme for him to undertake any such action but he is not a man to always act within reason. I think it would be unwise for Rosie to accompany you to Raydale until we see what his reaction really will be. We might persuade Robert and John to spend some time with you, as both a matter of prudence and as a help in the work on the house. I am sure you would want that to be in a fit state before Rosie joins you in any case. In the meantime I shall write to the Sheriff in York in my capacity as a Justice of the Peace and warn him of the possibility of trouble."

It was only when he heard his father make that statement about contacting the civil authorities in the county, that Joseph realised how seriously he was taking the threats. He began to realise that his bland assumption, that all would be well, was perhaps ill considered and, no, he certainly did not want his wife to be placed in any peril. On the other hand he was not going to be terrorised into relinquishing the rightful ownership of the estate and he bethought him that some stout-hearted helpers might be of great value. He decided to ride up to Appersett directly and consult his brother in law, Robert. Meanwhile, William had been recasting his own thoughts about the menace posed by Sir Thomas and his threats of violence. He decided to summon help now in order to prevent any trouble, rather than take punitive action after it had occurred. He returned to his study and wrote to the Sheriff at York, requesting the raising of local militia in order to suppress a likely unlawful assembly and disturbance of the peace. He explained to that official that the local constable would be totally incapable of dealing with a body of armed men and troops would be needed to contain them. He wrote too to the chief

Constable at Northallerton, informing him of the situation and the requesting that he forward his letter to the Sheriff as quickly as possible. Carefully sealing both letters he rode into Aysgarth and sought out the Constable, ordering him to ride at once to Northallerton. This done, he felt he ought to be able to relax but found that he couldn't. Was he justified in causing so much trouble? Of course it was the Metcalfe who was the basic cause of the problem but was he handling things in the right way?

It was too late now to change his mind for it was all arranged. Both John and Robert were to accompany Joseph to Raydale and take possession of the house. It was better that there be no delay and so on the next morning, at an early hour, a wagon set off loaded with provisions and tools, some useful balks of timber and a cow trailing along behind. The men were universal in their demand for fresh milk on a morning. John had ridden down to join his father as he set off, and they met with Robert at a prearranged place on the road near Buttersett. Joseph was startled to see that Robert had brought a longbow and a quiver full of arrows.

"I have two questions for you Robert," he said. "Do you really think it necessary to be armed and if so, can you really use it?"

"Impertinent man!" replied Robert. "I am no ancient hero from Agincourt, perhaps, but I can bend strongly and discharge with good accuracy. You may be glad of my precaution if we are attacked by the Metcalfe."

There was much jocularity about the age of the weapon and its place in the armament of the modern man, when the arquebus and musket was widely employed to greater effect, but Robert insisted upon its value. He claimed that it was a much more reliable weapon, there being no chance of a misfire, and its relative silence could be of advantage in skirmishing. Joseph and John looked at each other in silence for a moment before Joseph said

"I see you take the threat seriously, Robert, and perhaps you are right to do so. But we must be careful in our response to any move against us. We would all be horrified if any death should occur, my father most particularly. Better we lie low and simply bar them from entry to the house. If indeed there is an assault upon us then we shall be justified in using appropriate force in defence but that is all."

Joseph went on to say that his father had already alerted the Sheriff in York to the possibility of trouble and would not hesitate to call in the armed forces to protect them and suppress any violent action which Metcalfe would undertake.

"Aye, just so they arrive in time to save us," said a thoughtful John.

It was a beautiful summer's morning as they drove along the track on the west bank of the lake. The air was clear and their destination of Raydale could be seen, although not the actual house, which was hidden by a fold of the hills. John drew his companion's attention to a rider, who could be seen on the opposite bank of the lake. He had been using the track across the shoulder of the fell towards Stalling Busk but had now reined in and appeared to be watching them. Suddenly he turned his horse and made off back along the track, soon disappearing down the hill towards Bainbridge. Joseph expressed his opinion that they had probably been shadowed since their departure from Worton and, now that their destination was no longer in doubt, he was reporting back to Nappa. The tell tale presence of a milking cow was a good guide to their intentions to make a long stay and so Sir Thomas would soon be in a position to take action, if he so decided.

Having arrived at Raydale House, the first task was to make the place habitable but also defensible. John was set to work cleaning the rooms of the accumulated rubbish of many years' desertion, which included the sweeping up of numerous cobwebs, animal droppings and fragments of birds' nests which had dropped down the chimney. He made a good attempt to clean up the kitchen and wash down the ancient but serviceable table which had been left there and, after cleaning out the fireplace, he laid a fire ready for any cooking which might be attempted that evening. Meanwhile, his father and uncle had examined the fabric of the walls of the dwelling and set about repairing any defects. The walls appeared to be sound enough but the door was in a sad condition, the wood having rotted around the hinges. Clearly a new door had to be made and Joseph set about this at once, using timber they had brought with them as well as sound pieces from the old door and some timbers discovered in the outbuildings. Robert had climbed up onto the roof and examined the slates, several of which had slid down exposing the roof timbers beneath. He was relieved to find that the structure was basically sound and set about restoring the tiles to their correct positions. Those that were broken he replaced by scavenging from the old byre roof and quite soon he had produced a roof which was at least weather proof, even if a little patched and untidy.

They worked hard and unceasingly until John emerged from the house with a lunchtime plate of cheese and bread with ale to wash it down. They sat outside the door enjoying the sunshine and gazing far down the valley towards Semerwater. It really was a beautiful situation, the house being placed in a sheltered position, close to a forty-foot high limestone cliff and with a commanding view of the whole valley. Nothing stirred, but then they had hardly expected any contact to be made by the Metcalfes so soon. Nonetheless, they restarted work with a feeling of some urgency, as it was borne in upon them how isolated they were up here, the nearest dwellings being at Marsett and out of sight of the house.

When he had completed his unaccustomed and thoroughly detested domestic chores, John joined the older men outside and assisted his uncle Robert in contriving to protect the well. It was situated a few yards in front of the house, to the left of the doorway. They had tested the water by lowering a bucket and sampling the contents when drawn up. There seemed to be no contamination from green slime or other deposits and a cautious sip or two suggested that it was drinkable. It was essential that they protect their water supply, given the possibility of interference from the Metcalfe clan, and Robert set about constructing a wall which would enclose a passage from the door to the well. It was a huge task and one in which he welcomed the help of John, who transported stone from the debris at the foot of the limestone cliff behind the house. There were also fragments of stone nearer to hand which Robert made use of but such was the length of the wall necessary to reach the well that huge amounts were needed and their hands were scraped raw and bloody by the time darkness fell and still the wall was not long enough.

All through the day each man had been keeping his own watch on the valley but no person had been seen and, at nightfall, they considered it unnecessary to keep a watch. Perhaps, however, it was not strange that, despite their exhaustion, none of them passed an unbroken night of sleep. The following morning dawned as pleasantly as the previous day and they were all up and at work as soon as possible. There was still no sign of movement at the bottom of the valley but there was an air of tension about them now, as if they knew that something would surely happen that day. Steadily they worked and by mid-morning Jospeh had completed the new door. He engaged the help of the others to hang it in place and after goose grease had been applied to the hinges it opened and closed in a satisfactory manner. There was no refinery of smart handle provided but Joseph had constructed a strong bar to slide into the recess he had cut into the wall. The whole thing was very stoutly built and he was congratulated by the others on its solidity, if not its decorative appearance.

They had a break for a meal and then all resumed work upon the wall. It was shortly after this that the band of riders was discerned, entering the valley. It was disconcerting to see so many, two dozen or more, and all proceeding purposefully towards the house. It was a long climb for them and so, whilst time allowed, John made haste to draw as much water as could be stored within the house. Sadly there was no time to complete the wall but at least the well was partly concealed and they could but hope that the invaders would not notice it immediately.

It was time now to withdraw inside and bolt the door. Each took station at a window and awaited the arrival of the party. The horses were strung out and quite blown, when they breasted the final rise, so that the first arrivals simply sat and stared at the old house without moving until they were joined by Sir Thomas himself. He pushed his way to the front of the group and hailed the house.

"Robinson, I have come to take possession of my property," he called. "You must quit the place at once and return to your home. No harm shall come to you if you do as I say; you will be allowed to depart unmolested but I warn you that I shall use force to eject you if you do not comply with my wishes."

There was a slight pause and then Joseph answered from behind the window.

"No, Sir Thomas, I stay here. This house is now owned by my father, Mr William Robinson, and it is my home. I will not leave at your behest nor indeed for any other."

"I shall lose patience unless you leave this instant," came the reply. "Now, I shall be generous and give you five minutes. Five minutes to assemble your possessions and then deliver over the house to me. Otherwise I shall let loose my men."

"If you offer violence to us, Sir Thomas, you will be breaking the law and will render yourself liable to prosecution at the hands of the Sheriff. Meantime you shall not pass this door."

Joseph spoke with a firmness born from his annoyance at the high-handed attitude of this arrogant man, who thought he could force through his every wish against all reason and moral right. That resolution was obvious from his steady tone and the knight could not doubt but that he meant every word. He turned to the leader of his men.

"Break down that door," he ordered and a few men dismounted to carry out his instruction. They hammered ineffectually with their fists for a while but then one of them produced an axe. He swung some mighty blows with this and was unpleasantly surprised at his lack of immediate success. He resumed more scientifically and was rewarded with some splinters of wood. As he paused to take breath, Joseph spoke quietly to him through the door.

"T'will be a long tiring task for you, my friend, and, should you make the smallest hole, there will be a pitchfork for your eye. Be sure I will keep my word on't."

The assailant renewed his attack but with noticeably less enthusiasm and eventually he stopped and handed over his axe to another man. Again Joseph uttered his warning and to reinforce the point, he had Robert and John brandish their wicked two pronged forks at their respective windows. The man stepped back, unwilling to subject himself to this risk, but in truth little impression had been made upon this solid door and even if the outer boards had been destroyed, there were solid timbers behind them that would withstand hours and hours of axe work. There was a bellow from Sir Thomas:

"A battering ram. Find a timber big enough and we will batter down that door no matter how thick the wood."

But there were no timbers to use. All such pieces of wood had been painstakingly collected and brought into the house and Joseph was grateful that he had been persuaded of the seriousness of the Metcalfe threat by his father and had taken all these precautions. He still could hardly believe that he was in the middle of this violent conflict, besieged in a totally unlawful manner by a man who was oblivious to the eventual consequences of his actions, whatever the result of his attack. And these were no reivers or brigands. This was the retinue of a knight of the realm, supposedly a stalwart upholder of the peace of his country. It beggared belief that he was arrogant enough and old-fashioned enough to believe that he could bend or bludgeon his neighbours to his will, irrespective of the illegality of his actions. Surely he realised that those days of suppression of the people by force were over with the passing of the powers of the old medieval barons? It must be that he was a man led by his rage and hatred of his historical enemies, the Robinsons. But, incredible though it was, he had gone ahead and launched this attack upon the house.

It had not been unobserved. Just over a half mile away on the slopes of Faw ridge, a solitary watcher had been keeping the farmhouse under observation, as he had been instructed to do. Looking down and across the Raydale beck, he had noted the preparations made by the Robinson men, followed the progress and arrival of the party from Nappa and had watched intently what had followed. He saw the sun glint upon the upraised axe and even heard the dull thud of its blows upon the door. There was no need to wait longer, indeed there was an imperative haste to take home the intelligence he had gathered, and so he mounted his horse and totally unseen by the company on the opposite side of the valley, he made straight for Marsett, the trail back into Bainbridge and thence to Worton. His master, Mr Robinson's, worst fears had been realised and there was need to send for help.

There was now something of an impasse as defenders and besiegers glared at each other powerless to achieve anything. John had been gazing intently from a window when suddenly there was a sharp crack of stone and splinters rained down on him from the mullion. It had been struck by a quarrel fired by a crossbowman who lurked near the byre door. John had missed death by inches and suddenly this adventure was no longer fun. He kept his head as far out of sight as possible now but still tried to observe the activities of the besieging party.

Suddenly there was a cry of triumph from outside. When they peered out cautiously, they saw a man holding aloft the wooden bucket from the well.

"Well now, my pretty gentlemen, and how will 'ee fare without water? We shall deny you the well and so thirst ye out."

The man was startled by a great blow, the force of which knocked the bucket out of his hand, and was horrified to see a long goose feathered arrow sticking in the wooden pail, just a few inches from where he had been holding it.

"And no more will it serve for you my man," called Robert, another arrow already notched in his bow. "The next man who approaches that water will be pinned to the wall."

But this was not an equality of advantage, as Joseph well knew. Although it was a nuisance, it was perfectly possible for the besieging men to climb down the hill and drink at the beck, whereas they were totally cut off from any supply. The water John had drawn was all they had and just a little milk left over from the morning milking. Food they had in reasonable quantity, but without water they were doomed to eventual defeat. Joseph immediately organised a rationing of their supply and prayed that help would arrive before they succumbed. The one happy result of Robert's quick reaction with his bow was that the attackers were now aware of the fact that their opponents were armed and willing to use those arms. What had started out in many minds as an enjoyable excursion into the country to perform a simple eviction (which might be accompanied by the opportunity for a bit of looting), had now turned into something a good deal more serious, with the possibility of harm coming to any one of them. There was certainly no stomach now for an assault upon the house and it was a relief to know that Sir Thomas was happy to entertain the idea of a siege. Just so long as the besiegers themselves did not become too hungry in the process.

The afternoon wore on into evening and, as dusk started to fall, camp fires were lit. The men were clearly settling in for a long and patient wait, happy in the knowledge that thirst would eventually win the day for them without undue effort on their part. Sir Thomas left for the comforts of Nappa before dark, having first entered into a conference with a young man of gentlemanly bearing whom he was clearly designating as leader in his absence. None of the Robinsons could identify this person but were inclined to mark him down as a kinsman of the Metcalfe. Inside the house, they had decided to do without a light, as this might be too dangerous, but they portioned out the food and a measure of water each, whilst keeping an eye on activities outside. At one point there was an agonised bellow, a thrashing about in the byre and then silence. The three looked at each other in horror and rage. Their cow had just been slaughtered and was presumably being butchered even now to feed this miniature army camped outside. Joseph was furious. By God but he would seek full reparation if he could only get out of this situation! He grinned faintly as he bethought him that the cow was actually rather old and would provide a very stringy and tough beef for the hopeful men. It was very short sighted of them to slaughter the beast, as they had now lost a valuable supply of milk. It had been short sighted of himself of course, not to have brought the cow into the house for protection; he simply had not thought of it. He was continually reminded of his omission during the rest of the evening, as the smell of roasting beef permeated the air around the farm, but it was not the matter of food which really troubled him. He had estimated another two days supply of water at the most and only on the very barest of rations. If the siege persisted beyond then they were in serious trouble.

....

In York the Sheriff was musing over the recent problem with which he had been faced. He had been astounded to receive a request to raise the militia to quell an episode of civil disturbance; a matter which apparently could not be dealt with by the local constabulary. He would have been inclined to regard this request as totally unwarranted, a gross exaggeration of some petty village outburst of lawlessness, had it not be for its source. The request for military aid had come from none other than William Robinson, Justice of the Peace for upper Wensleydale, a man who he had met several times at the quarter assizes, and he had been impressed by this conscientious and level-headed magistrate. He was certainly not a man to exaggerate wildly and, if he thought there was need for armed intervention in, where was it now – ah yes Worton – well then it must be arranged. The very fact that the Sheriff and his officers were not sure just exactly where Worton was, except at the far end of a far flung dale, could account for the fact that no hint of this disturbance had reached the ears of the authorities in York or Northallerton.

On a second reading of the letter, he had been struck by the diplomacy and courtesy employed. Mr Robinson knew full well that the raising of the militia was no longer in the hands of county sheriffs, that responsibility having passed to the Lord Lieutenant or his deputies, but he also knew that his request would be taken more seriously, if it were passed on through the office of the sheriff, and furthermore he knew that one such deputy lieutenant resided in the city of York. The Sheriff was gratified that Mr Robinson had not seen fit to go straight over his head in this matter, as he might well have done. He was glad to be able to help in expediting the request and, at an appointment with the deputy this morning, they had thrashed out the logistics and arranged for a company of fifty men and two officers to set out immediately for Wensleydale. A fast riding messenger was despatched to take the news to Worton.

The morning dawned bright and sunny in Raydale and it was clearly going to be hot on this, the third day of the siege. Joseph looked at the rapidly diminishing supply of water with alarm. It would definitely be exhausted by the end of the day and there was no way they could reach the well without being cut down, as had been threatened by the investing party. He knew his father had written to the Sheriff a day or so before they had come up to the house but there was no way of knowing if his request would be met or how long it would take to arrive if he had been successful. What was it from York? A two or three day march? They could be here today, more likely tomorrow.

If they came at all. There had been little or no activity within the ranks of the Metcalfe party. They were apparently content to await the inevitable surrender when the water ran out and he shuddered to think how they might be treated in that event. Maybe a fighting escape would be the best plan, even if it was a forlorn hope.

During the morning there was a visit from Sir Thomas, who repeated his demand that they surrender the building to him and promising to curtail the activities of his men if they did so whilst he was here. Receiving only a curt refusal, he rode away again with the taunt that another day or two of thirst would make them change their minds.

At Worton Hall William was awaiting anxiously the help he had solicited, hoping that it would arrive in time. The messenger had come during the previous day with the welcome news that the militia were on their way but would they arrive before it was too late? For the hundredth time William examined his conscience over this awful development in the matter of the Metcalfe loan. Had he been totally honest in his decision to appropriate the house? It was certainly an option open to him under the law but was it the right one? Should he have relied upon the due but slow process of the law and referred the matter to the Court of Chancery? That might have taken years to reach a conclusion but he could afford it; they were wealthy enough to wait for the Court to rule. The problem was that and even then the money might not have been available, if for example the knight opted to go bancquaroutta, as had happened in several other cases to his knowledge. In some instances debtors had invested all the money they could borrow and then declared themselves bankrupt. They went to debtor's prison but could live high on the income from their investments whilst their debts remained unpaid. William had been determined that this should not happen to his loan. His error had been in completely underestimating the reaction of Sir Thomas and not putting in adequate safeguards before taking over the house. As it was, he had subjected his family to a grave risk to their safety. If harm came to Joseph, Robert and John he would never be forgiven by Bess and the other ladies. What is worse, he would never be able to forgive himself.

Young William could see that his grandfather was torturing himself with worry and he made a decision. Having assured himself that his absence from the farm would not cause a problem, he saddled up and quietly rode off without anyone knowing that he had gone. He didn't want to make explanations or be talked out of his little plan but he did leave a note to inform them what he was doing. He rode to Stalling Busk but then cut up Cragdale in order to approach the house from the east. When he estimated that he was level with the house, he dismounted and led his horse up the steep side of Billinside Moor. There was now a steep and tricky descent through thick woodland and so he tied his horse to a branch and made his way on foot until he reached the brink of the limestone clint above the house. Here, for the first time, he was able to see the besiegers' camp and took heart from the fact that they had not yet taken the house. Working his way to a point immediately behind the house, and making sure he was within sight of a window. He rose to his feet and filling his lungs hailed loudly:

"Ho there, the house! T'is I, William who calls you. Is all well with you?"

He watched intently and thought he discerned a cautious movement at the window. Immediately there came an answering hail from his father.

"William we are all well but what do ye do here lad? Have a care not to be taken by these rogues."

"I come to tell you father that the militia is on its way. They will be with you on the morrow so hold fast. I must go now!" He had spotted a small group of men working their way to a point of the cliff where it would be possible to climb up and decided to make a hasty retreat. He soon reached his horse again and galloped off to safety. He made good time getting home to Worton and reported to a relieved grandfather that all was well with the Robinson party, although they were still besieged by a large group of men. There had been no sign of Sir Thomas, which was a pity, as he might have called off his men once he heard of the impending arrival of the troops. But the men had heard and a council of war was held. There were some who, alarmed at the prospect of facing troops, were in favour of giving up the siege now and returning to Nappa. But their leader reminded them of the likely reaction of their master should they return without staying until the last possible moment. They had time, he said, to effect something against the occupants, if only someone could come up with an idea. And someone did have an idea.

Within the house spirits had been raised by the news William had brought although it did nothing to assuage the thirst which was already beginning to make itself felt by virtue of the very strict rationing which Joseph had imposed. John in particular was suffering and Joseph determined to secretly reduce his own ration until relief came. From what he had surmised that relief was not likely to arrive until sometime on the following day and it was too much to hope that the besieging party would abandon their position before the last moment. It would be desperate but it could be done. They would hold out. But the hours dragged slowly by and the heat of the day made conditions worse, despite the thickness of the walls, which generally kept the inside of the building cool. It was with relief that they noted the evening shades starting to fall and they apportioned out the little remaining food and last drops of water. The food was more than enough for it was difficult to eat with their mouths as dry as they were. Please God they could survive another day without water. Perhaps it would rain and leaks would provide a few drops. But it didn't. They settled down for the night, taking turns to watch as had happened each night so far.

It was Robert who was on watch in the early dawn when it happened. He thought it had been his imagination at first but then there came an unmistakeable noise. It was the sound of stone scraping on stone and it was above his head. Grasping his pitchfork, he silently ascended the crooked stair into the chamber above. There was only the one room up there and they had disregarded it as a source of danger. The two little windows were merely slits, through which not even a child could have passed. But something was happening up there and Robert guessed what it was. Standing quietly under the roof he felt a smattering of dust fall onto his head as a tile was levered sideways. A small hole had already been made and now an arm and shoulder were thrust through the gap seeking to enlarge it. Robert did not hesitate. Lancing his pitchfork upwards he impaled the limb and was rewarded with a howl of pain. The arm jerked free but its owner was unbalanced and rolled down the roof to fall heavily on the stone paving below. There was noise as his friends dragged him away out of sight but no further assault was launched upon the roof. Nonetheless the defenders were now all alerted and maintained a joint watch until the full light of day dawned and another day began with its promise of torture through thirst.

It was in the mid morning that the officer galloped into the yard at Worton, to be received rapturously by the Robinson family. He had merely called to ascertain the latest situation and had left his force marching along the road to Bainbridge. It would take them another two hours or so to reach the farm but he had accepted the offer of a guide in the shape of William for the last part of their journey and the two rode off to catch up with the marching column.

It was midday and the heat was stifling. Whilst Joseph and Robert were suffering, their case was not as bad as John's who had now lapsed into a coma from which a delirious raving emanated from time to time. There was also the possibility of an outright assault on the house as a result of the events of the night. The man who fell from the roof had died from a broken neck and his friends were infuriated. They were now desperate for revenge and were prepared to consider rushing the door with axes and taking casualties in their attempts to break it down. It was a matter of someone summoning up the courage to make the first move and their intentions were becoming clear to Joseph and Robert. The latter notched an arrow in preparation for the attack but Joseph had noticed movement and a splash of colour at the bottom of the hill and he laid a restraining arm upon his shoulder. Then, going to a window, he hailed the men outside and bade them look down towards the beck where a file of men, led by three horsemen, were crossing and making to ascend the hill.

"It is all over now," he called. "If you value your freedom you must depart now."

"Not quite over yet," came an enraged shout and the quarrel from a cross-bow came through the window and hit Joseph on the shoulder. He staggered back clutching his shoulder with blood spurting through his fingers. Robert leapt to the window and discharged an arrow at the retreating form of the bowman but missed his aim. The arrow however did have the effect of speeding the departure of their enemy and Robert turned his attention to Joseph. He ripped off his shirt and tore it into a rough bandage, which when tied tightly arrested the flow of blood. It had been agonising for Joseph but he knew that it was necessary and suffered the operation with gasps of pain. When he was assured of the safety of his brother-in-law, Robert wrenched open the door and rushed out to obtain a bucket of water, taking it straight to the recumbent form of John. He splashed it over his face, making sure that some of the liquid entered his mouth and then passed the remainder to Joseph who drank greedily. Then it was Robert's turn and he drained the rest before rushing out again to replenish the bucket. John was responding slowly to his first intake of water and Robert supported him, whilst feeding him some more in carefully small quantities. Then it was Joseph's turn again and in this manner Robert was kept so busy that he did not notice the arrival of the militia officer and William. It was a relief to let everything go into the hands of his rescuers who made the necessary arrangements to transport the injured Joseph and the still-weakened John back to Worton Hall. The body of the man who had fallen from the roof had been abandoned by his friends as they made their hasty retreat and that too was to be transported down to Bainbridge.

And so ended the siege of Raydale, which had taken four days and one life as well as inflicting a grievous, if not life threatening injury, which would leave a lifetime legacy.

Epilogue

William was not feeling well. His problems had begun a few months ago shortly after he had embarked upon an ill-advised stint of hard work on the farm. It was all because of this feeling of guilt which he felt and which he was trying to expiate by helping out the son who had been crippled on his behalf. Joseph had recovered from his injury but had been left with a left arm which hung at an odd angle and could bear little in the way of weight. He had accepted this physical disability philosophically and brushed aside his father's heartfelt apologies, saying that what had happened at Raydale had been a necessary stand against the tyranny of their neighbour. His father's fears about the risk of losing his investment, by taking the course of a necessarily prolonged legal process, had been supported by events following the siege. The matter had gone to court and Sir Thomas had been fined a large sum of money for his actions, as a result of which he had been compelled to mortgage the entire Nappa estate to meet his debts. So extensive were these debts that the generally accepted view was that he would never be able to discharge that mortgage. He had left Nappa Hall and was now living temporarily with a kinsman, Ottiwell Metcalfe of Swinithwaite, who, it was suspected, had actually taken a significant part in the organisation of the siege, and whose son had probably been a member of the besieging party. Since the court case they had heard nor seen nothing of him and were content to let things stay that way.

It was ironic however to realise that the retention of the Raydale estate had not proved to be successful as far as the family were concerned. John went so far as to say that he never wanted to see the place ever again and even Robert was unenthusiastic about taking it over. He had now inherited his father's farm and was not inclined to move. It was comparatively difficult to sell the lease for two reasons. In the first place it was rather remote for the taste of most people. Secondly there was the stigma attached to the farm after the notorious siege and the death of a Metcalfe retainer and so the farm remained empty and the land unused. William was not too concerned as he felt that someone would take it in the end.

Now life had returned to something like normality at Worton Hall, with Joseph relying heavily upon his fit young son, William, the aforementioned help from his father now having been abandoned. He had been quite cross about the old man's attempts to carry out work which was really beyond him and which had resulted in his current bout of ill health. It had begun with a pain in the left arm, which William had put down to lifting some large bales of wool. Then there had been some chest pain and a local physician had suggested that it was likely that he had strained his heart. He recommended rest and a total cessation of physical labour. William had grumbled a little but Bess had enthusiastically endorsed the doctor's prescription and fussed over him, making sure he did not attempt anything too strenuous and eventually he came to appreciate the arguments in favour of a life of leisure, confining himself to his correspondence and legal work. This had seemed to be working well until last week, when he had experienced a really bad attack of chest pain after partaking of a large meal. He had realised at once that this was not an episode of indigestion and wisely taken to his bed of his own volition. He was there now and had been told to remain there even during the party, which had been arranged to celebrate John's visit from Oxford. Despite his disappoint-ment, William was secretly glad that he did not have to rise and dress but could play host in his own chamber to the various members of the family. He felt so tired these days but it was a pleasant tiredness and he enjoyed the short visits of family and friends.

Bess seemed to have put on a grand party this time he thought, as he lay in bed sipping at a glass of malmsey. There was an inordinately large number of people in his room, some of whom he did not recognise. The doctor was there, hanging over him and John was there of course. Dear son John, with whom he was now such good friends; and Joseph too, refusing to be embit-tered by his disability. The grandchildren were all present and some little great grandchildren who he had yet to get to know properly. Martha and Rosie were looking after them. It was especially nice to see some old friends. There was Gervaise Tennant chatting to Mr Allcot and he thought he could recognise Mr Armstrong and his daughter, whatever her name was; and good heavens that was young Kit talking to Sculley! Sir Christopher had come too and he appreciated that courtesy, hoping to manage a chat with him in due course. At the end of the room in the shadows there was a beautiful, red-haired lady, attired in green and he knew her instantly. She was arguing vehemently with another tall, and also red-haired, lady who he did not recognise at all. She certainly bore herself in a very regal fashion and he wondered if he had been honoured by a visit from another monarch. It was not impossible, for she had written to him once.

It was pleasantly warm and the malmsey tasted delicious. Best of all, however, was the reassuring pressure from the hand of Bess, that wonderful and lovely woman who had been at his side for so many years and who he loved now as strongly as he had always done. She was speaking to him but he found it difficult to hear her. That rushing sound, probably the great grand-children, drowned out all other noise. He was unable to hear the sound of the glass breaking, as it slipped from his lifeless hand.